THE INHERITAN

JUN 3 0 2018

Tilly Bagshawe is the international bestsellin
eleven previous novels.

A single mother at seventeen, Tilly won a place
University and took her baby daughter with her.
to an American and a mother of four, Tilly an
divide their time between the bright lights of Los
the peace and tranquility of a sleepy Cotswold

Before her first book, *Adored*, became an interna
hit, Tilly had a successful career in the City. Later, a
she contributed regularly to the *Sunday Times*, *L*
Evening Standard before turning her hand to nov
in the footsteps of her sister Louise. These days, wherever
she's not writing or on a plane, Tilly's life mostly revolves
around the school run, boy scouts and Peppa Pig.

See more at www.tillybagshawe.com

Also by Tilly Bagshawe

Adored
Showdown
Do Not Disturb
Flawless
Fame
Scandalous
Friends & Rivals

Sidney Sheldon's Mistress of the Game
Sidney Sheldon's After the Darkness
Sidney Sheldon's Angel of the Dark
Sidney Sheldon's The Tides of Memory

To find out more about Tilly Bagshawe and her books,
log on to www.tillybagshawe.com

THE INHERITANCE

HarperCollins*Publishers*

This novel is entirely a work of fiction. The names,
characters and incidents portrayed in it are the work of the author's
imagination. Any resemblance to actual persons, living or dead,
events or localities is entirely coincidental.

HarperCollins*Publishers*
77–85 Fulham Palace Road,
Hammersmith, London W6 8JB

www.harpercollins.co.uk

This paperback edition 2014
1

A catalogue record for this book
is available from the British Library

ISBN: 978-0-00-747252-9

Set in Meridien by Palimpsest Book Production Limited,
Falkirk, Stirlingshire

Printed and bound in Great Britain by
Clays Ltd, St Ives plc

MIX
Paper from
responsible sources
FSC C007454

FSC™ is a non-profit international organisation established to promote
the responsible management of the world's forests. Products carrying the
FSC label are independently certified to assure consumers that they come
from forests that are managed to meet the social, economic and
ecological needs of present and future generations,
and other controlled sources.

Find out more about HarperCollins and the environment at
www.harpercollins.co.uk/green

For Sarah and Kris Glynn

The

Tittles...

Village Store

High

Furlings Estate

May Day Fête

St. Hilda's Church

Village Green

Fox

Cricket Ground

St. Hilda's School

owns

To Chichester

Greystones Farm
Tatiana
Flint-Hamilton

mbe

Post Office

Willow Cottage
Max Bingley

Street

Wragsbottom Farm
Gabe & Laura
Baxter

River Swell

Brockhurst Wood

Woodside Hall
Penny Harwick

Foxhole Lane
Pub

To Brockhurst

Wheelers Cottage
Santiago
de la Cruz

Swell Valley

Welcome to Swell Valley

The Cast of Characters

Furlings ancestral home of the Flint-Hamilton family. Original Queen Anne architecture with extensive grounds, built between 1702 and 1714.

The Flint-Hamiltons

Rory Flint-Hamilton the tenth Flint-Hamilton to rule Furlings as lord of the manor. Widowed, with Tati as his only child, and contented with the quiet life of a country squire.

Tati Flint-Hamilton young, blonde and stunningly beautiful wild child, due to inherit Furlings from her father.

Mrs Fiona Worseley housekeeper, widow, Mrs W has worked for the Flint-Hamiltons for over 30 years. She has no children of her own.

Jennings Estate gardener, as gnarled and solid as a Furlings oak tree.

The Cranleys

Brett Cranley Australian property developer
and serial adulterer. Founded Cranley Estates at
the age of 20 and turned it into a multi-million
dollar business before marrying Angela,
the love of his life.

Angela Cranley fragile and fair-skinned,
angelic in looks as well as in heart.

Jason Cranley the Cranleys' painfully
withdrawn eldest son. As kind and
loyal as the beloved family basset, Gringo.

Logan Cranley dark-haired and olive skinned
like her father, she is the apple of Brett's eye –
a bewitching Daddy's girl.

Michelle Brett's *very* efficient secretary
in London.

Gringo a portly basset hound of advanced years,
with a voracious appetite for all life's pleasures.

The Villagers of
Fittlescombe

Harry Hotham former headmaster of St Hilda's, the village school, for 25 years, now retired.

Gabe Baxter local Fittlescombe heart-throb. A farmer with ambitions, and eyes for no one except Laura, his wife.

Laura Baxter née Tiverton, a successful screenwriter.

Max Bingley the new headmaster at St Hilda's, a widower. Persuaded to move to Fittlescombe by his loving but bossy daughters, Rosie and May.

Stella Goye a local potter.

Dylan Pritchard Jones the handsome (and vain) young art teacher at St Hilda's School, married to Maisie.

Santiago de la Cruz preposterously handsome cricket star. Plays for England, Sussex and Brockhurst, Fittlescombe's great village rivals.

Penny Harwich artist, engaged to Santiago de la Cruz. Her first husband, Paul, left her on their twentieth wedding anniversary for another man.

Emma Harwich Penny's daughter. Fittlescombe's first home-grown supermodel and all-round brat.

The Fittlescombe Cricket Team
(notable members)

Seb Harwich son of Penny Harwich, brother of Emma, loves cricket and girls (in that order), has just about forgiven Santiago for playing for Brockhurst last summer.

George Blythe the local carpenter and Fittlescombe's captain.

Will Nutley funny and self-effacing batsman, blessed with immense charm. Formerly besotted with Emma Harwich.

Timothy Wright a retired stockbroker and star bowler at Eton in his youth.

Frank Bannister sweet-natured church organist, and an appalling cricketer.

The network in London, New York, Sydney and St Tropez

Edmund Ruck the Flint-Hamilton family solicitor.

Hannah Lowell chief stewardess of Brett's boat, the Lady A. Frighteningly efficient and apparently impervious to Brett's charms.

Tricia Hong Brett's ruthless long-time mistress from Sydney.

Didier Lemprière a French lawyer. Smooth as café au lait.

Marco Gianotti an Italian-American investment banker at Goldman Sachs.

Leon di Clemente a famous angel investor on the US East Coast. Leon's father, Andrea di Clemente, made a small fortune in mining in the Congo. His son has turned it into a large one.

Key Board members of Hamilton Hall

Lady Arabella Boscombe former deputy editor of the Times Educational Supplement. Her family owns half of Chelsea, with property holdings second only to the Duke of Westminster.

Eric Jenkins a senior partner at one of the largest City accountants.

Michael Guinness one of Hamilton Hall's largest individual investors.

PROLOGUE

Dawn broke late over the Swell Valley. The May sun rose sleepily into a cloudless sky, streaking it first red, then pink, then a gorgeous, deep, burnished orange, like melted rose gold. Bathed in this magical light, Furlings House shimmered above the village of Fittlescombe, tranquil and magnificent. The family seat of the Flint-Hamiltons for over three hundred years, Furlings was frequently referred to as the most beautiful estate in Sussex, if not the whole of England. Certainly it lived up to that accolade this morning, a study in Georgian splendour, with nothing to puncture the peace of its rolling parkland and idyllic views except the occasional whinny of a pony in the top fields, or plaintive bleat of a lost lamb somewhere on the Downs.

'You fucker!'

A loudly slamming door sent a slumbering heron soaring into the air above the river.

'You lying, shallow lowlife! Go to hell!'

Each word was screamed at deafening volume. It was a woman's voice, delivered in a cut-glass accent, and it was followed seconds later by the woman herself, crunching

1

over the gravel. She was striking for two reasons. The first was that she was young, blonde and stunningly beautiful. And the second was that she was stark naked (unless one counted the pair of Wellington boots she'd slipped on as she exited the kitchen; or the heavy, cast-iron frying pan she was brandishing menacingly above her head, like a Zulu warrior with a machete).

'For God's sake, Tatiana, calm down. You'll wake up half the village.'

Her intended victim, a much older man with dishevelled salt-and-pepper hair, was half running, half limping towards his car. Barefoot, he'd only managed to partially dress himself before the Amazon had beaten him out of doors. In an unbuttoned evening shirt, with his suit trousers slipping repeatedly towards his knees, he cut a pathetic, cowering figure. Only the keenest of political observers would have recognized him as Sir Malcom Turnbull, Secretary of State for Trade & Industry, married father of three and tireless champion of family values.

'You think I give a flying fuck about the village?' the girl hissed at him like a snake. 'I'm Tatiana Flint-Hamilton. I *own* this village. Besides, why shouldn't people know what a lying, cheating scumbag you really are?'

Sir Malcom had only just managed to scramble into his Porsche when Tatiana caught up with him. Lifting the frying pan high above her head, she brought it down with a deafening *thwack* on the car's roof, leaving a dent the size of a small meteor strike and missing the minister's skull by inches.

'Jesus *Christ*.' Shaking, Sir Malcom rammed the key in the ignition and turned it, but the bloody thing was jammed. 'Have you lost your mind?' he stammered. 'You knew I had a wife.'

'Yes. And you told me you were going to leave her! At least twenty times.'

'My dear girl, I will. But it's not that simple. Henrietta's terribly fragile at the moment. And Nick's got his GCSEs this summer . . .'

'Spare me.' Tatiana Flint-Hamilton lifted the pan again, like a shot-putter about to let rip.

'No! Please. Perhaps after the next election . . .' Sir Malcom spluttered.

'The next election?' Tatiana laughed out loud. 'That's years away. What about the money?'

'Money?'

'The money I need to fight for my inheritance. The money you promised me, along with using your influence in the High Court. That was all bullshit too, wasn't it? You treacherous snake!'

Wham! The pan struck again.

Wham! And again.

At last the Porsche's engine roared into life and the panicked minister sped away. Thank God it was still early and Furlings was so remote. *Just imagine if I'd taken her to the London flat. The paparazzi would have seen us for sure.* Sir Malcom Turnbull shuddered at what might have been.

Tatiana Flint-Hamilton was an incredibly beautiful, sexy girl, but the tabloids were right when they referred to her as a 'wild child'.

Forget 'tigress'. The young lady was a velociraptor.

The minister wasn't a religious man but as he drove away he prayed fervently that he never saw Tatiana Flint-Hamilton again.

Tatiana stood and watched as the battered Porsche disappeared into the distance.

Like my future. Like my house. All of it's disappearing, she thought morosely. But she quickly pulled herself together.

What a bloody cliché to drive a red sports car in your fifties, anyway?

Tosser.

A cool dawn breeze made her shiver. Tatiana looked down at her own nakedness, and the frying pan hanging limply from her hand, and laughed. All of a sudden a pair of knickers, or even a dressing gown, had a certain appeal. Come to think of it, so did a bacon sandwich. The combination of sex and rage had made her ravenous.

Striding back into the kitchen, she pulled a Barbour jacket off a peg by the door and wrapped it round her. Opening the fridge to look for bacon, she discovered there wasn't any, so poured herself an ice-cold vodka instead and wandered through to the drawing room, taking the bottle with her.

She tried not to think about how much she was going to miss this place.

I mustn't give up. Not yet.

In a few hours, the entire population of Swell Valley would be milling around in Furlings' lower fields for Fittlescombe's annual May Day fete. *I can't face them,* thought Tati, slumping down onto her father's old sofa and knocking back four fingers of Stoli before refilling her mug. *I truly can't. They've all come to gloat.*

Glancing up, she saw her grandmother's portrait staring down at her disapprovingly from above the fireplace.

'What?' Tatiana challenged the canvas angrily, throwing open her jacket to reveal a perfect pair of round breasts, smooth, flat belly and glossy dark triangle of pubic hair. 'Didn't you always tell me to use my gifts. Well *these* are my gifts!'

She was drunk and angry, with herself more than anything. What on earth had possessed her to trust a slimy toad like Sir Malcom Turnbull? Everyone knew politicians were worse than drug dealers. Tears welled up in her eyes, but she didn't allow them to fall.

'I'm doing my best, Granny, OK?' she slurred. 'I am doing my fucking best.'

PART ONE

The Usurpers

CHAPTER ONE

'Well I think it's crap.'

Gabe Baxter, a blue eyed, broad-shouldered farmer and local Fittlescombe heart-throb, leaned forward over the table and took a long, cool sip of his Merrydown cider.

'Tatiana Flint-Hamilton hasn't bothered to show up for a village fete in five years. But now she wants local support to get her precious house back, suddenly she's swanning in like Lady Muck offering to judge the cakes. It's so contrived. She doesn't give a shit about the community.'

'That's a bit harsh.' Will Nutley, another local lad and a friend of Gabe's from the village cricket team, stretched out his long legs contentedly. Will was drinking Abbey Dry, a local competitor to Merrydown. Gabe described it as 'cat's piss', but this hadn't deterred Will from ordering himself a third pint. 'I think it takes guts to come back, under the circumstances.'

'The circumstances,' as the entire valley knew, were that the late Rory Flint-Hamilton, long-time lord of the manor at Fittlescombe and owner of Furlings, had sensationally disinherited his only child, his daughter Tatiana. Until now, Tatiana

Flint-Hamilton had been most famous for her model looks and her taste for scandal, both of which had made her a favourite with the tabloids. With her long, caramel-coloured hair, slender figure and angular, almost cartoon-like face – huge green eyes, high cheekbones, wide, impossibly sensual mouth – at twenty-four Tati Flint-Hamilton exuded not only sex appeal but class. Breeding. Like a racehorse, or a rare, perfectly cut diamond. Unfortunately she also had a penchant for powerful, high-profile, and often married men, not to mention a well-documented drug habit. What set Tati apart from other society 'It girls' was her intelligence, her wit (she could always be relied upon for a suitably pithy and amusing quote) and her refreshing lack of remorse about any of her wild antics. On the scale of Great British Don't-Give-A-Shitness, she was right up there with Simon Cowell.

The media loved her for it. But her own father had spent his last years in a misery of embarrassment and despair over Tatiana's behaviour and, in the end, the idea of handing over his beloved Furlings to his tearaway daughter had proved too much. Rory had changed his will, apparently without breathing a word to anyone. Rumour had it that Tatiana had turned up at the lawyers' offices in high spirits, fully expecting to take possession of her inheritance. Only to be told by her godfather Edmund Ruck, senior partner at Jameson and Ruck, that a house that had been in Flint-Hamilton hands for over three hundred years had in fact been left to distant cousins, and she was out on her pretty little, diamond-studded ear.

'Guts?' Gabe spluttered. 'Come off it.'

'I'm serious,' said Will. 'It must be bloody humiliating, wandering around the village trying to act normally, when everyone knows her old man cut her off.'

Gabe grunted noncommittally.

'Imagine how you'd feel if your dad had disinherited you?' Will went on. 'If he'd left Wraggsbottom Farm to some random Aussie family.'

Brett Cranley, Rory Flint-Hamilton's appointed heir, was an Australian property magnate. Famous in his native Australia, he was evidently extremely wealthy in his own right. Somehow that made the whole inheriting Furlings thing worse, at least in Will Nutley's eyes.

'The Cranleys aren't random,' said Gabe. 'They're relatives.'

'Barely,' said Will. 'I heard Rory never even met them before he carked it. They're total strangers.'

'Yeah, well, whatever,' said Gabe. 'It wouldn't have happened to me because I'm not a vacuous socialite with no sense of responsibility who'd let the whole estate go to hell in a handbasket before you could say "pass the cocaine".'

Gabe and Will were sitting in the beer tent at the annual Fittlescombe village fete on what had blossomed into a blisteringly hot May morning. Always held on May Day and in Furlings' sprawling lower meadow, this year's fete had been given an added frisson of excitement thanks to the gossip surrounding Tatiana Flint-Hamilton's disinheritance. The latest word was that Tatiana had decided to take Furlings' new owners to court over it. Apparently she had some scheme brewing to have her father's will declared invalid. Although nobody seemed clear quite how such a challenge might succeed. Rory Flint-Hamilton was old but quite sane when he died. And by all accounts the Cranleys were as surprised by the contents of his will as his daughter was, so they could hardly be said to have coerced him.

In any event, the case had split the village, and the entire Swell Valley, down the middle. There were some who approved of Rory's decision to leave his ancient family estate in safer hands than those of his feckless, scandal-prone daughter. But many others felt aggrieved on Tatiana's behalf. After all, it wasn't as if all her Flint-Hamilton forefathers had been saints and angels, especially in their youth. Tati should be given a chance to grow up and prove herself. The fact that Rory's appointed heirs, the Cranleys, were not only card-carrying nouves but, worse, Australian, only served to fan the flames of local ire.

Of course, no one had actually met Furlings' new owners yet. The Cranleys were due to arrive next week. But that hadn't stopped the rumour mill from going into overdrive. Mrs Worsley, Rory Flint-Hamilton's old housekeeper, was the only person with first-hand information, having apparently Skyped with Brett Cranley and his wife on numerous occasions. On the basis of these conversations, the housekeeper pronounced her new employers 'charming' and 'terribly down to earth'. Of course Fiona Worsley had more reason than most to support Rory's Australian heirs over his daughter. Mrs Worsley had been there through the very worst excesses of Tati's teenage years and had seen first hand just how spoiled, destructive and Machiavellian she could be. She was fond of Tatiana deep down, but the thought of working for her, not to mention sitting back and watching helplessly while she and her rich, druggie London friends turned Furlings into some sort of party-house, was more than the old woman could have borne.

On Mrs Worsley's advice, Brett Cranley had already won over a few cynics by giving permission from Sydney for the village fete to go ahead as usual, and for the meadow to be used.

'You see what I mean?' Furlings' housekeeper had purred. 'He's as nice as pie and generous with it.'

What Furlings' new owner hadn't anticipated was that his absence had left a window for his cousin Tatiana to swoop in unannounced and effectively take over proceedings. She'd even demanded that Mrs Worsley put her up in her old room at Furlings for the week of the fete.

'I presume I'm welcome as a guest, at least? In my own bloody home,' she fumed.

Once installed, Tati had begun the Herculean task of trying to win over the locals. Her challenge to her father's will was based on the premise that Furlings had never really been Rory's to leave. That there was an effective entailment, inferred from generations of local practice. It was a shaky case, to say the least, but it was all she had. In order for it to stand a snowball's chance in hell of succeeding in court, she would need extensive local support. Hence, in Gabe Baxter's view, her cynical 'sudden interest' in the village.

'You have to admit, she's done a good job running the fete committee,' said Will Nutley, draining the dregs of his cider and wiping his mouth on his sleeve. 'This must be the best turnout we've had in a decade. Loads of celebs have shown up because of her.'

'So?'

'So it's all money for the village, isn't it? I saw Kate Moss earlier at the craft stall. And Seb Harwich said Hugh Grant was milling around somewhere.'

'Probably complaining,' said Gabe, downing the rest of his Merrydown in a single gulp. 'He's such a miserable git.'

Will grinned. 'Sure you're not just jealous because he's getting all the female attention?'

Gabe gave his trademark, arrogant laugh. 'Jealous? Please. Anyway, he's not getting Laura's attention,' he added proudly. 'That's the only female I'm interested in.'

At the top of the meadow, Laura Baxter, Gabe's pretty young wife, mopped her brow with a handkerchief. Christ it was hot today! The weather at least seemed to be on Tatiana Flint-Hamilton's side. At this rate the fete would raise a fortune, and Tati would get all the credit.

'I'll 'ave five tickets for a pound, please.' Mr Preedy, the proprietor of Fittlecombe Village Stores, gazed appreciatively at Laura's breasts, straining for escape from her pale pink linen shirt-dress.

In the grip of some temporary fever, Laura had agreed weeks ago to man the tombola, without doubt the most boring job at the entire fete. She passed a handful of tickets to the little bald shopkeeper and watched as he carefully unfolded and examined each one.

'Look at that! I've got a winner!' Practically hopping with excitement, Mr Preedy handed his last ticket back to Laura. 'Five hundred and ten. Winners end in a zero, right?'

'That's right.'

'Well, what've I won, then? Don't keep me in suspense.'

Laura looked along the table. She found the appropriate ticket taped to a peeling packet of Yardley bath salts.

'Erm . . . these?' She handed them over apologetically.

Unperturbed, Mr Preedy beamed as if he'd just won a luxury cruise. It was so sweet, Laura quite forgave him his earlier breast-ogle.

'Smashing! I never win anything, me. You must be my lucky charm. I'll give 'em to the wife,' he said, clutching the salts to his chest. 'Earn meself some brownie points. You can't put a price on that now, can you?'

'Indeed you can't.'

Laura smiled as he disappeared into the crowd. She loved the way that such small things seemed to give people here pleasure. Especially on days like today. The Fittlescombe fete really was a throwback to another, gentler, happier world. And what a wonderful turnout this year, thanks to the

14

combination of the glorious bank holiday weather and the undoubted star power of Miss Flint-Hamilton, returned from her jet-setting life in London to 'recommit' to the village.

Not that Laura, of all people, had a right to judge Tati for that. This time two years ago, Laura had been living in London herself, working all hours as a television writer, completely immersed in city life as she climbed the greasy pole. But she too had returned to the Swell Valley, the place where she'd been happiest as a child, at a low point in her life. And now here she was, utterly immersed in the rhythms of the countryside, married to Gabe – a farmer's wife, no less – and happier than ever. It was incredible how quickly, and totally, life could change.

Of course, she and Gabe had their moments. He could be a terrible flirt sometimes, but Laura wasn't really worried by it. She knew he loved her, and was faithful. It was annoying though, especially after he'd had one too many drinks at The Fox. Then there was his ambition, which for some reason always surprised her. He'd already started talking about trying to buy some of Furlings' farmland from the new owners.

'Rory Flint-Hamilton swore blind he'd never sell a single blade of grass. But he mismanaged that estate something terrible. Maybe the new bloke'll be more amenable? Just think what we could do if we owned all that land along the valley.'

'Go bankrupt?' offered Laura.

The unfortunately named Wraggsbottom Farm had been in Gabe's family for almost as long as Furlings had been in the Flint-Hamiltons' hands, and was just as beautiful in its own way. It was, however, altogether a more modest enterprise. Like all the working farming families they knew, Gabe and Laura struggled financially, a fact that Gabe conveniently forgot during his fantasies of empire-building.

'We're barely breaking even as it is,' she reminded him. 'You're talking about doubling the size of the farm.'

'I know,' Gabe grinned. 'We'd be a real estate. If I can only convince this Aussie to let me buy those fields . . .'

'With what money?' Laura asked, exasperated.

'Mortgage.'

The nonchalant shrug with which Gabe offered this solution sent chills down her spine.

'I don't want to be lady of the manor, darling.' She wrapped her arms around his neck and kissed him. 'I just want a lovely, quiet life here. With you. Preferably not in a debtors' prison.'

They'd dropped the subject before it turned into a proper row. But it was only a matter of time before it reared its ugly head again. Laura adored Gabe, but it did sometimes get tiring, always having to be the boring grown-up in the family.

Down the hill from the tombola, Tatiana Flint-Hamilton was chatting up villagers waiting in line at the coconut shy. She'd swept down from the house earlier, making sure that everyone knew she'd been staying at Furlings – staking her claim – and looking more beautiful than ever in a demure, pale buttermilk shift dress, with her long blonde hair tied up with a whimsical blue ribbon. It was a far cry from the raunchy, barely-there outfits with sky-high stilettos she was known for in her tabloid days. But, of course, a lot had changed since then.

She wants people to like her so badly, thought Laura, pityingly. *This time two years ago, she had it all. And now look at her, a guest at her own house.*

Unlike Gabe, Laura Baxter felt sorry for Tati. She didn't blame her for fighting her father's will. *If I grew up in a house like Furlings, I'd fight like hell to keep it too*, she thought, glancing

16

over her shoulder at the Queen Anne mansion perched serenely at the top of the hill.

The house looked more gorgeous than ever today, dazzling in the May sunshine with its sash windows dripping in wisteria and its lawns criss-crossed by box hedges and winding gravel paths, dotted with elaborate topiary. How awful to think of it being lived in by strangers! And how hard for Tati to have to stay there now as a guest, even before her hated cousins had arrived. Secretly Laura was rather rooting for Tati to turf the interlopers out, although that was highly unlikely. The bylaw that Tatiana was hoping to invoke was properly ancient. As for convincing the naysayers in the village that she was suitable lady of the manor material? With her history, that was going to be a tall order. It would certainly take a lot more than a Julie Andrews dress and a hair ribbon.

'It's impossible,' Tatiana complained good-naturedly to the woman standing next to her at the coconut shy. 'I'm sure it wasn't this hard when I was a girl. Are you sure it's not rigged?'

'Pretty sure,' the woman laughed.

'I reckon they've glued them onto the stands.'

'Nonsense.'

A wildly attractive Latin-looking man whom Tati dimly recognized appeared at her elbow. 'You just need the right technique.'

In chinos and a blue linen shirt that matched his eyes and perfectly offset his olive skin, the man was easily the best-looking specimen Tati had seen since her return to Fittlescombe. With the Cranleys due to arrive in a week, she would soon be kicked out of Furlings and have to find herself more modest accommodation in the village while she put together her legal case against her disinheritance. The prospect of months spent living in some dismal local hovel had been filling Tati's heart with gloom for weeks now. As had the idea of begging for a job as a lowly teacher at the village primary school.

The real kicker in Rory's will, the part that no one in the village even knew about yet, were the conditions the old man had placed on Tatiana's trust fund. Not content with robbing her of Furlings, he'd effectively taken steps to cut her off from all family money unless she, as he put it, 'got her life in order.'

With this in mind, the old man had stipulated that if Tati agreed to take a teaching job at St Hilda's Primary School in the village, he would authorize the trust to release a 'modest' monthly stipend. Even then, the money would only ever be released to her in the form of regular income payments. At no point would Tatiana receive a large lump sum of money.

For Tati, this had been the final twist of the knife. She recalled the scene in her godfather's London office as if it were yesterday.

'You're telling me I'm penniless?' She'd glared at Edmund Ruck accusingly.

'Hardly,' London's most eminent solicitor responded evenly. 'You have the equivalent of a modest trust fund for the time being. As long as your life remains stable, the monthly payments will go up considerably every year. Any capital remaining at the end of your life will pass to your children.'

'It's a fucking pittance!' spat Tatiana.

'It's more than most people earn in a lifetime, Tati.'

'I don't care what "most people" earn. I am *not* "most people".' Tati's arrogance hid her fear and profound shock.

'And I won't get any money coming in at all till I'm thirty-five. Thirty-fucking-five! I might as well be dead.'

Edmund Ruck suppressed a wry smile. He'd known Tatiana all her life and was fond of her, but he understood why Rory had declined to trust her with the family fortune, still less with the magical historic seat at Furlings. Even so, leaving the estate to a distant cousin he'd never met had been a surprising move on the old man's part. The will had raised Edmund Ruck's eyebrows, so he could hardly expect it not to raise his goddaughter's.

'Some money can be released to you earlier,' he explained, 'as long as you comply with the conditions set out in your father's letter of wishes.'

Tati let out a short, derisive laugh. 'As long as I go back to Fittlescombe and become a schoolteacher, you mean? Don't be ridiculous, Edmund.'

'Why is that ridiculous?'

Tati looked at him witheringly, but Edmund pressed on.

'You trained as a teacher, didn't you?'

It was true that Tatiana had studied, abortively, for a teaching degree at Oxford Brookes, before dropping out. She'd always been incredibly bright, especially at maths, but had never worked hard at school, or cared about her grades. The world of yachts and private jets and wealthy lovers, of winters in Kitzbühel and St Barth's and summers in St Tropez and Sardinia, had exerted an irresistible pull. Besides, why bother with university when one was never going to need to get a job?

'Did my father seriously think, even for a moment, that I was going to agree to become a village school ma'am? That I would be content to live in some poxy cottage, while Furlings – *my* house, my bloody *birthright* – was occupied by some jumped-up bloody Australian and his family, the *Cranfords*?'

19

'Cranleys,' her godfather corrected, patiently.

'Whatever.'

Tatiana had been full of fight that awful day in Edmund Ruck's offices. And yet she *had* returned to Fittlescombe, just as her father had demanded. And she *would* take the job at the school, because she needed that money. But anyone who interpreted those things as her acceptance of Rory's will would be making a grave mistake. Tatiana was here for one reason and one reason only: to fight for her real inheritance.

The Adonis standing next to her at the coconut shy might at least provide a welcome distraction while she did what had to be done.

'You hold the ball like this.' He slipped one arm confidently around Tati's waist, placing the ball in her hand. 'And throw overarm, aiming downwards. Like so.'

'I see,' said Tati, inhaling the delicious, lemony scent of his aftershave as she released the ball into the air. She looked on as it sailed skywards in a perfect arc before dipping to strike the coconut clean onto the ground.

'That's amazing,' she said delightedly, spinning around to face her instructor. 'Thank you. I'm Tatiana, by the way.'

The handsome man smiled and shook her hand.

'I know who you are, Miss Flint-Hamilton. Santiago de la Cruz. A pleasure to meet you.'

De la Cruz. The cricketer. Of course! Santiago played for Sussex. Tati had heard he'd moved to the valley last year. After a week holed up at Furlings with nothing but Mrs Worsley's scowling face for company, or trapped in deathly dull fete committee meetings with the church flowers brigade, it felt wonderful to be flirted with again. Tati tried to remember the last time she'd had enjoyable sex or even been on a date with an attractive man – she didn't count this morning's disastrous encounter with the semi-fossilized Minister for Trade and Industry – and drew a complete blank. It must have been before that awful day in Edmund Ruck's office. Before the world stopped spinning and her life fell apart. She smiled at Santiago coquettishly, tossing back her long ponytail of honey-blonde hair. 'Santiago,' she purred. 'What a glorious name.'

'And this is my fiancée, Penny.'

A middle-aged woman wearing a hideous gypsy skirt and a T-shirt covered in paint splatters had appeared at Santiago's side. Tati's smile wilted. From the look of pride on Santiago's face, you'd think he'd just introduced her to Gisele Bündchen. *Talk about love being blind*, thought Tati. Still, ever mindful of her charm offensive, she shook Penny's hand warmly.

'Lovely to meet you.'

'We've met before,' Penny Harwich reminded her, although it was said without reproach. 'I'm Penny Harwich. Emma's mother.'

Oh yes. Emma Harwich. The model. Tati vaguely remembered the family, although not particularly the ragamuffin of a mother.

'Of course. How silly of me.' Her smile didn't waver. 'Your fiancé just won me a coconut.'

'Did you, darling? How sweet.' Slipping her arms around Santiago's neck and standing up on tiptoes, Penny Harwich kissed him blissfully. Tatiana felt the envy as a physical pain, like a cricket ball lodged in her chest. Not because she fancied Santiago. Although of course she did. But because she didn't have anyone herself. She was alone, now more than ever. Other people's happiness felt like a personal affront.

'Is that the time?' She glanced at her Patek Philippe watch, an eighteenth birthday present from her father. 'You must excuse me. I think I'm wanted at the duck racing.'

Turning away, Tati walked towards the pond, nodding and smiling at villagers as she went till her jaw and neck both ached. There was old Frank Bannister, the church organist, and the Reverend Slaughter who'd been the vicar of St Hilda's Church in Fittlescombe for as long as Tati could remember. There were new faces too, scores of them, whole families that Tati didn't recognize. It was so long since she'd spent any time here, she thought, a trifle guiltily. Although really her father ought to bear some responsibility for that. In the last five years of his life, Rory had been so disapproving, so resolutely unwelcoming.

He practically drove me away. And now he wants to punish me for it from beyond the grave.

'Tatiana!' Harry Hotham, Tati's old headmaster at St Hilda's Primary School and a lifelong friend of her father's, waved from the gate that linked Furlings' lower meadow to the village green. It was less than two years since Tati had last seen Harry, at the same Hunt Ball where she'd infamously run off with Laura Tiverton's boyfriend, but he'd aged two decades in that short time. Stooped and frail, leaning on a walking stick, his remaining wisps of hair now totally white and blowing in the breeze like tufts of dandelion seeds, he tottered towards her.

'How marvellous to see you. And how divine you look, my dear. Yellow is definitely your colour. I'd heard you were back in the village. Do tell me you're staying?'

Harry's enthusiasm, like his smile, was utterly genuine. Tati was touched.

'That rather depends,' she said, kissing him warmly on both cheeks. 'You heard about Daddy's will?'

'Yes.' Harry nodded gravely. 'Bad business, that.'

'Well I'm not giving up,' said Tati, jutting her chin forward defiantly. Harry Hotham remembered the look well from

Tatiana's days as his pupil, a tearaway even then but charming with it, at least in Harry's eyes. 'I'm contesting it.'

Harry frowned. 'Yes. I heard that too. Are you sure that's wise, Tatiana?'

'What do you mean?'

'Only that, knowing your father as I did, I imagine he took very thorough legal advice. I'd hate to see you ripped off by some ghastly lawyer.'

Tati waved a hand dismissively. 'Every lawyer has a different opinion. And I'm already *being* ripped off. I don't see that it can get much worse.'

'That's because you're young, my dear,' said Harry, patting her hand affectionately. 'It can. Believe me.'

'Well, it's early days yet but I need funds to pursue my case,' Tati went on, ignoring Harry Hotham's warnings. 'A war chest, if you will. I wanted to talk to you about that actually.'

'My dear Tatiana, I'd happily give you my last farthing, but I'm afraid you are looking at a very poor man,' Harry said matter-of-factly. 'There's no money in teaching, you see. Not a bean.'

'Oh, no!' Tati laughed, embarrassed. 'I wasn't asking you for money. It's a bit of an odd request, but I . . . I was hoping for a job.'

'A job?'

'Yes. Did Daddy not say anything to you before he died?'

'Say something?' Harry looked confused.

'It would just be for a few months, while I sort out my legal situation,' said Tati. She explained about her trust fund, and the codicil in Rory's will that would release money to her but only on the condition that she move back to Fittlescombe and work as a teacher at St Hilda's.

'Dad always had a ridiculous fantasy about me settling

down and teaching one day. Ever since I did that awful course at Oxford Brookes.' Misinterpreting Harry Hotham's pained face, she added, 'Look, I know it's madness. But you'd be doing me a huge favour. When I get my inheritance restored to me, I promise to fund a new school building and anything else you want.'

'It's not that my dear,' said Harry. 'The job would be yours if it were mine to give. But I'm afraid I retired.'

'What?' Tati frowned. 'When?'

'At Christmas. I had a fall and I . . . well, I realized I wasn't up to snuff any more. Physically, I mean. I recovered and all that. But I still need this blasted thing.' He shook his walking stick reproachfully. 'Running a school is a younger man's game.'

'Oh, Harry. I'm so sorry,' said Tati, truthfully. 'I can't imagine St Hilda's without you.'

'Yes, well, things move on. And the new chap's terribly good,' said Harry, graciously. 'Bingley, his name is. He's a widower and rather a dish, so I'm told. All the yummy mummies are after him. He could probably use one of these himself,' he waved his walking stick laughingly, 'to beat them all off with!'

Tati forced a smile, but this was not good news. Working at St Hilda's would always have been tough, a desperate measure for desperate times. But at least with Harry Hotham she'd have known where she stood. They'd have worked out some arrangement to satisfy her trustees – a few hours volunteering in the library or helping the girls play netball – and no one would have been any the wiser.

But this new fellow, Bingley, was an unknown entity. No doubt he'd already heard all kinds of bad things about her from village gossip, if not from the *Daily Mail*'s society pages.

'Cheer up,' said Harry Hotham, taking her arm. 'You look like you've lost a shilling and found sixpence.'

'Do I, Harry?' Tati laughed. Somehow being around Harry Hotham reminded her of all the good things about her father and the past. Harry was part of her history, of Furlings, of all the things she was fighting for. 'I'm off to judge the duck races. Would you like to come with me?'

'*Dearest* Tatiana,' enthused the old man. 'I'm sure I can think of nothing I would like more.'

CHAPTER TWO

'Wow.'

Angela Cranley gasped as she drove her Range Rover over the crest of the hill.

'Wow.'

'Stop saying "wow", Mum. You sound like a dork.'

Logan Cranley, Angela's ten-year-old daughter, rolled her eyes in the back seat. After the long flight from Sydney, Logan was tired and grumpy. She hadn't wanted to leave her old school, or her friends, and couldn't understand what had possessed her parents to uproot themselves overnight and move to the other side of the world, just because some old guy had died and left them a house. Even at ten, Logan understood that her family were extremely wealthy. Her father, Brett, was a real-estate developer and one of the richest men in Sydney. The Cranleys already had a bunch of houses, including a grand apartment in London. What was so special about this one?

Secretly though, she too was impressed by the stunning scenery that surrounded them as they got nearer to their new home. Narrow ancient lanes flanked by high hedgerows guided them through the rolling chalk hills of the Downs; they passed a Tudor pub, The Coach and Horses, that looked exactly like Logan's dolls' house back home in her playroom in Australia, all white wattle walls and criss-crossing black beams, with mullioned windows. There were meadows full of buttercups, picture-postcard villages made up of clusters of flint cottages, medieval churches and the occasional grand Georgian manor house. Queen Anne's lace, grown wild and as tall as the top of the car, reached over from the grass verges and brushed the windscreen as they passed, like delicate white-gloved fingers waving an ecstatic welcome. And everywhere the late spring sunshine, light, bright and clear, bathed the countryside in a glorious, magical glow.

In the front passenger seat, Logan's older brother gazed vacantly out at the patchwork of hills and fields. At just turned twenty, Jason Cranley was painfully withdrawn. Tall and thin, with a pale, freckly complexion and sad, amber eyes, it was hard to believe that he was genetically related either to Logan, or to their father, Brett. Both Jason's little sister and his father were dark-haired, olive-skinned and bewitching, like gypsies, or members of some exotic tribe of Portuguese pirates. Jason took more closely after his mother. Angela was blonde and fair-skinned, the sort of colouring that could easily have gone to red and that had zero tolerance for sun. Jason glanced across at her now, smiling, enchanted by this new world unfolding before her.

She's so brave, he thought. *So optimistic. After everything that's happened, she still believes in fresh starts.*

How he wished that he did, too.

'This is it. Fittlescombe. We're here!'

Angela Cranley squeezed her son's leg excitedly as they passed the sign for the village. The Range Rover had descended a steep escarpment, then forked sharp right at the valley floor. The village was completely hidden from the main road above, folded into the downs like a baby joey enveloped in its mother's pouch. It made it feel like a secret place, a hidden jewel only to be discovered by the chosen few. Despite herself, Angela felt her excitement building and her hopes start to blossom like the first buds of spring. This, surely, was a place where people were happy. Where the miseries and betrayals of the past could be left behind.

The most recent betrayal, in the form of Brett's mistress Tricia Hong, a pushy young news reporter for SBS who had done everything in her power to destroy Angela's marriage, was now a satisfying ten thousand miles away. Brett had been unfaithful before, of course – countless times. But Tricia had been a threat of a different order: intelligent, ruthlessly ambitious and utterly without scruple. Perhaps it was no surprise that she and Brett had been drawn to one another. They were so very alike. Still, in the end, even Brett had been taken aback by the beautiful young Asian's tenacity. He, too, had begun to feel under siege. Rory Flint-Hamilton's surprise bequest could not have come at a more opportune time. Nor could it have brought them to a more idyllic spot.

'Oh my God, look at the post office! Isn't that the cutest, with the roses round the door? And the school. Look, Logan. St Hilda's. That's where you'll be going. What do you think?'

Logan made a noncommittal, grunting noise. She refused to get excited about her new school, however idyllic it might look. She still hoped there was a chance her father would change his mind and that they could all go home to Sydney and reality and forget this whole thing. Her mum kept telling her that she and Rachel and Angelica would stay friends, that they could Skype. But it wasn't the same. She was going to miss Wellesley Park Elementary's summer fair. She was going to miss *everything*. Rachel and Angelica would become best friends and wear the best friend necklaces, the ones with two pieces of a heart that fit together perfectly. She, Logan, would be forgotten. Erased. She'd probably start speaking with an English accent, God forbid.

'Stop.'

Jason's voice rang out, startling his mother. He hadn't said a word since they pulled out of Heathrow. Having watched him go through a series of depressions, Angela wasn't surprised by his silence. She had learned to sit with her son's sadness, to stop trying to snap him out of it. But she still found it hard.

'That was it. Furlings. There's a sign at the bottom of the drive.'

Angela reversed. Sure enough, there it was. Damp and faded, and partially covered by overhanging trees, a simple wooden sign: 'Furlings – Private Property'.

The driveway had seen better days. The four-wheel drive bounced and juddered over potholes, rattling its occupants like cubes of ice in a cocktail shaker. But after about a hundred yards of winding their way up the hill that overlooked the village, the private track widened into a grand, gravelled forecourt with a stone fountain at its centre. The house stood back from the gravel and was set slightly above it, atop a flight of six wide stone steps. A grand, square central section was flanked by two, lower symmetrical wings, all in the same red brick typical of Queen Anne architecture. Elegant sash windows peeked out shyly beneath thick fringes of wisteria, and the formal gardens at the front of the house gave way to stunning, oak-dotted parkland below, the green hills rolling all the way down to the village green.

It was quite the most exquisite house Angela Cranley had ever seen, combining elegance with an undeniable grandeur. It was also, to Angela's way of thinking, enormous. If this was a small stately home, she struggled to imagine what a large one might look like.

'It's a palace!' Logan squealed delightedly, forgetting all her heartfelt objections in the joy of the moment as she tumbled out of the car and ran towards the steps. 'Oh, Mum, isn't it gorgeous?'

Angela also got out of the car, stretching her aching legs. 'It is, darling. It is gorgeous.' She craned her neck and stepped back, trying to get a sense of the scale of it. 'What do you think, Jase?'

'Yeah. It's very nice.'

Jason pulled the two heavy trunks out of the boot, wishing that Furlings' beauty could affect him the way it ought to. Wishing that anything could. The cases thudded onto the ground with a crunch. Most of the family's furniture and effects were arriving by separate plane in the coming days, but they'd brought a few 'essentials' with them. Jason's father was supposed to come down to see the new house in a week. Brett had business in London, and preferred to stay in town than to deal with the hassle of moving in. 'Your mother can do that. Women love all that nesting crap.'

'It's a lot of work, Dad,' Jason had protested. Unusually for him. Jason Cranley was afraid to provoke his father. Everybody was afraid to provoke Brett Cranley.

'Rubbish,' said Brett. 'There'll be a housekeeper there to help her. Mrs Worsley. Old man Flint-Hamilton asked me to keep her on. And you can pitch in, can't you? God knows you've got nothing else to do.'

Ever since Jason had dropped out of college, his father had been berating him for laziness, for failing to get a job and a life. Brett Cranley did not believe in depression. 'We've all got our shit to go through,' he told the family therapist at the one and only session Angela had convinced him to attend. 'Wallowing in it doesn't help. The problem with Jason is that he doesn't realize how damn good he's got it.'

Logan had already raced up the steps and run inside, darting in and out of the house like an over-excited puppy. Behind her, a smiling, soberly dressed woman in her mid-sixties appeared in the front doorway, plainly amused by the little girl's high spirits.

Angela climbed the steps, her hand extended. 'Mrs Worsley?'

'Mrs Cranley. Welcome. You must be shattered after such a long journey.'

The older woman's hand was cold and her grip firm, her Scottish accent clipped and efficient. She had grey hair, swept up into a neatly pinned bun, and wore no make-up, but her bright eyes and warm smile stopped her from appearing severe.

'I suspect I'll be tired later,' Angela smiled back. 'To be honest I think we're all a bit too excited now. Excited and overwhelmed. What a house!'

'Indeed.' Mrs Worsley beamed with pride, as if she'd built Furlings herself, brick by brick. 'Everyone in the village is so excited about your arrival,' she lied. 'It'll be wonderful to have a family here again. Mr Flint-Hamilton was on his own for such a terribly long time.'

Jason had begun dragging the heavy cases up the steps but Mrs Worsley hurried forward, assuring him that Mr Jennings, the gardener, would 'see to all that'.

'He's not really called Jennings, is he?' The faintest of smiles traced Jason's lips.

That boy looks ill, thought Mrs Worsley. *As pale and pasty as rolled-out dough. With any luck the country air will sort him out.*

'He is,' she said aloud. 'And he'd be mightily upset to see you manhandling your own luggage, Mr Cranley.'

'Jason,' said Jason, embarrassed.

'Jason.'

Mrs Worsley smiled. First impressions weren't everything, of course, but she liked this family. The rambunctious little girl; the shy, polite son; the beautiful, perhaps slightly sad-looking mother. She felt certain that dear Mr Flint-Hamilton would have liked them too.

Fiona Worsley had worked at Furlings for over thirty years. She had known Tatiana's mother, Vicky, and loved her dearly, grieving with Mr Flint-Hamilton when she died, and helping him to raise his infant daughter. A few years after Tati's mother's death, Mrs Worsley's own husband, Mick, had also died, suddenly from a heart attack aged only forty-one. Rory Flint-Hamilton had returned the favour, supporting his housekeeper through her loss. The bond forged between them through mutual grief was a strong one. Never romantic. But as unique and powerful as any marriage.

Without children of her own, Mrs Worsley had focused all her love and attention on the young Tatiana, although she was a strict mother-figure and not especially demonstrative. In an odd, unspoken way, she, Rory and Tatiana had become a family unit of sorts up at Furlings, although none of them would ever have described the relationship in those terms. It had broken Mrs Worsley's heart, watching Tatiana throw her life away on parties and unsuitable men as soon as she got into her teens, both for Tati's sake but also for her father's. Rory Flint-Hamilton had been a lovely man and, in her own way, Fiona Worsley had loved him. She'd particularly hated watching dear Mr Flint-Hamilton agonize over his will and Furlings' future during the last, painful months of his life, and she laid the blame for his suffering squarely at Tatiana's door. As such, she was firmly in the pro-Cranley camp when it came to the dispute over Rory's will.

It wasn't that she didn't love Tatiana, or that she resented her, as many people in the village assumed. But at this point, after so many years of bad behaviour and broken promises, the housekeeper shared her former employer's view that tough love was Tatiana's only chance of salvation. And then there was the estate to think about. Furlings was as much a part of Mrs Worsley's life as it was of Tatiana's. At least now the estate would be preserved. Not only that, but it would become a family home again, cherished and brought back to life as a great house should be. She couldn't understand why so many people in Swell Valley seemed unwilling to give this young Australian family a chance.

'Come and see my bedroom!' Logan was shrieking, circling her mother like a deranged shark as Angela finally made it across the threshold of her new home. 'I've picked it out already, it's right at the top and it's *amazing*! There's room for bunk beds. Can I have bunk beds? I really really *really* want bunk beds, and yellow wallpaper.'

'I don't know about the yellow wallpaper,' said Angela. All of a sudden she *did* feel tired, and achy and sore and in desperate need of a shower and change of clothes. 'Let's see what Dad says.'

Furlings wouldn't be home until Brett got here and gave it his seal of approval. It was hard to imagine how he couldn't love it – how anyone couldn't. But Angela intended to spend the next week making the house as perfect and homely and welcoming as was humanly possible.

If Brett's happy, we'll all be happy.

We'll settle down here. Put down roots.

Angela Cranley closed her eyes and willed it to be so.

Brett Cranley closed his eyes and willed himself to come. Normally he had no trouble in that department, but the stress of opening up new offices in London combined with family pressures and physical exhaustion had taken their toll. Either that, or the girl just wasn't hot enough.

'Oh, that's good! That's so good.'

The secretary moaned, arching her back and giving her new boss a better view of the eagle tattoo across the top of her buttocks. Brett was not an admirer of tattoos, on men or women. He found himself becoming irritated – *why had the stupid girl gone and done such a thing?* – which was not helping him to orgasm. He closed his eyes again. *Focus, for fuck's sake.*

Reaching around, he grabbed hold of the girl's breasts which were large and heavy, like two water balloons. Her nipples were small and erect, twin pink diamonds between his thumb and forefinger. *Better.* She was pretty, sexy in a slightly chubby, accessible sort of way, with short hair – a pixie cut, he believed it was called. Tricia had had glorious long hair, black as tar and silken. Thinking about it now, Brett felt his erection strengthen and his excitement start to build at last.

'Oh Brett! Brett!'

Thrusting harder and faster, he wanted to say her name but realized he'd forgotten it. Michelle, was it? Or Mary? Something with an 'M'. He'd only hired her a week ago as the receptionist for Cranley Estates' new London office. He couldn't be expected to remember everything.

Reaching behind her, the girl cupped a hand underneath his balls and began to stroke them. That was it. 'Oh . . . Jesus.' He came, finally, collapsing on top of her, sweat pouring from his brow.

'That was nice.' The girl smiled cheerfully, wriggling out from under him.

'Wasn't it?' Brett sighed, rolling onto his back. The carpet felt rough and scratchy underneath him, but he was too tired to move. Bending over him, the girl expertly removed his condom, carried it over to the waste bin in the corner of the office and dropped it inside. Then, still stark naked, she grabbed a few sheets of printer paper, balled them up and dropped them on top, concealing the evidence.

Brett grinned. *She's thorough. I like that in a secretary. A self-starter, too.*

He wondered how things were going down in Sussex. Whether Ange and the children had reached the house yet. He must call them in a minute, once what's-her-name had gone.

He glanced at the clock on the wall: 4.30 p.m. The secretary was already almost fully dressed, doing up the top buttons on her silk blouse and straightening her hair as if she'd just got back from the gym. Clearly she had no expectation of post-coital affection from him: another huge plus. Tricia had been painfully demanding in this regard. In every regard, come to think of it. Brett missed his mistress's lithe, gymnast's body, but nothing more. Tricia had broken the sacred code of the other woman and made a nuisance of herself with Angela, calling the house, showing up at events where she knew his wife would be present. She'd become a threat to his marriage, to his family. Brett Cranley couldn't tolerate that. His own parents had divorced when he was young, and Brett saw himself decidedly as a family man. Sure he played around. Who didn't? But he loved his wife and it would be a cold day in hell before he left her for another woman.

But this girl – *Michelle. It's definitely Michelle* – she seemed to have a much clearer idea of the boundaries. She also seemed nice, sunny natured, a good sort of chick to have around. Perhaps he could overlook the tattoo and the hair?

*　　*　　*

35

Brett Cranley had not grown up poor. His father had run a successful dry-cleaning business and his mother, Lucille, was a hairdresser. What Brett had done was grown up quickly. Both his parents were dead by the time he turned fourteen, his father from a car accident on Christmas Eve, hit head-on by a drunk driver, and his mother from breast cancer. It was Lucille's death that had affected him the most. An only child, Brett had always adored his mother. And while the loss of his father was shocking and sudden, Lucille Cranley's protracted illness, her pain and fear, her desperate, dashed hopes of remission, had profoundly changed Brett's psyche. The teenage boy lost his faith, not only in God and modern medicine, but in other people altogether.

There was no point in loving people, because the people you loved would eventually be taken away from you.

There was no point relying on people, because they would let you down.

There was only one life: this life. And in this life, you were on your own.

These were the lessons Brett Cranley learned from his parents' deaths.

In some ways they changed him for the better. Having always been a rather lazy pupil, with no fixed goals or plans for his future, Brett suddenly threw himself into his studies. Living with his aunt Jackie and her two children, who were jealous of his good looks, intelligence and modest inheritance, and made sure he knew he was tolerated rather than loved within the family, Brett spent hour after after locked in his room, cramming for exams. When he won a place at a prestigious boarding school on a mathematics scholarship, his aunt didn't want him to go.

'It's six hundred miles away, Brett. You won't know a soul. Won't you be lonely?'

'No.'

'Your mum wanted you to live here, with us. She thought that'd be best for you.'

'She was wrong.'

Aunt Jackie looked pained. 'It was what she wanted. I promised her . . .'

'It doesn't matter what she wanted,' Brett said angrily. 'She's dead.'

'Brett!'

'I'm alive and I know what's best for me. I'm going to St Edmund's.'

In the end Brett had had to apply to the executors of his father's will to release funds for his education and had petitioned the family courts to be allowed to go away to school. He never returned to his aunt's house, or to Burnside, the Adelaide suburb where he'd spent his childhood. It was the first of many battles that he would win in his determined pursuit of wealth and worldly success, the only 'security' that meant a damn in Brett's book. By his sixteenth birthday he was fully legally independent, the top performing scholar at the top school in Sydney, and the youngest-ever applicant to be awarded a place at ANU, the Australian National University in Canberra, for applied mathematics.

ANU was to change Brett Cranley's life. Not because he graduated with first-class honors and went on to Melbourne Business School to begin an MBA he would eventually be too successful to have time to finish. But because it was at ANU that he met the two women who transformed him from a boy into a man.

The first was a professor's wife by the name of Madeleine Jensen. Maddie spotted the dark, angry-looking boy on campus in his first week in Canberra.

'Who is that?' she asked her husband. Professor Jamie

Jensen was the head of the math faculty at ANU, a quiet, scholarly man considerably more interested in Fermat's Last Theorem than he was in his wife's sexual needs. Or any other needs, for that matter.

'That's Brett Cranley. The prodigy, or so they say. Ridiculous to send a child of that age away to college in my view, but there we are.'

'I wouldn't call him a child,' said Maddie, catching Brett's eye and the wild hunger beneath his brooding exterior. 'He's very good looking.'

'If you say so, my dear,' Professor Jensen muttered absently.

Maddie did say so. Not just to her husband, but to Brett himself when she approached him after lectures a few days later. 'Are you a virgin?' she asked him bluntly.

Brett replied in the affirmative. Since his mother's death he'd undergone a self-imposed ban on all interaction with the opposite sex. Not that he had no libido. Quite the opposite. But the strength of the physical longing welling up inside him was at war with the terrible fear of loss and abandonment that had become as much a part of him as his own flesh and bones. Brett adored women – both sexually and for the warmth and intimacy they offered, warmth and intimacy that he desperately longed for – but he was afraid of them.

'Do you want to be?'

Whether it was Madeleine's directness, her utter lack of guile, or the fact that she was almost old enough to *be* his mother; or whether it was her beauty, or her own deep sexual need speaking to his, Brett didn't know. What he did know was that he wanted to go to bed with her. Very, very badly.

'No.'

'Good.' Maddie smiled. 'Follow me.'

38

Sex opened up a new and glorious world for Brett Cranley. Before long it rivalled ambition as the key driver in his personality. His relationships with women were wildly conflicted: needy, passionate and adoring on the one hand; angry, frightened and controlling on the other; each one a reflection of his feelings for his mother, frozen in suspended animation at fourteen. He and Maddie Jensen remained lovers for over a year, but there were many, many others, too many to count, let alone remember, a sea of faces and bodies and, before long, a trail of broken hearts left in his wake. Brett needed sex like a plant craving sunlight. Both the physical rush and the emotional validation fuelled his confidence and ambition like a shot of adrenaline in the arm.

He'd been sure of himself before ANU, before Maddie Jensen.

Now he felt invincible.

It was in his last year, his last few months at ANU, that Brett Cranley met the second woman who was to change his life forever.

Angela Flynn was not a student at the university. A shy, sweet, quietly funny eighteen-year-old girl, with no life experience and no particular ambition, she worked in the Belwood Bakery close to the mathematics faculty building. Brett used to see her when he bought his lunchtime sandwich and was immediately drawn to something about her. It was a combination of innocence, kindness and fragility. Angela was so pale she looked almost like a ghost, with her white-blonde hair and amber eyes, oddly translucent beneath her spun gold lashes. She was the sort of girl who looked as if she might faint if exposed to too much sun, or cold. And yet her disposition belied her appearance. As Brett got to know her, he discovered she was a relentless optimist, as hopeful and trusting of the world as he was cynical and dismissive. He also discovered that she was a virgin. For some reason that he couldn't define, even to himself, this was important.

His attraction to Angela was different to that with all the other women he had gone to bed with, something that would remain the case throughout their long marriage. He wanted to own her, to protect her, to carry her around with him in a glass case, like a guardian angel. His angel. His Angela. He was sure that his mother would have loved her.

As it turned out, marrying Angela Flynn was not the easy feat he'd assumed it would be. She had a father, and three older brothers, all of them Irish Catholic, deeply protective and not remotely inclined to let their teenage sister 'throw herself away' on a kid not much older than she was and well known to be a player on campus. Nevertheless, Brett persisted, proposing to Angela before he went away to business school and agreeing to a chaste, three-year engagement at the Flynn family's insistence. Even after he founded Cranley Estates at only twenty years old, backed by MacQuarie Bank, then dropped out of business school and became a multimillionaire almost overnight, Angela's family held firm. They finally married on Angela's twenty-first birthday, not a day before, in a tiny local church in Canberra.

The bride wore white.

It was the happiest day of Brett Cranley's life.

'You'd better get dressed,' Michelle said, matter-of-factly.

She was back in PA mode now, as if the sex had never happened, scrolling through the rest of the day's agenda on her Samsung phone while Brett lay sprawled out naked on the carpet with his arms and legs outstretched, like Leonardo da Vinci's Vitruvian man.

'The guy from Goldman Sachs Asset Management's gonna be here in ten minutes.'

'Oh, God. Really?'

'Really. And I don't think *those* are the assets he's interested in, do you?' She looked down at her boss's wilting dick and grinned broadly.

'I certainly hope not.' Brett grinned back, feeling happier by the minute that he'd hired this girl. If they didn't give him an 'Investor in People' award next year, there'd be no justice in the world. 'Be an angel and hand me my clothes, would you? And call down and order a pot of tea for . . . what's his name, the GSAM bloke?'

'Kingham. Anthony Kingham. Will do.'

Brett had forgotten completely about the Goldman meeting. He must be tireder than he thought. He'd have liked to cancel, but it was too late now.

Never mind. The call to Angela and the kids would have to wait.

CHAPTER THREE

Max Bingley walked down Fittlescombe High Street with a spring in his step.

'Good morning, Mrs Preedy!'

The village shopkeeper's wife smiled and waved. She was wearing an old-fashioned apron with deep front pockets and had a wicker basket, filled incongruously with leeks, under one arm. She reminded Max of Mrs Honeyman, the village gossip from *Camberwick Green*, a 1960s children's programme made with puppets that he and his younger brothers used to watch as kids. There was something wonderfully innocent and timeless about Fittlescombe that regularly took Max back to earlier, happier times. The Preedys' shop was at the heart of it all, along with the excellent village pub, The Fox.

'Enjoying the break, Mr Bingley?'

Mrs Preedy had unloaded her leeks into a crate of fresh vegetables outside the front door of the shop and was now polishing apples with the front of her apron.

'I am indeed. Hard not to with such lovely weather.'

It was indeed a perfect day, blue-skied and warm for May, with the faintest hint of breeze carrying the scent of honeysuckle and early flowering jasmine on the air. Half-term had run late this year, and school wasn't due to start again for another week, so the unexpected sunshine was an added boon. Max Bingley was thoroughly enjoying his new job as headmaster of St Hilda's Primary School, and didn't mind the idea of going back. But nothing could quite beat a week's walking and fishing in the glorious Downs countryside. Not for the first time, Max said a silent prayer of thanks that he'd had the good sense to take the St Hilda's job when it was offered to him.

When Harry Hotham, St Hilda's headmaster of over twenty-five years, unexpectedly announced his retirement last year, and the governors approached Max about the position, he found himself on the receiving end of a relentless campaign by his daughters to accept the job. Max had been depressed since his wife, their mother, had died two years earlier.

'You need a fresh start, Dad,' said Rosie, now in her fourth year of medical school at Cambridge. 'The Swell Valley is supposed to be ridiculously beautiful.'

'You need a challenge, too,' chipped in her sister May, already Dr Bingley and now studying for a second PhD in Medieval History in London. 'Mum would hate to see you wasting away like this. You're still young.'

'I'm not young, darling,' Max smiled, 'but thank you for saying so.'

'Well you're not old,' said Rosie. 'More to the point, you're a wonderful teacher. You have so much more to give professionally. And Fittlescombe's a lovely village. I went there once for a wedding.'

'I'm sure it is . . .'

'We should at least go and take a look.'

All Max's objections – he'd never taught in a state school,

the pay was awful, he was a rotten administrator – were swatted aside by his daughters like so many pesky, insignificant flies.

'You should have made head years ago, but you never pushed for it. And where better to make a difference than in a state school? Why should the wealthy kids get all the good teachers? Anyway, St Hilda's is a charter school so there won't be that much admin. The governors run it, and they obviously like you and your methods. You'll have free rein.'

Little by little, Max had been worn down. Then he'd come to Fittlescombe, and walked into the cottage that May and Rosie had already found for him online. Half the size of his present house, Willow Cottage was utterly charming with its flagstone floors, open fires and enchanting sloping garden leading down to the river.

'Private fishing rights, dad,' May said with a wink. 'And you wouldn't need a mortgage.'

So Max took the job of headmaster at St Hilda's, more because he lacked the energy to fight than for any positive reason. Now, nearly five months later, things were very different. *He* was very different. Revived and energized professionally in a way he wouldn't have believed possible a year ago, he'd already had a profound impact at the school. Not everybody loved his old-fashioned methods – desks in rows, teacher at the front, blackboards and chalk and weekly tests on everything from spelling to times tables to French verbs. But the OFSTED report in March had given the school a glowing review, and if the current Year Six performed as well in their SATs as they had in the Easter mock exams, St Hilda's had every chance of topping the West Sussex league tables. Quite an achievement for a four-room village primary school with a tiny budget and over thirty children to a class.

But it wasn't only the school that had transformed Max Bingley. Day by day, week by week, the village of Fittlescombe had worked its magic on him, drawing him in and making him one of their own. The community was friendly, but it went far beyond that. It was the place itself, the solid stone walls of Willow Cottage, the church with its yew hedges and ancient tombs, the houses and shops squeezed together along the high street, like the last line of resistance against all that was ugly and vulgar and painful in this modern world. And then, of course, there were the Downs, surrounding Fittlescombe like protective giants, as vivid green as wet seaweed and as softly undulating as feather pillows. Max walked, and fished, and drank in the beauty of his new home like a humming bird gorging on nectar. And although his daughters despaired over the state of his cottage, and his utter lack of interest in painting a wall or hanging a picture, or even curtains, the truth was that the move to Fittlescombe had brought Max Bingley back to life.

At the end of the High Street he turned left, along the lane that led to the bottom of Furlings' drive. Everybody in the village knew that a family of rich Australians had moved into the big house, the first non Flint-Hamiltons to live there in three centuries. Max Bingley had been surprised but delighted to learn that the new owners intended to send their daughter to the village school. Typically families with that sort of money sent their little darlings off to prestigious prep schools, like the one where Max had spent most of his career. Then again, Australians were supposed to be more down to earth and egalitarian by nature, weren't they? Perhaps the Cranleys were champagne socialists? Either way, Max wasn't above buttering up St Hilda's new, mega-rich parents in the hope of a future donation to the school. He'd only been there a term and a half himself, but he already had a wish list for St Hilda's as long as both his arms. More teaching assistants would be a start. And a central heating system that stood at least a fighting chance of seeing them through the next winter.

Straightening his tweed jacket, he headed purposefully up the long, bumpy drive.

'Jason? Have you seen those cushions? They were in the big box. The one from the General Trading Company. Jason!'

Angela Cranley ran an exhausted hand through her hair. Brett was coming home tonight, for the first time. *Home.* It was funny how quickly Angela had come to think of Furlings in those terms. But nothing, nothing, was ready. The twin Knole sofas she'd ordered from Peter Jones had been the wrong colour and had had to go back. Her and Brett's bed, shipped over from Sydney at Brett's insistence because it was the most comfortable bed in the world, had been damaged in transit and now sat in the master suite with a huge crack in its antique mahogany headboard. The food order from Ocado *had* arrived, but the bloody people in Lewes had made a bunch of substitutions, including swapping out the seabass Angela had planned for Brett's welcome-home supper with cod. Brett hated cod. And now the cushions – four large, down-stuffed squares of hand-embroidered Belgian lace, designed to cover the dreaded headboard crack – appeared to have gone missing in action.

To top it all off, Mrs Worsley had been called away to a family emergency, something to do with her sister and a boiler (Angela had only been half listening), and was not due back until tea time, only a few hours before Brett walked through the door. Which left Jason, who'd been in a world of his own these past few days, as Angela's sole helper. (Unless you counted Logan who, last time Angela had seen her, had been painting her toenails in rainbow stripes with a packet of felt tip pens on the kitchen floor.) Now Jason, too, was gone.

Perhaps my son and four Belgian lace cushions are together somewhere, knocking back sour apple martinis and enjoying themselves while I lose my mind? Angela thought hysterically. She'd been pacing the library like a madwoman for the last five minutes, as if a two-by-three-foot crate from the General Trading Company were going to magically materialize before her eyes, simply because she remembered leaving it there yesterday.

The ringing doorbell did nothing to calm her jarred nerves.

'Coming!'

Running into the hall, she collided with Jason, still in his pyjamas and looking as if he hadn't slept a wink. Insomnia was one of the worst parts of depression, but Angela was too frazzled to offer much sympathy this morning.

'Where have you been?' she wailed. 'I need you.'

'In bed. Sorry.'

'Have you seen the new cushions? They were in that big box . . .'

'They're in your dressing room. Mrs Worsley carried them up last night, remember?'

Clearly, Angela didn't remember. She hadn't felt this stressed since the day that horrendous Tricia woman showed up at the house in Sydney and announced, cool as a cucumber, that she and Brett were 'madly in love'. The doorbell rang again.

'Yes, yes! I'm coming. Give me a chance, for God's sake.'

She pulled open the door, unaware of quite how deeply she was frowning, or how far her voice had carried.

'I'm s-so sorry,' the man on the doorstep stammered. 'I do apologize. I've come at a bad time.'

The man was older, maybe a decade older than Brett, with a fan of wrinkles around each eye, but he wasn't unattractive. Tall, and still only partially grey, with a slightly military bearing and a kind, intelligent face, he looked quintessentially English in his tweed jacket and bottle-green corduroy trousers. Angela could see at once that she'd embarrassed him by being so unwelcoming.

'Not at all. God, please. *I'm* sorry. What must you think of me? I'm not normally so rude. Or so scruffy.' She looked down at her crumpled jeans, stained at the knees with wood polish, and at the chipped nail enamel on her bare feet, and blushed what she knew to be a perfectly hideous tomato-red. 'How can I help?'

She's not at all what I expected, thought Max Bingley. He'd imagined diamonds and perfectly coiffed hair and a fleet of servants answering the door, not a harassed housewife with bags under her eyes dressed like a charwoman. Perhaps the Cranleys were not as well off as local gossip suggested?

'Max Bingley.' He proffered his hand. 'I'm the new head-master at St Hilda's, the primary school in the village. I understand your daughter will be joining us next term?'

'You're Logan's headmaster? Oh, crap.' The words were out of her mouth before she knew she'd said them. Angela's colour deepened. 'I can't believe I just said that out loud! I am soooo sorry.'

Max laughed. Her discomfiture clearly amused him.

'That's quite all right, Mrs Cranley. I promise I won't be sending you to my office. Or your daughter. Not yet, anyway. What did you say her name was?'

'Logan,' said Angela, smoothing down her dishevelled hair.

Max resisted the urge to say 'like the berry?' and merely smiled politely.

'We have a son too. Jason. But he's twenty so I doubt you're going to want him in your classroom, ha ha ha ha!'

What's wrong with me? thought Angela. *Why am I babbling away like a lunatic?*

'No. Quite so.' Max shifted awkwardly from foot to foot. This was the moment when he'd expected her to invite him inside for a cup of tea, or at least to ask a few polite questions about the school. Instead she just stood in the doorway looking flustered. *I shouldn't have come. I should have waited to meet her at school like everybody else.* 'Well, I won't keep you. I just wanted to say welcome and I look forward to meeting . . . Logan.'

He turned the word over in his mouth as if it were some strange fruit he'd never tasted before. There weren't too many Logans to the pound in Fittlescombe. Or in England, come to that.

'Right, well. I look forward to seeing you both at school,' Max finished awkwardly. 'Goodbye!'

He smiled and gave a cheery wave, but it had clearly been an embarrassing encounter for both of them.

Angela walked back into the hall, closing the front door behind her. 'I just made a total dick of myself in front of the village headmaster,' she told Jason.

'I'm sure you didn't,' said Jason, not looking up from the box of books he was unpacking.

'I did. I said "crap".'

Jason smiled. 'I reckon he'll recover, Mum. Crap's not that bad. It's not even a real swear word.'

'It fucking well is,' said Angela. They both giggled.

'You need to chill out, you know,' said Jason. 'It's only Dad coming home. It's not the pope.'

'I know,' Angela sighed. 'But I promised him the house would be ready and it's a bloody disaster.'

Jason hugged his mother. He hated to hear the fear in her voice. But the truth was, Angela was afraid of Brett. They all were. Not physically afraid. But afraid of his disapproval, his censure, his disappointment. Brett Cranley was a bully.

So what if you promised him? Jason wanted to scream. *What about all the promises he made to you, and didn't keep? Anyone would think you were the one who'd been unfaithful, not him.* But he knew it would do no good.

'The house is not a disaster. It's beautiful. Dad's gonna love it, you'll see. Now go and have a bath and get changed.'

'A bath? I can't. The cushions . . .'

'I'll do the damn cushions. And I'll unpack the rest of these boxes too,' said Jason. 'Please, go and take a chill pill before you hurt yourself. You're no use to anyone in this state.'

Once she'd gone, reluctantly and only after leaving a barrage of instructions about what needed to be done in the next hour, Jason returned to unpacking. The few books the family had had shipped from Australia looked ridiculous in Furlings' enormous library. Rory Flint-Hamilton had bequeathed his vast collection of Victorian first editions to Sussex University, so the endless shelves in the grand mahogany-panelled room were bare. *Like the mouth of an old man who's lost all his teeth*, thought Jason. He couldn't imagine how they were ever going to fill them.

Perhaps he could persuade his parents to turn it into a music room? The acoustics would be perfect for a Steinway grand piano. Jason's father had never encouraged his music, partly because he considered it to be a useless attribute in a man, and partly because, as he told Jason brutally, 'You're not good enough, mate.'

In this latter observation, however, Brett was correct.

Jason was a good, solid pianist, but he lacked the talent and flair to make it professionally, at concert-level. The idea that a person might want to play the piano for pleasure, without making any money from it, was anathema to Brett Cranley.

'Why don't you do something useful? Something you can make a living at?' Brett would ask his son. Jason had long ago given up trying to reason with his dad. It would be like an eagle trying to communicate with a gorilla. Utterly futile.

The doorbell rang again. People were seriously social in this village. Jason hesitated – he was still in his pyjamas – but he knew if he didn't get it, Angela would heave herself out of the bath like something out of *The Kraken Wakes* and run dripping down the stairs. She'd probably open the door stark naked, she was in such a bloody state about Dad and the house.

Skidding back into the hallway, sliding along in his socks like Tom Cruise in *Risky Business*, he opened the door.

'Oh my goodness. Hello.'

The most beautiful woman Jason Cranley had ever seen stood before him, looking him up and down, curling her upper lip with a combination of amusement and disdain.

'Do you know who I am?'

No, thought Jason. *But suddenly, I want to.* The girl was tall and slim, with a cascade of honey-blonde waves falling onto her shoulders and down her back. She was wearing tight jeans tucked into riding boots, a dark green cashmere sweater that clung unashamedly to her large, pert breasts, and aviator sunglasses that hid her eyes but could not conceal the chiselled beauty of her features. Her cheekbones looked as if they could cut through glass.

'I'm Tatiana Flint-Hamilton,' the goddess announced,

51

without waiting for an answer. Just as well, as all Jason seemed able to do was to open and close his mouth like a guppy. 'I'm here for my painting.'

Pushing past him, Tati strode into the hall. She'd both longingly anticipated and dreaded coming here today to face Furlings' new owners. Or rather, to face the imposters who had, temporarily, appropriated her birthright. Tati would never, ever view the Cranleys as anything other than squatters, no matter how many pieces of paper they or their lawyers waved in front of her. This was her home. She had no intention of giving it up without a fight, and indeed had already engaged a solicitor to contest Rory's will on her behalf.

She clung tight to her indignation now, as a tumult of emotions threatened to overwhelm her. Nostalgia. Grief. Regret. Ignoring Jason completely, she stormed off down the corridor, pushing open doors into rooms that were either bare or filled with strange, jarring, modern furniture. Other people's furniture. Tati found herself fighting back tears. She'd stayed here herself only a few weeks ago for the fete, and it had still felt like home. She'd inhaled the smell of stone and wood, faintly infused with smoke from last winter's fires, and run her fingers lovingly along the heavy, damask curtains in the drawing room. She used to like to hide behind those curtains as a child, eating Carlsbad plums she'd stolen from the pantry, much to Mrs Worsley's fury. But now the curtains were gone and the house smelled of lavender and some Godawful room spray from The White Company. Like a bloody hotel!

Tatiana turned on Jason, who'd been following her around silently like a confused puppy since she arrived.

'Where's Mrs Worsley?'

She said it accusingly, as if Jason had kidnapped the

housekeeper, or murdered her in her bed and concealed the body.

'She took the day off.'

'Don't be ridiculous. She never takes days off. To do what?'

'Erm, I think her sister . . .' He left the sentence hanging, both intimidated and enthralled by Tatiana's beauty and her astonishing confidence. She hadn't asked if she could come in, or even inquired as to his name. She'd simply swept past him, like a queen reclaiming her castle.

'Is there anything I can help with? I'm Jason by the way.'

Tatiana deigned to remove her Ray-Bans. 'Jason. How do you do? I would say it's nice to meet you but, under the circumstances,' she smiled thinly, 'I won't bother. When will Mrs Worsley be back?'

'I'm back now.'

The disapproving Scottish voice that Tatiana knew as well as her own rang out behind her, filling the room that until a few months ago had been Rory Flint-Hamilton's study.

'What do you want, Tatiana?'

Tatiana looked at the housekeeper with narrowed eyes. She was certain the old witch must have known about the changes to her father's will. She'd probably encouraged him. God knows she'd had enough opportunity to sow the seeds of doubt in Rory's mind. Tati could hear her now:

'It would be tragic to think of Furlings going to wrack and ruin.'

'Poor Tatiana's her own worst enemy. The last thing she needs is more cash in her hand.'

She probably thought Daddy would leave her something as a token of his appreciation. The sanctimonious, money-grubbing, scheming old shrew.

Underneath Tatiana's anger there was love there, and a grudging respect for the woman who had practically raised her. But, as on Mrs Worsley's side, the hurt feelings ran deep, with both women feeling let down and betrayed by the other.

Tatiana had insisted on staying at Furlings in the run-up to the fete, but Mrs Worsley clearly hadn't wanted her there. Perhaps unsure of her status since Rory's death, she had given in and allowed it anyway, despite her better judgement. But now, with the Cranleys safely installed, she obviously felt emboldened.

'You know you shouldn't be here,' she chided.

'I've come for Granny's painting,' Tatiana responded stiffly.

'I see. Well, you know where to find it.'

'Obviously.'

While the two women glared at one another, arms folded, the doorbell rang yet again.

What now? thought Jason, irritated to have to go back to the front door rather than stay and watch the standoff.

'Can I help you?'

It was a man at the door this time, blond and stocky and with a disarmingly genuine smile.

'Gabriel Baxter. We're neighbours.' Gabe offered Jason his hand. 'Is your father at home?'

Just at that moment, Angela came downstairs. Fresh from the bath, with her still damp hair tied up in a bun, she looked younger than her forty-two years in a plain white Gap T-shirt and a pair of cut-off jeans. She wore no make-up and seemed fragile and tiny in her bare feet.

'My husband's still in London.' She smiled at Gabe. Having made such a poor impression on Max Bingley, she was determined to be friendly to any other villagers who showed up on the doorstep. 'We're expecting him this evening. I'm Angela. Would you like a cup of tea?'

Tatiana, her painting tucked under one arm, marched back into the hallway. She was about to storm straight out but stopped in her tracks when she saw Gabe.

'What are *you* doing here?' she asked rudely, her eyes narrowed in suspicion. Tatiana knew Gabe was one of the leading voices against her in the village. She also knew that when her father had been alive, Gabe had tried relentlessly to convince Rory to sell off parcels of Furlings' land. She didn't trust him an inch.

'Just being neighbourly,' lied Gabe. 'How about you?'

I live here, Tati wanted to shout. *It's my fucking house.* But she managed to restrain herself.

'I'm collecting a painting. My grandmother's portrait. One of the few pieces of my inheritance that wasn't stolen from me,' she added caustically. Belatedly catching sight of Angela, she introduced herself, extending the hand not holding the painting with regal disdain.

'Tatiana Flint-Hamilton.'

'Oh!' Angela smiled warmly. 'Hello. I didn't know you were coming. I'm Angela. I'm so sorry about the mess. You should have called.'

'Should I indeed?' Tati's voice quivered with resentment and hostility.

'I didn't mean it like that,' Angela blushed. 'I just meant . . .'

'Don't apologize,' Gabe Baxter interjected. 'It's your house.'

Tati shot him a look that would have turned a lesser man to stone.

'Besides, you're quite right. Tatiana *should* have called.'

'Don't you have a ewe that needs lambing, Gabriel?'

sniped Tati. 'Or an episode of *The Archers* to listen to? Gabriel's terribly *rustic*,' she added patronizingly to Angela and Jason. 'A real local character. If you ask him nicely, I expect he'll come round and do a spot of Morris dancing for you, won't you, Gabriel? It's really quite adorable.'

Gabe's features hardened. He looked at his watch.

'My goodness, is that the time? You'd best get home to your rented cottage, Tatiana. It's almost coke-o'clock.'

Blushing scarlet, Tatiana pushed past him and stormed out, throwing the painting into the back seat of her Mini Cooper and driving off. Gabe Baxter followed swiftly after, promising to come back and call on Brett at the weekend.

Once the door closed behind him, Angela and Jason exchanged shocked glances.

'Is everybody in Fittlescombe so . . . dramatic?' Angela asked Mrs Worsley.

Or so attractive? thought Jason. Watching Gabe and Tatiana going at it was like watching a pair of peacocks fanning out their tails for battle. Terrifying but beautiful.

'No ma'am,' said Mrs Worsley with feeling. 'I can assure you that most of your neighbours are quite normal, sane and friendly people. Miss Flint-Hamilton – Tatiana – I'm afraid she can bring out the worst in folk. Especially around here.'

Angela bit her lower lip anxiously. She'd already heard whispers in the village about Tatiana's legal challenge to the will. Brett had assured her that the legacy was watertight, and Furlings was theirs. But having seen Tatiana in the flesh, Angela got the strong sense that Rory Flint-Hamilton's daughter was a force to be reckoned with. Perhaps Brett had underestimated her?

'You don't think she plans to cause trouble, do you?'

She looked at Mrs Worsley nervously.

'Unfortunately Mrs Cranley, Tatiana's done nothing but cause trouble since the day she was born. And since she turned fifteen . . .' She rolled her eyes heavenwards. 'Her father was always too soft on her, bless his soul. Try not to worry, though,' she added, noticing Angela's tense expression. 'She's full of hot air about the will.'

'Do you really think so?'

'Oh, yes. She would need the support of the whole village to be able to launch a challenge, and she certainly hasn't got that. Even if she did, Mr Flint-Hamilton was a clever man, and a thorough one. These so-called loopholes are all in Tatiana's head.'

'I do hope so,' said Angela.

The thought of packing everything up and returning to Sydney, Tricia and their old life now was more than she could bear.

Twenty minutes later, pushing open the stiff door of Greystones Farm, Tatiana collapsed on the ugly, brown sofa feeling exhausted and depressed.

It had been a pretty devastating two days.

Unable to afford a decent London lawyer, she'd retained a local, Chichester man, Raymond Baines of Baines, Bailey & Wilson. Their meeting yesterday had been less than Tati had hoped for.

'To be perfectly honest with you, Miss Flint-Hamilton, I don't believe you have a case.'

Short and bald, with thick, owlish glasses and a distinctly passive, mild-mannered, absolute-opposite-of-a-go-getter-lawyer demeanour, Ray Baines looked at his would-be client steadily.

'But I already have half the village behind me,' Tati protested. 'The tide of local opinion is definitely turning. Nobody wants some upstart Australian installed at Furlings. I made good headway running the fete committee, and by the time it comes to court I'm sure I can—'

'It won't matter,' Raymond Baines cut her off, not unkindly. 'That's what I'm trying to tell you.'

'Are you saying you are unable to act for me, Mr Baines?' Masking her disappointment with anger, Tatiana bristled with aggression.

'No, Miss Flint-Hamilton. I am *able* to act for you. And technically speaking you are correct. We could mount a challenge based on the premise that Furlings was subject to an 'effective' entailment which your father had no legal authority to break. However I am advising you that it is my legal opinion that such a challenge will fail. With or without local support.'

'Yes, but you don't know that. You only think it.'

'I think it very strongly.'

Tatiana knew she was clutching at straws. But drowning as she was in a sea of shattered hopes, she had no choice but to clutch on regardless.

'What are your fees, Mr Baines?'

Raymond Baines told her. The number was modest, a tiny fraction of what Tati's godfather's firm would have charged for the same service. But it would still represent a dent in Tati's meagre savings that she could ill afford.

'Savings' was perhaps the wrong word for the few thousand pounds remaining in Tatiana's bank account. Having split from Piers, her latest wealthy lover, and moved out of his Belgravia flat, Tatiana had taken the jewellery he'd given her, along with any other gifts from former paramours she suspected might be of value, and auctioned the lot at Christie's. The resulting windfall had been enough to pay off her debts, rent Greystones for six months, and leave a modest sum to fund a legal battle with the Cranleys.

Unfortunately, she would need a lot more than a modest sum. At a minimum, she would need full access to the pittance of a trust fund her father had deigned to leave her. That would mean crawling cap-in-hand to St Hilda's new headmaster, Harry Hotham's replacement, to beg for a job. So far Tati's pride had prevented her from availing herself of this much-needed source of funds. It was bad enough having to leave London and return to Fittlescombe, but that was a necessity. Ending it with Piers meant she'd lost the roof over her head, and rents in any part of London where she might actually want to live were astronomical. Still, if the court case dragged on as long as Raymond Baines seemed to think it might, the fact was she was going to need a job of some kind. And as the school job was the only one that unlocked her trusts, this was the obvious path to take.

The prospect terrified her. Tatiana Flint-Hamilton had never worked a day in her life. As for teaching, she wished she shared her godfather's faith in her abilities. Or her father's, for that matter. The simple truth was that she no more knew how to control a class full of children than she knew how to mill flour or discover a cure for cancer.

She'd hoped that going back to Furlings today and seeing the new owners installed there might revive her fighting spirit and boost her courage. Remind her that the fight was worth it. In fact, all it had done was make her desperately sad. The fact that the Cranley family seemed so nice and friendly, and so *ensconced* already, only made Tati feel worse. Mrs Worsley was already firmly on their side, defending their right to be there like the wretched dragon that she was. It didn't seem to bother her in the least that Furlings might end up in the hands of a boy named Jason with a sister who, if local gossip was correct, appeared to have been named after a berry. Granny Flint-Hamilton would be rolling in her grave! As for Gabe Baxter, he was little more than a jumped-up farmhand himself. It was hardly any wonder that he was pro-the Cranleys, already hanging around Furlings like a bad smell. People like Gabe ran on envy the same way a car runs on petrol.

Shit-stirring little Bolshevik. I wonder what he's after, exactly?

Getting up from the sofa, Tati wandered into the kitchen and put the kettle on, more for something to do than anything else. It was a long time since she'd felt so profoundly alone. Greystones, the farmhouse she'd rented, was simply furnished, almost to the point of sparseness, and Tati had brought nothing with her from London, beyond some bed sheets and a preposterously expensive couture wardrobe, wholly unsuitable for country life. Her shoe collection alone, more than fifty pairs of Jonathan Kelsey, Manolo Blahnik and Emma Hope stilettos in a rainbow of gleaming, candy colours, would have been enough for a deposit on a house like this one, if only she'd spent her money a little more wisely. Then again, she'd assumed she would always be rich. And why wouldn't she? How was she supposed to know that her vengeful bloody father had been plotting to disinherit her all along, in some sort of macabre, sick joke from beyond the grave?

Having never put roots down anywhere other than Furlings, it had never occurred to Tati to acquire furniture or clocks or books or favourite cushions, the things that would have helped to turn a house like this into a home. She hated the poo-brown sofas, and the incongruously modern, sixties-style Ikea plastic chairs around the dining-room table. As for her landlady's rugs, they were so vile – swirly affairs in orange and lime green and other colours that had no place in a beautiful, Grade II-listed Sussex hall house – that Tati had rolled them all up on the day she'd arrived and stacked them en masse in the back of the garage. The original flagstones and wide-beamed oak floors beneath were infinitely preferable. But without a single rug of her own to warm the place up a bit, the overall effect was one of bareness. Stark and barren, like a tree stripped of its leaves after a storm.

The kettle switched itself off with a click, the steam from its spout fogging up the kitchen window. Tatiana wiped the glass clean with her sleeve and looked out into the garden. It was a stunning day, blue-skied and clear, like the summers of her childhood. Greystones Farm was really little more than a cottage on the outskirts of Fittlescombe, but its garden was enormous, its various sections – rose garden, orchard, vegetable patch and lawn – tumbling into one another willy-nilly, as each exploded and overflowed with colour and scent and fruit and life. There must have been a planting plan once, a design. Tatiana could see where the crumbling walls and overgrown beech hedges had once delineated and organized more than an acre of space. But now, untended, other than a weekly lawn-mowing by old Mr Dryer from the village, the garden was a joyously jumbled eruption of blossoms and greenery. Gazing out at it, watching a rabbit skip about in the white carpet of fallen apple blossom, even Tatiana's spirits lifted a little. Making herself a cup of Earl Grey and two slices of toast and honey, she pushed open the back door and wandered outside.

Could I be happy here? She wondered, savouring the deliciously sweet, buttery toast as she strolled through a towering row of hollyhocks. Tati hadn't lived in the countryside, or spent more than a week at a stretch here, since her childhood. And those weeks had always been spent at Furlings, riding her beloved horse, Flint.

There were times when Tati thought she missed Flint even more than she missed her father. The grey stallion was a former racehorse, and had been a wildly extravagant tenth birthday present from Rory Flint-Hamilton to his daughter. Mrs Worsley had disapproved from the start, but Tatiana would never forget that magical day. Rory leading her, blindfold, around to the stable yard and telling her to open her eyes as Flint pranced majestically out of his horsebox.

'For you, my darling. What do you think?'

'Oh, Daddy!' Tati had gasped, fighting back tears of joy. 'He's beautiful. He's so beautiful! Is he really mine?'

'All yours, my angel. You deserve him.'

Memories of that day still brought Tati to tears. Perhaps because it represented a time before it all went wrong? A time when her father adored her unconditionally. A time before she'd disappointed him. Before she grew up.

Six years later, Flint had also been the cause of one of their worst-ever rows, a terrible turning point in their relationship. Blind drunk after breaking into Furlings' wine cellar and stealing Rory's Pierre Ferrand 1972 Vintage Cognac, Tati had ridden Flint bareback up to the main A27 road. Terrified by a passing lorry, the stallion had bolted into a nearby field, badly injuring his right foreleg.

'How *could* you be so irresponsible!' Rory had chastised her the next day. The vet was still not sure whether or not Flint would be permanently lame.

Tati, severely hungover and secretly riddled with guilt, had lashed out defiantly, refusing to apologize. 'He's my horse. I can do what I want with him.'

'He could have been killed, Tatiana. You both could have been killed.'

'So? It's my life. I can do what I want with that as well,' Tati snarled at her father before throwing up violently all over the tack-room floor.

Looking back now she couldn't for the life of her remember what she had been so angry about. She only remembered that she was angry, and out of control, and that somewhere deep down, even back then, she knew it.

Standing in the garden at Greystones Farm, she wondered whether that episode with Flint had been the turning point. The horse had recovered and been sold, and Tatiana pretended not to care. But losing Flint had marked the end of an era.

And now I've lost Furlings, too.

It was Furlings that had brought her back to Fittlescombe. The house itself had always been the draw. It was the house that kept calling to her, through all the later dramas and distractions of her adult life.

Now, banished from Furlings, and with her former London party life gone up in ashes and smoke behind her, she found she was noticing Fittlescombe village and its glorious surroundings almost for the first time. This garden, for example: humble and gone to seed, a far cry from the formal grandeur of Furlings, was equally idyllic in its own way. So were the rolling chalk giants behind it, and the lane leading down from Greystone's front gate to Fittlescombe High Street with its shops and church and green and wisteria-covered pubs. It was all beautiful. A wonderland, really. Tati couldn't imagine what had prevented her from seeing it before.

But as time passed and she meandered through Greystones' garden, Tati's heart began to harden. *Wonderland indeed. Get a grip. You're not some tourist on a sodding walking holiday*, she told herself sternly. *You're here to get Furlings back.* If she lost sight of that purpose, that goal, there would be nothing left at all. No point to her life. No identity. No future. No hold on the past.

She shivered. It was cold, and getting dark. How long had she been out here, walking and thinking? Too long, clearly.

Inside the house she turned on the central heating and all the lights, forgetting the expense for once in her dire need for some cheer. What else did she want? Noise. Something mindless. She turned on the television and flipped channels, settling for Kelly Osbourne on *Fashion Police* poking fun at celebrities' outfits. It didn't get any shallower or more distracting than that. Finally, she opened the larder cupboard and pulled out a packet of Pringles and a bottle of cheap red wine, liberally filling glass after glass as she ate and watched, watched and ate, pushing all deeper considerations out of her head.

By the time she *thought* she heard the doorbell ring, Tati was in a warm, alcohol-induced glow. The process of deciding definitively that the bell had – indeed – rung, standing up, brushing the Pringles crumbs off her jeans and weaving her way unsteadily to the door took another few minutes, by which time the caller had gone. Leaning on the porch step in the darkness, however, was a tightly bubble-wrapped package.

Pulling it inside, Tati closed the door and ran to the kitchen for scissors. With drunken abandon she sliced away at the plastic wrapping, finally wrenching the contents free with her hands. It was a set of miniatures, tiny, intricately painted portraits of Tati's grandmother Peg and her three siblings. Of course! She'd completely forgotten that her father had left her these too. Perhaps because, unlike the large Sutherland portrait of Peg, they weren't particularly valuable. Not that Tati had any intention of selling any of them.

Tati turned each of the miniatures over in her hands. Granny, Uncle John and the two older sisters, Maud and Helen, whom she never knew. For a moment she thought it might be Mrs Worsley who had sent them in a moment of forgiveness. But the note was from Angela Cranley, who realized she'd forgotten them and had them sent over. Even Tati had to admit that that was kind and thoughtful. She tried not to resent it as she propped each of the tiny pictures up along the kitchen countertop. Picking up the large painting, she set it beside them, studying it closely for the first time.

There was her grandmother Peg, a young girl of twenty-one in the portrait but with the same sharp, knowing eyes she'd had as an old woman, and that Tati remembered so vividly from her own early childhood, in the years when her mother had still been alive. Peggy was Tati's mother's mother, but the two women hadn't been remotely physically alike. Tatiana's own mother, Vicky, was all softness and curves, a round, gentle loving woman, as welcoming as a feather bed or a favourite cushion. Peggy, by contrast, was intelligent and cynical, a tall, slender person of angular proportions and gimlet stares, rarely seen without a strong French cigarette in one hand and a tumbler of whisky in the other. *Much more like me,* thought Tati.

Sinking down into one of the ugly plastic dining chairs, Tati gazed at the painting for a long, long time. Her grandmother would have been horrified to see a family of Australians installed at Furlings, of that Tati felt sure. She was less sure as to whom Granny Peggy would have blamed for the situation: Rory, for changing his will? Or her, Tati, for driving him to it?

It doesn't matter anyway. She's dead. They're all dead except for me. Peggy and her siblings. Mum and Dad. I'm the last. I'm the living. It's what I think that matters.

She didn't realize until hours later, when she got up to go to bed, that her face was wet with tears.

CHAPTER FOUR

Angela Cranley tied the silk belt of her kimono robe loosely around her waist and smiled down at her husband.

'Come back to bed,' growled Brett, reaching for her hand and pulling her towards him.

'I can't. You know I can't,' giggled Angela. 'It's Logan's first day at school this morning.'

As always after they'd made love there was a glow about her. Brett loved his wife the most like this, with her tousled hair and flushed cheeks and that smile that said more about her love for him than words ever could. Thank God he'd left Sydney and that bitch Tricia! He didn't know what he would do if he ever lost Ange.

It was three days since Brett had first arrived in Fittlescombe and walked through the front door of the house that was to be his home for the foreseeable future. All Angela's anxieties about Furlings not being ready had been for nothing. Brett had instantly seen past the teething problems of the move and fallen almost as deeply in love with the house as he was with his wife and children. (Well, one of them, anyway. Jason still seemed miserable and distracted, but then that was becoming a permanent state of affairs with him.) Brett had seen numerous images of Furlings online, of course, so he'd already known the house was a beauty. But this was one of those rare cases where reality had trounced anticipation. Brett Cranley had grown used to having lovely things, to buying whatever he wanted and designing his life to order. Despite this, ever since he'd learned of Rory Flint-Hamilton's will and seen those first pictures, Furlings had seduced him. It was a bit like having an arranged marriage and then discovering your bride was a supermodel.

He noticed that Angela had been nervous at dinner that first night, but he put it down to the house call she'd received earlier in the day from old man Flint-Hamilton's daughter. Apparently Tatiana was threatening to challenge the will.

'She seemed awfully determined about it,' Angela said, refilling Brett's wine glass and re-folding his napkin like an over-attentive Geisha. 'She's clearly heartbroken about losing the house.'

'I don't give a shit,' Brett said brutally. 'She had no right turning up here unannounced and worrying you like that.'

Angela didn't say that her only real worry had been how Brett would take the news. Her husband doled out law suits the way that other people sent out Christmas cards. She couldn't face beginning their new life in this idyllic village under a cloud of conflict and rancour.

'She lost the house because of her own shitty behaviour. Rory's letter of wishes made that very clear. She's no one to blame but herself. As for challenging the will,' he drained his wineglass, throwing the burgundy liquid down his throat angrily, like a man trying to put out a fire, 'she hasn't a snowball's chance in hell. Forget her.'

In her relief that Brett was happy, and that they were going to stay here, Angela had forgotten Tati. She'd sleep-walked through the last two days in a blind stupor of contentment, helping Mrs Worsley sew name tapes into Logan's uniform and ordering expensive lingerie online to surprise Brett, who was always trying to get her into negligees and stockings, usually with no success.

'Jason can take Logan to school,' Brett said now, refusing to release Angela. Slipping one hand beneath her kimono he cupped her left breast, simultaneously kissing her ear and neck as he dragged her back beneath the covers.

'He can't,' Angela protested half-heartedly, her lips finding her husband's as she kissed him back. 'Not on the first day. She'll be nervous.'

'Logan?' laughed Brett. 'Nervous? Please. She'll be eating those poor teachers alive. That kid's got more confidence than Muhammad Ali on steroids.'

It was true. Logan took after her father in that regard, as in every other.

'I have to take her, darling.' Angela smiled. 'Jase can pick her up this afternoon. The school's only down the lane, I'll be back by nine.'

'Just make sure you are,' said Brett, his voice thick with desire as he reluctantly released her. 'I don't like being kept waiting.'

'I don't like being kept waiting.'

Tatiana Flint-Hamilton's cut-glass voice ricocheted off the walls of St Hilda's school office like a shower of diamond-tipped bullets. It was three o'clock in the afternoon on the first day back after half-term. With only half an hour until the bell went, the school office was calm and quiet for the first time all day. Or rather it was until Tati walked in.

'How long is he going to be?'

'Mr Bingley's exceptionally busy this afternoon,' said the school secretary tersely. It had been a long and trying day. The last thing she needed was attitude from Fittlescombe's self-appointed Lady Muck.

'Yes, well so am I,' lied Tati.

She realized she was being obnoxious and that her rudeness wasn't helping matters. But her nerves were out of control. It had taken all of her reserves of courage to steel herself to come here today in the first place, to swallow her pride and ask for the job that her father had arranged for her before he died.

But Rory had been dealing with Harry Hotham. Harry had known Tati all her life. He'd taught her as a child and flirted with her gently but incorrigibly as she blossomed into womanhood. Harry would have adored the tight-fitting Gucci skirt suit and vertiginous Jimmy Choo heels she'd chosen for today's interview. But suddenly Tati felt nervous that the new man, Bingley, might not be so appreciative. With her long hair cascading down her back like a river of honey and her wide, pale pink lips glistening with Mac gloss like two delicious strips of candy, her look did not scream 'village schoolmistress'.

Not that it mattered what she wore if the new headmaster couldn't even be bothered to see her.

'This is ridiculous.' Snatching up her Chanel quilted handbag, Tati headed for the door. If she hurried she'd miss the first of the parents arriving to collect their little darlings and be spared the embarrassment of being seen loitering around a primary school as if dressed for a *Vogue* cover shoot. 'Tell Mr Bingley I'll call to reschedule.'

But just as she pushed open the double doors, Max Bingley emerged from his office. 'Miss Flint-Hamilton? Do come in.

I've only got a few minutes but I can see you now if it's quick.'

Tati hesitated, wildly unsure of herself and feeling particularly foolish in her teetery heels. Max Bingley was younger than Harry Hotham but he had far more gravitas, and none of Harry's playful twinkle in his eye. With his military bearing and craggy but handsome face, he radiated authority like a star radiates heat. In one sentence he had successfully asserted his dominance over Tati and taken complete control of the situation, a state of affairs that Tati was neither used to, nor enjoyed.

'I . . . erm . . . all right,' she stammered, following him back into his room and sitting meekly in the chair that he indicated.

'How can I help?' Max asked. His tone was friendly but brisk.

'I . . . well. It's about the job,' Tati began uncertainly.

Max raised an eyebrow. 'What job?'

'Well, my father . . . you see, he and Harry Hotham . . .' Tati blushed. What on earth was she doing here? The last thing she wanted to do was get into the ins-and-outs of her father's will with this complete stranger, some second-rate schoolteacher from who knows where. She took a deep breath.

'Harry Hotham was a friend of my family,' she blurted. 'My father and he were keen that I should teach at the school. But then I learned Harry had retired.'

Max Bingley frowned. 'I see. Are you a qualified teacher?' He looked Tati up and down with what she took to be a combination of curiosity and distaste.

'Well, no. Not exactly. I'm a . . .' Tati searched for a word to describe herself. 'Socialite' made her sound vacuous. 'Heiress', sadly, was no longer accurate. She cleared her throat. 'I did train as a teacher.'

'But you never qualified?'

'No.'

'Have you ever worked in a school?'

'Not until now.'

Tati smiled and flicked her hair alluringly.

Max Bingley's frown deepened. 'So let me get this straight. You have no experience or qualifications. But my predecessor offered you a *teaching* position here?'

'Yes,' Tati said defiantly. 'With respect, Mr Bingley, I hardly think that teaching a few five-year-olds is beyond me. We're talking about the village primary school, not a fellowship at Oxford!'

She laughed, earning herself a withering glare from across the desk. The interview wasn't going at all the way she'd hoped.

'Look, it wasn't a formal offer or anything,' she back-tracked hastily. 'I don't have a letter. Harry didn't operate like that.'

'Didn't he indeed?' muttered Max Bingley.

'My father was keen I should use my training,' Tati ploughed on. 'Now due to . . . family circumstances, I find myself back in Fittlescombe for a while. So I thought, you know, why not?'

She leaned back languorously in her chair and re-crossed her legs, giving St Hilda's new headmaster a front-row view of her perfectly toned upper thighs. He wasn't so easily manipulated, but realizing the game she was trying to play, for a split second it was Max Bingley's turn to feel flustered and unsure of himself. But he quickly regained his composure.

'I'm afraid I can think of a number of reasons why not, Miss Flint-Hamilton, the main one being that the children of this village, of this school, deserve a decent education. I can't parachute in a completely inexperienced teacher on the back of some vague offer that may or may not have been made to you by my predecessor! The very idea's ridiculous.'

Tati got to her feet, stung. 'There's no "may or may not" about it,' she said hotly. 'Harry Hotham promised me a job. Do you think I'd be here otherwise?'

She looked so terribly upset that for a moment Max Bingley relented. He had two daughters of about the same age as Tatiana and flattered himself that he understood young women. Behind the cocky façade, Max realized, this girl was terrified. Terrified and embarrassed in equal measure.

'Sit down,' he said kindly. 'I'm not doubting your word. I'm merely saying that it wouldn't be right for me to give you a job as a teacher here, even if I had a position available. Which, as it happens, I don't. Without experience, you wouldn't succeed at it, Miss Flint-Hamilton. The children would suffer and so would you.'

Tati sat down, deflated. She was hardly in a position to argue with any of the above. On the other hand, if she were going to stay and fight for Furlings, she needed the money from her trust fund. And if she were going to eat, never mind buy any furniture for Greystones, she needed a salary. She needed this job.

'I'm sorry,' she said, picking up her handbag. 'I've clearly wasted both of our time.'

'Not necessarily,' said Max. 'If you're seriously interested in teaching and would like to gain some experience, I might consider taking you on as a classroom assistant.'

Tati brightened. *Classroom assistant.* Would the trustees go for that?

'You'd have to do a three-month trial first, so I could assess your suitability for the job.'

'A trial?' Tati frowned.

'Yes. Unpaid, although we'd cover your basic expenses.'

'*Unpaid*?' There was no disguising her outrage now. 'Thank you, Mr Bingley, but if I'd wanted to volunteer my time I'd have gone directly to Oxfam. No doubt I'll see you around the village.' And with that she stormed out, slamming Max Bingley's office door shut, the smell of burning olive branches lingering in the air behind her.

The bell must have rung while she and Max were talking. Outside the playground was thronged with overexcited children and weary mothers, rolling their eyes at one another as lunchboxes, backpacks and discarded items of uniform were thrust into their outstretched arms.

Blinded with rage, at herself as much as anyone, and desperate to get out of there, Tati stumbled in her high-heeled shoes and careered into one of the fathers. Dropping her Chanel bag onto the asphalt she looked on in horror as its contents spilled everywhere.

'For fuck's sake,' she hissed through gritted teeth.

A stunningly pretty ten-year-old girl, resplendent in what looked like a brand-new St Hilda's summer uniform of red and white gingham dress, white ankle socks and straw boater with a red ribbon, gasped.

'She said the "f" word!' Did you hear her, Jase? She said the "f" word!'

Belatedly, Tati caught the Australian accent. Looking up she saw that the 'father' she had bumped into was not a father at all but Jason Cranley, the mute, freckled guy she'd met up at Furlings a few days ago. The little girl must be the daughter, Logan.

'She's got cigarettes in her bag!' Logan squealed accusingly, picking up a half-empty packet of Marlboro reds and shaking them in Tati's direction. 'Don't you know smoking is the most dumbest thing you can ever do? You can die! And you can get wrinkles.'

For some reason this last rejoinder made Tati laugh.

'Wrinkles? My goodness. That sounds *very* serious.'

'It is.' Logan's huge, dark eyes widened beneath her long lashes. She really was an extraordinarily pretty child, although it struck Tati that she looked nothing like either her mother or brother. 'I'll throw them in the bin for you if you like.'

Jason, who'd watched silently until now, finally found his voice. 'You can't throw other people's property in the bin, Logan.' Taking the cigarettes from his little sister, he handed them back to Tatiana.

'No. But you can steal it from under their noses, apparently,' Tati shot back waspishly, 'by conning a dying man into leaving you his home.'

Jason blushed. 'I'm n-n-not the enemy, you know,' he stammered. 'None of this will business has anything to do with me.'

'No, well. I suppose not,' Tati conceded grudgingly, appraising him more closely than she had done at Furlings a few days ago. He wasn't bad-looking. But he was very much a *boy* rather than a man. There was a fragility about Jason Cranley, one might even say an innocence, that made one want to protect and mother him. Perhaps it was the freckles? Tati couldn't imagine him having sex, although it was clear from the way he blushed and avoided eye contact that he was attracted to her.

'I'd like it if we could be friends,' he mumbled.

Tati considered this. She had no problem with Jason Cranley. Only with his greedy, conniving, inheritance-pilfering father. Besides, it might turn out to be useful to have a Cranley family member on her side. She may lack experience as a teacher, but when it came to pulling a young man's heart strings, or fanning his sexual obsession, Tatiana Flint-Hamilton was very much an old hand. Jason could be her 'man on the inside' at Furlings. If she were going to win this legal battle over the will, she would need all the help – and inside information – she could get.

'Me too,' she smiled. 'I had a shitty day, that's all. Of course we can be friends.'

Reaching out, she touched his arm in a conciliatory gesture and was gratified when Jason blushed as if he were on fire.

'What was so shitty?' Jason asked. In her sexy, expensive clothes, exuding glamour like a movie star or a royal princess, it was hard to imagine Tatiana's days being anything other than gilded and wonderful.

'Oh nothing.' She waved a hand dismissively in the direction of the school buildings. 'The new headmaster doesn't think I'm capable of ascending to the dizzy heights of village schoolteacher. He wants me to *audition* to be some PGCE nark's *assistant*. An "unpaid trial", that's what he offered me. Can you believe the nerve?'

Jason Cranley couldn't. From his limited first impressions, Tatiana Flint-Hamilton seemed capable of absolutely anything. He certainly wouldn't have the balls to cross her.

'Anyway,' Tati smiled, pulling a cigarette out of her packet 'I'll definitely be needing one of these to calm my nerves.'

'No!' Logan, who'd been watching this exchange between her brother and the very beautiful lady with interest, shook her finger up at Tati disapprovingly. 'Wrinkles, remember?'

Tati shook her finger back and lit up. 'Wrinkles Schminkles.'

To Jason Cranley's delight, and the other parents' slack-jawed astonishment, she winked at him as she sashayed out of the playground.

Back at Furlings, Brett Cranley was in the kitchen. Sitting at the table with his shirtsleeves rolled up and his arms folded, he was listening intently to his new neighbour, Gabriel Baxter.

'They can't be developed,' Gabe was saying. 'The whole valley's an area of outstanding natural beauty. The only thing they're good for is farming. And your yields – the estate's yields – over the last ten years have been dismal.'

'So why do you want them so badly?' asked Brett. He liked the young farmer sitting opposite him. In jeans and an open-necked shirt, his naturally pale skin tanned the colour of just-cooked-toast from long summer days spent out in his fields, and with his blond hair flopping over his eyes messily like a handful of straw, Gabriel Baxter came across as honest, ambitious and direct. But Brett Cranley took nothing at face value when it came to business.

'Because I'd do a better job at farming them,' said Gabe bluntly. 'Farming's my business. It wasn't Rory's and it isn't yours. Plus, they abut my land directly, so I could almost double my holdings and benefit from all those economies of scale.'

'Why do you want to double your holdings?' Brett asked.

Gabe looked puzzled. 'Why not? Wouldn't you?'

Brett smiled broadly. He liked this boy more and more. 'I'll think about it.'

Gabe was itching to close the deal. He'd wanted those fields for years, for all the reasons he'd told Brett, and because they were just so bloody pretty. He wouldn't be happy till he'd nailed a new 'Wraggsbottom Farm' sign onto the gate at the bottom of the lower meadow. For the first time since he'd inherited the farm from his father, he could sense they were within reach. But this was his first meeting with Brett Cranley and he knew he mustn't push too hard.

'Thank you.' Standing up he shook Brett's hand. Just then the kitchen door opened and Logan came skipping through the door, with Jason trailing in her wake, carrying her schoolbag, blazer and straw hat like a put-upon courtier.

'Have you met my kids?' asked Brett, his eyes lighting up at the sight of his daughter, who looked exactly like him.

Gabe smiled at Jason. 'I met your son.'

'Oh yeah?' said Brett, uninterested. 'Well *this* is my baby girl.' He pushed her forward proudly, as if she were a prize vegetable he'd just grown.

'Hello,' said Gabe.

Logan stared up at him, her dark eyes like saucers beneath her long, camel-like lashes. She didn't think she'd ever seen such a handsome man in her life. He looked like a prince, or a knight, or a—

'Say hello to Mr Baxter, Logie,' Brett prompted. 'She's not normally shy,' he added to Gabe. 'I think she likes you.'

'*Daddy*,' Logan hissed, blushing vermilion.

'Oh, come on, pumpkin,' Brett ruffled her dark hair. 'I'm only teasing you.'

Gabe said his goodbyes and left. Once he'd gone, Logan swiftly changed the subject. 'Guess what?' she asked Brett, making herself an orange squash that was practically neat syrup.

'What?'

'Jason's got a girlfriend.'

Brett looked at his son, half amused and half amazed. 'Have you? That was quick work. Who is it?'

'It isn't anyone. Stop being silly, Logie.'

'She's the most beautiful lady I've ever seen in my life,' Logan gushed, between gulps of teeth-rotting orange squash, helping herself to a fistful of McVitie's chocolate fingers from the jar. 'She had very tight clothes on and long hair and big boobs. And she winked at Jason in the playground. Everyone saw her.'

'Who knew the school run could be so exciting?' said Brett. 'I should have gone myself.'

He was playing it cool, but inside he was delighted. It had long bothered him that his son was so hopeless with the opposite sex. Brett viewed Jason's shyness, like his on-and-off depression, as some sort of personal affront. It was almost as if the boy was deliberately asserting his complete 'other-ness' to Brett and everything he stood for, throwing it in his father's face: *I don't look like you, I don't act like you, I don't think like you.* A gorgeous girlfriend – any girlfriend – would be a welcome development indeed.

'So come on, Jase, spill the beans. Who is this mystery woman?'

'There's no mystery,' muttered Jason, wishing the kitchen floor would open up and swallow him. How was it that his father always managed to take every good thing in his life, however small, and ruin it? 'Logan's talking about Tatiana Flint-Hamilton. I ran into her briefly at school, that's all.'

Brett stiffened. 'What was that scheming bitch doing at the school?'

'She's not a bitch,' said Jason. 'She's actually quite nice once you get to know her.'

'I've no intention of "getting to know her". She's already been round here, I gather, causing trouble and upsetting your mother. I won't have that.'

Why? Because nobody's allowed to upset Mum except you, you hypocrite? Jason thought darkly.

'And I won't have you dating her either,' Brett ranted on.

'For God's sake, I am not dating her,' said Jason, exasperated. 'I barely know the girl.'

'Logan said she winked at you.'

'She did!' Logan insisted through a mouthful of chocolate biscuit crumbs.

'She was being friendly. Jesus.'

'Winking isn't friendly. It's flirtatious. She's up to something, and you're too dumb to see it. You shouldn't even be talking to her.' Brett's anger was building, like a steaming kettle about to sing. 'Where's your family loyalty?'

'She *is* family, in case you've forgotten,' Jason shot back. 'We wouldn't be standing here in her house if she weren't.'

'Furlings is not *her house*!' Brett erupted.

Disturbed by all the shouting, Angela walked in. After spending the better part of the day in bed with Brett, she positively beamed with contentment. Until she saw the expression on her son's face. Angela knew that look. Angry. Detached. Shut-down.

'What on earth's the matter?'

'Ask him.' Jason glowered at his father before storming out of the room.

'Come back here!' Brett roared. 'Don't you walk away from me, you little shit!'

'Don't say shit, Daddy,' said Logan, utterly unperturbed. Knockdown drag-out fights between her father and brother were a daily occurrence. Stuffing more chocolate fingers into her pockets, she went up to her bedroom to think about Gabe Baxter in peace. She wondered if she could see his farm from here, and whether or not her binoculars had been unpacked yet.

Once she'd gone, Angela put a tentative hand on Brett's arm. 'What happened?'

Brett's face was set like flint. 'Apparently Jason and that Flint-Hamilton woman were all over each other outside the school gates this afternoon.'

Angela frowned. 'That sounds *highly* unlikely. Are you sure?'

'I'm sure she was there. Logan said she winked at Jason.'

'Well, maybe she did. But I'm sure it was quite innocent.' Angela could not imagine the poised, sophisticated, drop-dead gorgeous Tati in any sort of romantic entanglement with her cripplingly shy, depressive son. Much as she might like to. 'Or maybe Logan made a mistake.'

'She's staying in the village, isn't she? Tatiana?'

'Yes. At Greystones Farm. Why?'

Brett picked up his car keys from the kitchen counter.

Angela looked alarmed. 'You're not going over there?'

'Damn right I am.'

'Oh darling please, don't. What will you say?'

'That I don't want her sniffing around my son, upsetting my wife, or stalking my bloody daughter on her first day at school.'

Angela wrung her hands miserably. 'You're being ridiculous, Brett. If you go over there it'll only stir up trouble, and you know it.'

But it was no use. Brett was already striding down the hall towards the front door. Angela stood and watched from the kitchen window as he jumped into the driver's seat of his new Bentley Continental GT V8 and sped off down the drive like a maddened bull. He could fuel that car on testosterone alone, she thought sadly, as the gravel sprayed up into an angry arc behind him. Testosterone and rage.

Standing at the window she offered up a silent prayer.

Please, please, don't let him start a war with Tatiana Flint-Hamilton.

Some sixth sense told her that Tatiana was every bit as angry and stubborn as Brett. Once begun, this was not a war that would be over by Christmas.

CHAPTER FIVE

Tati lay back in a bath full of Badedas bubbles and inhaled deeply on her cigarette. Even now, a grown woman, half of the pleasure she derived from smoking in the bath was the knowledge of how vehemently both Mrs Worsley and her father would have disapproved of it.

'Unladylike,' Mrs Worsley would have called it. Rory would have said it was vulgar, or worse, 'common': the ultimate insult in Tati's father's book. What they had both failed to appreciate was the deep, profound sense of relaxation the combination of warm water and a shot of nicotine to the bloodstream had on the human body. Fuck yoga. This was the only way to de-stress. Better yet, it was guilt and hangover free, unlike red wine and Pringles . . .

Flicking ash into a horrid, fish-shaped soap dish on the ledge above the bath (her landlady's taste really was abysmal; she must get around to putting more of her ghastly tat into boxes and out of sight), she reflected again on her interview with St Hilda's new headmaster.

Max Bingley had rejected her. Worse, he had patronized her, humiliated her, treated her like a spoiled child who needed to be slapped down, taught a lesson. His voice in her head now made Tati's stomach churn with shame:

'I can't parachute in a completely inexperienced teacher. The very idea's ridiculous! I might consider taking you on as an assistant . . .'

How had her life come to this? How? This time last year she'd been sunning herself on a yacht in the Caribbean, enjoying a much-publicized dalliance with an Arab prince. By now the whole village would know that she'd come crawling to the sanctimonious Max Bingley today, begging for work, and been turned down. The humiliation was almost more than Tati could bear. She didn't even have the luxury of not caring what the locals thought of her. She needed them and their good opinion now, more than ever.

As the bubbles and nicotine worked their combined magic, a small part of her – tiny – admitted the possibility that Max Bingley might, in fact, have been trying to help her this afternoon. That he'd thrown her a lifeline with the offer of a trial position when he really didn't have to. That in reality it was *she* who had been rude and surly and entitled, not the other way around. But Tati squashed that part, snuffing it out ruthlessly. Letting it live would mean admitting weakness. That was something she could never do. Not even to herself. Not if she wanted to survive.

Be that as it may, and despite her wounded pride, she already knew that she would accept Bingley's offer. The job might be unpaid, but without it her trustees would leave her penniless. Of course she could always find herself another rich boyfriend, as she had in the past. But in Tatiana's experience, while men were more than happy to pay for clothes and trinkets and expensive suites in hotels, they were less likely to stump up for their paramours' protracted legal battles. Especially when said battles had been consistently advised against by a veritable fleet of lawyers. When it came to fighting for Furlings, she was on her own.

Stubbing out her cigarette, she pulled herself up out of the bath and stood in front of the mirror. Clumps of bubbles stuck to her wet skin like cuckoo spit on a stem of sticky jack. Tendrils of wet hair escaped from the wide white linen hairband she always wore in the bath, coiling themselves into spring-like ringlets that kissed the top of her neck and shoulders. Naked and without make-up she looked younger than her 24 years, except for the green eyes that stared back at her, knowing and cynical beneath dark, wet lashes.

Tatiana was beautiful and she knew it. A small smile escaped her as she admired her reflection. But it soon turned to a shriek of terror. The figure of a man suddenly appeared behind her, looming ominously in the bathroom doorway.

'Get out!' Panic manifested itself as anger as Tati reached for the nearest heavy object – a solid pottery vase filled with plastic poppies that stood beneath the mirror – and hurled it at the intruder's head. He ducked, narrowly missing being knocked out cold, then lunged forwards, grabbing Tati by the wrists.

'Calm down. I'm not here to hurt you.'

Luckily for Tati her skin was still wet from the bath. With a quick twist of her arms she was able easily to escape his grip. Having no other weapons to hand, she lashed out wildly, kicking, scratching and biting, before finally aiming her left knee towards the man's groin.

Unluckily, his reactions were as quick as her own. Turning to one side so that her knee collided with nothing more sensitive than his thigh bone, he advanced towards her, forcing her back against the bathroom wall. There he was easily able to pin her down, his weight and strength more than compensating for the lack of a firm grip as he pressed her against the plaster, waiting for her breathing to calm down and her struggling to cease.

'Please stop screaming.'

'Fuck off!' Tati screeched. 'There's nothing here to steal, you aresehole!'

'I'm not a burglar.'

'I don't care who you are. Get out of my fucking house!'

'I'm Brett Cranley.'

It took a few seconds for this information to sink in.

Feeling Tati relax beneath him, Brett cautiously released her. 'I'm sorry I frightened you. The front door was open. I called your name but there was no answer so I came in.' Turning around he grabbed a towel, holding it out to Tatiana at arm's length, waving it like a white flag.

'Here. You'd better take this.'

Tati stood in front of him, quivering with rage. Brett felt his libido start to stir, like a roused lion. Stark naked, her perfect, high round breasts jutting out at him defiantly, Tatiana was quite simply magnificent, one of the most beautiful girls Brett had ever seen. And he'd seen quite a few. Slim but not skinny, her long legs tapered up perfectly into softly curving hips and waist, like the sides of a cello. A sleek, dark triangle of pubic hair, like the wet hide of a mink, nestled proudly beneath a perfectly flat stomach. Brett did like a woman with some hair down there. Back in the early nineties the explosion of bare, Brazilian-waxed pussies had been new and exciting. But these days it was so commonplace, he'd come to prefer the mystery of the more natural look. It showed confidence. Although not as much confidence as the way that Tatiana steadily met his gaze, acknowledging the hunger in it, taking the proffered towel slowly rather than jumping to grab it. Clearly she was not remotely embarrassed by her nakedness.

'Get out of my house.'

Her voice was quiet now, and controlled, but there was no mistaking the anger in it.

'Not yet. I need to talk to you,' said Brett.

He knew he ought to leave but he was congenitally incapable of taking orders, especially from a woman. He fully expected Tati to lose it and start pushing him out the door, and/or calling the police. But to his surprise she merely said icily 'Fine. Go downstairs and wait while I dress.'

Ten minutes later, perched uncomfortably on the ugly brown sofa in Tati's sitting room, Brett began to wish he'd left when she'd asked him to. He'd made a complete balls-up of his first encounter with the Flint-Hamilton girl. Barging up the stairs uninvited had been a foolish thing to do. But he'd been so damn angry, and the open door had felt like an invitation. Now he was very much on the back foot, waiting around for Tatiana to grant him an audience like a nervous kid on a first date. Worse, he now very obviously owed *her* an apology, which was not the way he'd hoped to begin this evening's tête-à-tête.

'So, Mr Cranley. You want to talk.'

Tati came downstairs in a pair of chocolate brown corduroy trousers and an old, sludge-green sweater that looked bizarrely good on her. She was barefoot, her wet hair pulled back in a messy bun, and hadn't bothered to put on make-up. It was a look that told Brett very clearly, 'You are not important to me.' A second jolt of desire surged through him, like the aftershock of a major earthquake.

'Yes,' he said gruffly. 'I apologize for startling you earlier. It was stupid of me to barge in on you like that.'

'Yes, it was. Not to mention illegal. But perhaps they don't have breaking and entering in Australia? I daresay in a nation descended from convicts, one shouldn't be surprised.'

Brett's eyes narrowed. *You arrogant little minx.*

'The door was open,' he said coldly. 'As for stupid, I guess you would know. Challenging your father's will is downright moronic. You haven't a prayer of getting Furlings back, you do realize that?'

'Well, we'll see, won't we?' Tati said brazenly. She knew she must not show weakness in front of this usurper. 'You'll find I'm not the only person in this village who wants you out, Mr Cranley.'

'I don't give a fuck what the village thinks. I won't have you coming around *my* house upsetting *my* wife.'

'It's not your house,' Tati hissed.

'You can explain that to the police when I have you arrested for trespassing,' said Brett.

'*You* have *me* arrested?' Tati laughed. 'You just assaulted me, naked, in my own bathroom!'

'Don't be so melodramatic.'

He stood up and started wandering around the room, picking up random objects and examining them idly. In her shocked state up in the bathroom, Tati hadn't got a good look at her enemy. Although clearly he'd got a *very* good look at her. Now, she examined Brett Cranley more closely. Her first thought was how much he looked like his daughter, or rather how much Logan looked like him. Man and girl both had the same dark eyes and blue-black hair, the same swarthy, pirate-like complexion. But whereas Logan was a slender, delicate little thing, Brett had the broad, stocky build of a cage fighter. Moving around Greystones' drawing room now, he seemed too big for the space, like a bear stumbling around a tea room.

He's not especially tall. But he has presence, thought Tati.

She'd witnessed the same effect before in countless other powerful, successful men, men who she'd delighted in seducing and bending to her will. Brett Cranley, she suspected, might prove a more difficult fish to catch. Not that she had the remotest interest in him romantically. All Tatiana wanted from her obnoxious third cousin was the deeds to her house. That and his handsome head on a platter.

Brett gave her a questioning look. 'What are you doing here, Tatiana?'

She glared at him. 'What do you mean?'

'I mean, why are you in this house? This village? You know damn well you're never going to get Furlings back. Why don't you go back to London, find some nice, rich schmuck to marry and live happily ever after? A girl like you could get a score of beautiful houses if she wanted to.'

'I don't want to,' said Tati with feeling. 'All I want is Furlings. Anyway, what do you mean "a girl like me"?'

Brett's questions were the same ones she'd been asking herself less than half an hour ago. But she instantly bridled hearing them from him.

'Oh, I think you know what I mean,' Brett sneered. He had moved close to her now, too close. Tati could smell the faint, patchouli scent of his aftershave and feel the warmth of his breath on her neck. Before she knew what was happening, he had slipped one hand around the small of her back and begun gently stroking her bare skin beneath the tatty sweater, a gesture at once affectionate, erotic and breathtakingly presumptuous.

It was the latter that Tati reacted to, pushing him away violently.

Brett laughed. 'Why so affronted? You're a sexy girl and you know it.'

'And you're a revolting old lech, whether you know it or not. You don't seriously think I'd be attracted to you?'

'Oh that's right, I forgot. You prefer boys now, don't you? Like my son,' Brett said archly, walking away. 'Strange, that's not what I read in the papers about you.'

'I haven't the remotest interest in you or your son,' Tati insisted furiously. 'All I want is my house back. And whether you like it or not, I'm going to get it.'

'You're out of your league,' Brett said languidly. He was mocking her now, a cruel, amused smile playing on his thin lips as he pulled his car keys out of his pocket and tossed them from hand to hand. 'Pretty girls like you should stick to what they're good at.'

'Oh really. And what's that?'

'Shopping and shagging. And looking decorative.'

'That's what your wife does, is it?' said Tati, touching a nerve at last. 'How proud you must be.'

Brett's face darkened. 'You stay away from my wife.'

'I'll be glad to. Just as long as *you* stay away from *me*. I'll see you in court, Mr Cranley.'

Brett said nothing. He merely walked back to his car, laughing.

Once he'd gone, Tatiana stood frozen to the spot, too angry to breathe, let alone move.

Disgusting, arrogant, entitled, sexist pig!

I hate him.

I hate him more than I've ever hated anyone in my entire life.

It was a miracle that both the Cranley children had turned out so sweet. Clearly Angela Cranley must be quite a mother, far from the 'decorative' doll of her revolting husband's imagination.

Conceited little shit.

Shopping and shagging indeed . . .

Tati had been determined to contest the will even before Brett Cranley showed up at her door. But now? Now she'd sell her own organs to get Furlings back if she had to. Brett Cranley was going to rue the day he underestimated Tatiana Flint-Hamilton.

Laura Baxter brushed her teeth and spat furiously into the basin.

'I don't know why you're so angry,' said Gabe. Lying on the bed in his boxer shorts in Wraggsbottom Farm's beautiful, beamed master bedroom, he had a James Bond novel open in one hand and a packet of Maltesers in the other. It was a warm night and the lead-mullioned window beside the bed was open, revealing a glorious view of the valley, with the river Swell at its base and the Downs rolling away to the sea. Gabe had lived here since birth and loved his farm as if it were a person. Since marrying Laura he loved it even more, with all the promise it now held for the future. Their future.

'I went to see a neighbour,' he said, popping another Malteser into his mouth. 'I wasn't selling our first-born child to Pol Pot.'

'We don't have a first-born child,' said Laura. 'And we're not likely to if you keep lying to me.'

She came back into the bedroom looking as furious as it was possible to look in a floral Laura Ashley nightdress covered in pale pink rosebuds.

'I didn't lie to you,' said Gabe indignantly.

'You went behind my back. It's the same thing.'

'It is not the same thing. Christ, what is wrong with trying to buy a few fields anyway?'

Throwing back the covers, Laura climbed into bed, punching the pillows as if she had a grudge against them. She hated it when Gabe was deliberately obtuse. Not to mention deceitful.

'It is not "a few fields". It's hundreds of acres of land that we can't afford. *And* that may not even be Brett Cranley's to sell. You know as well as I do that his inheritance is disputed.'

'All the more reason to buy now, while we've got the chance.'

Laura let out a stifled scream of frustration and turned out her bedside light. Pulling the covers around her like a shield, she pointedly turned her back on her husband.

Gabe was equally frustrated. Running the farm was his job. He didn't tell Laura how to produce television programmes or write scripts. What gave her the right to meddle in his business decisions? On the other hand, he hated fighting with her. Putting down his book and sweets, he wrapped his arms around her stiff, angry body.

'I love you,' he whispered in her ear.

Laura didn't move.

'I know you want to know what they're like,' Gabe teased, slipping a warm rough hand under her nightdress and caressing her wonderful, full breasts. 'The Cranleys.'

Despite herself, Laura moaned with pleasure. It was utterly infuriating, how good he was in bed.

'I'll tell you if you're nice to me,' Gabe whispered, his hands moving slowly down over her belly, his fingertips just skimming the soft fur between her legs. Unable to keep up her resistance any longer, Laura turned around and kissed him, luxuriating in the solid warmth of his body. God, he was beautiful.

'Go on then, tell me,' she said, releasing him at last. 'What are they like?'

'Ha!' said Gabe. 'So you do want to know. I knew it! You're just a sad old village gossip, Mrs Baxter.'

'What's *he* like?' asked Laura, ignoring him. 'Brett Cranley.'

'Actually, I liked him,' said Gabe. 'I mean, I can see how he could be seen as arrogant.'

Laura frowned. 'In what way?'

'He's a big personality. Maybe even a bit of a bully. He obviously favours his daughter over his son, and the wife seems a bit afraid of him.'

Gabe told her about his brief encounter with Logan and Jason today, and about Angela's nerves the first time they met.

'He sounds vile,' said Laura. 'What on earth did you like about him?'

'I don't know, exactly,' said Gabe, thinking. 'He's direct. Honest. I don't think he'd cheat you in business.'

'Well he certainly cheats in his private life,' said Laura with feeling. 'At least if the press coverage is anything to go by.'

'Oh, yeah, but that's different,' said Gabe.

'Why? Because it's OK to cheat on women? Just as long as you're honest with men, is that it?'

Laura felt her hackles rising again. She loved Gabe but sometimes he could be so . . . unreconstructed.

Gabe sighed. 'Give it a rest, Germaine Greer. You asked, I answered. I liked him. Sorry if you and the rest of the village lynch mob have already decided he's the Swell Valley's answer to Vladimir Putin. But I do have the advantage of having actually met the guy.'

'Well, bully for you. I hope the two of you will be very happy together,' said Laura.

Turning away from her, Gabe turned off his own bedside light.

'And I'll tell you something else,' he added defiantly. 'I'm going to get him to sell those fields to me. So put that in your bra and burn it.'

CHAPTER SIX

'Have you seen that stack of marked Year Three homework anywhere? The robot sketches?'

Dylan Pritchard Jones ran a hand through his curly chestnut hair and scanned the mess that was his kitchen. Aside from the detritus of breakfast, almost every surface was covered with copies of *Country Living*, *Elle Décor*, *Period Homes* and every other conceivable variety of interiors magazine. Dylan's wife, Maisie, was expecting their first child and had gone into a frenzy of what the pregnancy websites called 'nesting'. Apparently this was a woman's primitive urge to spend thousands of pounds on expensive Farrow & Ball paint and decorative antique rocking chairs. Dylan prayed it would soon pass. On an art teacher's salary, it was not easy to make Maisie's *Homes & Gardens* dreams come true.

'Last I saw them they were upstairs on the landing.' Maisie chewed grimly on a piece of dry toast. 'I passed them on my way to the loo at about five a.m.'

Pregnancy had not been kind to Dylan's young wife. Relentless morning sickness had turned Maisie's former peaches and cream complexion an unattractive shade of greenish-grey. At only a few months gone she was already thirty pounds heavier than usual, and her legs were covered with revolting varicose veins that reminded Dylan of mould running through a slab of Stilton cheese. Apparently there were men who found their pregnant wives uniquely attractive and desirable. Dylan Pritchard Jones could only imagine that their wives looked more like expectant supermodels – lithe amazons with compact little bumps beneath their lululemon tank tops – and less like the swollen, exhausted figure of his own other half. He tried to be a patient and understanding husband. But he couldn't help but count down the days till it was over, and prayed that Maisie intended to get her figure back quickly afterwards. His suggestion last week that she think about hiring a trainer had been met with what he felt was excessive frostiness.

'Thanks, you're an angel.' Kissing her on the head, Dylan raced upstairs, grabbed the work and ran out to his car, a piece of peanut butter toast still clamped between his teeth. St Hilda's art teacher was perennially late. It was part of his charm, along with his broad, boyish smile, twinkly, bright blue eyes, and the mop of curls that made him look years younger than his actual age of thirty-three, and that women had always found hugely attractive. Dylan Pritchard Jones enjoyed being the 'cool' teacher at St Hilda's, the one whose classes the children actually looked forward to, and with whom all the pretty mothers flirted at parents' evening. Yes, Fittlescombe's primary school was a small pool. But Dylan was the prettiest fish in it, if not the biggest. He loved his life.

In the staff room at St Hilda's, tempers were fraying. The Year Six SAT exams were less than a month away now, but the government had seen fit to choose *this* moment to dump an enormous amount of additional paperwork on its already overloaded state teachers. This morning's staff meeting had been called to agree a consensus on whether or not Max Bingley should hire an additional administration person. Cuts would have to be made to pay for such a hire, so it was vital that all the departments be represented. The art department, as usual, was late.

'We really can't put this off any longer.' Ella Bates, one of the two Year Six class teachers, voiced what the entire room was thinking. 'If Dylan can't be bothered to turn up for the vote, he doesn't deserve a say in it.'

'It's not a matter of what he deserves,' Max Bingley said calmly. 'We need consensus, Ella.'

In Max's long experience, all staff rooms were political snake pits, even in a tiny, tight-knit school like this one. It had been the same story at Gresham Manor, the private boys prep school in Hampshire where Max had spent most of his career, as head of History and, latterly, deputy head of the school.

Max Bingley had loved his job at Gresham Manor. He would never have taken the St Hilda's headship had his beloved wife not died two years ago, plunging him into a deep depression. Susie Bingley had had a heart attack aged fifty-two, completely unexpectedly. She'd collapsed at the breakfast table one morning in front of Max's eyes, keeled over like a skittle. By the time the ambulance arrived at Chichester Hospital she was already dead. Max had kept working. At only fifty-three – with a mortgage to pay, not to mention two daughters still at university – he didn't have much choice. But without Susie, life had lost all meaning, all joy. He moved through his days at Gresham like a zombie, barely able to find the energy to get dressed in the mornings. The Fittlescombe headship offered a new start and a distraction. Max had taken it under pressure from his girls, but it had been the right decision.

Right, but not easy, either personally or professionally. When Max first arrived at St Hilda's he'd been forced to cut back a lot of dead wood. Inevitably his decisions to fire certain people had angered some of the remaining staff. As had his hiring choices. The staff room was already divided into 'Camp Hotham', the old guard hired by his predecessor and championed by Ella Bates, a heavy-set mathematician in her late fifties with a whiskery moustache, brusque manner and penchant for pop socks that drew an unfortunate amount of attention to her wrinkly knees; and 'Camp Bingley', made up of the new teachers and those amongst the old who, like Dylan Pritchard Jones, approved of Max's old-school teaching style and relentless focus on results. Even Camp Bingley, however, had been resentful of Max's hiring of Tatiana Flint-Hamilton as an assistant teacher. The fact that Tati was unpaid did little to assuage the anger.

'We don't have time to waste training charity cases,' was how Ella Bates had put it. 'She's a drain on resources.'

With the notable exception of Dylan, the other teachers all agreed. So far Max Bingley had held his ground: 'If we do our jobs and train her properly she could be a vital addition to resources at a fractional cost,' he argued. But, in truth, he too had doubts about the wisdom of bringing Tatiana on board, doubts made worse by the new administrative pressures they were under.

'Sorry I'm late.' Dylan breezed in, looking anything but sorry. Mrs Bates and the headmaster both gave him angry looks, but the rest of the (mostly female) staff swiftly melted beneath the warm glow of the famous Pritchard Jones smile.

'Traffic,' he grinned. 'It was bumper to bumper on Mill Lane this morning.'

This was a joke. There was no traffic in Fittlescombe. Tatiana laughed loudly, then clapped a hand over her mouth when she realized that no one else was following suit. 'Sorry.'

She'd made the mistake of inviting a girlfriend from her party days, Rita Babbington, down to Greystones for the night last night. Inevitably the two of them had begun reminiscing – Tati's days and nights had been so unutterably boring recently, just *talking* about excitements past felt like a thrill – and Rita had demanded cocktails. Multiple home-made margaritas later – Tati might never have had to pay for a drink in her life, but she certainly knew how to make a world-class cocktail and after four lines of some truly spectacular cocaine that Rita had brought down with her 'in case of emergency', Tatiana had collapsed into bed with her heart and mind racing. She'd woken this morning with a dry mouth and a head that felt as if she'd spent the night with her skull wedged in a vice, tightened hourly by male-volent elves. It was a testament to her friendship with Dylan Pritchard Jones that he still had the capacity to make her laugh.

Not for the first time, Dylan reflected on how beautiful St Hilda's new teaching assistant was, and how out of place such a stunning young creature looked in their grotty staff room. Although he did notice the shadows under Tatiana's feline green eyes this morning. Clearly she'd had a lot more fun last night than he had.

The headmaster's voice cut through his reverie. 'Right. Now that we're all here, a vote. To hire an additional PA for a year will cost us thirty thousand pounds. That's money we don't have. It would have to be funded out of a combin-ation of cuts to nonessential classes – that's art, music and games – and salary cuts. I don't have all the numbers worked out yet. I just need to know if, in theory, this is something you're open to or not. So. A show of hands please for making this hire.'

Nine hands, including Mrs Bates's, went reluctantly up. Dylan Pritchard Jones's did not. Nor did Orla O'Reilly's, the reception teacher, or Tatiana's.

'I can't afford a pay-cut,' said Orla. 'I'm sorry.'

'And I don't see art as nonessential,' said Dylan. 'I'm not sorry,' he added, winking at Tatiana.

'What about you, Tatiana?' Max Bingley asked.

'What?' Sarah Yeardye, the Year Two teacher, failed to conceal her outrage. 'You can't seriously propose giving *her* a vote? She doesn't teach here. None of this affects her.'

A chorus of angry 'hear-hears!' rang out around the room.

'I assumed I didn't have a vote,' Tati said meekly.

'Well you do,' said Max. He believed in consulting his staff and gaining consensus where he could. But he was headmaster here. He wasn't going to be dictated to by Miss Yeardye and Mrs Bates. He also suspected, rightly, that a lot of the antipathy towards Tati from the other teachers was rooted in nothing more worthy than old-fashioned envy. Before Tati came along, Sarah Yeardye had been widely acknowledged as the most attractive teacher at St Hilda's, the one that all the fathers fancied. Now she was as good as invisible.

'Yes or no?'

Surveying the sea of hostile faces, Tati locked on to Dylan Pritchard Jones's encouraging smile.

'No,' she said boldly.

Fuck them all. They're never going to like me, even if I vote yes. And Dylan could use the support.

'That's still nine to four in favour,' said Ella Bates stridently.

'Nine to five. I also vote no,' said Max Bingley. 'It's an unnecessary expense.'

'It is *not* unnecessary!' Mrs Bates snapped.

Things looked set to deteriorate into a full-on slanging match until Sarah Yeardye piped up: 'Why can't Tatiana take on the extra paperwork?'

Everyone fell silent.

'She's a free resource we already have just sitting here,' said Sarah.

The entire room brightened up at this suggestion. Even Max had to admit it was quite a good idea. Before long the chorus of 'yes, why nots?' was quite deafening.

'Tatiana,' Max asked. 'Would you be willing?'

'Of course,' Tati said through gritted teeth. Bloody Sarah. That bitch had been out to get her since day one. 'I mean, I may need some guidance . . .'

'I'm afraid none of us has time for handholding,' Ella Bates barked unkindly. 'If you can't fill in some simple administrative forms, then you've no business being here in the first place.'

Ella Bates's chin was so whiskery and wart-ridden, she reminded Tati of a Roald Dahl character. Mrs Twit, perhaps. The fact that there was apparently a Mr Bates somewhere, or had been once, astounded her.

'I have time,' said Dylan, helping himself to coffee from the machine in the corner. 'If Tati's prepared to help me save the art programme for our children, the least I can do is give her some guidance.'

'Marvellous.' Max Bingley rubbed his hands together with satisfaction just as the bell went. 'That's settled then. Let's get to class.'

'Thanks,' Tati said to Dylan as they all filed out.

'What for?' said Dylan. 'You just saved *my* neck. All our necks, although those old clucks are too blind to see it.'

'They hate me,' Tati sighed.

'No they don't.' Dylan put a friendly arm around her shoulders. 'They hate change, that's all. They're set in their ways. And maybe just a wee bit jealous. Don't let them get you down.'

Dylan dashed off to his art class while Tati headed to the library. On the rare occasions she was actually allowed to help with teaching, she felt flashes of happiness and confidence. But most of her days were spent on menial chores such as today's, when she was scheduled to spend the morning re-cataloguing the school's library books. It was a boring, mindless job. But it gave her much-needed time to think about her legal battle and the all-important next steps.

Tatiana's challenge to her father's will was due in court in September, only three months hence. Raymond Baines, Tati's lawyer, had asked her to put together a dossier of all emails, letters and conversations in which Rory had alluded to her inheritance of Furlings. She was also supposed to be getting him detailed research on the estate's history, particularly anything that might smack of an historic entailment; *and* a list of villagers prepared to attest to the fact that they understood the local manor would always be owned by a Flint-Hamilton and who were actively supporting Tati's claim. So far she had about thirty definites on the list, including Mr and Mrs Preedy at the Village Stores, Danny Jenner, the publican at The Fox, who'd always fancied her, Harry Hotham, St Hilda's ex-headmaster, and Lady Mitchelham, a prominent local magistrate. Will Nutley, Fittlescombe's cricketing hero, was a highly probable, and a smattering of other families had agreed to help Tati in her fight to oust the Cranleys. She was touched by their support – she'd worked hard for it – but the case was still a long shot at best. Collating the documents her solicitor needed was a painstaking, time-consuming and frequently frustrating job, which was already monopolizing all Tatiana's evenings and weekends. Just how she was supposed to fit in a boat-load of St Hilda's paperwork on top of all that, she had no idea. But she had to try, or the money would stop dead. And it might help her win round some of the staff to add to her list of supporters.

So far her trustees had been as good as their word and released a monthly income to her as soon as she accepted this poxy unpaid job at the school. Tatiana's father had what he wanted – for now. She was back in the village, working with children, keeping out of trouble.

But not for long, she told herself, pulling stacks of the Oxford Reading Tree down from the shelves and dumping them on one of the library tables for sorting. *After September I'll have my life back. First Furlings. Then all of the rest. This whole period will seem like a bad dream.*

An image of Brett Cranley's arrogant, taunting face popped into her mind, strengthening her resolve. This would be her first and last term at St Hilda's, putting up with the back-stabbing and bitchiness of Ella and Sarah and the rest of them.

Thank God for Dylan Pritchard Jones. Without his kindness and good humour, Tati wasn't sure she could survive even that.

'What the hell is this?'

Brett Cranley waved the presentation document in his son's face furiously, as if it were a weapon. Which, in some ways, it was.

'I put you in charge of this. I gave you more responsibility, which you *said* you wanted. And this is the best you can come up with? Jesus Christ, Jason. It's embarrassing.'

Jason stared out of the window of his father's London office, wishing he were somewhere else.

103

Had he said he wanted more responsibility? He certainly couldn't remember doing so. It seemed most unlike him. Jason viewed coming to work in the family business the way that most people needing root-canal surgery viewed a trip to the dentist. As something deeply and profoundly unpleasant that could not be put off forever.

Brett's office had great views across the Thames to Tower Bridge. All Brett's offices had had killer views. The one in Sydney, looking out across the harbour towards the iconic opera house, had been jaw-dropping. Jason assumed it was a power thing, this need for a big, swanky corner office and huge windows and a view that said, *Look at me, world. I've made it.*

Most of Cranley Estates staff worked in modest cubicles on the floor below, with the little natural light coming from windows overlooking the car park and council estate housing blocks to the rear of the building. As they had in Sydney. Brett might have changed things up geographically, but he was still the same bullying megalomaniac he'd always been.

'I'm sorry you don't like it.' Jason spoke in a monotone.

'It's not a question of me not *liking* it,' Brett goaded. 'This isn't a matter of taste. It's crap. It's full of typos. The artwork's shit and what there is of it is out of focus. I've seen school kids put together more professional-looking work on Photoshop. This is for McAlpine, for fuck's sake. They're a huge potential client.'

'I know. I'm sorry,' Jason said again, staring at his shoes.

'Look at me when you're talking to me,' Brett commanded. 'You really don't give a shit, do you?'

About the real-estate business? No, I don't. About you being a dick? Yes, Dad, I give a shit about that. But what can I do?

To his intense distress, Jason found his eyes were filling

with tears. He fought them back desperately, forcing himself to meet his father's angry, disappointed gaze. How he wished he didn't care! How he wished he had the strength to shrug off Brett's relentless, soul-crushing criticism and become his own man, making his way in his own world. But that was like a penguin wishing it could fly.

'I should have asked the art department for help,' he stammered. 'I can see that now.'

'So why didn't you?'

'I didn't want to bother them. They seemed to have a lot on their plates already.'

Brett put his head in his hands and groaned. 'God give me strength.' Picking up the phone, he summoned Michelle from reception into his office.

'Sweetheart, would you see what you can do with this in the next hour?' He handed her the offending document. 'Jim Lewis and I are going in to McAlpine this afternoon at two. We sure as hell can't offer them that load of old bollocks.'

'Sure. I'll see what I can do.'

Jason noticed the way Michelle's hand brushed his father's as she took the document, and the conspiratorial flash of eye contact that followed. It was an exchange he'd seen scores of times before.

They're having an affair.

He felt the anger rise up within him. Mostly for his mother – how could Brett do this to her again? Here, in England, what was supposed to be their 'fresh start'? But also because, in his quiet way, Jason had liked Michelle and hoped she might become a mate. With her short hair and her raucous laugh and her slightly wrong, too-sexy-for-the-office clothes, she seemed kind and irreverent and a laugh. A breath of fresh air in a corporate world that Jason found choking and stifling in the extreme. Now he would have no choice but to avoid her. Another door closing.

As soon as Michelle left the room, Brett turned on him again.

'What's wrong now? You look like you've swallowed a wasp. I'm the one who should be pissed off here, Jase, not you. You've let me down. Again.'

'You're sleeping with her, aren't you?'

Jason was almost as astonished to hear the words come out of his mouth as Brett was.

'I beg your pardon?'

Brett sounded dangerously angry, but it was too late to back down now.

'M-M-Michelle,' Jason stammered. 'She's your new mistress, isn't she? I saw the chemistry between you just now. How could you? How could you do it to Mum?'

'Now you listen here.' Brett grasped his son by the shoulders. Although Jason didn't think so, Brett loved him. He hated Jason's depression because it was a problem he couldn't fix, and he resented the boy's sensitive, open nature because he was congenitally incapable of such emotions himself. But he did love him, and he valued his family more than anything. 'I don't know what you think you saw. But you're wrong. I'm not "doing" anything to your mother. I don't have a mistress, and if I did, it wouldn't be one of my employees. Understand?'

Jason nodded, willing it to be true.

'Go out and get yourself some lunch,' Brett added gruffly. 'Clear your head. I'll see you after the meeting.'

'OK.'

Brett watched his son leave, shoulders slumped, feet dragging, as defeated as any retreating infantryman. He sat back down at the desk, punching the polished teak in frustration.

What the fuck was wrong with the boy? He just didn't understand it. It was as if he didn't want to be happy, didn't want to succeed.

Whatever Jason's weaknesses, he certainly wasn't stupid. At least not emotionally. He'd picked up on the vibe between him and Michelle in an instant, like a bloodhound stumbling upon a scent.

I'll have to be a lot more careful if I'm going to continue to have him work here.

Although it pained Brett to admit it, perhaps he'd been rash in forcing Jason to join the family business. At the time it had seemed an obvious solution to his listlessness. Ever since they arrived in England Jason had been moping around like a wet weekend, hanging around the house and the village, getting under Angie's feet. It seemed clear to Brett that he needed something to do, some structure to his life. An eight-to-six job interning at Cranley Estates fitted the bill perfectly. Add in the commuting time – Brett spent at least three nights a week at his London flat, but Jason took the train back and forth from Fittlescombe daily – and he wouldn't have time to dwell on whatever it was that was bothering him.

The theory still sounded solid. But the reality was that Jason loathed the rhythms of office life and found no excitement, no thrill in business, in the daily battle to beat one's competitors and make money. All Brett had done was to inadvertently parachute a spy into his London life, a spy with the potential to cause serious damage to his family idyll down in Sussex.

Because it *was* an idyll. Angela was happy to a degree that Brett hadn't seen in years. Logan seemed to have settled in at school. And Brett felt his own heart soar and spirits lift on a warm Friday evening, leaving grimy, gridlocked

London behind, driving through lanes lined with cherry and apple blossoms as he weaved his way through the ancient Downs. Turning into the driveway at Furlings, walking into his beautiful home, to be greeted by his beautiful, smiling, loving wife . . . It all gave Brett a sense of security and deep contentment that he hadn't felt since before his mother died.

London, the office, Michelle – not to mention all the other girls he brought back to the flat during the week: that was all part of a different life, a life that Brett had gone to great lengths to compartmentalize, both practically and emotionally.

The thought of Jason jeopardizing this perfect balance sent iced water through Brett's veins. As did the prospect, remote though it was, of losing Furlings to Tatiana Flint-Hamilton.

Brett Cranley had grown used to scaring off would-be competitors or threats to his interests through a combination of bullying and flexing his economic muscle. If a rival real-estate developer showed an interest in a property Brett wanted, for example, he either simply outbid that developer, or intimidated him into backing down by making multiple threats to his business. And Brett Cranley's threats were not idle. Renowned as one of the most maliciously, aggressively litigious players in the market, Brett had a legal war chest bigger than the GDP of many small African countries. By dragging out lawsuits, he was able effectively to filibuster smaller players out of the game.

Unfortunately, this strategy did not seem to be working with the tenacious Tatiana Flint-Hamilton. Despite her lack of funds, or even any serious legal case, she'd managed to rally significant support in the village. A County Court judge had already ruled there was enough there for the challenge to be heard in the High Court, and a date had been set for September.

Brett had already spent a fortune employing a team of

legal experts to look into every possible loophole that Tatiana might conceivably exploit in court. Although he hadn't paid her another visit in person since their first, ill-fated but memorable encounter, he'd had lawyers send an array of bullying letters in an attempt to get her to drop the case. Tatiana had responded to none of them, and had even had the nerve to hand the last, most aggressive missive to Logan at school. Sealed in a fresh envelope, with 'Return to Sender' written boldly on the front, she'd instructed the little girl to deliver it to her father.

'What is it?' Logan asked.

'It's a birthday card.'

'But Daddy's birthday's not till August.'

'It'll be his first then, won't it?' Tati smiled sweetly. She was very fond of Logan, who was in her remedial reading group at school, and did her best to forget that the child was a Cranley.

Brett opened the envelope that evening at dinner. Inside was his latest lawyer's letter and a two-word note from Tati.

'*Bugger Off.*'

That was the night he'd decided to take Gabriel Baxter up on his offer and sell off two hundred acres of Furlings' farmland. Once the deal was done, Brett had played Tati at her own game and sent copies of the new deeds with Gabe's name on them to school, via Logan. His envelope also contained a two-word note.

'*Give Up.*'

But of course Tati hadn't.

Even more infuriating than his inability to bully her out of court were the erotic dreams Brett found himself having about her almost nightly. The whole of England knew about Tatiana Flint-Hamilton's wild sexual exploits in the years leading up to her father's death. But as far as Brett could see, since she'd returned to Fittlescombe and hunkered down on his doorstep, like a fungus asserting its unwanted presence at the roots of a giant oak, Tatiana had lived the life of a nun. Once or twice Angela had reported seeing her looking chummy with the married art teacher at St Hilda's, Dylan Pritchard Jones, a jumped-up popinjay of a man if ever Brett saw one.

Curious, Brett had asked Gabe Baxter in conversation what he thought of Dylan.

'He's all right,' Gabe had shrugged, but he said it in a tone that made it plain he wasn't a fan. 'We used to be mates. We play cricket together.'

'But . . .?'

'He's vain. I'm not surprised he and Tatiana are getting friendly. They're like two peas in a pod.'

The thought of Tatiana's perfect, youthful, curvaceous, sinfully sensual body being plundered by a vain village school-teacher was not a pleasant one. But it was hardly worse than the idea of her going to bed alone every night, less than a mile from the spot where Brett himself was trying and failing to go to sleep, twitching with anger and frustration. It wasn't simply that *he* couldn't have her, although that certainly rankled. It was the idea of all that youth and beauty going to waste. In far too many ways, Tatiana Flint-Hamilton felt like a thorn in Brett Cranley's side. He longed for September, for the court case to be over and done with, and for the girl to go crawling back to her old, dissolute lifestyle somewhere far, far away from Furlings and from him.

And yet . . .

Michelle knocked on his office door.

'Is the coast clear?' she asked conspiratorially. She held a mug of hot tea in each hand, one for her and one for Brett. Pushing the door closed behind her with her bottom, she handed Brett his tea, kissing him fleetingly on the lips as she did so. Brett put the mug down on his desk and slipped a hand under her sweater, more out of habit than desire.

'We're going to have to cool it,' he said, caressing her wonderfully full, heavy right breast. 'Jason's suspicious.'

'I see. And this is you cooling it, is it?' Michelle smiled, closing her eyes and enjoying the sensation of Brett's warm hands on her bare skin. She knew Brett Cranley was a shit. That their affair – if you could even call it that – was going nowhere. But he was so funny and charming and exciting and so interested in her. When Brett looked at her, she didn't feel like Michelle Slattery, secretary from Colchester. She felt like somebody important, somebody who mattered. Like a *muse*. Josephine to Brett's Napoleon, Cleopatra to Brett's Caesar. It was that ego boost, more than anything, that she couldn't quite bring herself to give up.

Reluctantly, Brett removed his hands. 'I'm serious. Just for a while, while Jase is here. I wouldn't want to upset the apple cart, if you know what I mean.'

Michelle knew exactly what he meant. If it upset her, she hid it well, changing the subject with her usual good-humoured briskness.

'He's a sweetheart, your son, but he did make a bit of a pig's ear of that document.'

Brett rolled his eyes. 'Can you fix it?'

'Oh yes.' Michelle said confidently. Brett loved her competence almost as much as he loved her warm, welcoming, womanly body. 'I'll whip it into shape. Drink your tea now. I'll be cross if you let that get cold.'

By late June a heat wave had descended over the whole south of England. In London this meant office workers in rolled-up sleeves eating their lunches in the park, and restaurants shoving tables out onto pavements, doing their best to look as if they were in Rome. Fittlescombe, like the rest of the Swell Valley, opened its back doors and spent an inordinate amount of time lounging about in its collective gardens in deckchairs. Whittles, the off-licence in the village, sold out of Pimm's. Red-faced children sucked greedily on Wall's ice lollies. And everywhere a holiday mood prevailed.

At Furlings, Angela Cranley finally felt as if she were getting into her stride. She'd hired Karen, a girl from the village, as a cleaner to help out Mrs Worsley, as well as a boy to assist Jennings in the garden. The Flint-Hamiltons' old gardener was highly resistant to the idea.

'I know me way about,' Jennings muttered stubbornly when Angela first suggested it. 'I don't need some bloody little Herbert getting under me feet.' But in fact, he *did* need it. His arthritis was so bad at times that he could hardly hold a pair of secateurs, still less get on his hands and knees to weed the rose and lavender beds at the front of the house. Angela didn't know exactly how old Mr Jennings was. (Nobody did, it seemed, not even the man himself.) But he was certainly over seventy. His face was as gnarled and weather-beaten as a pickled walnut and his chest made a terrible wheezing, rattling sound as he shuffled about, like a concertina punctured by a sword.

Happily, however, once eighteen-year-old Alfie finally arrived and began tidying potting sheds, mending tools and making Jennings cups of tea like a whirling dervish, the old man relented. Sitting out on the terrace at the back of the house, overlooking the lawn and rolling acres of parkland beyond, Angela watched happily as man and boy tended the flowerbeds, Alfie pruning and Jennings given directions, waving his spindly old arms about like a general on a battlefield.

Noticing that her own arms were turning pink and freckly, despite the lashings of factor fifty sun block she'd applied only an hour ago, Angela retreated indoors. It was half past two on a Friday afternoon, almost time to collect Logan from school. Logan, thank God, seemed to have settled in brilliantly both at school and in the village. Sweetly, she'd developed a thumpingly enormous crush on Gabe Baxter, the local farmer to whom Brett had just sold some fields. Angela suspected Brett had only done the deal to get back at Tatiana Flint-Hamilton, but that was by the bye. A few nights ago she'd been tidying Logan's room when she'd found four sheets of A4 paper stuffed under the bed, covered in practice signatures, all of them either Logan Baxter, Mrs Logan Baxter or Mrs Gabriel Baxter.

'Should we be worried?' Angela asked Brett. 'She's only ten, for God's sake. Surely we should have a few more years before this starts?'

But Brett had been enchanted, insisting that they keep the papers and frame them. 'It's adorable. We should give them to her as a birthday present on her twenty-first.'

Brett would be coming home tonight, along with Jason, whose low moods were starting to worry Angela again. She'd hoped that the job up in London might have opened up some new friendships for him. The village was lovely, and Jason seemed to appreciate it, but there weren't many opportunities for him to socialize with people his own age. Other than the pub, but Jase had never been the sort of confident man's man who can strike up easy conversation in a room full of strangers. Unlike his sister, Jason seemed lonelier than ever since their move.

Grabbing a sun hat and a wicker shopping basket (she needed to stop at the greengrocer's for some white cherries on the way home), Angela set off for the village, pushing her worries about Jason out of her mind for the time being. It was such a glorious day, with the dappled sunlight pouring through the trees and the heady scents of honeysuckle and mown grass hanging thick in the warm air. Turning right out of Furlings' drive towards the green, she heard the church bells of St Hilda's toll three times, and watched the front doors of the cottages open one by one as the other village mothers began their various school-runs. They reminded her of the little wooden people that used to come out of her father's weathervane back home in Australia. There was a woman with an umbrella who popped out if it was raining and a male peasant in breeches and shirtsleeves if it was fine.

Life here can't have changed much since Elizabethan times, she thought happily. It was odd to feel a connection to the past generations of Fittlescombe dwellers – essentially to dead people – but Angela found that she did, and that the idea of being one in a long line of people who had lived here and loved the place gave her a profound sense of belonging.

Relations with her living neighbours were a little more problematic. Thanks to Tatiana Flint-Hamilton's negative PR campaign, a solid third of the village had taken against the Cranleys before they'd even arrived. Angela had done her best to reverse this, knocking on doors, mucking in at school events, making sure that everyone knew the door to Furlings was always open. But it wasn't easy, not least because the antipathy wasn't personal, but rooted in age-old traditions that Angela could barely understand, let alone change.

As Mrs Preedy at the shop put it, 'It's not about you, dear. I'm sure you're lovely. It's not about that Tatiana either. It's about what's right and proper and fair. Not having a Flint-Hamilton at Furlings would be like not having a river in the valley. Old Mr F-H should have consulted local feeling before he went out and changed things, all secretive like, behind people's backs.'

Not having ever met Rory Flint-Hamilton, there was little Angela could say to this. Even those who approved of the inheritance kept their distance. As the new, rich, foreign owner of 'The Big House', Angela was treated with polite deference by the other mums at school, rather than being met as an equal. Without equality there was little chance of friendship. Gabe Baxter's wife Laura had been kind, even though she obviously disapproved of Brett. As had Penny Harwich, another local engaged to Sussex cricketing hero Santiago de la Cruz. Penny had gone out of her way to include Angela in village WI meetings and girls' nights out. But Angela still missed her girlfriends back home, and wondered if she would ever truly fit in in the Swell Valley, as much as she loved it here. Of course, if Tatiana won her court case in September, it wouldn't matter. They'd all have to move again. Angela couldn't imagine that Brett would agree to stay in Fittlescombe if they lost Furlings. With a shudder, she pushed the thought out of her mind.

She'd arrived at the school gates now. Hovering behind a group of mothers in Logan's class, about to steel herself to go and join them, she stopped when she overheard a snippet of their conversation.

'Apparently he's a total sex addict,' one of the mums was saying. 'Worse than Tatiana Flint-Hamilton. He was known for it in Australia.'

'Well I don't know about that,' said her friend. 'But Oliver saw him in The American Bar at the Savoy on Tuesday night with a girl half his age on his lap, acting like he didn't have a care in the world.'

'Yes, well, he doesn't does he?' a third woman piped up.

'He's got his lovely house, his lovely wife, his lovely life in London. Cat that got the cream, I should say.'

'Is Oliver sure it was him?' the first mother asked.

They all laughed at that. 'You can hardly mistake him. He's so bloody good looking.'

'Do you think so?' The first mother wrinkled her nose. 'I've only met him once but he gives me the creeps. Anyway, what was *your* husband doing at The Savoy on a Tuesday evening, that's what I'd like to know? Oliver might have made the whole thing up to cover his own tracks!'

'Yeah, right. Somehow I don't think my Ollie has quite the pulling power of Brett Cranley.'

The mothers' conversation moved on. Behind them, Angela Cranley stood rooted to the spot. She felt dizzy all of a sudden. The sounds of birdsong and chattering voices and the school bell ringing all merged into one muffled dirge that grew louder and louder until she found herself clutching her head. Spots swam before her eyes.

'Are you all right?'

Someone was touching her arm. Angela turned to look at them but could see nothing but blackness. She felt herself falling, sinking. Then nothing.

'Mrs Cranley. Mrs Cranley, can you hear me?'

Angela opened her eyes. Max Bingley, Logan's headmaster, was standing over her. He had one hand on her forehead and the other on her wrist, apparently taking her pulse. When he saw her look up at him he smiled reassuringly.

'Thank goodness. You had us all worried there for a moment. Mrs Graham, would you fetch Mrs Cranley a large glass of water?'

While the school secretary scuttled off, Angela took in her surroundings. She was in the headmaster's study, stretched out on the sofa. Copies of the latest OFSTED report lay neatly stacked on the coffee table, and the walls were covered from floor to ceiling with bookshelves. Bingley had an eclectic collection, everything from teaching manuals and curriculum guidelines to Victorian novels and books on travel and adventure.

'You're a reader,' Angela croaked.

'I should hope so, in my job,' Max Bingley said amiably. 'I think you must have had a touch of sunstroke out in the playground. How do you feel?'

'Embarrassed,' said Angela. 'I can't believe I fainted.'

Painfully, the mothers' conversation came back to her. *It doesn't mean anything*, she told herself angrily. *It's just gossip. A man in Brett's position gets that sort of crap all the time.*

The secretary returned with the water and Max handed it to Angela, propping her up with cushions.

'Nothing to be embarrassed about,' he said kindly. 'Its ridiculously hot out there. I suspect you got a bit dehydrated, that's all.'

In fact, Max knew what had happened. After Angela passed out, one of the mothers admitted they'd been talking about Brett.

'We had no idea she was there. None of us would have said a word otherwise.'

'And you're sure she overheard you?' Max asked.

'I'm not sure, no. But she keeled over right afterwards, so I'd say it's a fairly safe bet. We all feel dreadful.'

Max loathed gossip, but unfortunately it was the very lifeblood of almost all schools, and St Hilda's was no exception. In any case, the whispers about Brett Cranley could be heard well beyond the school gates. Everybody in the village knew that Furlings' new owner was an inveterate womanizer, and that the Cranleys had moved here at least in part to escape an impending sexual scandal back in Oz.

Max Bingley for one couldn't understand it. Angela Cranley was a beautiful woman, and not just on the outside. There was something luminous about her, a glow that could only come from a truly kind spirit within. If Max were married to a woman like Angela, he wouldn't dream of playing the field. Then again, he suspected that he and Brett Cranley had very little indeed in common, in this area or any other. There was a reason that Max was headmaster of a tiny village primary school and Brett was an international real-estate mogul, a reason that went far deeper than their respective sexual mores.

'Where's Logan?' Angela asked. She didn't know why but she suddenly felt an overwhelming urge to get out of this room, away from Max Bingley's kindness and sympathy.

'Bertie Shaw's mother Harriet took her home. She's fine.'

Bertie Shaw, aka Naughty Bertie, was a great friend of Logan's.

'She's going to have tea with Bertie and Harriet will drop her off at Furlings later. Or she can stay the night there, whatever you prefer. Have you got her number?'

Angela nodded weakly. Logan was bound to want to stay the night, which was fine with her. It was about time her daughter had a night off from perching at her bedroom window clutching binoculars, hoping to catch a glimpse of Gabe Baxter. Plus it would also be easier to talk to Brett with Logie out of the house . . . if she *wanted* to talk to Brett. Right now she wasn't sure. It was so much easier, so much safer and less troubling to believe that what she'd overheard this afternoon was idle gossip. To dismiss it, refuse to allow it into their lives.

'I gave Dr Grylls a call.' Max Bingley's voice brought her

back to reality. 'Once he's taken a look at you I can run you home, if you like.'

'Oh, no. God no, please. I don't need a doctor.' Finishing her water, Angela sat up straight, then gingerly got to her feet. 'I'm completely fine.'

Max Bingley frowned. 'I think you should see someone, Mrs Cranley.'

'Angela, please. And I assure you there's no need. Please,' she turned to Max's secretary, 'ask Dr Grylls not to come.'

Mrs Graham looked to Max for approval. He nodded, although his expression made it plain he was still concerned.

'I don't need a lift home either,' said Angela hurriedly. 'I appreciate the offer, but I'm perfectly capable of walking. Despite appearances, I assure you I'm not some pathetic, feeble damsel in distress.'

She laughed, but Max Bingley answered seriously.

'I never for a moment thought of you as either feeble or pathetic,' he said. 'Far from it.'

There was something terribly intense about him. When he focused his attention on you, it was like sunlight burning through a magnifying glass. Angela felt as if she might burst into flames at any moment.

'However, I'm afraid I do absolutely insist on driving you home.'

Max Bingley said this in a tone that made it clear he would brook no argument. Tired suddenly, Angela acquiesced.

Max drove a very old Land Rover, the back seat of which was piled high with books, papers and classical music CD cases. The CDs themselves were strewn liberally on the front passenger seat. Scooping them up, apparently unashamed of the mess, he chucked them into the glove compartment so that Angela could sit down.

'They'll get scratched, you know,' she warned him.

'I know,' said Max, pulling out of the school and heading along the green in the direction of Furlings. 'I'm awful about putting them back in their cases. But I like having them to hand. CDs are my one extravagance. I love music.'

'So do I,' said Angela. She found herself telling him about Jason's talent as a pianist. How she'd always encouraged him, but Brett disapproved.

'That's a shame,' said Max. He'd yet to meet Brett Cranley in the flesh, but he was finding it harder and harder not to dislike the man. 'What about Logan? Is she musical too?'

Angela laughed. 'Unfortunately not. She's tone-deaf like her father.'

'She's a sweet little thing,' said Max. 'Seems to have settled in really well.' Angela could hear in his voice that he had a genuine love of children. It made her like him even more.

'She's a handful. She's growing up so fast,' Angela sighed, thinking about the sheet of signatures in Brett's drawer.

'Oh, they're all a handful,' Max grinned. 'Some of them just wait a little longer than others to let it show, that's all.'

'Do you have children?'

They'd arrived at Furlings just as she asked the question. Angela hadn't even noticed them turning into the driveway before the car juddered to a halt.

'Two daughters,' he said. 'They're both grown now, of course.'

Angela longed to ask about their mother. She knew that Max lived alone, but she wasn't sure if he were divorced or widowed. For some reason she was curious, but she didn't want to be rude or to overstep the boundaries.

'Well. Thank you. For the lift and . . . everything.' She opened the passenger door. 'Sorry again for all the drama.'

'Not at all.' Max smiled, but it was a brisk, distant smile, the smile that a headmaster would usually employ when addressing a parent of one of his pupils. The fleeting intimacy Angela had felt hovering between them on the short drive was gone now. Although perhaps intimacy wasn't the right word? It was more a sort of paternal affection. Angela realized with a pang that she missed her own father. She would call him tonight. Hearing his voice, even from thousands of miles away, always made her feel safe.

Standing outside the front door of Furlings, she watched Max Bingley drive away.

Then she turned and went inside, smothering her doubts and fears like someone throwing a wet blanket over a fire.

CHAPTER SEVEN

'Through Him, With Him, In Him. In the Unity of the Holy Spirit, One God, for ever and ever.'

Reverend Slaughter enjoyed the sound of his own voice as it resonated throughout the packed church. Few things pleased him so much as seeing St Hilda's full to the rafters. Clearly his Fittlescombe flock had been as eager to hear his sermon on Our Lord's passion and its relevance today as he was to deliver it. No one ever gave sermons on the passion outside of Easter week. Reverend Slaughter was convinced it was the way that he 'changed things up' and kept his parishioners guessing that was tempting them back to Sunday services in ever-increasing numbers.

It hadn't occurred to him that it might be the soap opera being played out in the front three pews that had actually dragged seo many of the reluctant faithful from their beds. The war over Furlings was the most interesting thing to have happened in Fittlescombe in many a long moon, not least because both factions were so glamorous and attractive. Up till now, the key battlefields had been the school, the pub and the village shop, where Tatiana Flint-Hamilton had been relentlessly campaigning. But, perhaps sensing he was losing ground, Brett Cranley had decided belatedly to make his presence felt in the village. Last week Brett had attended church for the first time and had ostentatiously led his wife and children to the front left-hand pew, a bench that for three hundred years had been the exclusive preserve of the Flint-Hamilton family.

Naturally this had instigated a frenzied round of gossip in the village. Once news reached Tati, suitably embellished (by the time Tati heard the story, Brett had been 'strutting like a rooster, as if he owned the place') it was only a matter of time before she would show up in person to defend her birthright.

It was all wildly diverting. From the moment the first bells had begun pealing for the ten o'clock service, at nine forty-five that morning, it had been standing room only in St Hilda's Parish Church.

Max Bingley, who had somehow managed to rise above the drama and was out of the 'Pew-gate' loop, sat in his usual spot in a pew about halfway down the nave. He'd arrived early to light a candle for his wife, as he always did on Sunday mornings, and exchanged a few kind words with Angela Cranley, until her husband appeared and hurried her away. Max couldn't be sure, but he got the sense that Mr Cranley didn't like his wife talking to other men, even if those men were years older and the headmaster of her child's school. It was clearly one rule for the goose and another for the gander in the Cranley marriage.

He wondered why Angela Cranley put up with it. *Like one of those kidnap victims who fall in love with their captor.* Then again, Max was old enough to understand that one could never really know anything about another person's marriage. There were those who'd thought that he and Susie weren't right for each other. How very, very wrong those people had been. Max still missed his wife every day, even if the sharp agony of eighteen months ago had dulled now to a slow and steady ache.

'The Lord be with you.'

'And also with you.'

Five rows back from where Max Bingley was sitting, Dylan Pritchard Jones said a silent prayer that the Lord might do something about his hangover. Dylan's wife Maisie was away visiting her parents, which had left him free to spend a leisurely Saturday evening at The Fox last night. He didn't remember having drunk so very much. Then again, he didn't remember anything at all after about ten o'clock, when Chris Edwards, the local bobby, had suggested a round of 'I have never'. The next thing Dylan knew he was waking up fully dressed in his marital bed at five o'clock this morning with a sandpaper-dry mouth, a stomach that churned and curdled like a vat of cottage cheese and a headache that felt as if it might at any moment burst through his skull and run around the room shrieking like some mad leprechaun. Four Alka-Seltzers, a hot shower and a fried breakfast later, he'd felt well enough to put on a clean shirt and stagger to church. He'd only come to support Tatiana, but so far she'd failed to show up, to the entire congregation's immense disappointment.

Almost the entire congregation. Logan Cranley, wedged between her father and brother in the disputed front pew, couldn't have cared less about Tatiana, so delirious was she with happiness that Gabe Baxter had decided to come to church this week. Logan had to turn around and crane her neck to get a good look at him, which was annoying. And of course there was his wife, looking pretty but (in Logan's opinion) far too old for him, selfishly imposing herself on

Logan's fantasy by sitting next to him and occasionally whispering things in his ear that made Gabe smile. Still, if she pretended that Laura Baxter wasn't there, Logan found it was easy enough to lose herself in Gabe's mesmerizing blue eyes and to imagine his strong arms beneath his Thomas Pink shirt wrapped tightly around her. Thank God she'd vetoed that hideous, babyish dress Mummy had picked out for her and gone for jeans and her new blue top with sequins from Zara. That looked far more teenager-ish. Obviously she was too young for Gabe today. But if she wanted him to notice her in a few years, she needed to plant the seeds of romance now. She was hardly likely to do that in a smocked number with pink bows that made her look about six.

Four rows back, on the other side of the aisle, Laura whispered in Gabe's ear. 'I think you've got a fan in the Cranley pew. And I don't mean your buddy Brett.'

It had been a tough few weeks in the Baxter household. Gabe had ignored Laura's wishes and bought the land from Brett Cranley, raising the money through a combination of a second mortgage on their house plus a hefty bank loan. Laura, whose parents had lost their own home back in the early Nineties and had almost lost their marriage as a result, was horrified by the scale of their debts, and even more horrified by Gabriel's devil-may-care attitude to their finances. They'd had some bitter, horrible rows. But last night they'd made love again for the first time since the sale went through. Laura was trying hard to put both her fear and resentment behind her.

Looking up, Gabe saw Logan staring and winked, prompting a blush that could have earned a place in the *Guinness Book of World Records*.

'She's a sweet kid,' he whispered back to Laura, squeezing her possessively around the waist. Gabe had also felt miserable and unglued after all the fighting and was deeply relieved to be back in Laura's good books.

'She is,' said Laura. 'You shouldn't encourage her though.'

Gabe grinned. 'I can't help it if all females find me irresistible.'

The congregation stood up, preparing to shuffle up to the front for communion. Dylan Pritchard Jones was just thinking that this might be as good a moment as any to slip away unnoticed – Tatiana had clearly thought better of a confrontation with Brett Cranley at the Sunday service, which was no bad thing – when the rear doors of the church swung open.

'Bloody hell,' Will Nutley whispered to Santiago de la Cruz, who'd been dragged to church by his fiancée Penny. 'Talk about an entrance!'

Dylan almost didn't recognize Tatiana. With her long hair swept up elegantly beneath a veiled, pillbox hat, and her to-die-for figure modestly encased in a 1930s-style skirt suit, exquisitely cut in ultra-fine lightweight wool, Tatiana looked like a vision from another time. Serene, mature, effortlessly classy, radiating that unique confidence and entitlement that only the true upper classes seemed to possess. Every head swivelled to gawp as she glided up the central aisle towards the altar, meekly bowing her head in front of Reverend Slaughter as she took the first host.

'The body of Christ,' the vicar intoned pompously, handing the wafer to Tatiana.

'Amen.'

A line of parishioners had formed behind Tati as she made her stately way to the front of the church. Turning around she paused, giving all of them a chance to get a good look at her chilly composure, before turning sharp right into the first pew and sitting down right next to Logan Cranley.

Oh my God, Dylan Pritchard Jones winced. *She's sitting right next to them!* The entire congregation held its collective breath.

'Miss F-H!' said Logan in an awestruck voice, loud enough for the entire church to hear. She knew Tatiana from school and the two of them had always got along well. 'I didn't know you came to church. You look so pretty!'

'Thank you, Logan,' Tati smiled. 'You look very pretty too. I love your top.'

Logan grinned like the Cheshire cat. At the other end of the pew, Brett Cranley looked as if someone had just pissed in his champagne. Nostrils flared, lips drawn into a tight line of loathing, he seemed unprepared and had clearly been caught off guard by Tatiana's bold assertion of her ancestral rights.

'Can you scoot along a bit and make room?' Tati asked Logan sweetly.

'Of course.' Unaware that there was anything amiss, the little girl did as she was asked, bumping into Jason, who in turn squeezed up against his mother. In order to give Angela room to breathe, Brett found himself being pressed uncomfortably against the wall.

Aware that he looked like a fool, he stood up, muttering expletives under his breath and indicating with an angry jerk of the head that the family should do the same. One by one they filed out to take communion, right past Tatiana. To Brett's immense irritation, Logan gave Tati a hug. Jason smiled shyly. Angela kept acknowledgements to a brief but cordial nod. Brett deliberately knocked into her as he pushed past, his face like thunder.

'What are you doing here?' he hissed in her ear.

'Praying,' Tatiana responded pithily. 'For strength.'

'You could have sat somewhere else,' Brett growled.

'I could indeed.' Tati met his gaze unwaveringly 'And so could you. You'd better hurry, Mr Cranley, or there'll be no more salvation left.'

Once communion was over, the Cranleys filed back into their seats. Brett had hoped to shove Tatiana down to the wall end and wedge *her* in there, but Logan was the first back to the pew. When Tatiana stepped to one side to let her in, she obligingly skipped along to the end herself, leaving Jason and Angela no choice but to follow suit. This left Brett in the uncomfortable position of standing next to Tati for the final hymn – 'Guide Me Oh Thou Great Redeemer' – and being forced to sing, one of the few things in life he was profoundly bad at.

Tatiana wisely said nothing, staring resolutely ahead until the church doors opened and people began pouring out onto the village green. But Brett was sure he saw the faintest hint of a smirk playing around her lips beneath that oh-so-demure veil.

One of these days I'm going to fuck that girl and hear her beg me not to stop, he thought furiously.

On the face of it, all Tatiana had done this morning was to arrive late to church and sit down in her normal seat. If Brett took issue with her publicly he would look like a prize fool. Yet he couldn't shake the feeling that he'd already been made a fool of, shown up as a charlatan. By reclaiming her pew with such dignified, quiet entitlement, she'd made him look as though he was *playing* at being lord of the manor, in front of the entire village. It was the same strategy she was trying to use in court, to turf him out of Furlings. Next to Tatiana, Brett Cranley and his family had been made to look like cheap, shoddy imitations of the real thing. From her attention-grabbing entrance to that outfit that made her look like Lady Mary from Downton bloody Abbey, Tatiana had succeeded in embarrassing him in as subtle, underhand a way as possible.

His face reddening like a ripe pepper, Brett rounded up his family and practically dragged them out of the churchyard.

Sidling up to Tatiana, Dylan Pritchard Jones slipped an arm around her waist.

'Bravo,' he whispered in her ear. 'I do believe you rattled him.'

'I'm not sure one can rattle a snake,' Tati said dolefully.

'You know, the funny thing is, for a moment there, all wedged into the same pew like that, you almost looked like a family,' said Dylan.

Tati looked horrified. 'We did *not*. Please, don't ever say that.'

'But it's true,' said Dylan. 'Logan obviously adores you.'

'Yes, well. She's a sweetie,' Tati admitted.

'And the brother was all smiles.'

'Jason's sweet too,' said Tati.

'Exactly. And Angela Cranley's a lovely woman.' Catching Tati's questioning look, Dylan added swiftly, 'I mean she's nice. Kind. Not the sort of person who'd try to do anyone down. If it weren't for the horrible dad, I reckon they'd welcome you with open arms.'

Tati looked at him frostily. God, she was magnificent in that suit and hat. Like Wallis Simpson without the vulgarity.

'I don't want to be *welcomed* into the Cranley family, thank you very much,' she said caustically. 'I want my inheritance. And I'm damn well going to get it.'

'Come on,' said Dylan, who suddenly felt in desperate need of a hair of the dog. 'Let's go to the pub. I'll buy you lunch and let you rant for a whole hour.'

Spotting Gabe and Laura Baxter about to leave, Tati said, 'Sounds good, thanks. I'll meet you there.'

Running across the green, she tapped Gabe hard on the shoulder.

'I suppose you think you're clever, do you?' she said accusingly. 'Getting your grubby little hands on my fields.'

'Good morning, Tatiana,' Gabe smiled. Turning to Laura he said, 'You go on ahead, darling. I'll catch up with you.'

'When I win my court case in September, I'll have your deeds to that land revoked,' Tati told him furiously.

'Uh huh,' said Gabe. 'And when the aliens invade and take over the earth, they'll turn my farmhouse into their intergalactic headquarters.' He started walking away. 'Get a grip, Tatiana.'

'You know, I'm not surprised you and Brett Cranley have teamed up. There are so few low-lives in this village, it must be lovely for you to have found a kindred spirit at last.'

Against his better judgement, Gabe stopped and turned around. 'You know, you're right. There *aren't* many low-lives – although I see you've adopted one in Dylan Dick-Hard Jones.'

'What do you mean?' Tati said crossly.

'I mean that all he's interested in is what's between your legs, sweetheart. Then again, that's all you've got to offer these days, isn't it?'

Tati blushed scarlet, but for once had no comeback.

'Still, there may be a lack of low-lives but at least there are plenty of snobs,' Gabe went on, twisting the knife. 'You'll have plenty of people to commiserate with over croquet and cucumber sandwiches while I'm busy working *my* land. Enjoy your afternoon with Dick-Hard,' he called over his shoulder, walking away for good this time. 'Just don't say I didn't warn you.'

As always on a Sunday lunchtime, The Fox was packed.

Outside, the pretty beer garden was full of families, parents enjoying their ploughman's lunches and pints of shandy while their children played on The Fox's excellent rope swing, a veritable death-trap that propelled one off a high bank right across the river Swell and back again at bone-rattling speed.

Inside, Fittlescombe's single males propped up the bar, arguing over last night's football and debating the merits of the new series of *Top Gear*. Wandering in, in search of Dylan, Tatiana noticed that Archie, the new gardener's boy at Furlings, was amongst them, although at eighteen he was too young and too shy to join in with the adult banter. He was good looking, though, in a floppy-haired, blond, freckly sort of way. Back in Tatiana's day, the only gardener allowed to set foot in Furlings' grounds had been the wizened and taciturn old Jennings. It crossed her mind how much she'd have enjoyed having a toyboy like Archie on the estate, and how much fun it would have been to take him to bed and play Lady Chatterley. *If I hadn't been so lonely there, perhaps I'd have stuck around*, she thought wistfully.

Tatiana found Dylan inside, at a small table close to the bar.

'Everything all right?' Dylan asked. 'Gabe Baxter looked as if he was giving you a hard time outside church.'

Tati waved a hand dismissively. '*Gabe*. He's such a pleb. He's got it in for me for whatever reason. I suspect it's to do with his wife.'

'Laura?' Dylan waited for her to elaborate.

'Yes,' Tati said casually. 'I might have accidentally slept with her boyfriend once. Ex-boyfriend. The one before Gabe.'

Dylan chuckled. 'How do you "accidentally" sleep with someone?'

'I didn't know he had a girlfriend,' Tati explained. 'He certainly didn't behave as if he did. Anyway, I did Laura a favour. He turned out to be a total dickhead and she and

Gabe got together that very night. But of course, now he has decided to rewrite history and paint me as the villain of the piece.'

Dylan changed the subject. He didn't want to waste his lunch talking about Gabe Baxter, a man with whom he maintained a nominal friendship but whom he'd always secretly envied. Before long he and Tati were chatting away happily about school, and some of the pupils they had in common, over a long, lazy lunch. A couple of Boody Marys and a mouth-watering steak and kidney pie put paid to Dylan's hangover, and Tati positively glowed with contentment after her second ice-cold glass of Chablis, remembering her bettering of Brett Cranley at church this morning.

By the time they paid the bill and emerged onto the green, it was almost three o'clock on a gloriously warm Sunday afternoon.

'What are you doing now?' Dylan asked casually.

Tati's face clouded over. 'Paperwork, unfortunately,' she groaned. 'I stayed late on Friday but I still have a stack of forms to finish for Years Three and Four. You've no idea how time-consuming it is.'

'Oh, I do,' Dylan reminded her. 'I've been a teacher for eight years. I've done my fair share of mindless form-filling, believe me. If you like you can bring them over to mine and I'll help you. Maisie's away and I'm not really doing anything this afternoon.'

'Are you sure?' asked Tati. She loathed the education department paperwork with a passion, not least because half of it made no sense to her and she had to cross-reference answers between one exam board and another. An experi-enced teacher like Dylan could get the job done in half the time. 'You really don't mind?'

'Course not. Go and get the files and I'll nip home and put some coffee on.'

By the time Tatiana arrived at the Pritchard Jones's house, having changed into more comfortable denim shorts, flip-flops and a faded Rolling Stones T-shirt, a delicious smell of fresh-roasted coffee was already wafting through the kitchen. Maisie's interiors magazines and piles of fabric samples lay scattered over the oak table, and pictures of Dylan's very pretty young wife were everywhere, from the fridge door to the pinboard to the walls, covering every inch of space not already taken up by Dylan's landscape paintings.

'Your wife's gorgeous,' said Tati admiringly, and truthfully.

'Thanks,' said Dylan, a tad stiffly.

'How come I never see her at school?'

'She used to pop in a lot.' Dylan handed Tati a mug of coffee and poured another for himself. 'But she's pregnant now and she gets very tired, especially in the afternoons. She's usually napping when I get home.'

'Is she a designer?' Tati flipped idly through the magazines, clearing a space on the table on which to plonk her giant stack of paperwork.

'God no. This is all just for the baby's room. She doesn't work,' Dylan said, a touch dismissively, Tati thought.

She sat down at the table, but Dylan gestured towards the sofa, kicking off a sleeping tabby cat to make room for the two of them.

'Let's work over here. More comfy.'

For a second, Gabe Baxter's 'Dylan Dick-Hard Jones' jibe replayed in Tati's mind. *He's only interested in what's between your legs.* But she quickly pushed the thought aside. Gabe Baxter was poisonous, an obnoxious little wide boy on the make. What did he know about Dylan's intentions? Tati

133

wouldn't let Gabe ruin the one, genuine friendship she'd made since coming back to Fittlescombe.

In the end, she and Dylan got through the paperwork in record time. Once Dylan had shown her the ropes, it was easy. Of course, no one at St Hilda's, least of all the poisonous Year Six teacher Ella Bates, had bothered to talk her through the system. Tati realized now she'd spent untold hours chasing her tail, quite unnecessarily.

'I can't bloody believe this,' she complained to Dylan. 'Those cows. They could easily have told me what to do. I hate working at that damn school.'

'You don't mean that.' Dylan smiled his twinkly smile and cleared away the papers, his hand accidentally brushing Tati's bare leg as he reached over to the coffee table.

'I do,' said Tati. 'I mean, I love the kids.'

'That's because you're a natural teacher.'

'Do you really think so?'

Despite her outer confidence, she'd always doubted her own abilities. For whatever reason, Tatiana wanted to be a good teacher, to have a genuine skill that people valued and respected. That her father would have valued and respected.

'I do.' Dylan smiled. There was something so good about his face, so kind, beneath those unruly auburn curls. He wasn't small-minded and petty like the other staff, or cold and austere like Max Bingley. 'Just look at how far Logan Cranley's come on since you've been helping her with her reading. That didn't happen by magic, you know.'

'Thanks,' said Tati, suffused by a warm glow of pride. Used to compliments about her looks, it was rare for her to be admired for anything else. Since her father's death, and losing her birthright to the Cranleys, her self-esteem had been particularly low. 'I don't know why you're so nice to me,' she told Dylan.

'Don't you?'

His voice had taken on a rough, throaty edge. He touched her leg again, but this time there was nothing accidental about it.

Tatiana watched his fingers lazily move up and down her thigh. At first it was almost as if it were happening to someone else. But the rush of desire that shot through her was most definitely all her own. God it had been so long, so very long since she'd had a man. She'd never really thought about Dylan sexually, perhaps because he was older, and married, although that had never hindered her libido in the past. Since her father's death, Tati had effectively shut down that side of herself completely. Apart from that one, disgusting yet disturbingly erotic touch from Brett Cranley weeks ago, she hadn't had anything approximating to an enjoyable sexual experience in well over a year.

'You're so beautiful.' Dylan was whispering in her ear now, his hands creeping upwards, playing with the frayed hem of her shorts. On autopilot, Tati reached around the back of his neck, pulling him towards her and kissing him. The kiss was more curious than passionate, like someone reminding themselves of a familiar, favourite food that they've always loved but haven't eaten in a long time. Dylan's response was unequivocal. Pushing her down onto her back so she was stretched out full length on the couch, he kissed her back hard, pressing his entire weight down on top of her. The combined sensations of his stubble grinding against her cheek, the smell of his aftershave and excitement, and his hand sliding under her T-shirt to grab her bare breasts made her gasp out in pleasure. But a few seconds later reality reasserted itself. Feeling Dylan's rock-solid erection pressing down on her groin through his khaki trousers, Tati suddenly panicked. *Dick-Hard Jones.* All she could hear was Gabe Baxter's mocking voice in her head:

You've adopted a rat of your own.

Opening her eyes, like a hypnotized patient emerging from a trance, the first thing she saw was a photograph of Dylan's wife staring down at her from the kitchen wall.

'We can't do this.' She tried to wriggle out from under him, but Dylan seemed oblivious. 'Dylan,' she shouted louder. 'Stop.'

'Stop? Why?' He raised his head a fraction, but was still lying on top of her, his weight pinning her down.

'You know why,' said Tati. 'Your wife.'

'She's away. She won't know,' Dylan murmured, resuming his exploration of Tati's magnificent left breast.

'That's not the only reason,' said Tati, trying not to enjoy the sensation. 'We work together. We're friends.'

'You are so fucking sexy.' Ignoring her, Dylan reached down and began to unbutton her fly. Tati froze, lust replaced by anger, at Dylan, at herself, and at Gabe bloody Baxter, for being right all along.

'I said Stop!'

With all her strength, she drew her right knee upwards into Dylan's groin.

It was more of a nudge than anything, but he jumped off her all the same. A look of profound annoyance flashed across his face. 'Are you kidding me?'

'No. Why would I be kidding?' Tati sat up, shaking, and straightened her clothes. 'Come on, Dylan. You know as well as I do this is a bad idea.'

'That's not what you thought five minutes ago.' He ran a hand through his hair, a picture of frustration and fury. His erection, sticking out like a tent pole at the front of his trousers, looked ridiculous now, and not remotely sexy.

'You led me on,' he whined petulantly.

Tati would have laughed, but there was a cold glint in Dylan's eye that made her think better of it. Instead she picked up her papers, clasping them to her chest like a shield.

'That wasn't my intention. Look, you're an attractive man. It's not that.'

'Please,' Dylan snapped. 'Don't patronize me.'

Tati felt like crying suddenly. It was true, she had kissed him back. And she had been tempted. But only for a moment. Dylan was behaving as if she'd made the first move. As if she'd come here with the express purpose of seducing him, which couldn't have been farther from the truth.

'I'd better go,' she mumbled, backing away from him towards the door. 'Thank you for the help with the papers.'

She longed for him to say something, to relent, to admit that he was sorry and had gone too far and that they could still be friends. God knew Tati needed a friend in Fittlescombe, and up to this point, Dylan Pritchard Jones had been it. All she needed was a smile, a small gesture, anything to break the tension. But instead Dylan turned away, his face set like flint.

'You can see yourself out, I assume,' he said bitterly.

Tati fled.

CHAPTER EIGHT

Monday morning saw a break in the weather and the first rainy day southern England had endured in weeks.

Jason Cranley sat at his desk, staring through a grimy window at the grey London skyscape. It struck him that the city seemed somehow more *right*, more *real*, in the drizzle than it did in the sunshine. Tower Bridge had looked fake last week against a backdrop of blue sky and sunshine, like a prop from a movie set. The rain seemed in an odd way to suit it, to bring it back to life. Or perhaps it was just he, Jason, who suited the rain? He who needed the grey world outside because it reflected the grey world inside, the ever-present clouds inside his head?

Wearily, he dragged his attention back to his computer. Ever since his 'epic fail' with the pitch document for McAlpine, Brett had had him churning out market research, trawling through the internet and London newspapers looking for data on property transactions. It was perfectly obvious that no one, least of all Brett, needed this stuff; that it was a task Jason had been given to fill his time and keep him out of trouble. But he couldn't really complain. It wasn't as if he had a burning ambition to work at the sharp end of his father's business, and at least the research gave him time to pursue the one aspect of London life that did interest him: music.

He'd discovered that a number of jazz venues within a ten-mile radius of Cranley Estates' offices held open auditions for new performers on a fairly regular basis. Jason had played piano at a couple of tiny, coffee-shop gigs back in Sydney, before his depression had returned with a vengeance. The mere act of sitting at a keyboard soothed him, the way that lighting up a cigarette or sipping a glass of whisky or sinking into a hot bath soothed other people. But performing, on the rare occasions when he found the courage to do it, filled him with a sense of contentment and wellbeing and fulfil-ment that nothing else on earth could compare to. Having a room full of people applaud him for doing what he loved most in the world – no matter how small a room – was like having a brilliant surgeon restart his heart.

Surreptitiously opening the website for Joe's Diner in Borough Market, and clicking on the 'Performers' tab, Jason allowed his mind to wander deliciously into fantasy as the rain drummed on the windowpane.

'Buying restaurants now, are we? I didn't know we'd diversified.'

The secretary's voice was like a jug of ice cubes down his shirt. Jason jumped, accidentally shutting down his screen altogether in his clumsy attempts to close the web page.

'Was that a porn-slam?'

Michelle looked at Jason archly. She was clearly joking with him. Ever since the day of his botched presentation, when Jason had accused his father of sleeping with her, he'd noticed Michelle's attempts to make-nice. Part of him wanted to respond in kind. She seemed a sweet girl, and had always gone out of her way to be kind to him. And technically, he supposed, there was a possibility he was wrong about her and his father. But then he remembered the way they'd looked at one another that day and he knew he hadn't been.

'I don't look at porn,' he mumbled, refusing to meet her eye.

'I know. I was only kidding. You just looked so guilty when I came in.' Michelle grinned. 'Planning a night out, were you? There's nothing wrong with that. You should get out more, a bloke your age.'

'Says who? My father?' Jason snapped.

Michelle bit her lip awkwardly. 'I've been to Joe's,' she said, trying to move the subject on. She'd only come in to check the printer, which had been playing up lately, and wished she hadn't. 'It's a fun place. We could go together one night if you like.'

Jason couldn't take the fake camaraderie a moment longer.

'He's just using you, you know.' Swivelling around on his chair he fixed Michelle with a searing, intense stare. 'He'll take what he wants until he gets bored and then he'll sack you and move on. You're probably not the only one he's ch-cheating on my mother with even now. You're not special.'

Michelle's mouth opened, then closed again. She looked as if she'd just had acid thrown in her face.

Jason knew he was being cruel. It pained him, because he wasn't a cruel person. But he wanted to get through to her, to jolt her out of her complacency, or blindness, or whatever it was that made attractive, fun, decent young women like her fall for his bastard father.

'You're very sure of yourself,' she said eventually. The words were challenging but her tone was quiet and defeated. 'What makes you think you know?'

'That there are other women, you mean? Besides you?' asked Jason.

'That we're having an affair,' said Michelle. 'What if I told you that you were wrong?'

'I wouldn't believe you,' Jason said, his voice devoid of emotion. 'Brett's sleeping with you because you're there. Unfortunately, when it comes to my father's extramarital tastes, that's all he needs. Availability. He's not looking for some perfect woman. He already has that in my mother.'

'Perhaps *he* doesn't think so,' Michelle snapped back defiantly. But her lower lip was wobbling. Jason could see his words had hit home.

'He does think so,' he said quietly. 'I'm not trying to hurt your feelings. I'm telling you the truth, for your own sake as well as my mum's. You seem like a nice person.'

'I am a nice person,' said Michelle.

'Then end it,' said Jason. 'Get out while you still can.'

A few days later, Angela was chopping carrots and parsley in the kitchen at Furlings. The break in the summer heat wave was enough to warrant a hot evening meal, and she'd decided to try out a Jamie Oliver recipe for chicken chasseur.

Estate agents would probably have described Furlings' kitchen as being 'in need of updating', but to Angela it was perfect. An enormous, cast-iron range cooker, similar to an Aga but about twice the size, fifty years older and covered with a century's worth of encrusted casserole remnants, dominated one wall. To the left and right of it stood two enormous butchers' chopping blocks, above which a row of gleaming copper pots and pans hung from hooks on the ceiling, like shiny carcasses in an abattoir. The adjoining wall overlooked the lawn and deer park beyond, glistening green after the rain in the soft, early evening light. Mrs Worsley and the cleaning girl did most of the washing-up, but Angela had been known to spend a full ten minutes rinsing out a single cup in the huge, chipped Belfast sink, transfixed by the loveliness of the view. Directly opposite the sink, in the middle of the room, a large round oak table sat lopsidedly on a sloping flagstone floor, worn dangerously smooth and slippery by generations of stockinged feet scurrying back and forth across it. Usually this table was covered in clutter – Logan's school books, Angela's half-read newspapers, Jason's sheet music – but today Mrs Worsley had cleared it to make space for a large jug of slightly overblown peonies, cuttings from the garden that she'd caught Jennings about to chuck in his wheelbarrow and throw away.

Chopping away at her vegetables, soaking up the cheerful, homely atmosphere of the room, Angela jumped a mile when she felt two arms encircle her waist from behind.

'You should let Mrs Worsley do that,' Brett whispered, nuzzling into her neck. 'That's what we pay her for.'

Angela spun around, beaming. 'What are you doing home?'

Brett invariably spent the midweek nights at his London crash pad. On the rare occasions when he made it down to Furlings before Friday, he always called to let Angela know.

'Do I need an excuse to come and see my beautiful wife?'

'No, of course not. I'm just . . . surprised. Why didn't you catch the train with Jason earlier?'

'I still had some work to finish up,' said Brett. 'I love you,' he added, kissing her again.

Angela felt relief wash over her like a gentle wave. Ever since that awful afternoon at the school, when she'd overheard the other mothers gossiping and so embarrassingly fainted, a nagging seed of doubt had been planted in her mind. She didn't really believe that Brett was cheating on her again. But at the same time, she couldn't be certain that he wasn't. Which left her in a sort of awful, silent limbo that had put a strain on the marriage. Neither she nor Brett had acknowledged it, but they both knew it was there. And Brett's behaviour had been off in other ways, too. He'd been distinctly standoffish with Max Bingley at church last Sunday, for example, and seemed irritated when Angela so much as spoke to the headmaster in passing. Ridiculously, Angela found herself feeling guilty as a result, perhaps because Brett still knew nothing of the fainting incident. As if by winding up on Bingley's couch that day she had somehow betrayed her husband. Which, of course, was pure nonsense. But the feelings remained, and Angela had gone out of her way to avoid bumping into Max at school this week as a result of them.

Then there was Brett's growing obsession with Tatiana Flint-Hamilton and the looming court case over Rory's will. Brett's face still darkened ominously whenever Tati's name was mentioned, which in a small village like this was a real problem. Especially given that Angela ran into Tati almost daily at school, and Logan positively adored the girl, who'd done more to help her with her reading than any of the expensive tutors back in Australia.

Of course, none of these things added up to much in isolation. But Angela had been unable to shake the feeling that something was amiss with Brett. That the dynamic in their marriage had become skewed, off-kilter, dangerous in some inexplicable way. She felt like an actor in a play, thrust onto the stage but with no idea what her lines were, or even what part she was supposed to be playing.

Feeling Brett's arms around her now, however, she instantly relaxed.

I've been worrying about nothing. Overthinking things, like I always do.

'So where is Jason?' Brett asked casually, picking up a piece of raw carrot and crunching it between his teeth.

'I think he's in his room, I'm not sure,' said Angela. 'Is everything OK?' she added anxiously.

'Everything's fine,' Brett smiled. 'Why wouldn't it be?'

'Daddy! What are you doing back?'

Logan sauntered into the kitchen, looking more pre-teen than ever in a punk tutu skirt and skull and crossbones T-shirt teamed with high tops with the word 'Grrrrrl' emblazoned on the side in black sequins. Brett was taken aback by how pretty she was becoming, with her high cheekbones, dark eyes and long black hair flapping behind her like a trail of smoke.

'I missed Mummy's cooking,' he said, kissing the top of her head. 'Are you wearing perfume?' he frowned.

'No,' lied Logan, making a hasty exit.

'She was over at Wraggsbottom Farm after school, supposedly helping Laura with the chickens,' Angela explained. 'It's her parent–teacher meeting tomorrow afternoon. Do you think we should say something to Max Bingley about the whole Gabe Baxter obsession?'

'Absolutely not,' said Brett firmly. 'It's a crush, not an "obsession". And it's none of Bingley's business. Anyway, what do you mean "we"? There's no way I can come. I've got far too much on at work.'

Logan, who'd suddenly reappeared in the doorway, heard the last part of Brett's comment.

'You're not coming to my parents' meeting?' she pouted.

'I can't, pumpkin.' Brett tried to sound conciliatory. 'You know I'm not a big one for school events. Mum'll be there, though. And if your grades are good, I'll get you a toy from Hamleys. What Barbie are you after?'

'*Barbie?*' Logan curled her upper lip contemptuously. 'I'm almost *eleven years old*, Dad. I don't want a doll!'

'Well, what do you want?' asked Brett.

'I want you to come tomorrow,' said Logan. 'I'm doing amazing with my reading.'

'Amazing*ly*,' Angela corrected on autopilot.

'Miss F-H says I'm the best pupil in my whole class and I've made the most progress.' Her dark eyes shone with pride. 'And I've got two stories – *two* – up on the wall in our classroom. No one else has that, not even Bertie and he's like Dexter from *Dexter's Laboratory*. That means he's a total brainiac,' Logan explained, seeing the blank look of incomprehension on her mother's face.

In fact, Angela had tensed up, waiting for the mention of Tatiana to plunge Brett back into his usual angry, dark mood. But instead she heard him say in a calm, measured voice: 'Miss F-H said that, did she? Hmmm. You know what, Logie? I *will* come tomorrow. As you've made such an effort.'

'Really?' Logan was as astonished as her mother by this turnaround. 'Brilliant! Can I go and tell Jase?'

'Of course.'

Once she'd gone, Brett pulled Angela into his arms and kissed her softly. 'I'm sorry I've been in a bit of a funk lately.' He stroked her hair. 'Work's been stressful, setting up the new office. And of course, this ruddy court case . . .'

'I know,' Angela said soothingly.

'But I do love you.'

Looking into his eyes, the same eyes that had first met hers all those years ago across the counter of her father's bakery, Angela could see that he meant it.

'I love you too, Brett,' she said, truthfully.

'I'm gonna be around a bit more from now on. You know, for Logan. Do more family stuff.'

Angela smiled. *That* she would believe when she saw it.

Jason skipped dinner. When Logan told him Dad was home, he miraculously lost his appetite.

Afterwards, Brett went upstairs and found him in his bedroom.

'I want a word with you.' He closed the door behind him.

Jason said nothing, not moving from his reclining position on the bed, like a possum playing dead. As if by remaining still and closing his eyes he could somehow will his father away.

'What did you say to Michelle the other day?'

There was an edge to Brett's voice that made the hairs on Jason's forearms stand on end.

'Did you hear me?' he said. 'I asked you a question.'

'Yes, I heard you,' said Jason.

He wished he weren't so afraid, so pathetically intimidated by his father. His own cowardice disgusted him. Number one hundred and twelve on the list of things he hated about himself.

'Then answer me,' said Brett. 'What did you say to her?'

'I didn't say anything she didn't already know,' Jason answered cautiously.

'Oh really? And what the hell do *you* know, may I ask?' Brett erupted, unable to rein in his temper any longer. 'You're a twenty-year-old kid! You don't know a damn thing. She gave in her notice today, do you realize that? One of the best secretaries I ever had quit a perfectly good job because of what *you* said to her.'

'You're blaming me?' Jason's eyes widened in disbelief.

146

'Yes, I'm blaming you,' said Brett. 'Why wouldn't I? You told her to quit.'

'You're the one who's been sleeping with her!' Jason blurted.

'I have *not*,' Brett hissed. 'And keep your voice down, for Christ's sake.'

The lie hung in the air between them, ugly and obvious. Father and son looked at one another. Brett broke the silence first.

'I love your mother,' he said gruffly.

'I never said you didn't, Dad.'

'I don't want you ever to speak of this again. Not at home, not at work, not with anyone. Ever.'

'Fine.' Jason turned his head away to face the wall.

'I'm serious, Jason.'

'So am I. I said fine, didn't I?'

Brett headed for the door. A torrent of emotions, none of them good, pressed heavily on his heart making it hard to breathe.

'Maybe it's best if I don't come back to work,' Jason called after him. 'I'll find another job, something local. We both know I'm not cut out for the real-estate business.'

'No,' said Brett dully.

'Why not?' Jason sounded close to tears.

'Because I said so,' said Brett. 'Because we're Cranleys. We don't quit when the going gets tough. And because . . . you're my son.'

He left, closing the bedroom door quietly behind him.

Only once the last of his footsteps had died away did Jason allow the tears to flow.

CHAPTER NINE

'I'm not sure I quite understand what you're saying.'

Max Bingley looked at Dylan Pritchard Jones suspiciously. St Hilda's art teacher was one of the few members
of staff whom he had never fully managed to get a handle
on. On the one hand, there was no doubt whatsoever that
Dylan was marvellous at his job. An accomplished artist in
his own right – not always the case with art teachers,
especially not at primary level – he was also a natural and
instinctive teacher. Patient, committed, inspiring. Someone
like Dylan could easily have found a job in a private school
that paid many multiples of what he earned here. Max
didn't doubt that he'd been approached by rivals, and he
was grateful that Pritchard Jones had decided to stay. Clearly
Dylan felt the same way about St Hilda's, and Fittlescombe,
that Max did: that it was unique; somewhere that couldn't
be replicated, still less bettered.

And yet their common love of the school and of their
profession had failed to create a bond between the two men.
For all his positive qualities, his charm and affability and
the staunch support he'd given to Max's changes since he'd

taken over from Harry Hotham, there was something 'fishy' about Dylan Pritchard Jones. Something that, despite himself, Max Bingley didn't quite trust.

It was that something that Max saw in Dylan's handsome, twinkling blue eyes this morning as he danced around the subject of Tatiana Flint-Hamilton.

'Has something happened between you and Tatiana?'

'No!' Dylan laughed, tossing his curly head from side to side dismissively. 'Nothing's happened, headmaster. I felt I ought to come to you privately, that's all, and talk off the record. Man to man, as it were. She's very . . . young.'

He weighted this last word, implying some mysterious significance.

'Yeeees,' said Max. 'And?'

'And young girls can be prone to crushes.' Dylan spoke smoothly. 'They're not always . . . how should I put this? Their behaviour isn't always appropriate.'

'I do beg you not to use that word,' Max said tetchily. 'It makes you sound like Bill Bloody Clinton. *Appropriate*. Whatever happened to right and wrong? Has Tatiana done something *wrong*, Dylan? Is that what you're trying to say?'

'No, no no.' Dylan's smile was starting to look rather forced.

'I thought you two were friends?'

'We are.'

'Then why are you here?'

There was an awkward silence. Max Bingley was beginning to lose his patience.

'Has she propositioned you, Dylan? Is that what you're getting at? Because you'll forgive me, but I'm afraid I find that rather hard to believe.'

'I can't think why.' Dylan looked put out.

'So she *did* proposition you?'

'Not exactly.'

Dylan squirmed in his seat. The old fossil wasn't making this as easy as he'd hoped. Dylan had always had Max Bingley pegged as an old-school sexist, a bit of a military martinet beneath the firm-but-fair exterior. He hadn't expected Bingley to play this with such a relentlessly straight bat.

'All right,' he said eventually. 'This weekend she did rather, you know, try it on. Nothing happened, but there was an awkward incident at my place, while I was helping her with some of the SATS paperwork.'

Max waited for him to elaborate.

'I'd prefer not to go into details. I handled it, and I'm not making a formal complaint or anything. She's a nice girl.'

'But?'

'But she's *young*, Max, and flighty! Come on. You know what I'm getting at here. Her lifestyle . . . Girls her age, they like to party. They drink, they dabble in drugs, they take their eye off the ball. You can't tell me you haven't noticed how exhausted Tatiana's been looking in the staff room lately?'

Max had noticed. He'd put it down to her heavy workload, combined with the stress of contesting her late father's will. The entire village was abuzz with gossip about the looming David and Goliath court case between Tatiana Flint-Hamilton and Brett Cranley.

'Dylan, I must ask you outright. Do you have any concrete reason to believe that Miss Flint-Hamilton has been using drugs whilst working at this school?'

Dylan flushed. 'I don't have any proof, if that's what you mean.'

Max shook his head. 'Then if you're not making a complaint, the matter is closed.'

Dylan stood up. Clearly coming to Bingley had been a mistake.

Panicked after Tati had rebuffed him last weekend, he'd taken the last three days off school with 'flu' while he tried to figure out what to do. There was bound to be tension between him and Tati at school, and other staff were bound to pick up on it. This was how rumours got started, and in a small village like this one, with a very pregnant, very paranoid wife at home, Dylan could not afford to come off looking like some sort of sexual predator. He had to take control of the situation, to hit back first. A few days at home, buttering up Maisie, followed by a man-to-man chat with Max Bingley had seemed like the best strategy. But from the moment he had sat down in Bingley's office, the old man had made him look and feel like a fool.

'I just hope you don't look back at this conversation in a few months' time, headmaster, and wish you'd taken me seriously,' he said pompously. 'I'm thinking of the good of the school.'

Like hell you are, thought Max. He didn't know what had gone on, but he didn't trust Pritchard Jones an inch.

'She's not even interested in teaching,' Dylan scoffed. 'She's only doing this to pay for her legal fees, you know.'

'I believe Tatiana is interested in teaching,' Max said stiffly. 'What's more, I believe she has a natural gift for it. Like you. Just look at the impact she's made on the remedial readers. Look at Logan Cranley. She deserves our encouragement, Dylan. So whatever issue you have with her, I suggest you sort it out between yourselves.'

Dylan left, and Max pushed their awkward encounter out of his mind. Today was the parent–teacher meeeting at St Hilda's. He had better things to do than referee some squabble between his art teacher and Tatiana Flint-Hamilton.

* * *

151

'Yeah, but I don't geddit.' A vastly overweight mother fixed the Year Two teacher, Sarah Yeardye, with a hostile glare. 'If I tell Kai to go and buy a packet of crisps, he can go and buy a packet of crisps.'

Sitting on a wooden classroom chair that looked as if it might collapse at any moment, rolls of legging-encased fat spilling over the chair's edge like excess pastry flopping over a pie dish, Kai Wilmott's mother did not accept Miss Yeardye's assessment of her son's mathematics ability as being 'well below average.'

'With the greatest respect, Mrs Wilmott, I don't quite see how being able to buy a packet of crisps is relevant.'

'Course it's relevant. Packet o' crisps is sixty p or whatever, right?'

Miss Yeardye nodded wearily.

'So my Kai knows he should give 'em a pound coin and get the change, like. That's maths, innit?'

'Well, yes, it is. But—'

'There you go then. 'E's fine.'

It took a lot to make Tatiana to feel sorry for Sarah Yeardye. The Year Two teacher had gone out of her way to dismiss Tati's contributions at St Hilda's and had rarely missed an opportunity to be bitchy and mean-spirited in the staff room. But Tati wouldn't wish Karen Wilmott on anybody.

The entire parents' meeting had been a real eye-opener. Some of these mothers were monsters! Half of them, like Mrs Wilmott, were insistent that their little darlings were Einstein and utterly blind to any/all evidence to the contrary; and the other half displayed a dispiriting lack of interest in the whole proceedings. Carefully prepared folders of work were skimmed through half-heartedly or not at all. Watches were glanced at repeatedly and questions asked again and again about how long 'all this' was going to take because they really needed to get back to work/gardening/*watching TV*, picking their toenails.

But the Year Two parents had been particularly dire. On reflection, that might have been why Mr Bingley had put Tati in here, alongside Sarah Yeardye. Perhaps he wanted her to get a taste of things at the sharp end. If so, the main lesson Tati had taken away was that, without a saintly disposition and superhuman patience, neither of which she possessed, there was every danger of these meetings descending into an out-and-out brawl.

This hadn't been a good week for Tati. Her short-lived triumph over Brett Cranley at church had been blighted by the unpleasantness with Dylan. Returning to work anxious and depressed on Monday morning, she'd hoped to try and set things straight between them, but Dylan had chickened out and called in sick. He'd seemed fit as a fiddle the day before, climbing all over her like an ant on a melted ice lolly, but now apparently he was all but bedridden with flu.

Then this morning he'd bounced back into the staff room, ignoring Tatiana completely, and immediately closeted himself away in the head's office in a manner that made Tati feel distinctly paranoid.

Was he saying something about her? Making up lies to get her into trouble with the head? Tati prayed not. She couldn't afford to lose this job, and up until now Dylan had been her only ally.

'Tatiana? Do you have a minute?'

Max Bingley stuck his head around the door of Year Two. Sarah Yeardye cast him a pleading look as Kai Wilmott's mother leaned forwards, her white, fat forearms shaking like two cylindrical lumps of lard. But Max was focused wholly on Tati.

'Of course.'

She was glad to get out of the stifling classroom, but braced herself for what the head might have to say. This was bound to be about Dylan. The thought of discussing what had happened last Sunday with Max Bingley made Tati's stomach churn. It would be like discussing sexual positions with your dad. To her surprise, however, Max didn't mention Dylan at all.

'The Cranleys are here,' he said matter-of-factly. 'They've specifically asked to talk to you about Logan's reading.'

'The Cranleys?'

'Yes.'

Cranleys, plural. Did that mean Brett? But Brett never came to school. Never ever. It was one of the things that had made working at St Hilda's bearable for Tati.

'Are you quite sure it's me they want to see?'

'Tatiana, I am not yet quite senile,' Max said drily. 'Although I'm beginning to wonder if you might be.' He did so hope that Pritchard Jones wasn't right about Tati experimenting with drugs. She certainly seemed dazed and confused right now. 'They're waiting for you in the Year Four classroom.'

Angela turned and smiled nervously as Tatiana walked in. She was also worried by Brett's sudden interest in Logan's academic progress and prayed he hadn't come here to cause a scene with Tati. But early signs were good. He barely looked up when Tati walked in, smiling and projecting a confidence she did not feel.

In wide-fitting grey trousers paired with flat shoes, and a simple white shirt with a sleeveless cashmere sweater pulled over the top, Tatiana looked professional and pulled-together, like any young teacher. But not even the dowdy clothes could fully disguise her knockout figure, or that perfectly structured face that seemed to grow more beautiful each time Angela saw it.

Tati pulled up a chair, keeping a few feet of distance between herself and the Cranleys. 'You asked to see me?'

'Yes.'

It was Brett who spoke, looking up suddenly, his eyes boring into Tati's with that same half-lustful half-disdainful gaze that had so unnerved her when he'd burst into her bathroom at Greystones. She wondered whether she would ever be able to look at Brett Cranley again without feeling naked. 'I understand you've been doing some work with my daughter.'

Tati noticed the way he said 'my' rather than 'our', and the way he had instantly taken over the conversation, to the exclusion of his wife. Was that what their marriage was like, she wondered? Brett, bullying his way through while Angela sat meek and cowed at his side? Clearly Brett Cranley was a man unused to having people stand up to him, especially women. Tatiana felt her confidence returning.

'That's right,' she said. 'Logan's made tremendous progress. She's really very bright.'

Brett snorted. 'Is that so? Funny how she's always bottom of the class then, isn't it?'

'That's not fair, darling,' chided Angela. 'Logan's maths has always been good. It's only in English where she's struggled.'

'And she still struggles,' said Tati, deliberately addressing herself solely to Angela. 'I'm not saying she doesn't find reading hard, because she does. But she's made immense progress. And her difficulties don't reflect a lack of intellect, or effort.'

'What are they caused by, then? Black magic?' sneered Brett. 'Because I can tell you, in the time it takes my daughter to read "Danger: Keep Out", she'd already have been mauled to death by bears or fried to a crisp on a live railway track.'

'Brett!' Angela was shocked. She'd expected Brett to be rude to Tatiana, but not at Logan's expense.

'What?' Brett shrugged, registering his wife's horrified expression. 'I adore Logan, you know I do, she's the light of my life. But I'm not gonna sit here and be told that she's some sort of genius when you know as well as I do it's a crock.'

Tati felt the anger welling up in her chest. She knew what it was like to have a father who didn't believe in you, who undermined all your achievements and triumphs and saw only what he wanted to see.

'I'm not saying she's a genius. But she *is* clever, whether you choose to acknowledge it or not. As for her reading, I strongly suspect that Logan may be dyslexic.'

Brett rolled his eyes. 'Dyslexic? Please. What a load of old horseshit.'

'I think you should have her tested,' Tati ploughed on.

'Oh yeah? And what do you know? You're not even a qualified teacher,' said Brett.

'No, I'm not. But I'm the one who's been reading with her.' Tati's nostrils flared defiantly as she glared back at him. 'Besides, her class teacher agrees with me.'

'Do you really think she's dyslexic?' Angela asked meekly. Tati had quite forgotten she was even in the room.

'I do,' said Tati. 'But it needn't be any great handicap. Quite the opposite. So much is known about the condition these days.'

'Condition?' Brett snorted. 'Give me a break. These are kids that can't spell.'

Angela Cranley opened her mouth to say something but her husband cut her off.

'Listen,' he said rudely to Tati. 'None of this matters. My daughter's gorgeous. With her looks and her name, no one's going to care if she can spell or not. She's at school to make friends and have fun, that's all.'

'Why's that? Because she's a girl?' Tati challenged him. She was half joking, but Brett responded quite seriously.

'Exactly,' he said, utterly unapologetic. 'Now, maybe if she looked like the back of a bus, or if she showed any interest in books, things might be different.'

Tati didn't think she'd ever heard such an outrageously, obnoxiously, outdated sexist comment in her life. Brett Cranley made Gabriel Baxter sound positively enlightened. He clearly had a profound problem with women. Tati glanced at his wife, who looked mortified, as well she might, but said nothing. *Stand up for yourself!* Tati wanted to shout at her. *And if you can't stand up for yourself, at least stand up for your daughter.* But she restrained herself.

'Has it ever occurred to you that perhaps Logan doesn't show much interest in books *because* she's dyslexic?' she said to Brett. 'Until now they've been a closed world to her. They might as well have been written in code.'

'Change the record,' Brett yawned.

Tati knew he was doing it to provoke her. The really infuriating thing was that it was working. She found herself wanting to lean over the desk and hit him. To punch and scratch and claw at his handsome, arrogant, smirking, sexist face and have him fight her back until all the frustration and rage drained out of her. She remembered the pressure of his body against hers in her bathroom at Greystones that day he'd walked in on her, the weight and strength of him, and felt an incongruous jolt of desire slicing its way through her anger. That only made her more furious.

'Mrs Cranley?' Max Bingley stuck his head round the

door, breaking the almost unbearable tension. 'So sorry to interrupt, but do you have a second?'

Angela couldn't remember the last time she'd been more pleased to see a person. She loathed confrontation, especially when it involved Brett. She also strongly suspected that his acting out with Tatiana reflected an underlying sexual attraction, a thought too hideous in its implications to be dwelt upon, even for a moment.

'Of course,' she said gratefully. 'Excuse me.' Bolting out of the room like a fox out of a hole, she left Brett and Tatiana to it.

'So.' Tati looked at Brett.

'So.' Brett looked back.

His dark eyes appeared almost black when he was angry, Tati noticed. Although there was something other than anger flickering beneath the surface now, a sexual tension so thick she could almost touch it.

For Brett, simply being in a room alone with Tatiana was intoxicating. He hadn't admitted, even to himself, how excited he'd been by the prospect of seeing her again today. Their argument earlier had brought out the best in her, the fire and antagonism in her eyes and body language belying her prim and proper teacher's outfit. He wanted her, badly.

'I'm just wondering if all this caveman, sexist nonsense is for my benefit,' she said, retreating behind her professional façade. 'Or if you genuinely don't care about your daughter.'

'I care plenty about my daughter,' said Brett.

'You just don't think girls need to be educated? Is that it? We're all second-class citizens?' She laughed mockingly. 'What happened, Brett? Didn't your mother give you enough attention when you were little?'

Brett's eyes flashed dangerously.

Oh good, thought Tati. *I've hit a nerve.*

'Don't speak about my mother.'

'Why not?' said Tati, delighted to have discovered a weak spot in the mighty Cranley armour. 'What happened? Let me guess. You caught her in bed with a lover?'

'I said shut up.'

'So that's where this pathetic Madonna/whore crap comes from. Fascinating! Mummy turned out not to be the perfect angel after all, eh?'

Brett clenched his fist. The loathing in his eyes was so intense that for a moment Tati thought he was about to explode. Instead he said quietly, 'She died.'

Tati detected the faintest tremor in his voice.

'When I was a kid.'

The emotion was so raw and unexpected, Tati almost felt sorry for him. But then she remembered the way he'd bullied his wife and belittled his daughter just now, and pulled herself up short.

'My mother died too, you know,' she told him. A look of profound surprise registered on Brett's face. 'You lost your mother? When you were young?'

Tati nodded. 'I was eight.'

'I'm sorry.' His concern sounded sincere, but you could never quite tell with Brett Cranley.

'Do you remember her?'

'Yes, of course, a bit – but the memories fade so quickly. You remember your mother?'

'Every day.'

A momentary empathy flashed between them, but Tatiana quashed it ruthlessly. She couldn't afford to let her emotional guard down. *This is Brett Cranley*, she reminded herself sternly. *He's your enemy.*

'Well, I'm sorry. But if your mum's death is your excuse for being a total arsehole to women, it's not good enough,' she said robustly, jumping back on the offensive. 'What kind of a man needs to put down his own daughter to boost his ego?'

'My ego doesn't need boosting, sweetheart,' Brett drawled. 'And when I want parenting advice from you, I'll ask for it.'

They glared at one another, an almost unbearable electric silence crackling in the air between them for what felt like an eternity. Then Brett took a breath, took a step back.

'Playing teacher doesn't suit you, you know.'

The flash of vulnerability he'd revealed when discussing his mother was completely gone now. He eyed Tati's clothes disparagingly. 'You look ridiculous in that get-up.'

'Is that so?' said Tati. 'And what should I wear to parents' meetings, I wonder, in the world according to Brett Cranley? Crotchless panties and nipple tassels, I suppose?'

Brett couldn't fully suppress a smile. 'That's a great mental picture.'

I hate you, Tati thought furiously. 'Perhaps all the female teachers at St Hilda's should be issued with stripper poles?' she snapped.

'Not all of them. Just you.' Brett was still smiling. 'You're as out of place here as a whore in a nunnery, and you know it.'

The irony was, Tati did know it. But she wasn't about to give Brett Cranley the satisfaction of hearing her admit it.

'Yes, well, luckily I won't be here for very long.'

'Amen to that,' said Brett.

'After my inheritance is restored to me in September, I'll be too busy undoing all the damage you've done at Furlings and reversing your shady land deals to stay on at school. Sadly.'

Brett rolled his eyes. 'You're living in a fantasy.'

'We'll see,' said Tati.

'I'm curious. What will you do when you lose?' Brett leaned back in his chair, stretching his legs out in front of him. It was a small gesture of control, of power. Having let his guard down earlier, he was determined to reclaim the upper hand. 'Stay on in the village and carry on the charade? Or crawl back to London with your tail between your legs?'

'I won't lose,' said Tati.

'Hypothetically.'

He was toying with her again now, with a disturbing hybrid of flirtation and disdain that made Tati's mouth go dry, despite herself.

'Hypothetically. *If* I lost the case? Then yes, I might well carry on teaching,' she said defiantly.

'Do you know,' Brett smiled, 'I don't think I've ever met someone with less self-awareness than you, Tatiana. You could no more settle down to a quiet life as a village school-teacher than I could settle down as a Buddhist monk.'

'I agree, orange isn't your colour,' quipped Tatiana. 'But you're wrong about me. I love country life.'

'Bullshit. You love money. You love excitement. I know what you love,' Brett whispered, leaning forward so that he was close enough for her to smell his cologne.

How can someone so poisonous and hateful be so sexy? thought Tati.

'Of course, if you were a man, or had any skills,' Brett went on, enjoying the effect he was having on her, 'I'd tell you to start your own business.'

'Fascinating.' Tati yawned pointedly.

'But for a society party girl like you, marriage is really the only option.'

'You know, you really need to be in therapy,' Tati responded. 'You're not well.'

Brett laughed. The black eyes were turned on Tati in their

full intensity now. She felt her stomach flip over unpleasantly and wished, not for the first time, that Brett Cranley didn't have such an uncanny ability to toss her emotions like a pancake. He was a complicated man, more complicated than he appeared on the surface or liked to admit. But he was also an unreconstructed bastard, who would stop at nothing to deny her her inheritance. With an effort, she managed to keep her own gaze steady.

'I'm just being honest,' said Brett. 'You should play to your strengths.'

'And what are my strengths, Mr Cranley? In your warped opinion?'

Standing up, Brett reached across the desk, and ran one finger slowly across Tatiana's cheek. Gently lifting a single strand of hair that had fallen across her face, he placed it back behind her ear. It was a small gesture, but it was slow and intimate and unbearably erotic. It took all of Tatiana's willpower not to gasp out loud.

'One of these days, Tatiana,' Brett whispered, 'I'll show you exactly what your strengths are.'

Outside in the corridor, Max Bingley was still chatting to Angela Cranley, trying to talk her into sponsoring the school's upcoming Gala, when Tati burst out of the classroom and practically knocked them both flying.

'What on earth's the matter, Tatiana?' Max said reprovingly.

'Nothing,' said a thin-lipped Tati, exchanging only the briefest of glances with Angela, who could see at once what had happened. Brett must have picked a fight with her. Pushed things too far, as usual. 'I need to get back to Year Two, that's all. I promised Sarah I wouldn't be long.'

Max watched Tati dash off, frowning slightly before

162

returning his attention to Angela. 'So you'll be gone for the whole summer, then?' he said. 'That's a shame.'

'It is,' Angela sighed in agreement. 'Brett adores St Tropez, but to be honest I can take it or leave it. All those beautiful people, showing off. The smell of effort's enough to put you quite off your Bellini.' She laughed, then blushed, wondering if perhaps that was a crass thing to say to man like Max Bingley, who almost certainly holidayed in Cornwall and drank nothing more exotic than the local pale ale. 'I hope you don't think me a show-off,' she began, awkwardly. 'I didn't mean—'

'Nothing could be further from my mind,' Max assured her.

'I know our life probably sounds awfully glamorous. But the truth is, I'm afraid I'm old before my time. I can't bear the thought of leaving my garden for six whole weeks. Sad, isn't it?'

'Not at all,' said Max. Although he did wonder how this sweet, private woman had ever fallen for a shallow, party-loving shark like Brett Cranley. It was the oddest pairing he'd seen in many years.

'Will Furlings be empty then, over the break?' he asked Angela.

'No. Jason will be there. He has to work. None of Cranley Estates' junior staff get more than two weeks' holiday allowance in their first year. It wouldn't be fair to change the rules for Jase. That's what Brett says, anyway.'

'He's quite right,' said Max. 'Well, we shall miss you. *I* shall miss you. But you can rest assured I'll be roping you into Gala committee meetings the moment you return in September.'

Just then Brett emerged from the classroom looking highly pleased with himself, and as relaxed as Tati had seemed stressed. He snaked a possessive arm around Angela's waist.

'What's this about September?'

'I was just saying I look forward to seeing you both again after the summer,' said Max Bingley. 'Your wife tells me you're off to the South of France for the duration.'

'That's right. Can't wait,' Brett grinned. 'My yacht, the *Lady A*, should be in St Tropez by this weekend.'

Pompous arse, thought Max. *And why not 'our' yacht?*

Aloud he said, 'How lovely. Well, I'd better get on. Lots of parents to see and all that.'

As Max walked off down the corridor, Brett turned to Angela.

'I don't like that guy,' he said abruptly. 'He's such a stiff.'

'Oh, he's all right,' said Angela. 'He's kind.'

'Hmmm.' Brett sounded unconvinced. 'He was all over you like a rash.'

'Don't be ridiculous!' Angela laughed, taking Brett's arm. 'And don't try to distract me either. What happened in there after I left? With Tatiana?'

'What do you mean?'

'What did you say to upset her? She came out looking as if someone had squirted lemon juice in her eyes. You promised you wouldn't cause trouble today, remember?'

'I didn't cause trouble,' said Brett. 'I told the girl the truth, that's all. It's not my problem if she doesn't want to hear it.'

Jason Cranley gazed out of the train window at the glorious Sussex countryside as they hurtled towards London. He'd worked from home today, while his parents were at Logan's school, finishing up some meaningless and deathly dull research project his father had given him on retail rental yields. Now he was taking the five o'clock train back up to town.

Graham Jones, an irksome, rabidly ambitious VP at Cranley Estates, only a few years older than Jason and clearly one of Brett's 'favourites', had insisted that Jason present the file in person at seven o'clock tomorrow morning.

Graham Jones drove a pillarbox-red Audi, had loud telephone conversations in public places, and used hideous corporate speak around the office, asking Jason whether or not he had the 'bandwidth' to perform such-and-such a task, and assuring him that he was eager to 'blue-sky' any ideas that might arise from Jason's rental yield research. Rather than face the prospect of a 5.30 a.m. train from Fittlescombe tomorrow, followed by a stressful sprint across London to the office to present to the odious Jones, Jason had decided to head up to town tonight and stay at his father's flat. At least that way he could make it into the building early and try to come up with a single idea about retail rental yields that didn't involve suffocating himself with a plastic bag out of sheer, mind-numbing boredom.

Switching his iPod to a new recording of Shostakovich's *Piano Quintet in G Minor* that he'd downloaded last night, he allowed the rolling waves of music to crash over him and flood through him until all thoughts of work and Graham Jones and his father had been washed away. Jason loved commuting, and the train journeys back and forth to town were often the best parts of his day. He enjoyed the romance of train travel, especially on the Victoria to Brighton line where they still used the old, 1950s rolling stock, with its roughly upholstered seats, wooden tables and windows that you could slide up and down to open and that rattled rhythmically and constantly as the train trundled along. Most of

165

all, though, he enjoyed the peace of it. The sense of being alone, and yet not lonely – sitting in a carriage with other travellers made it companionable, yet there was never any danger of being drawn into unwanted conversation or bothered in any way. For one and half glorious hours Jason had nothing to do but listen to the sublime piano, admire the idyllic scenery, and be lulled into a state of profound calm by the gently rocking movement of the carriage.

A sharp tap on his shoulder made him jump a mile. Accidentally yanking the cord of his headphones, they fell out of his ears, pulling the iPod with them off his lap so it fell with a clatter onto the train floor.

'I'm so sorry. I startled you.'

Tatiana Flint-Hamilton stood over him. Still wearing the trousers and sweater she'd had on for the parents' meeting earlier, she had loosened her top button and let down her hair, which cascaded around her shoulders now, as shiny and inviting as golden syrup.

'Oh, no. Please. It's fine. Please. How are you? Sit down. I mean, if you want to, obviously,' Jason babbled stupidly. He wasn't the most socially adept of young men at the best of times, but around Tatiana he always seemed to regress to a state of complete, dribbling idiocy.

Tati took a seat in the empty seat opposite him. The five o'clock train up to town was almost empty. Only two other people shared the carriage, both of them elderly and deep in their books.

'You're going to London?' Jason scrabbled on the floor for his iPod, stuffing it back into his bag.

'Yes.' Tati smiled. She was amused by his awkwardness, but the smile was kind rather than mocking. 'Unless I'm on the wrong train.'

'Of course. Silly question.' Jason blushed. It was a wonder

the rest of his body still functioned, with so much blood rushing to his cheeks.

'I'm actually going out for dinner and drinks with a girl-friend tonight,' said Tati, helping him out. 'I hardly ever get up to town any more, but there's a teacher-training day tomorrow and I decided I needed a break.'

'Bad day?'

Tati considered lying, but in the end decided there was no point. 'I'm afraid so,' she said. 'Mostly thanks to your bloody father.' Reaching into her handbag, she pulled out a cigarette and lit it, ignoring the disapproving look she got from one of the pensioners.

'I don't think you're supposed to do that in here,' Jason said gently, gesturing towards one of the many 'No Smoking' signs underneath their window.

'You aren't,' Tati said cheerfully. 'But at this point I'm afraid I couldn't give two hoots. If they fine me, I'll send the bill to your old man.'

Jason grinned. How he wished he had even a fraction of Tatiana's chutzpah, especially when it came to Brett.

'Sorry,' she added. 'It's not personal.'

'Please, don't apologize. My dad makes my life miserable – and I'm his flesh and blood. I get it, believe me.'

'Hmmm.' Tati studied him more closely. 'Yes. I suspect you do.'

Inhaling deeply on her cigarette, she released the smoke in a slow, sultry trail through her pursed lips, looking at Jason all the while. Anyone who thought of smoking as a dirty, unattractive habit clearly hadn't seen Tatiana Flint-Hamilton doing it.

It *had* been a stressful day. Brett's comments about marriage to a rich man being her only option had been no more than a childish attempt to put her down. Playground spite. And yet deep down Tati feared there might be some truth to them. He was certainly right that she could never settle down as a teacher in a sleepy Sussex village. That she needed excitement, and drama, and that she missed the high life she'd left behind in London.

The problem was that having always expected to inherit Furlings, and a fortune to go with it, she'd never given much thought to making her own way. But now the question had become pressing. If she didn't win her court case in September, what *would* she do? What would her future look like? Brett had been typically scathing about her ability to start her own business. Then again, Brett Cranley was so sexist he probably believed women were incapable of tying their shoelaces without a man's help.

Tati told herself firmly that if an intellectually challenged emotional retard like Brett Cranley could become a self-made millionaire, then so could she. Besides, she *wasn't* going to lose the court case. But the lingering feeling of self-doubt and depression refused to leave her. She was coming up to London to escape.

'So, what takes you up to town?' she asked, turning the conversation back to Jason.

'Work.' He sighed heavily.

'You don't sound too thrilled about it!'

'I'm not.' Partly out of nervousness, and partly because he liked Tatiana and she seemed genuinely interested, Jason started to elaborate on how much he hated working at his father's company and how useless he was at anything connected to business. He described Graham Jones to her, reducing Tati to tears of laughter, and did his best to convey the almost indescribable tedium of his work at Cranley Estates.

'Wow,' she said when he finally stopped talking. 'That does sound ghastly.'

'It is.'

'Almost makes me feel lucky to be stuck making the tea at a village primary school. Although your father was kind enough to suggest today that I quit my job, and my court case, and focus on snagging myself a rich husband.'

Jason shook his head. 'I'm sorry. He's a Neanderthal.'

'Why *is* that?' asked Tati.

Jason looked thoughtful. 'I don't really know. It's odd because in one way he loves women. He's always been much closer to Logan than to me, and he loves Mum, even though he sometimes doesn't act like it. The only time I've ever seen him cry was talking about his own mother. But then, in another way . . .' He trailed off. 'I don't think he likes to be challenged.'

'That's an understatement,' said Tati. 'Not that I give a monkey's what your father thinks about me. But I do feel sorry for Logan. I was trying to tell Brett today about how bright she is, if she just had the right help. But he didn't want to hear it.'

Jason felt the anger rise up inside him, hardening into a solid ball in his chest. The idea of Brett stifling Logan the way he'd stifled him filled him with impotent rage.

'Doesn't he want his children to succeed?' Tati questioned.

'Oh, he does,' Jason said bitterly. 'It's almost funny; family is everything to him – but he doesn't quite know what to do with us. But only on *his* terms. *His* definition of success.'

'Which is?'

'Dad wants me to be an entrepreneur, the next Sol Kerzner, and Logan to marry a prince.' Jason laughed, but there was no joy in the sound. 'I'd say Logie's got a better chance than I have.'

Tatiana looked at Jason more closely. She still couldn't

entirely decide whether or not he was handsome. He had huge, soulful eyes, beautiful in a sad sort of way, but also strange-looking, too big for the rest of his face, like a possum's eyes. His skin was pale like his mother's, with delicate features and a sensual, expressive mouth. *He'd be a stunning girl*, Tati found herself thinking. It was bizarre how all the male traits that Brett exemplified – confidence, charm, ambition – seemed to have been inherited by his daughter; while his son and heir was a gentle lamb who completely broke the mould.

Tati found herself empathizing with Jason. They might not have much in common in other ways, but they both knew what it was like to have a father who was constantly disappointed in them. Who wanted them to be someone else, someone they were intrinsically incapable of being.

'What would you like to do?' she asked Jason. 'For a job, I mean. If it were entirely up to you?'

His face lit up. 'Perform.'

'At what?'

'The piano. But unfortunately I'm not good enough to play professionally.'

'Says who? Your father?'

'Well, yes. But I'm afraid he's actually right on that one. I would never make the grade as a concert pianist.'

'I bet you would.'

Jason shook his head and gave her a small, self-deprecating smile. 'Nah. But even just a gig at a jazz club or a little wine bar somewhere would be incredible. All I really want is to play. I could teach music on the side maybe, for extra money. I don't know.' He blushed, as if this modest little scheme were a preposterous pipe dream, like becoming an astronaut or discovering Atlantis. 'It doesn't matter anyway. It's not gonna happen. Not in this life.'

They fell silent as the train made its way through the outskirts of London. After East Croydon they began to make more frequent stops, moving slowly through ugly suburbs. The mishmash of architecture fascinated Jason: Victorian red-brick terraces, their walls stained black from years of coal pollution, stood cheek-by-jowl with sixties tower blocks in unforgiving grey concrete, and modern office buildings, gleaming, sterile behemoths of glass and steel. London was like a living museum, a pop-up history book that never ceased to surprise and amaze him. Compared to Australia, everything here was on a tiny, doll's-house scale. But he appreciated the city's quirks and idiosyncrasies, and he loved the feeling of it being a genuine melting pot – economically, ethnically, culturally and in every other way.

By the time they pulled into Victoria, he'd almost forgotten Tatiana was sitting opposite him.

'It was nice talking to you,' he said shyly as they stepped down onto the platform. 'Enjoy your party.'

'It's only dinner,' said Tati. 'But I will. And good luck with your work thing.'

'Thanks.'

'God, that smells good.'

Tati closed her eyes and inhaled. The pungent scent of warm dough and chocolate from the Millie's Cookies kiosk wafted over them deliciously.

'Shall we get one?'

They strolled onto the concourse together and bought two white-chocolate-chip cookies, still soft and warm from the oven.

She's really nice, thought Jason. He didn't understand where Tati's scandalous, rich-bitch reputation had come from. Suddenly reluctant to let her go, he asked about her plans for the summer.

171

'I'll be in Fittlescombe,' she said gloomily.

'Working on the court case?'

She nodded. It felt awkward, talking to Jason Cranley about a legal battle that, if she won, would see him turfed out of his home. She changed the subject.

'What about you? Logan said you're off to the South of France.'

'My parents are, not me. I've got to work.'

Tati's ears pricked up. 'So you'll be at Furlings over the holidays then?'

Jason nodded. 'Logan's been begging to be allowed to stay too. I'm not sure she can bear the thought of a whole summer away from Gabriel Baxter.'

He told Tati about Logan's crush on Gabe, which showed no signs of abating.

'I'd be careful if I were you,' Tati said archly. 'I wouldn't trust Gabe as far as I could throw him. But you'll be on your own then, will you? At the house?'

'Yup. Just me and Mrs Worsley. And the dog.'

The cogs in Tati's brain began whirring. She hadn't set foot in Furlings since the day she'd collected her grandmother's painting. Brett's presence, and the looming court case over the will, made any sort of social call impossible. But with Jason Cranley home alone, she'd be able to drop in whenever she pleased. Here was a perfect chance to invade enemy territory! Perhaps even snoop around in Brett's office, or scour the attic for papers of her father's? Who knew what she might unearth that could help her case?

She'd have to get round old Mrs Worsley, of course. Rory's dragon of a housekeeper had made no secret in the village of her disapproval of Tatiana and her support of the Cranleys' claim to Furlings. But at least old Ma Worsley was a known enemy. With a little advance planning, Tati was confident she could think up some scheme to get rid of her.

'We must have lunch.' She bestowed her most dazzling smile on Jason. 'Or dinner. Or both. As we're stuck in Sussex together.'

Jason couldn't imagine anything more wonderful. Thanks to the ambrosial melting cookie in his mouth, an enthusiastic nod was the most he could manage by way of response.

'Lovely,' said Tati, kissing him on the cheek. 'I'll call you.'

She slipped off into the crowds and was gone.

CHAPTER TEN

'Good morning, Mrs Cranley. Would you like breakfast on the upper deck this morning, or down here?'

Hannah Lowell, the *Lady A*'s frighteningly efficient chief stewardess, handed Angela Cranley her morning newspaper as she emerged onto the yacht's lower deck. In flip-flops and a simple blue shirt-waister sundress, with her hair tied back and a pair of toirteshell Ray-Bans covering her eyes, Angela looked relaxed as she stepped out into the Côte d'Azur sunshine. (Unlike Brett, who'd been awake since dawn, pacing the boards and yelling into his mobile phone at some hapless private banker who'd evidently made a mistake on a deal.)

'Who's upstairs?' she asked Hannah. 'Is everybody up already?'

'Most of them, yes. Jeremy Curzon and his . . . friend . . . are still in their cabin. But the O'Mahoneys, the Gassinghams and Mr Morgan are all at breakfast. Monsieur Lemprière, the lawyer, left last night after dinner.'

As usual, the relaxing family holiday that Brett had promised her had been hijacked by a slew of rich and famous

174

guests and their hangers-on. Brett loved entertaining on the yacht. What was the point of spending forty million on a boat you used twice a year at most if you didn't at least get to show it off to your mates?

'Is Mr Cranley with them?'

'He is.'

'And Logan?'

'Danny took her out on the jet-ski an hour ago. Don't worry,' Hannah Lowell added, seeing her mistress's face cloud over with anxiety. 'She had her headgear on. Danny's super, super safety-conscious. He's one of the best deck hands we've ever had.'

'All right. I think I'll stay down here,' said Angela. The thought of making small talk with Brett's chest-beating playboy friends and their vacuous young wives did not appeal. 'Don't tell Mr Cranley I'm up. And I don't want breakfast yet, just a large mug of coffee. Thanks.'

Hannah left, and Angela sat down on one of the outdoor sofas, carefully choosing a section that was shaded by a large, blue canvas awning. To Brett's irritation, and Angela's huge relief, they were moored offshore and not in St Tropez harbour itself. The harbour was the place to see and be seen, which was of course why Brett liked it. But Angela always felt like a monkey in the zoo there, being gawped at by all the tourists strolling around the port.

At this time in the morning, and seen from a little distance, St Tropez looked idyllic, with its sloping cobbled streets and red tiled roofs tumbling down the hills, one on top of one another, punctuated only by the occasional medieval church spire. The Mediterranean sparkled bright blue in the sunshine, like liquid lapis, and seagulls swooped and cawed overhead, excited by the nets of wriggling fish being hauled up onto the quayside for today's market.

Take away all the yachts and Ferraris and arseholes, all the Club 55 poseurs and diamond-encrusted Russian whores at Nikki Beach, and this would be a charming village, Angela thought wistfully. Still, it was hard to feel too depressed, sipping fresh coffee on the deck of the beautiful yacht that her husband had named in her honour, reading yesterday's edition of the *Daily Mail* while the sun warmed her back. *We have an amazing life*, she told herself sternly. *I must try to appreciate it more.*

Her attention was caught by an item in Baz Bamigboye's gossip column about Tatiana Flint-Hamilton and her latest squeeze, described as 'City whizz-kid, Marco Gianotti'. Whizz-kid or not, judging by the picture of the two of them leaving Annabel's arm in arm, he was certainly very good looking. How odd it must be for Tatiana, flitting between her two lives as village primary schoolteacher and 'It girl' about town. The former took up considerably more of her time than the latter, but clearly someone at the *Daily Mail* believed that Tati's photograph could still sell newspapers.

'What are you doing down here on your own?'

Brett appeared out of nowhere. Angela hastily folded the paper and put it aside. Tatiana Flint-Hamilton was not a subject likely to be conducive to marital harmony. In white linen shorts and an open-necked, cornflower-blue polo shirt, Brett looked fit and tanned, far younger than his forty-five years. Angela had never stopped wanting him, even after all the storms and heartaches of their marriage.

'You startled me.'

He kissed her on the cheek. 'Come up and join the party. Jeremy and Miriam just sat down to breakfast.'

Angela folded her newspaper disapprovingly. 'All the more reason for me to stay down here. Poor Rachel. She'd be horrified if she knew.'

Brett rolled his eyes. 'You're not still on about that, are you?'

Rachel and Jeremy Curzon were old friends from Hong Kong. The Curzons had married the same year as Angela and Brett, and the couples became instant friends. This was back in the early days of Cranley Estates, when they were all still in their twenties. Then, last year, Jeremy had walked out on Rachel and their four children and set up home with a twenty-four-year-old Persian model named Miriam Kashani. Angela had choked on her cornflakes when Brett announced he'd invited the two of them on the yacht for a week.

'Jeremy and Rachel are separated,' Brett said wearily.

'So?'

'They'll be divorced by Christmas, Ange. It's not like Rachel doesn't know the marriage is over.'

'Yes, and why is it over? Because of that bloody tart,' Angela said angrily. 'And you expect me to have breakfast with her? Make small talk over the frittatas, as if I approve?'

'You don't have to approve,' said Brett gently. 'You just don't have to *dis*approve quite so pointedly. After all, it's not going to change anything, is it?'

No. I suppose it isn't.

Angela closed her eyes. Brett was massaging her shoulders, being unusually affectionate. She didn't want to start the holiday off by fighting with him.

'Besides,' he said smoothly. '*I'd* like to have breakfast with my wife. Especially as you're sodding off to the mainland without me later.'

Angela had quite forgotten. It was market day today, a jolly affair in the Place des Lices. Local artisans sold everything from soap to hand-sewn baby clothes, lavender oil and stinky, unpasteurized cheeses. Over the years they'd been coming to St Tropez, Angela had scored some surprising bargains at the market, including kilim rugs and antique jewellery. She adored pottering around the square, soaking up the atmosphere of France and the local flavour of the Var, but Brett had always hated it.

'Who wants to waste time on bloody tourist tat when you could be enjoying a nice cold flute of Bollinger at Nikki Beach?'

They had long ago made a pact to split up on market day, regrouping in the evening for dinner on the yacht, mutually refreshed after a day pursuing their respective pleasures.

Cheered by the prospect of a whole day in town to herself, Angela agreed to join Brett for breakfast.

'I suppose I can manage a slice of toast. But I'm not sitting next to Miriam.'

'Damn right,' said Brett, kissing her. 'You're sitting next to me.'

A few hours later, weaving her way aimlessly through the market stalls, Angela felt deeply happy. Breakfast had not been the ordeal she'd expected. Jeremy's mistress had had the good sense to keep her head down and contribute little or nothing to the conversation. And the other guests had been good company, Johnny Gassingham in particular regaling the table with hilarious stories of his recent trip to India, where he'd somehow managed to fall foul of local police and get himself arrested for shoplifting. (Worth comfortably north of a hundred million, Johnny was apparently suspected of stealing a banana.)

More importantly, Brett had gone out of his way to make her feel comfortable and happy. One of the reasons Angela had always disliked St Tropez in the past was that it seemed to bring out the very worst, most insecure side of her husband's nature. Brett became louder, brasher, more bullying, less considerate from the moment they set foot on the yacht. But this time he seemed genuinely to be making an effort. He'd even arranged for Logan to spend the day at Luna Park, a local funfair, so she wouldn't be bored while her mother was in town.

Picking up a beautiful lace tablecloth, Angela began to haggle with the stallholder in broken French. It took a few minutes to agree on a price. Reaching into her wicker shopping basket for her purse, Angela's stomach suddenly lurched.

'Oh god,' she blanched. 'It's gone! Someone's taken it.'

The woman stallholder looked at her curiously.

'*Voleur*,' said Angela. '*Mon sac à main*. Stolen. *Volé. Vous avez vu quelqu'un?*'

The woman shook her head. Angela tried not to be suspicious, but one read so many stories about sellers at French markets being in cahoots with local pickpocketing gangs. There wasn't much cash in her purse, but she felt quite sick. Violated, as if the beautiful rose she'd just been smelling and admiring had suddenly erupted with maggots.

Pushing through the crowds, she made her way back to the harbour. She was about to call Brett and have one of the tenders come and pick her up when she caught sight of Danny Michaels, one of *Lady A*'s crewmembers.

'Danny!'

'Mrs Cranley! I thought you were at the market.'

The boy seemed unaccountably nervous.

'I was.' Angela told him what had happened. 'It's lucky you're here. You can take me back to the boat. Come to think of it, why *are* you here?'

'I was dropping the other guests off, ma'am. The ladies have all got spa appointments at the Byblos and the gentlemen are lunching at the beach.'

'And my husband?'

179

'Mr Cranley . . . er . . . Mr Cranley is still on board. I believe.'

Working, thought Angela. You couldn't part Brett from his precious deals for long, not even here.

'OK. Well let's head back. I'll cancel my cards and get some cash, and then you can bring me back to town again.'

The boy hesitated. 'Shouldn't we tell the local police first? As we're here.'

'Oh, they're not going to do anything,' Angela said dismissively. 'One more robbed tourist. They couldn't care less.'

'Still,' Danny persisted. 'If no one reports these guys, it's hopeless, isn't it? They can act with impunity.'

'I suppose so,' said Angela. 'But I really don't feel like trudging up to the gendarmerie. I'll call them from the yacht.' Stepping past him, she began to climb down into the waiting speedboat. 'Better yet, I'll get Brett to do it. He's bound to have more joy than I am. The French are such sexists, they won't take a woman seriously.'

Danny stood frozen on the dock for a moment, as if unsure what to do next. Angela looked at him curiously.

'Is something the matter?'

'No, Mrs Cranley.'

'Well come on then!' Angela laughed. 'I don't know how to pilot one of these things by myself. The sooner we get back to the yacht, the sooner we can turn around again.'

The boy climbed in and started the engine.

Five minutes later, Angela was climbing the stairs up to the *Lady A*'s lower deck and the entrance to the family living quarters. Dropping her basket in the TV room, she headed towards the study.

'Brett?'

No answer. Pushing open the door she saw his computer open on the desk, but he wasn't there.

Everything on the boat was quiet. Danny must have been wrong. Had Brett joined the others for lunch at the beach after all? Walking down the corridor, she opened the door to the master suite.

'Oh my *God.*'

At first she thought she was seeing things. *It can't be her. Not here!* She closed her eyes and opened them again, but the apparition was still there, sprawled out on the bed in a pair of tiny Agent Provocateur knickers.

Tricia Hong, Brett's mistress from Australia, was exactly as Angela remembered her. The same tiny, gym-toned body, the same smooth golden skin and silken black hair, the same tiny, perky breasts like two glued-on apples. And the same ruthless look of naked hatred in her beautiful, snake-like eyes.

Tricia neither moved nor spoke. Both women remained frozen, like actresses in a play who've forgotten their lines. From the en-suite bathroom, Brett's voice ricocheted off the walls like a stray bullet.

'Hold on a minute, angel. I'll be right there.'

He was opening and closing cabinets. *Looking for a condom,* thought Angela numbly. She should probably scream or cry or throw something, but she was in absolute shock.

How could Tricia be *here*, now, in France? On her boat? In her bedroom? She was supposed to be in Australia, thousands of miles away. There was a time and a place for every enemy, a time and a place where Angela might have felt prepared for such a betrayal. A year ago, back in the Sydney apartment, she could have made sense of it. But not now, not like this. It was like going for a walk down the High Street in Fittlescombe and finding yourself face to face with

181

a tiger. The unexpectedness of the situation almost trumped the fear.

Brett burst into the room, a smile a mile wide plastered across his face. Then he saw Angela.

'Oh, shit,' he said quietly. There didn't seem much else to say.

Ashen-faced, Angela turned and ran staggering down the corridor.

Brett ran after her. 'Ange wait! Please.'

She quickened her pace. Tears bleared her vision, but she kept going, knocking against the walls as the yacht rocked gently from side to side on the water.

'Angie!' Brett grabbed her by the arm. She tried to wrench herself free but his grip was too tight.

'Let go of me,' she sobbed.

'No. I won't. I can't. Ange, I'm sorry.'

'Sorry you did it? Or sorry you got caught?'

'Both,' said Brett truthfully.

'She knew you'd be here! You've been in contact.'

Brett said nothing.

'Oh my God,' Angela shook her head in disbelief. 'Did you fly her out here?'

Again Brett didn't deny it.

'You *planned* this.'

The pennies dropped one by one, like acid on Angela's skin.

'Look, Ange, she called me. She was relentless. I know it was stupid of me and weak. She doesn't mean anything to me.'

'I have to get out of here,' Angela said quietly.

'Please! Don't go. I don't mean anything to her either, and that's the truth. She's got a new boyfriend. They're getting married . . .'

Angela put her hands over her ears and screwed her eyes up tight, like a child hiding from monsters under the bed.

'Stop!' she begged him. 'I don't want to hear it. I'll check into a hotel. You can have Hannah send a bag over later.'

'Please don't!' Brett pleaded. He knew it had been madness to fly Tricia over. But the week she'd called him in London, he'd been so whipsawed with anger and frustration over Tati Flint-Hamilton, his reserves of self-control had been low. And then he'd got the pictures texted to his phone: Tricia, her legs spread and lips parted, staring right into the camera, right into his eyes. The ticket was booked, the deed done. He'd genuinely believed Ange would never find out.

He grasped at straws, desperate to stop Angela from leaving. 'What about Logan? What will I tell her?'

Angela hesitated. She'd completely forgotten about their daughter. That complicated things. She needed to be alone, to think. But she couldn't very well abandon Logie without any explanation. Her mind was racing so fast, it was hard to make any rational decisions.

'Just tell her I've gone on a trip and I'll be back tomorrow.'

'Will you?'

There was no mistaking the vulnerability in Brett's voice. The need. Despite herself, Angela felt the tug at her heartstrings. But she was tired of being Brett's mother, his security blanket, tired of being the one whose job it was to forgive and forgive and forgive. *He* was the one who'd betrayed *her*. This was *her* time to be comforted and cherished, not his.

'Yes.'

His shoulders sagged with relief.

'For Logan, not for you,' Angela added sharply. 'I want you gone by the time I get back, Brett.'

Brett nodded. 'OK.' He was hardly in a position to argue

183

with her. 'I'll go back to London. Tell Logan it's a business trip.'

'Good.'

'What about our guests?'

Angela grimaced. 'I suppose they'll have to stay. I can't very well kick them out with no explanation. But they're going to have to fend for themselves. I'm not in the mood for entertaining.'

'I truly am sorry, Ange.' Brett tried to touch her shoulder but she shrugged him off. 'It's you I love. You do know that, right?'

With as much dignity as she could muster, Angela walked away.

CHAPTER ELEVEN

Angela checked into Le Yaca hotel. She'd just been handed her keys and was heading for the lift when she caught sight of Didier Lemprière, the French lawyer who'd been one of the guests at last night's dinner aboard *Lady A*.

Damn it, thought Angela. She vaguely remembered having liked Didier. He'd been more normal and low-key than most of the show-offs Brett had invited. Among other things he'd told a very funny story involving a camper van and a corpse that had reduced everyone to tears of laughter. But she was in no mood for small talk this evening.

Putting her head down she hurried across the lobby, praying that he wouldn't see her.

For his part, Didier Lemprière was having a trying day.

A successful tax lawyer from Paris, Didier was in St Tropez on business, visiting two wealthy clients. The first, Jason Morgan, was a decent enough guy. It was Jason who knew Brett Cranley and who'd invited Didier out to Brett's yacht for dinner, a fun experience but one that had left him with a hangover this morning that could have felled a rhinoceros.

Unfortunately, it was Didier's other client, a boorish German industrialist by the name of Helmut Schnetzler, who had invited him to dinner at Le Yaca tonight. Helmut had already completely hijacked Didier's day, insisting on an afternoon round of golf (a game Didier loathed). Helmut had arranged tonight's dinner for the sole purpose of 'talking through' his issues with the French tax authorities. As if he and Didier hadn't just spent the past week discussing nothing else!

An attractive man in his late thirties, with dark hair, brown eyes fringed with long, jet-black lashes, and a strong jaw that no amount of shaving could ever completely rid of a faint shadow of stubble, Didier was funny and charismatic – unusually for a member of his profession. He enjoyed all the good things in life: wine, music, food, classic cars and beautiful women. But he worked hard and was not a liar, never promising his many girlfriends more than he could realistically offer, i.e. great sex and amusing company but on a strictly time-share basis. Didier Lemprière was not so much of a commitment-phobe as a freedom-o-phile. He loved his bachelor life, and had yet to be presented with any compelling reason to end it.

As such, he'd been hoping to ditch Helmut early tonight and then settle in for an evening of flirtation at Le Yaca's famous poolside bar, trying his luck with the myriad stunning young women who flocked to St Tropez each summer, as long-legged and exotic as flamingos in their pink Cavalli minidresses and spiked Gucci heels. But Herr Schnetzler had put paid to that. With his booming German voice and his fat cigars and his bottle after bottle of expensive claret, he was clearly settling in for a long night.

'I hope I'm not boring you?'

Didier looked up. Helmut was halfway through an

interminable, boastful story about some deal he'd pulled off. Didier thought he'd stifled his yawn, but perhaps he hadn't.

'Not at all. I'm a little tired, that's all. Not all of us have your stamina, Helmut.'

'Ha!' The old man laughed, gratified by the compliment. 'Now, where was I?'

Didier let his client's voice wash over him, throwing in the occasional 'oh' and 'hmmm', and wondering when he could politely excuse himself, when a woman he recognized walked into reception. Slim and willowy, wearing an old-fashioned sundress in some sort of Liberty print, and with her blonde hair clipped up, it took Didier a moment to place her. But then he remembered. It was Angela Cranley, his hostess at last night's dinner.

He hadn't paid Mrs Cranley much attention last night. They were sitting too far apart and she'd been rather quiet. Looking at her now, he realized that everything about her seemed to belong to a different, more elegant era – the Fifties, perhaps; or at least to belong in a different town. Amid all the attention-grabbing miniskirts and silicone breasts and flashy diamonds of St Tropez, Angela Cranley was as out of place as a librarian in a Bangkok brothel.

Didier saw that she was checking in, which was very odd in itself. Who stayed at the Yaca when they had a palatial yacht moored offshore? But to show up at a hotel at so late an hour and with no luggage bar a small overnight case . . . something was up.

She was heading towards the lifts, obviously in a hurry.

'Excuse me.' Didier interrupted Helmut mid-sentence. 'I have to use the bathroom.'

By the time he reached the lift, the doors were about to close. Didier rushed forwards, leaping into the tiny space with seconds to spare.

'Mrs Cranley!'

Angela looked up and smiled politely. 'Monsieur Lemprière.'

'Which floor?'

'Oh, er . . . third. Thank you.'

Close up she was older than Didier had thought last night, with a faint fan of lines around her eyes, but she was still extremely beautiful. There was a sadness about her, too, that somehow pulled at him.

'I apologize for following you.'

'Were you following me?' Her eyes narrowed suspiciously.

'Well, not following exactly,' Didier corrected himself awkwardly. 'I saw you checking in and I wondered if every-thing was all right.'

'Everything's fine, thank you,' Angela lied. 'I wouldn't want to keep you from your guest.'

'Oh, God, please keep me from him.' Didier rolled his eyes. 'He's German and fat and so dull he brings tears to my eyes. Whereas you are absolutely stunning.'

Angela was so surprised, at first she wasn't sure how to react. It was a very long time, a decade or more, since a man had flirted with her quite so directly. Especially such an attractive man, and one who knew she was Brett's wife.

'Well, er . . . thank you,' she blushed.

The lift lurched upwards, stopping with a judder at the third floor. Angela hoped it was that that was making her stomach flip over, and not the attentions of Monsieur Lemprière. *A smooth, handsome Frenchman like him probably uses the same line twenty times a night*, she told herself firmly. *I expect every woman he meets is 'stunning'.*

The doors opened and they both stepped out into the corridor. Angela's room was immediately on the right. There was a moment of awkwardness as she stood outside with

188

her key card and Didier hovered beside her. *Surely he doesn't expect me to invite him in?*

'Well, goodnight, Monsieur Lemprière' she said at last, breaking the silence because one of them had to. 'This is me.'

'Have a drink with me,' Didier blurted. 'Downstairs, once you've settled in. And for God's sake call me Didier.'

'I appreciate the offer, Didier,' said Angela. 'But I honestly can't. I've had a very long day.' An image of Tricia, lithe and naked, sprawled out on her bed, popped unbidden into her mind. 'I'm afraid I'm exhausted.'

Didier's face fell. 'Tomorrow, then?'

Angela hesitated. She'd told Brett she'd be back on the yacht by tomorrow. It was the last thing she wanted to do – she desperately needed space – but with Logan on board she had little choice.

Impulsively, Didier grabbed both her hands and clasped them to his chest. 'I have to see you tomorrow. Please. Lunch, at least.'

'I'm married,' Angela heard herself saying. 'You know I'm married.'

'I also know you're checking into a hotel at nine at night on your own,' said Didier. 'Besides, married people still have to eat lunch, don't they?'

Angela smiled. 'I suppose so.'

There was something so earnest and endearing about him. Or maybe she was just flattered by the fact that he appeared to find her genuinely attractive? Perhaps as a by-product of Brett's affairs, Angela had long felt frumpy and middle-aged. Compared to the pneumatic perfection of girls like Tricia Hong, a forty-two-year-old mother of two had little to offer.

This whole encounter is ridiculous, she told herself, gently removing her hands from Didier's and sliding her key card into its slot, opening the door to her room.

'I'll pick you up at noon, then, shall I?' said Didier firmly, pressing his advantage

'Hold on. I never said I—'

'In the lobby. Just lunch.'

Angela hesitated, then nodded. What harm was there in one lunch, after all?

'OK.'

'Sleep well, Mrs Cranley,' said Didier.

'Angela,' she corrected, then closed the door to her room and leaned back against it, her heart pounding with adrenaline, as if she'd just robbed a bank. *What on earth had just happened?* Looking down at her left hand, she twisted her wedding ring round and round on her finger. Then, to her own surprise, she burst into laughter.

Downstairs at the dinner table, Helmut Schnetzler was getting impatient.

'Better?' he asked gruffly, as Didier returned to his seat.

'Much,' said Didier, smiling broadly.

He wondered how long it would take him to crack Mrs Angela Cranley.

Didier took Angela to a tiny fish restaurant, up in the hilltop village of Ramatuelle.

'I thought you might prefer to be out of town,' he said as they took their seats on the balcony, overlooking the rooftops of the village with the sparkling blue sea beyond. 'It's more peaceful up here, don't you think?'

'It's gorgeous,' Angela sighed.

She was waiting for the guilt to hit her, or at least the absurdity. What was she *doing*, having lunch with some French playboy at least ten years her junior? But in fact she felt sublimely content. Yes it was unreal, *sur*real even, to be sitting across the table from a handsome stranger while he poured from a bottle of chilled rosé. But after the events of yesterday, the reality of Angela's life had lost every shred of appeal.

To think, just yesterday morning she'd been sitting on the yacht eating breakfast and thinking how lucky she was. What a joke! All Brett's affection, all his warmth had been a front, designed to lure her into a false sense of security. All along he was just waiting for her to leave, so he could smuggle that whore into their bed. Angela felt a wave of nausea wash over her. The thought of going back to the yacht, of putting on a brave face for Logan and trying to act naturally in front of Brett's friends filled her with a lurching dread.

'Are you OK?' Didier asked.

'I'm fine, thanks.' She forced a smile. Brett was the one who should bloody well be feeling sick and anxious, not her.

Didier ordered for both of them, langoustines in white wine and garlic with a side of cold poached artichokes and a delicious selection of local cheeses. He talked easily and naturally about everything from his life in Paris to politics, music and art. Before long Angela felt as if she were lunching with an old friend. By the time he brought the conversation around to more personal matters, they'd already started a second bottle of wine, and Angela was feeling considerably more relaxed.

'So. You're married,' Didier observed casually, helping himself to more of the richly oozing Brie.

'Yes.' Angela swirled the pale pink liquid around her glass.

'Happily?'

She shrugged. 'Sometimes. Not always.'

'How about now?'

Her tongue loosened by the alcohol, she ended up telling him the whole story, from walking in on Brett and his mistress yesterday, to the history of the affair in Australia, and all the affairs that had preceded it.

'We moved to England to make a fresh start,' she laughed bitterly. 'Like a fool, I thought we had. But Brett hasn't changed. He arranged this whole thing.' She drained her glass.

Didier looked at her for a moment, weighing his words before he spoke.

'Well. Maybe now, *you* will change.'

'What do you mean?'

'Just what I say. Maybe you will grow tired of this life, waiting for the next affair, the next betrayal.'

I am tired, thought Angela.

'Look,' he took her hand. 'I am in no position to pass judgement on your husband. I 'ave not always been faithful to girlfriends.'

'Yes, but you're not married,' said Angela. 'You don't have kids. It's not the same.'

'Isn't it?' said Didier. 'A lie is a lie. Pain is pain, *non*? All I'm trying to say is, each one of us has our strengths and weaknesses, and we each justify our decisions to ourselves. Your husband may change, or he may not change, but *you* can't change him. You can only change yourself. So I am wondering . . . will you?'

Didier was caressing the underside of her wrist with his thumb. *Will I what?* thought Angela. *Will I change? Or will I have an affair with you?*

'You're very attractive,' she said, truthfully, withdrawing her hand. 'And I'm flattered. But my life is complicated enough right now without . . .'

She left the sentence hanging.

'Without what? Happiness?' Didier prompted. 'Without pleasure?'

Angela shrugged. 'Two wrongs don't make a right.'

'So what will you do?' Didier asked after a while, leaning back in his chair and sipping at his wine.

'I don't know,' said Angela. 'Go back to the boat. Take care of my daughter. But beyond that . . . I don't know.'

She couldn't imagine leaving Brett. She'd been with him her whole adult life. He *was* her life, in so many ways. But she also recognized the truth in what Didier was saying. The only way to break a cycle was for one person to change. And if it wasn't going to be Brett, it would have to be her. They couldn't go on like this forever.

Didier paid the bill and walked her back to his car.

'Can we keep in touch?'

He hadn't given up hope of seducing the lovely Mrs Cranley. But he sensed that coming on too strongly now would be a mistake. He must go slowly with this one, break her in gently like a frightened young foal.

'I'd like that.' Angela smiled.

For now, it was enough.

CHAPTER TWELVE

Tatiana fiddled with the strap of her watch and looked awkwardly around the restaurant. Daphne's on Draycott Avenue had been her choice, an old favourite from her 'It girl' partying days. But she regretted it now. It was so small and intimate, she felt as if every table of diners were watching her, wondering who it was who'd stood her up and how long she'd be hanging around at the bar like a spare part, waiting for him.

Of course, they probably *weren't* thinking anything of the kind. No doubt they had bigger fish to fry than worrying about a society has-been's romantic entanglements. Or lack of them. The truth was, it was so long since Tati had been on a date, she felt as wired and nervous as a racehorse on Derby Day morning.

Two more minutes. Two more minutes then I'll go, and never speak to that self-important dickhead again.

'Hello. Oh my God I am so sorry I'm late. There was a pile-up on the Embankment, it was insane. Please tell me you haven't been here long?'

And there he was. The self-important dickhead, aka Marco

194

Gianotti, an Italian-American investment banker whom Tati had been introduced to by her friend Katia a few weeks ago, the same day she'd bumped into Jason Cranley on the train, and who hadn't stopped calling her since.

'I was about to give up on you,' she said, more frostily than she'd meant to, but only because she'd forgotten just how unbearably attractive Marco was. Tall and broad shouldered with thick, wavy black hair and a flawless olive complexion, he looked more like an aftershave model than a banker. Although Goldman Sachs were known for hiring ridiculously good-looking employees. Back in her heyday, Tati had bedded quite a number of them.

'Please, don't do that.' Marco smiled. 'Not after keeping me hanging for almost a month. That would be too cruel.'

Tati felt the blood rush to her head then straight back down to her groin. It had been too long, far too long, since she'd had a decent man. Her abortive encounter with Dylan was hardly a night she wanted to remember.

The maître d' led them to their table, tucked away in a rear corner of the restaurant. Marco ordered champagne and a plate of oysters to share, then boldly reached across the table and took Tati's hand.

'You look incredible.'

This was no more than a statement of fact. In a cream Alaïa minidress with a flared tennis-style skirt and raffia wedges, Tati's flawless figure and famous, gazelle-like legs were showcased perfectly. Her make-up was minimal, just a sweep of bronzer and some lip gloss, but she radiated youth and health and natural beauty. The rose remained thorny, however.

'I bet you say that to all the girls,' she said coolly, reclaiming her hand.

'All what girls?' asked Marco.

'All the girls you've been screwing while I kept you hanging.'

Marco grinned. 'I love it when you talk dirty.'

Tati grinned back. 'I love it when *you* talk business. Tell me more about Avenues.'

When they'd met at Katia's party, Katia had introduced Tati as 'a teacher at a village school.' Marco had flatly refused to believe this. 'I'm sorry. I went to school. Teachers don't look like you and I know that for a fact.' Having successfully begun a flirtation, he'd asked Tati about her background and ambitions. She'd given him the edited version of her battle with Brett Cranley and the furore over her father's will.

'Once this damn court case is over, win or lose, I'm going to start my own business. Cranley's right about one thing, there's bugger-all money in teaching.'

'I wouldn't be so sure,' said Marco. 'Two good mates of mine were first-round investors in Avenues. They both made a fucking mint.'

'Avenues?' Tati looked blank.

'You know. The new hot school in Manhattan? Suri Cruise goes there. They've got a waiting list as long as your arm. I'm telling you, the guys who started that thing are printing money.'

It was a throwaway line, and the conversation had swiftly moved on. But Tati had thought a lot about Marco's comment since that night – almost as much as she'd thought about his hot body underneath that bespoke Savile Row business suit. This evening was a date, but she saw no harm in killing two birds with one stone.

Happily, neither did Marco. 'All right,' he said obligingly. 'What do you want to know?'

Tati wanted to know everything. Whose idea was it to start the school, how much seed money had they needed, did anyone have a background in education, what fees did they charge, how had they come up with that number, what was their marketing strategy? By the time they'd finished the oysters and their first courses had arrived, Marco had got the message.

'You're serious about this, aren't you? You're thinking of setting up a school?'

'I'm curious,' Tati said cautiously. 'I won't know what the future holds till after September. But it's something I'm considering.'

Marco took a slug of champagne. 'You need a concept. It's a bit like opening a restaurant. You need something that sets you apart from all your competitors.'

Tati nodded.

'Do you have one?'

'I might.' A small smile flickered flirtatiously across her lips.

'You also need money. A lot of money.'

'Ah.' Tati's smile faded.

'That's the biggest drawback, I think,' said Marco. 'It's not like other ventures where you can put your toe in the water for a couple of hundred grand. There's no way to get into the schools business without a whopping initial investment. You need the real estate, the facilities, the staff, the insurance – all of that jazz – before you even think about the marketing strategy. And marketing's the key, of course. If you don't hit the ground running and fill all your places from the day you open the doors, you've had it. You're deep in the hole, right off the bat.'

'Hmm.' Tatiana fell silent. Marco watched her mind working while she toyed with her seabass and thought for the hundredth time how badly he wanted to get her into bed. He appreciated intelligent, ambitious women. His last

197

two girlfriends had been models – gorgeous girls, and very sweet, both of them, but ultimately the lack of challenge had bored him. Katia had assured him that Tati Flint-Hamilton did not fit this mould.

'The last chap I knew who dated her said it was like putting your dick in a honey-pot and your heart in a shredder.'

'Better than the other way around,' Marco observed drily.

'She'll eat you for breakfast.'

'When?' Marco asked hopefully. He'd waited the better part of four weeks. That was quite long enough.

'That's enough business talk,' he announced firmly, declining the dessert menus and signalling for the bill. 'Let's get out of here.'

'And go where?' Tati asked archly.

'You'll see.'

'Salsa?'

At the grand old age of twenty-four, Tatiana liked to think it took a lot to surprise her. But when Marco asked the cab driver to stop outside a basement bar and club just off Kensington High Street, she looked at him in astonishment.

'Not just salsa. They do all kinds of dance here – flamenco, you name it.' He paid the cabbie and bundled her onto the street. It was ten thirty and cold for a summer's night. There was no moon but the streetlights burned too brightly to see any stars. *You'd see all of them in Fittlescombe*, Tati thought briefly. Not that she wanted to be anywhere but here, with Marco.

'I thought we were going to bed.' She leaned into him, relaxed at last after half a bottle of Bollinger.

'We are. Later. Come on.'

A burly bouncer with a shaved head let them into a dingy hallway that led directly onto narrow stairs. Leading Tati by the hand, Marco took them down into the basement. After such a grotty entrance she'd expected some smoky dive, but in fact the room was quite wonderful. It must have been an old wine vault originally. Now candlelit brick alcoves concealed plush, red-velvet loveseats, and a long, clear glass bar took up the whole of one enormous wall. Tables were arranged in a semicircle around a low dance floor, at the back of which a jazz trio were thumping out a tune. The clientele were sexy rather than glamorous: lots of slim, dark European girls in flapper dresses and costume jewellery and men in dark suits. It was like stepping back into the Twenties.

'This is great!' Tati's eyes lit up. It was so long since she'd been dancing, so long since her world had consisted of anything but children's homework, village gossip and legal papers. Just being here with Marco felt liberating, intoxicating.

'I'm so glad you like it.' Marco beamed back at her. 'Shall we dance?'

The floor was almost empty, but the room was so dark and the low, fast beat of the music so hypnotic, Tati didn't feel self-conscious. Feeling Marco's warm body pressed against hers as they swayed to the rhythm was better than any foreplay. Closing her eyes, Tatiana let go of her worries – school, her unpaid legal bills, Dylan Pritchard Jones, Brett Cranley. One by one they flew out of her head like so many bad dreams forgotten at dawn's first light. Because tonight *felt* like a dawn, a new beginning. Marco, London, the club had all reminded Tati of the person she used to be, the person she still could be, just as soon as she got Furlings back.

Opening her eyes as Marco leaned her back in a tango-esque move, she caught sight of the musicians at the back of the dance floor.

'Oh my goodness.'

'What?' Marco pulled her upright. 'I didn't hurt you, did I?'

'No no.' She rested her head on his shoulder, glad of the darkness and the noise and Marco's broad torso concealing her like a shield. 'It's just . . . the pianist. I know him.'

Lost in the music and his own performance, Jason Cranley hadn't seen her. But Tati had recognized his earnest, pale face immediately. *So, his parents are away in the South of France and he's taking the opportunity to spread his wings. Good for him!* She was astonished Jason had the balls to defy Brett so brazenly. He always seemed so afraid of his father, so overshadowed. It pleased her to think of Jason executing this small defiance. But at the same time she hadn't wanted any reminder of the Cranleys and home to creep into her perfect date with Marco.

'Should we go and say hello after their set?' Marco asked. 'I guess we should if he's a friend of yours.'

Tati shook her head. She didn't want to acknowledge Jason tonight, and she suspected he would feel the same. In their different ways, they were both trying to escape Fittlescombe and reality.

'That's OK. He's not really a friend, more of an acquaintance. Anyway, I'm not feeling sociable.' Reaching up so her arms were around his neck, she kissed Marco passionately on the lips.

'Nor am I,' Marco growled, his dick hardening rapidly. He'd brought Tati dancing because he wanted the evening to be special and memorable. With Katia's warnings ringing in his ears, he was determined to differentiate himself from Miss Flint-Hamilton's countless other lovers. But enough was enough. If he didn't get her home and naked within the next fifteen minutes, he was going to implode with frustration. 'Let's get out of here.'

Back in Swell Valley four days later, Jason Cranley wiped his brow as he climbed farther up the hillside into Furlings' woods. It was a swelteringly hot summer's day, and Gringo, the family basset hound, had decided to run off the moment Jason let him off the lead. Well, waddle off. Gringo wasn't the speediest of animals, with his squat, stumpy legs and barrel-round body, so it hadn't occurred to Jason to keep much of an eye on him. But while Jason walked on, lost in a highly pleasurable daydream involving him playing piano to a packed and rapturous crowd at Ronnie Scott's, Gringo had somehow managed to disappear completely from view. Despite having the biggest, floppiest ears known to dog, he was apparently deaf to his temporary master's repeated calls and whistles. Hot and irritated, Jason was starting to get worried. If anything happened to that dog, his mother and Logan would be heartbroken and Brett would have a fit.

'Gringo!' he shouted, his voice echoing through the valley. He'd reached the top of the hill now, the basset's lead dangling uselessly from his hand, the same bright red as Jason's cheeks. Following a steep, narrow path through the pines and silver birch, he descended to the valley floor. The river Swell was at its widest and shallowest here, on the very edge of Furlings' land. Dancing and burbling its way through the woods, its cool, crystal-clear water looked wonderfully inviting. Peeling off his sweaty T-shirt and discarding his shoes, Jason waded in, splashing ice-cold water onto his torso and face, and drinking a long cool draught from his scooped hands.

'You shouldn't drink it, you know. I know it looks clean, but you never know what microbes are in it.'

Tatiana Flint-Hamilton's voice made Jason jump out of his skin. Spinning around suddenly, he lost his footing and stumbled backwards, falling painfully and embarrassingly on his backside. By the time he scrambled to his feet, his shorts were soaked. Water dripped down his skinny legs as he wrung out his clothing like a wet rag.

'I didn't see you there,' he explained unnecessarily, pulling on his dry T-shirt. Tati was wearing cut-off jeans shorts and a pale green shirt tied at the navel. As usual she looked effortlessly stunning, already lightly tanned after two days sunbathing in the garden, and with her hair tied back in a simple ponytail.

She looked at the lead in his hand. 'Have you lost Gringo?'

Tati knew the Cranleys' dog well. Angela often brought him to school when she came to pick up Logan, and all the St Hilda's children were fond of him.

'You wouldn't think it was possible, would you, the great fat lug,' said Jason. 'But he wandered off somewhere almost as soon as we left the house.'

'I'll help you look for him if you like,' said Tati.

'Really? That's very kind but it might take a while.'

Tati shrugged. 'I've nothing else to do. Besides, I know these woods a lot better than you do. He's probably down at the rabbit warren, trying his luck. Come on.'

They walked along together, Tati leading the way and chatting idly about nothing in particular while Jason dried off.

'So how are you finding it, with your folks away?' Tati threw the question out casually. 'It must be quiet up at the house.'

'It is, but I don't mind that so much,' said Jason. 'I'm working most of the time anyway.'

'Yes. And moonlighting as a pianist in West London clubs,' said Tati.

Jason went white.

'I saw you playing at Bar Piccata last Tuesday night,' she explained. 'You were very good.'

'Please don't tell my father,' Jason blurted. He felt as if he might be about to throw up.

Tati stopped and turned to look at him. 'Why on earth

would I tell your father? This may have escaped your notice, but your dad and I aren't exactly bosom buddies.'

'I know, but he'd hit the roof if he knew. Even if you just let something slip by accident. It would be awful.' He gave a small, involuntary shudder.

'I'm not going to let anything slip,' said Tati. 'I think it's great you're following your dreams.'

'I don't know why,' said Jason, bitterly. 'It's not as if they can come to anything. Dad will be back at the end of the summer and everything will go back to normal. He'll be watching me twenty-four/seven, or having one of his minions do it for him.'

Tati found herself feeling angry, with Brett for bullying his son, but also with Jason for not standing up to his father. 'You are over age, you know,' she told him, holding on to a low branch for support as she hopped over a ditch, then waiting while Jason did the same. 'You can do what you like.'

'You don't know my father,' Jason said, matter-of-factly. 'He doesn't care how old I am. He can make my life hell if he wants to. Besides, this is really not the time to piss him off. It's my twenty-first birthday in May,' he confided. 'If I keep sweet with my father till then, I'll come into my trust fund. That should buy me some independence, at least on paper.'

Tati stifled an unworthy pang of envy. *Her* trust was tied up so tightly, she'd be lucky to get her hands on any capital before she turned fifty. And here was this boy, not only living in her home, but with talent and freedom and – soon – unlimited funds, but too frightened to take advantage of any of it. If Jason weren't such a sweetheart, it would be easy to dislike him.

'What were you doing in Bar Piccata anyway?' he asked,

changing the subject. 'I didn't have you pegged as a jazz and salsa fan.'

'That's because I'm un-peggable,' Tati laughed. 'Actually, I was on a date. This guy I'm seeing took me there. It's a great place.'

Now it was Jason's turn to feel jealous. Ridiculously, as of course Tatiana had boyfriends, probably an army of them; and even if she didn't, she was hardly likely to want to date a shy, nerdy, mildly depressed, social incompetent like him. But he flattered himself Tati was his friend. And Furlings linked them forever. That alone gave him a feeling of ownership, of entitlement, whether it was rational or not.

'Is he your boyfriend?' he heard himself asking.

Tati frowned. 'No. Not yet. I'm not sure if I have room for a boyfriend in my life right now. Not with this court case hanging over me. Plus, he works in London. I can spend time there now, while St Hilda's are on holiday, but once school starts again I'm stuck here.'

'There are worse places to be stuck,' said Jason, looking around them.

'Yes,' Tati sighed.

They'd reached a clearing in the woods. It was a place Tati knew well from her childhood, a rabbit warren of at least thirty years' standing. The ground was mossy, a virulent green carpet studded with hundreds of brown burrows. Birch and pine had given way to oaks and sycamores, their sturdy trunks and broad, shady branches providing a thick canopy, through which dappled rays of sunlight chinked their way to the forest floor. There were bright red toadstools underfoot and crunchy acorns and the scent of some sweet, cloying flower – honeysuckle perhaps – hanging heavy in the warm air. It was a magical place, a place to come with a lover, to lie down on a blanket and gaze up at the clouds as they drifted softly across the blue summer sky.

'Gringo!'

An exhausted but delighted-looking basset hound bounded out from behind a tree, in cumbersome pursuit of a rabbit that he had about as much chance of catching as Jason had of becoming the next Olympic hundred-metres champion. Sliding to a halt, his tail wagging stupidly as the rabbit shot down the nearest hole, the dog allowed Jason to clip the lead onto his collar. He was panting madly, his enormous, drooling pink tongue hanging out of his mouth like a wet sheet on a washing line.

'I knew he'd be here,' said Tati. 'We should get him home and give him a drink. He must be terribly overheated in this weather.'

Back at Furlings, Mrs Worsley was on her hands and knees, polishing the parquet floor in the drawing room, when she heard voices. Darting out into the hall, she couldn't hide her displeasure at seeing Tatiana arm in arm with young Jason Cranley, wandering into the kitchen as if she owned the place.

'Hello, Mrs Worsley,' Tati said brightly, filling Gringo's bowl from the tap above the Belfast sink and setting it down on the stone floor. As she bent over, the curve of her bottom was clearly visible below her very short shorts. Jason Cranley couldn't take his eyes off her. It was a close-run thing as to who was drooling more obviously, Jason or the dog.

'Long time no see. How are you enjoying the summer so far?'

'I'm keeping busy, thank you, Tatiana,' the housekeeper said frostily. 'What brings you to Furlings this morning? Do you not have anywhere you need to be?'

'Tati very kindly helped me find Gringo,' Jason explained. 'He ran off. We had a hell of a time catching him. It's so damn hot out there.'

'It is,' Mrs Worsley conceded, through pursed lips. *'Very kindly', my Aunt Fanny*, she thought. *Tatiana's up to something, and she's using that poor boy as a pawn.* Mrs Worsley looked up at the girl she had as good as raised, with intense suspicion written all over her face.

If she looked any more sour, she'd turn into a lemon, thought Tati. *Silly old witch.*

'I wonder,' said Jason, 'do you think you could find us a spot of lunch? I'm starving after all that traipsing around and I'm sure Tatiana is too, aren't you?'

'Famished,' grinned Tati, who was really starting to enjoy herself. Mrs Worsley's face was a picture.

'Just a salad or something would be great,' Jason said innocently, adding insult to injury. 'We'll be in the dining room when you're ready.'

Tati would have enjoyed the smoked salmon salad and fresh baked bread more had she not been wondering whether or not Mrs Worsley had spat in her helping. Certainly her father's former housekeeper maintained the pained expression of a cat chewing a wasp throughout the meal, making it hard to focus completely on conversation.

Despite the tension of having a self-appointed conscience spying on her every move, Tatiana enjoyed talking to Jason. She particularly enjoyed watching his shyness gradually fall away as they spent more time together in the dining room where Tati had eaten countless meals in the first twenty years of her life. Jason was clearly lonely, a state of mind Tati understood only too well. When he spoke about his mother and sister being away in France, it was clear that he missed them, even though their return would also mean the unwelcome return of his father and an end to his moonlighting as a pianist, at least for now.

Tati let him talk for a good hour before excusing herself to go to the loo. Mrs Worsley finally seemed to have made herself scarce, and Tati was able quickly and quietly to slip up the kitchen stairs to the first floor. Brett had turned the old servants' rooms into a set of adjoining offices. It was as good a place to start as any. Darting inside, Tati pulled open a filing cabinet at random and began riffling through papers. She didn't know what she was looking for specifically. Just anything that might help Raymond Baines to strengthen her claim on the estate. It didn't help that her heart was pounding against her ribs like a jackhammer and her palms were so sweaty she could barely separate one document from the next. *I'd make a useless cat burglar*, she thought, glancing anxiously at her watch. She couldn't be too long or that old dragon Worsley would smell a rat and come looking for her.

But it was no use. There was nothing here except old tax returns, at least six years' worth, together with carefully photocopied receipts and correspondence with the Australian tax office. Replacing the last of the documents, Tati was just about to close the drawer when she froze.

Footsteps.

They were faint at first. Tati hovered and listened, hoping to hear them recede. But instead they came closer. Was it Mrs Worsley, snooping around looking for her? No. The tread was a man's, heavy and purposeful. It must be Jason.

Glancing round the room, she searched in vain for somewhere to hide. The office was little more than an eight-foot-square box. It didn't even have curtains. There was a desk she could crawl under, but anyone who stepped more than a couple of feet into the room would see her there, crouching like a naughty child. She was still standing helplessly, like a deer in the headlights, when the footsteps stopped outside the door. The handle began to turn. Tati felt her stomach slide into her shoes. What excuse could she possibly give Jason? She could hardly say she was lost, in her own house. That she wandered into the office by mistake. *Oh God.*

Mrs Worsley's voice rang out like a siren.

'Mr Cranley! My goodness, whatever are you doing here? When I heard noises I thought it was an intruder.'

'I'm sorry.' Brett's growling, Australian baritone rumbled through the door. Tati would not have been surprised to see her heart leap out of her chest and start jumping up and down on the desk. 'I didn't mean to scare you. I had to come home on business for a few days. It was a last-minute thing or I would have called.'

'No need to apologize to me,' said the housekeeper. 'It's your house. But do let me make you something to eat and unpack your things. Jason's downstairs. With a . . . visitor.'

Tati waited for Mrs Worsley to elaborate, or for Brett to quiz her, but neither of them did. Instead, miraculously, Brett let go of the door handle and agreed to go down to join his son. Tati waited until she heard both sets of footsteps disappear down the kitchen stairs. Then she slammed closed the filing cabinet, bolted out into the corridor and ran as fast as she could to the front of the house, flying down the main staircase and into the loo off the entrance hall. Sixty seconds later, having washed her hands and face and regained her composure, she walked as casually as she could back into the dining room.

Brett and Jason were both standing, glaring at one another. As soon as Tati walked in, it was clear what their confrontation had been about.

'Speak of the devil,' said Brett, without humour. 'Thought you'd sniff around the place did you, while I was gone?'

'Exactly,' Tati replied mockingly. 'It was all part of some dastardly plan.'

'Dad, *please*,' Jason blushed. 'Tatiana was just—'

'I know what she was just doing,' said Brett. 'And now she's just leaving. Aren't you?'

Tati turned to Jason, bestowing him with her warmest smile. 'Thank you for a lovely lunch. We must do it again some time.'

'You stay away from my son!' thundered Brett as she walked away.

'Or what?' Tati called defiantly over her shoulder as she left the room. 'You'll put me over your knee?'

'Don't tempt me,' growled Brett, his eyes flashing dangerously.

Tati met his gaze for a split second, then turned and hurried away.

That had been far too close for comfort.

It was almost tea time by the time Tati got back to Greystones. The walk had been long enough for her to calm her frazzled nerves, although the close shave with Brett and her unexpected salvation by Mrs Worsley, followed by the disconcerting confrontation in the dining room, had left her feeling physically drained.

Closing the front door behind her, she felt a comforting sense of safety and relief. For all its drawbacks, the rented farmhouse felt like home in a way that it hadn't only a few short months ago. Somehow the whole place seemed more cheerful now that high summer had arrived. With no money to employ a gardener, Tati had let the long sloping lawn at the back of the house grow into a veritable forest of long grass and wild flowers. But the general eruption of flora had a joyous, riotous feel to it that she wouldn't have traded for neatly trimmed borders or sedate rose beds, even if she did have the money. As for the house itself, that was still a mess too. But with every window open and the summer light and scents pouring in, and with some plain white bedspreads thrown over the ugliest pieces of the landlady's furniture, it was not without a certain shabby-chic charm. A chipped jug sat on the kitchen table, rudely stuffed with peonies, and the fruit bowl on the sideboard overflowed with plums from the tree in the garden, which looked in danger of toppling to the ground any minute from the sheer mass of fruit weighing it down.

Making herself a glass of elderflower squash, Tati wandered out into the back garden. Dusting the cobwebs off a decrepit deckchair she found lurking in the shed, she sank down into it, enjoying the sensation of being completely hidden by the long grass. She remembered playing this game as a child. 'Boats', her father used to call it. Rory would sing her the song of the owl and the pussycat, and she would imagine the grass as the tall sides of a ship and herself sailing away for a year and a day. She didn't cry, but a wave of nostalgia overwhelmed her suddenly, bringing a lump to her throat.

It was hard to believe that it was still less than a year since Rory had died and Tati's world had been turned inside out. Yet, at the same time, when she thought about the school or the endlessly long, boring afternoons she'd spent in Raymond Baines's drab offices, it felt as if she'd been stuck in her present rut for a lifetime. Then, in the last few weeks, her mental landscape had suddenly shifted again. Brett Cranley's taunts at the parents' meeting had started it, sowing a seed of ambition in Tati that had never been there before. That very same night, as fate would have it, she'd met Marco, and the seed had been watered. Teaching was something she could do. Her father had believed that at any rate, and now Max Bingley believed it too.

Of course, Brett was right that she would never make a fortune on a teacher's salary. But what if there were a way to combine education and business? Wouldn't it be satisfying to prove Brett Cranley wrong, and with him every man who'd ever dismissed her as nothing more than a party girl with a pretty face? Marco could open doors for her, help to introduce her to the right people . . . Yes, it was a pipe dream. But it wasn't impossible. After all, if Jason Cranley could quietly pursue his dreams, his talents, with his vile father breathing down his neck, why shouldn't she do the same with nothing but her own fears holding her back?

The advantage of *this* particular pipe dream was that it was in Tatiana's own hands. Unlike the court battle over her father's will. Standing beside Brett's filing cabinet today like a fool, waiting to be caught red-handed, she'd suddenly realized how desperate she'd become. She knew now what she'd been looking for in those files: a miracle. Because, without a miracle, she was going to lose in court in September. Brett Cranley knew it. The lawyers knew it. Deep down, Tatiana knew it too.

So why can't I let it go? Cut my losses and walk away?

God knew she didn't relish the humiliation of being defeated by Brett in court. But at the same time, she couldn't bear him to see her as a quitter, or as someone he could bully into submission, the way he bullied poor Jason and so many others in his life. She had to see this through. As a child, everything Tati did was done to gain her father's attention. She had no mother or siblings. Rory had been her sole audience, and she kept dancing for him, long after the dance had ceased to be fun for either of them. As much as she loathed him, as much as he revolted her, the truth was that Brett Cranley made her feel the same way. In some sick, twisted way, he had stepped into her father's shoes. She yearned to impress him, like a lost dog yearning for home.

Closing her eyes and stretching out her legs, she tried to relax, focusing on the sunlight warming her skin and the soft hum of bees in the grass. An image of Marco's handsome face floated into her mind and she held it there like a talisman, pushing out the other face: the face with the angry flashing eyes; the face intent on her destruction.

She fell into a deep, mercifully dreamless sleep.

Up at Furlings, Jason Cranley stared at his bedroom ceiling.

He had never been in love before. Perhaps he wasn't in love now? With nothing to compare it to, it was awfully hard to tell.

All he knew was that when Tatiana left today, curling her lip at his father as if Brett were nothing, a mere irritant, a fly in her consommé, he'd wanted to pull her into his arms and never, ever let her go.

CHAPTER THIRTEEN

Angela Cranley sat bolt upright, gasping for breath.

'Ange?' Concerned, Brett shook her by the shoulders. 'Ange, what's the matter? Are you all right?'

She looked at his face, then around the room. One by one, familiar objects reasserted themselves. The thick red damask curtains she'd bought at auction in London. The antique French dressing table they'd had shipped over from Sydney. The horrible oil painting of the Sydney opera house that Brett adored and insisted on hanging directly opposite the marital bed, wherever they lived. Her panic attack subsided.

'I'm fine.'

I'm home.

At Furlings.

The summer's over.

It had all gone by so quickly, it was easy to imagine it had been a dream. Or should that be a nightmare? Finding Brett in bed with Tricia, meeting Didier, attempting to piece back together the shattered fragments of trust for the hundredth time. Now that she was back in Sussex, back in her role of wife and mother and mistress of the house, none of it seemed quite real.

But it was real. Brett had betrayed her again. And for all his apologies and promises, all his apparently sincere remorse, the wound felt deeper this time. About a week ago, Angela had allowed Brett to make love to her again. It was awful. Brett was tender, loving and apologetic, as he always was after he'd been caught out with another woman. Angela went through the motions, allowing her body to accept his apology. But inside she felt cold and dead and numb to a degree that frightened her.

Didier had texted and emailed a couple of times, while she was still out in France. It was obvious he wanted something more to develop between them. Angela didn't have the stomach for an affair, all the lies and deceit. But it did feel good to have a small, romantic secret of her own for a change. And Didier's attentions strengthened her in other ways too. She wanted to get her marriage back on track. But she didn't want to go back to the way things were before. Back to being passive. Back to being the frightened mouse of a woman she had always been with Brett, since the day he first walked into her parents' bakery. Something *had* to change. Going back would be death.

But then the holiday ended, they returned from France, and almost immediately the panic attacks began. Furlings, the house Angela had loved so much and felt such an instant connection to back in the spring, suddenly felt like a prison. It didn't help that Logan was ecstatic to be back.

'Do you think Gabe will notice my tan?' she'd asked her parents on the drive back from the airport, craning her neck out of the window as they passed Wraggsbottom Farm. 'I've matured a lot this summer,' she added, blowing an enormous bubble with her last piece of strawberry Hubba Bubba, then sucking it back into her mouth with a satisfying *snap*.

'Have you now?' laughed Brett. 'I'm sure Gabe Baxter has better things to do than check out your suntan. I don't want you hanging around that farmyard all the time, annoying people.'

'I don't annoy people,' said Logan, stung. '*You* annoy people.' She stuck out her bubble-gum-pink tongue in Brett's direction.

'Don't talk back to your father,' Angela said automatically. But Brett had just laughed. He was happy to be home too, to be going back to work, back to 'normal'. Only Angela, it seemed, was struggling to readjust.

Getting out of bed, she walked into the bathroom and turned on the shower in an attempt to avoid further conversation with Brett. She didn't want to be quizzed about her panic attacks, or the bad dreams that had plagued her ever since they got back. But to her surprise, Brett followed her into the shower. Pressing his naked body against hers, he wrapped his arms around her in an unusual display of tenderness.

'It's probably the stress,' he said, kissing her neck.

'Stress?' Angela frowned.

'The court case,' said Brett. 'This damn nonsense with Tatiana's been hanging over us for far too long. You'll feel better once it's over and we can relax in our own home.'

God, the court case. Angela had barely given it a thought, but it was next week, the same week that Logan went back to school. Although it was unlikely, there was at least a technical possibility that they might lose Furlings. While they'd been away in France, Tatiana had evidently been waging a relentless charm offensive on the locals, and had apparently obtained a stack of signatures supporting her claim to her father's estate. The thought of the ruling going against them made Angela shiver beneath the streaming jets of hot water. *I don't want to lose this place*, she realized suddenly. It wasn't Furlings that had been making her feel trapped, but her own state of mind. Ridiculously, she found herself wishing her father were here. He would know what to do.

Instead, she leaned back against Brett. He hadn't been much support lately, but he was all she had. She clung to him.

'It will be all right, won't it?' she asked him.

'Of course it will,' said Brett. 'Tatiana hasn't a snowball's hope in hell and she knows it.'

The Cranley vs Flint-Hamilton hearing was held at the High Court in London. Brett Cranley arrived early, dashing into the famous Royal Courts of Justice on the Strand beneath an umbrella held by his lawyer, Justin Greaves, London's pre-eminent probate and contested wills specialist.

'Is she here yet?' Brett asked Greaves, a wiry man in his fifties with coarse grey hair like a Brillo pad and thick-framed glasses that continually slipped down his nose.

'No. Her lawyer's over there,' he said, pointing to the anxious-looking figure of Raymond Baines. In a cheap suit two sizes too big for him, the fat Chichester solicitor looked shorter, balder and even less impressive than usual, completely out of place in such grandiose surroundings. 'That's the third time he's looked at his phone in the last minute. He's obviously lost her. Maybe she's bottled it?'

'I doubt that,' said Brett. Tatiana Flint-Hamilton had numerous weaknesses, but she wasn't one to shy away from a fight.

'Well she'd better show up soon or the judge will start

without her. Judge Sir William McGyver QC's presiding, which is good for us.'

'Is it?' said Brett.

'Yup. Sexist, patriarch, old as the hills and a stickler for form,' Justin Greaves said bluntly. 'Won't take kindly to Miss Flint-Hamilton playing the diva and wasting court time.'

At that moment, right on cue, Tatiana burst in. Her long hair was wet from the rain and had started to curl into damp spirals around her flushed face. She wore a beige macintosh raincoat, also wet, which she removed to reveal a sleek cream woollen suit. The look was conservative and professional, but somehow this only seemed to heighten her desirability. As if the wild, passionate creature beneath the demure clothes were begging to be unleashed. Brett couldn't take his eyes off her, but Tatiana ignored him completely, muttering apologies about traffic as she hurried over to join Raymond Baines.

Moments later they were called into court. Justin Greaves leaned over to whisper in his client's ear. 'You're staring. Try not to.'

'Sorry.' Brett forced himself to look at the judge, and not at Tatiana, who was crossing and uncrossing her legs on the other side of the aisle in a distinctly distracting manner. He'd told Angela he wanted this court case over, and Tatiana out of the village and out of their lives for good, and he meant it. The girl disconcerted him, attracting and infuriating him in equal measure. Something about her drew him in, but not in a good way. More like the Death Star, exerting an irresistible force over any stray spacecraft that happened to fly too close.

Judge McGyver was talking, his voice a droning irritant in the back of Brett's mind. He was calling for opening arguments. Justin Greaves and Raymond Baines both stood up.

217

For a split second, Tatiana looked across at Brett and their eyes met. A crackle of electricity passed between them. Brett wasn't sure if it was lust or hatred. Then she looked away.

The battle had commenced.

Later that same afternoon, Max Bingley was enjoying the drive back from Arundel. He'd been at an NUT conference, some nonsense about opting out of OFSTED reports. It had rained all day while Max was stuck inside, listening to a bunch of dreary, leftie graduate teachers bemoaning the state of the education system. But now that he was on his way home, free at last, the grey skies had miraculously cleared, and the still-wet fields around him glistened like emeralds beneath a bright September sun. The entire landscape seemed fresh and alive after the rains, the flint cottages of the villages washed clean, and even the winding lanes gleaming black, like newly poured rubber.

Max looked at his watch. It was still only four thirty, and he had no particular reason to rush home to Fittlescombe, other than a pile of SATs marking that could definitely wait till the weekend. On a whim, he turned left at a wooden sign for Alfriston, and soon found himself parking his Mini Cooper by the green and stretching his long legs in one of England's prettiest villages.

Max hadn't been here for years, not since he was a young married man and he had brought his girls to Drusilla's zoo nearby. Happily the village hadn't changed much. It was a more twee, slightly more touristy version of Fittlescombe, but deeply charming nonetheless, with its beamed Tudor sweet shop full of glass bottles stuffed with old-fashioned gobstoppers and sherbet saucers, its second-hand book shop and its wisteria-clad coaching inn, The George. It was the latter that called to Max, with its open front door, through which could be glimpsed both the bar and a pretty beer garden beyond. After the unrelenting tedium of today's conference, Max reckoned he deserved a pint at the very least. Taking off his jacket, he sauntered inside.

'What can I get you?'

The barman was young and ruddy-cheeked, a typical Sussex farm boy. Max cast his eye over the list of local ales written up on the chalkboard behind him when he suddenly froze. There, sitting a few tables away in a floaty blue dress with flowers printed on it – white daisies – and her blonde hair loose to her shoulders, was Angela Cranley. Max's first thought, other than surprise at seeing her here, was how young Angela looked, and how happy. Moments later he saw why. A man – a young, handsome man – returned to the table carrying two glasses of wine.

Max felt as if he were watching a scene from a movie. The tableau only lasted a few seconds. The man sitting down and smiling, making a joke that had Angela rocking back in her chair with mirth. They hadn't kissed or touched one another, but it was clear from their body language that there was a powerful attraction between them. This was a side to Angela Cranley that Max Bingley had not known existed.

An affair! Who would have thought it?

In those few seconds, Max felt all manner of things. Happiness, to see such a lovely, downtrodden woman looking happy for once; nostalgia, for his own days of passion – how very long ago they seemed now. And an uncomfortable, unwelcome emotion that he was loath to acknowledge, but at the same time couldn't deny: envy. Max envied the young man at Angela's table, bitterly. *He* wanted to be the one to make Angela smile that youthful, pretty, carefree smile. *He* wanted to be the one to rescue her from her ghastly husband and her lonely life, shut up at Furlings like the Lady of

Shallot. Before he'd had a chance to delve deeper into any one of these emotions, Angela turned and saw him. The colour drained from her face.

'Mate?' The barman broke Max's reverie. 'What can I get you?'

'Oh, erm . . . a pale ale please,' said Max. Angela said something to her companion, who looked at Max with ill-concealed irritation. Seconds later, they both made a hurried exit.

Max felt awful. He'd clearly intruded on a private moment. Entirely accidentally, of course. But he felt guilty all the same, as if he were some sort of revolting old peeping Tom.

His beer arrived. He drank it gloomily and had almost finished when he felt a tap on his shoulder.

'Hello.' Angela was alone. She still looked pale, although not quite as horrified as she had done when she first saw him. 'I suppose I owe you an explanation.'

'My dear Mrs Cranley . . .'

'Angela.'

'Angela. You owe me nothing of the kind. I'm mortified to have intruded.'

'You didn't,' said Angela, with a shy smile. 'Shall we go outside?'

The beer garden at the back of the pub was completely deserted. Angela and Max took a seat beneath a gnarled apple tree, its trunk bent double with age, and watched two pale blue butterflies flutter and weave their way across the sky. Across the meadow behind the garden wall the river Cuckmere could be heard burbling merrily, the only sound other than the constant chirrup of birdsong and the occasional lazy bleat of a sheep from the surrounding fields. The Cuckmere met the river Swell further down the valley, which meant that the same water they were watching now would be flowing through Fittlescombe in an hour or two. For some reason the thought made Angela happy.

'It's lovely here,' she said.

'Yes,' Max nodded. *You're lovely*, he wanted to add, but he was too old to make a fool of himself over a woman. Especially a woman a dozen years younger than he was, who was already encumbered with both a husband and, apparently, a lover.

'I know what it looks like,' Angela blurted, feeling silly and shy and a little sick. 'But I'm not having an affair.'

'Right,' said Max. He hadn't expected such a forthright declaration, and wasn't sure how to respond. 'I see.'

'Didier's just a friend.'

Didier. A Frenchman. Max didn't know why, but somehow it irritated him even more that a Frenchman should have been responsible for the look of pure, unadulterated happiness on Angela's face a few moments ago.

'It's the court case this week,' Angela continued, 'up in London.'

'Ah, yes,' said Max. 'Tatiana's challenge to her father's will. That must be stressful for you.'

'It has been,' said Angela. 'But it also means Brett's been staying up in town for a few days. Didier's a friend but he's . . .' she hesitated, searching for the right word . . . 'he's not a friend Brett would be comfortable about me meeting. That's why I agreed to meet today, and why we came here. I love Fittlescombe, but people do tend to gossip.'

Max laughed loudly. 'That's quite an understatement. Listen,' he said, keeping his tone friendly, 'you have nothing to explain to me. Your private life is absolutely none of my business.'

221

'Perhaps not,' said Angela. 'But I . . . I care what you think.'

Max was touched.

'*I* think that you're a very nice woman who's put up with a lot and who deserves some happiness of her own,' he said, truthfully.

'Really?' Angela brightened. 'It's just that you looked so shocked when you saw us just now.'

'Not shocked. Surprised,' corrected Max.

'And disappointed,' added Angela.

Max smiled. 'That's only because it was another man and not me.'

'We're not having an affair, you know. That's the God's honest truth. I think he wants to. But I can't.'

'Why not?' said Max.

Angela seemed floored by the question.

'Well I, er . . . I mean . . .'

'Because of the children?' Max prompted.

'Partly,' Angela admitted. 'I had a tough time this summer and Didier, well, he was there. He helped. I should have cut off contact when we got home, but I didn't. I suppose part of me liked the attention.' She gave another small, self-deprecating smile. 'Perhaps I'm having a mid-life crisis?'

'Well, all I can say is, you look very well on it,' said Max kindly, raising his glass to hers. *In another life*, he thought, *other circumstances, I could have been happy with this woman. I could have made her happy with me.* 'Now please, we must both forget this afternoon ever happened. I never saw you, and you never saw me. Agreed?'

'Agreed,' said Angela. 'Thank you.'

She'd always liked Max Bingley. But, as of today, she decided, he was a friend indeed.

She'd decided something else too. She wouldn't see Didier Lemprière again.

Tatiana Flint-Hamilton stood on the pavement in a daze. Her lawyer stood uselessly next to her, unsure what to do.

'Will you be all right to get home?' Raymond Baines asked. 'I'm getting a taxi back to Victoria. We could take the train together if you like.'

Home. Tatiana let the word tumble through her mind. Where was home now? Not Furlings. Judge Sir William McGyver QC had been brutally clear about that. 'Frivolous' was how he'd described Tatiana's challenge to her father's will. 'Wholly without merit.' Even Raymond Baines, who'd always been bearish about their chances, had thought that the hearing would run to two days. Instead the judge had dismissed their arguments out of hand, showing a partiality towards Brett Cranley and an utter lack of compassion for Tati from the very beginning that quite took her breath away.

There could be no further appeal from here. A 'no' from the High Court was binding and final. Winded with disappointment and grief, Tati felt as if her father had died all over again.

Baines was still standing next to her. 'I don't like to leave you here alone, Tatiana,' he said, looking anxiously at his watch. Raymond Baines badly wanted to get home to his wife, his sausage and mash supper and the latest episode of *DCI Banks* that he'd recorded on Sky Plus last night. The Flint-Hamilton case had been more stress than it was worth from day one, and though he hadn't expected the outcome to be quite so swift, he *had* expected it. Everyone had. Except his client.

'I'll be fine,' Tati said numbly. 'Thank you for your help, Mr Baines, but do go home. I'll make my own way.'

The fat little lawyer scuttled off, leaving Tati staring at the traffic in the fading afternoon light. All around her the world continued to come and go. Horns blared, rush hour rushed. But Tatiana felt frozen in time, stranded on the Strand like a lost puppy, bereft.

'Get in.'

A black cab had pulled up to the kerb beside her. Brett Cranley was in the back seat, holding the door open. Half hidden in the shadows, his dark hair and eyes looked blacker than usual, mirroring his dark suit. *And dark nature*, thought Tati. *Bastard.* When he smiled his teeth shone, like a wolf's.

'What do you mean "get in"?' she asked. 'I'm not going anywhere with you.'

'Yes you are,' said Brett. 'Don't be a sore loser. Come and have a drink with me.'

Tati almost laughed. 'Are you serious?'

'Deadly,' said Brett. 'Why? What else are you doing? If you stand there much longer the pigeons'll start to crap on you.'

Despite herself, Tatiana laughed. He was right about her having nothing better to do, and nowhere she wanted to go. Marco was expecting her call. She'd already arranged to stay at his place tonight, assuming that the case would run until tomorrow at the very least. But she couldn't face talking to him now, explaining the humiliation of today's proceedings, listening to his sympathy. At least with Brett Cranley she could be what she wanted to be – angry. She got into the cab.

'Where are we drinking?' she asked.

'The Ritz,' said Brett. 'Where else?'

The shock still hadn't worn off as they walked into the Rivoli Bar. The place was full of suits, almost none of them English, and busy, given that it wasn't yet six. Every man in the room turned to look at Tati, most of them because she was such a stunning girl, although one or two clearly recognized her from the newspapers. Nobody recognized Brett, which suited him perfectly. He steered Tatiana to a quiet corner table and ordered a bottle of vintage Dom Perignon 1990.

'No champagne for me,' said Tati. 'I'm not celebrating.'

'Suit yourself,' said Brett.

'I'll have a bourbon on the rocks,' Tati told the waiter, who nodded and left.

Brett looked at her appraisingly across the table.

'You know, you could look on today's verdict as an opportunity,' he said.

'For what? Penury?' Tati said witheringly.

'No. For moving on with your life. You've been clinging to the past for a year now. Let go.'

'I've been fighting for my birthright,' Tati said furiously. 'Fuck. Wouldn't you?'

'Not if I knew I couldn't win,' said Brett.

'I didn't know that,' said Tati.

'Yes you did.'

She glared at him in furious silence. The drinks arrived. Brett barely sipped at his champagne. He watched as Tatiana downed her Jack Daniel's in one, immediately ordering another. She'd kicked off her shoes under the table and untucked the camel silk shirt from the cream woollen waistband of her suit skirt. Little by little, the armour was coming off, but not the fighting spirit. There was something belligerent, almost violent in her self-destructive tendencies. Disastrous relationships. Court cases she couldn't win. Taking herself out with hard liquor, as if the answer to her problems lay at the bottom of a cut-crystal glass.

'I saw a lot of Jason while you were away,' she said, deliberately baiting him. 'He's such a sweet boy.'

225

'He is,' Brett agreed. Tati gave him a surprised look.

'If you really think so, why are you such a cunt to him all the time?'

Brett winced. He didn't like to hear women using that word. It made them sound hard and ugly. He didn't want Tatiana to sound hard and ugly. But he answered the question nonetheless.

'He's too sensitive. He needs to toughen up.'

'Says who?' said Tati, knocking back another huge slug of bourbon.

'Says me.'

'And who made you the expert on everyone else's lives?'

'I don't know. Who made my *son*'s life any of your business?' retorted Brett.

'He's my friend,' said Tati.

'Bullshit. He's just a kid. He fancies you rotten and you enjoy the attention.'

'Do I?' Tati was toying with Brett now, playing suggestively with an ice cube from her drink while she maintained eye contact.

'If you really cared about him, you'd stop encouraging him,' said Brett, unable to tear his eyes away from Tati's lips.

'Well *you* should let him be himself,' said Tati. 'Stop trying to turn him into a miniature version of you. Not everyone's cut out to be a heartless bastard, you know.'

'Is that what you think I am?'

Tati looked deep into Brett's dark eyes. She recognized something fragile there – she knew from their encounter back at Logan's parent-teacher day that Brett Cranley wasn't without weaknesses – but he masked them with so much aggression and ambition and testosterone that they were all but completely buried most of the time. Brett wasn't handsome in any classical sense. Not like Marco. But he was the most masculine man Tatiana had ever met, as strong and unyielding as a wall of flint.

'It's not what I think you are,' she said boldly. 'It's what you are.'

Brett's hand shot out across the table, like a spider lurching suddenly for its prey. He firmly held her wrist. Tatiana's heart rate shot up, a mixture of fear and desire taking over her body.

'Let's get out of here,' said Brett.

The cab ride was almost unbearable. Aware of his body next to hers, the rock-hard thigh beneath his trouser leg bumping occasionally against her skirt as they sped through the cobbled streets, Tatiana sat rigid and alert. It was as if she were preparing herself to react to danger, to a threat. And yet it was she who'd invited the danger in, she who wanted it like an addict craving a hit. She could stop the car at any time. Get out. Go back to Marco's place, end the madness. But the electrical sexual tension between her and Brett kept her rooted to the spot like an erotic force field.

Brett's flat was in Mayfair, so close they could almost have walked it. He paid the driver, then wordlessly took Tatiana's hand and led her first into the lobby, then the lift. His hands felt warm, his palms surprisingly rough, like a labourer's. The lift was of the old-fashioned type that closed with a metal cage.

I'm trapped, thought Tatiana. *Locked in with the tiger.* But when Brett increased the pressure with his fingers she returned it instantly, so wracked with desire she was half surprised that her clothes hadn't already melted off her.

They got out at the top floor. 'The penthouse,' said Tati wryly. 'Of course.'

They were the first words either of them had spoken since

they left the bar at the Ritz. Brett made no answer, other than to open the door to his flat and pull her inside. The moment the door was closed he kissed her, pinning her back against the wall, his hands grabbing at her hair, then sweeping down over her breasts to settle on her waist. It was tiny, like a doll's. For some reason that excited him even more. Tati closed her eyes as he picked her up and carried her into the bedroom, dropping her onto the bed. When she opened them again she found herself in a luxurious but utterly masculine room. The walls were lined with taupe silk paper, there were black and white photographs of old racing cars and some bizarre, red-tasselled piece of chinoiserie above the fireplace. All the furniture was in heavy dark wood, and even the silk quilted bedspread was brown. It was like lying on melted chocolate.

It's like a hotel, thought Tati. *Completely impersonal. There's nothing of Brett in here, nothing real, nothing revealing.*

As she thought it, suddenly all of Brett was on top of her, naked and demanding and as strong as an ox. *When had he got undressed?* Other than her shoes and jacket, which she'd somehow lost en route to the bedroom, Tati was still fully clothed. It was a shock to see Brett without his armour, exposed like an animal. But the bare skin of his broad boxer's back beneath her palms felt wonderful, and the sensation of his powerful legs and chest bearing down on her was wildly exciting, like being pulled into a riptide of pleasure. Reaching behind her, Tati started to unbutton her skirt, but Brett grabbed her hands impatiently, pulling them down to his simply enormous erection. Then he pushed her skirt up around her hips, tore off her underwear and launched himself inside her so suddenly and violently that Tati gasped. He let out a loud cry of relief, like a tortured prisoner finally breaking his chains. Then he relaxed, settling into a slower rhythm as she arched her back against him, tuning in to her responses and exploring her glorious body.

Somehow Tatiana managed to wriggle out of her blouse and bra. Marco was a good lover, inventive and patient and technically proficient. But he couldn't match Brett for raw desire. Brett wasn't making love to her, or even fucking her. He was devouring her; sating himself on her body like a bee gorging on nectar. For Tatiana, the release was incredible. Here, in Brett Cranley's bed, there was no room for grief or rage or pain or loss. There was nothing but the delicious sensations sweeping through her body, the bliss of knowing that in this moment she both owned Brett completely, and belonged to him completely.

Slipping off her skirt at last and running his hands languorously over her bare buttocks, Brett rolled her onto her stomach and took her from behind.

'You're incredible,' he whispered in her ear as he moved in and out of her with agonizing slowness. One hand was between her legs, teasing her, brushing against her clitoris but never quite giving her what she wanted. 'I want to feel you come.'

'Oh God, Brett, please,' Tati moaned, so excited and frustrated she felt close to tears.

'Tell me you want me. Tell me you love it when I fuck you.'

'No.' Tati shook her head, even as her hips bucked and squirmed upwards against him. 'I hate you.'

Brett moved both hands upwards to her breasts. Taking both nipples between his thumb and forefinger he squeezed hard, increasing the pace of his thrusts. Tati yelped with pleasure.

'Come for me,' Brett growled. He was past the point of no return himself now. Tatiana could feel it, even as her own orgasm rushed inexorably up from somewhere deep inside her, unstoppable, like a breaking wave. 'Come for me now.'

And she did, biting down on the pillow and digging her nails into the soft sheets as if clinging on for dear life. Brett smiled triumphantly, closing his eyes as he felt her muscles grip and spasm frenziedly around his cock. Cupping both of her perfect soft breasts in his hands, he exploded inside her.

A few moments later he lay back on the bed, arms spread wide, staring at the ceiling. Tatiana lay motionless, still face down beside him. Her back was still slick with sweat, her hair a tangled, tousled mop, cascading over the sheets and pillow. Brett had slept with countless women. Hundreds, certainly. But that, without question, had been the most satisfying fuck of his life. He wanted to do it again, immediately and repeatedly. He wanted to keep Tatiana Flint-Hamilton in his bed, at his beck and call, for the rest of his life.

Reaching out, he touched her bare back, stroking tenderly down to the tops of her buttocks. Tati rolled away from him. Sitting up in bed, pulling the sheet up to cover her breasts, she pushed her hair out of her eyes and looked at him coldly.

'Where's the bathroom? I need to pee. And take a shower.'

Her voice was businesslike. Distant. Brett frowned.

'Through there,' he said. 'What's the rush? Why don't you rest a little? I thought I'd order us some food. We can have a glass of wine. Talk.'

'What's there to talk about?' Tati was already walking to the bathroom. Brett noticed that her back was covered in scratches. He must have been rougher than he'd realized. 'If you want to be helpful you could call me a cab,' she called over her shoulder, stepping into the shower and turning it on.

Brett followed her. 'Are you serious? You're not staying the night?'

'Of course not,' said Tatiana, rubbing Floris shower gel under her arms and between her legs. 'Marco's expecting me. I suspect I'm late for dinner as it is.'

She said it as if it were an irritant. As if the mind-blowing sex they'd just had had been some boring chore that had delayed her plans and put a kink in her evening. Marching into the shower, Brett turned her to face him, his hand slipping on her wet, soapy skin.

'You're not seriously going to spend the night with another man. After this?'

Tati turned off the water. 'After what?' She thrust her chin forward aggressively. 'It was sex, Brett. A one-night stand. It meant nothing.'

'That's a lie!' shouted Brett. 'There's something between us. There always has been and you know it. '

'All there is between us,' hissed Tati, 'is what you stole from me.'

'And that's what you're going to tell your boyfriend, is it? When he sees *that*?' Pulling Tati out of the shower, Brett turned her around in front of the bathroom mirror, so she could see the marks on her back and thighs.

Tatiana shrugged. 'By the time I've finished blowing him, I imagine he'll be too happy to notice,' she taunted.

Brett could have hit her. The thought of that beautiful, cruel mouth wrapped around another man's dick made him want to scratch his own eyes out. Did she really feel nothing? Nothing at all?

'Besides, my boyfriend is my problem. I suggest you worry about your wife.'

Brett felt sick. He did not want to think about Angela. He loved Angela. But what he felt for Tatiana was different. Compulsive. Painful. Unstoppable.

Grabbing a towel, Tatiana dried herself, marched into the

231

bedroom and pulled on her clothes. In less than a minute she was at the door. Watching her, Brett felt a horrendous sense of helplessness. Half an hour ago he'd felt powerful, completely in control. He'd beaten Tatiana in court and he'd finally conquered her in bed. But now she was leaving, walking out of the door and perhaps his life, as if none of it had ever happened.

'This isn't over,' he called after her. 'You know that as well as I do.'

'Grow up, Brett,' Tatiana said witheringly.

She didn't look back.

CHAPTER FOURTEEN

Autumn turned into winter, then spring, with each new season bringing fresh life and hope to the Swell Valley. Having lost her legal challenge to her father's will, and all hope of regaining Furlings, Tatiana Flint-Hamilton had considered packing up and leaving Fittlescombe. She could always move in with Marco, get a job in London, resume some toned-down version of her old, carefree life. But she chose not to, partly out of stubbornness and a desire to maintain her independence, modest though it might be; and partly because she refused to give Brett Cranley the satisfaction of thinking he'd run her out of her own village. She *did* want more from life than a job as a teacher in a rural primary school. She hadn't given up her dreams, or her ambitions. But this was a time for healing and recuperation, for regaining her strength and picking her next battle wisely. The job helped. Tati was good at it, and the children all liked and respected her. Marco helped too. Their relationship was steadily building, and while Marco wasn't the most exciting boyfriend she'd ever had, he was attractive and successful and stable, a quality Tatiana had come to value more over the last nine months. Since her one, wild night with Brett Cranley last September, after the court case, she'd also remained faithful to Marco, an astonishing personal best for a girl who hitherto had only known 'fidelity' as an investment fund.

Perhaps wary of screwing things up, she'd kept her relationship and her life in the village wholly separate up till now, only ever visiting Marco in London during the holidays and at weekends. But Marco had been pushing to be allowed into his girlfriend's secretive country life, and Tati had finally acquiesced. Next weekend was the late May bank holiday and also Jason Cranley's 21st birthday party at Furlings. Tati was invited – she'd remained in contact with Jason, much to his father's chagrin. She decided she would bring Marco along. It would be as good a chance as any for them to make their debut as a couple, plus she could use the moral support. Jason's party would be the first time Tatiana had been back to the house, *her* house, since the court case. And of course, Brett would be there. She tried hard not to think about Brett.

Dylan Pritchard Jones held up two dinner jackets in front of his wife.

'Which one?' he asked, gingerly stepping out of range of his baby daughter Caroline, who was sitting in her high chair armed with a plastic spoon (aka catapult) and a bowl full of some revolting greenish mush.

Maisie Pritchard Jones glanced up from the Mumsnet Rules. 'I'm not sure it matters, does it? It's only a twenty-first birthday party. Besides, they both look exactly the same.'

Dylan struggled to keep his temper. 'They are *not* exactly the same,' he said stiffly. 'The Ralph Lauren clearly has a far wider lapel.' He waved the jacket on the right at her

234

meaningfully. 'And it is *not* just a twenty-first birthday party. Not only will the entire school and village be there, not to mention all the Cranleys' swanky London friends. But Jane Templeton is confirmed as coming. I'll never have a better chance to impress her. It wouldn't kill you to give me a little support.'

Maisie stared at her husband open-mouthed. She'd been up since five with Caroline (Maisie did everything with the baby; if Dylan changed a single nappy he expected a medal), and had somehow found time to pitch for two new design jobs in between pureeing vegetables, ironing a mountain of Dylan's shirts, playing pat-a-cake with a grizzly, teething infant and making supper. And now Dylan expected her to play fashion consultant? Just how much 'support' did one man need?

'I want this job for both of us, you know,' said Dylan, sensing that perhaps he'd gone a tad too far. 'The deputy headship at St Jude's would be a huge step up.'

Jane Templeton, a local bigwig and chair of the Fittlescombe Conservative Association, also happened to be the chair of governors at St Jude's, a prestigious prep school in neighbouring Brockhurst village. Having successfully charmed the old battle-axe at the Fittlescombe fete, Dylan was now actively lobbying to be considered for the deputy headship at Jude's. (Graham Marshall, the last deputy head, had considerately dropped dead of a heart attack last month.)

'I know that, darling,' said Maisie, conciliatory now that Dylan was making a token effort. She could see how vain and self-centred her husband could be, but unfortunately she loved him. 'But you're not going to win or lose the job based on the size of your lapels, are you?'

'I suppose not,' said Dylan, lowering the jackets with a disappointed pout. The truth was he had numerous reasons for wanting to look his best at the Cranley party, not least of them a desire to outshine Tatiana Flint-Hamilton's much-talked-about new boyfriend. Things had calmed down at school since Dylan's attempt to get rid of Tati, after his failed efforts to get her into bed. The headmaster, Max Bingley, seemed to have forgotten the incident, no doubt distracted by his new romance with Stella Goye, a local potter with whom he was spending more and more of his time. As for Tatiana herself, now an official special needs teacher and an accepted part of the staff room at St Hilda's, she treated Dylan with the same cool, cordial professionalism that he afforded her. Even so, Tati's rejection of him sexually, and his inability to outmanoeuvre her politically at work, both still rankled. He still wanted the little tease to know what she was missing.

Looking at Maisie he thought how tired and unattractive she looked, with her baby-food-stained clothes and the shadows under her eyes as dark as bruised plums. As for her body, since having the baby she'd completely lost her washboard tummy and her boobs had been totally destroyed. What had happened to the beauty he'd married? He prayed she was going to at least wash her hair for the party and put on a half-decent dress. It was so hard to make one's way in the world with a wife who couldn't be bothered to make an effort. Last month when they'd been invited to a drinks party at Max Bingley's place, Maisie had actually fallen asleep on the sofa and started snoring loudly, like a beached sea lion.

Please don't let her embarrass me like that again, thought Dylan.

Two days before Jason's party, Angela Cranley stood perched on a ladder in Furlings' hallway, tying balloons to a chandelier.

Cross-legged on the floor beneath her, Logan was thoroughly enjoying herself blowing them up with a manual pump like a giant cake-icer.

Before he left for New York on business, Brett had been scathing about Angela's decorating plans. 'He's twenty-one, not four,' he said sourly over breakfast, just hours before his flight. But the days when Brett's every word had the power to hurt her, or change her decisions, were behind her now. Angela had merely shrugged and said, 'Jase likes balloons, and so do I.'

'And me,' piped up Logan.

'Besides, it's a birthday party, not a bloody corporate meet and greet,' Angela added. 'I don't know why you've invited so many business contacts.'

'To make up the numbers,' Brett said bluntly. 'If we only invited Jason's mates, the house'd be deserted.'

This comment *did* sting, because it was true. They'd lived in England for a year now, but Jason still seemed very much like a fish out of water. Other than Tatiana Flint-Hamilton, and a couple of acquaintances from the village, drinking buddies from The Fox mostly, he hadn't made any friends. Work was still an obligation, something to be got through every day, rather than a place where he felt he belonged. Not once had Angela known her son to stay up in London for drinks or dinner with colleagues after work. If he'd made friends with anyone at Brett's office, he'd never brought any of them home, or mentioned anyone.

Even more worrying than his loneliness, and the way he still drifted through life, was how reliant he seemed to have become emotionally on Tatiana. It wasn't even as if they saw one another very often. Brett had banned Tati from the house and would stalk out of rooms in a huff if her name was so much as mentioned. Jason and Tati's 'friendship', such as it was, was based around chance meetings in the village or at Logan's school – nothing more. It was clear to Angela that Tatiana only bothered with Jason at all out of kindness and pity. Equally clear was the fact that Jason had a huge, hopeless and utterly unrequited crush on Tatiana. Ever since he learned she had a boyfriend in London, Jason had sunk into a morass of despair that at times had brought Angela close to panic. She tried to share her concerns with Brett, but he point-blank refused to talk about it. Bizarrely however, in the last month, Jason seemed to have emerged from his self-imposed funk all on his own. Turning twenty-one, and the prospect of a big party, seemed to have miraculously lifted his spirits. And the nearer the party drew, the happier he became. Even when the rumours began flying at school about Tatiana Flint-Hamilton bringing her boyfriend down to Fittlescombe for the event, Jason remained resolutely upbeat. He'd even started playing the piano again, a sure-fire sign that his mood was on an upswing.

'When's Dad getting back?' asked Logan, handing her mother a long, yellow balloon like a giant rubber banana.

'Hopefully tomorrow,' said Angela, carefully tying the tip of the balloon with twine and looping it around the chandelier with the others. 'There's a chance he might be late though.'

'He wouldn't miss the party, would he?' Logan looked stricken. Brett had only been gone for six days, but she always missed him terribly when he travelled. In the rare moments when Angela imagined life without her husband, one look at Logan's face banished the thought from her mind utterly.

'Definitely not,' she said reassuringly. 'Dad will be here.'

Brett had spent a small fortune on this party, which had morphed from being about Jason into a showing-off-Furlings

238

event, a chance for Brett to flex his muscles in the local community and establish himself properly as Fittlescombe's new lord of the manor. No way on earth would he miss it now. For an Aussie boy with humble beginnings, the truth was that Brett could be a terrible snob. Having a court validate and uphold his inheritance was one thing. Being accepted by the local British upper classes was quite another. Angela had long wondered whether her husband's bizarre, negative fixation with Tatiana Flint-Hamilton had something to do with insecurity on that score. Tatiana may have lost her inheritance to Brett but, poor as a church mouse or not, she was still resolutely, unquestionably 'top drawer' socially. Brett Cranley, on the other hand, an Australian entrepreneur, would always be considered a 'nouve', unflattering British slang for nouveau riche. Angela couldn't have cared less. She was proud of her heritage and thought the English obsession with class amusing to the point of ridiculousness. But image meant a lot to Brett.

'Did you tell Dad about my new dress?' Logan asked archly.

'No.' Angela rolled her eyes.

One of the mums from school had taken Logan shopping last weekend in Chichester, along with her own daughter Tamara. The girls had come back with matching red party dresses from Topshop. Both dresses were a size eight, but whereas on Tamara the hemline hovered demurely above the knee, on Logan it stopped a good three inches higher.

'It's only because I'm tall,' Logan pleaded, when Angela suggested she opt for something less revealing. 'It's the same exact dress.'

'I know that, darling. But I can almost see your knickers! Dad will have a fit if I tell him you're wearing a minidress to your brother's party.'

'Don't tell him then. He won't care if he doesn't know beforehand. Once all the guests get here, he'll be far too busy to notice what I'm wearing.'

Angela looked doubtful.

'Oh, come on Mum, pleeeease.' Logan twirled around, stroking the fabric of the dress lovingly as it clung to her skinny, almost-twelve-year-old figure. 'You have to admit it looks good.'

It did look good. That was the problem. That and the fact that Angela knew for a fact its intended audience was Gabriel Baxter. A year on, Logan's crush on their handsome, married, thirty-something neighbour showed no signs of abating. All the boys at St Hilda's fancied Logan, as did a number of their elder brothers from the village. Still not yet twelve, her height and confidence made her seem older than her years. Brett seemed oblivious to the dangers. In his eyes Logan was still completely a little girl. He couldn't imagine anyone seeing her differently. But Angela fretted constantly, every time an adult male so much as said hello to her daughter.

Despite this she'd given in on the Topshop dress, worn down by days of constant pleading. She hadn't said anything to Brett, and prayed that Logan was right and that he'd be too distracted to notice.

Climbing down the ladder, she took both Logan's hands, pulling her up to her feet.

'Just please make sure you wear the low heels, not those ridiculous spiky things. And if I see you spending the whole evening following Gabe and Laura around like a shadow, I'm going to put you to work in the kitchen.'

'I won't,' said Logan breezily. 'I never do.'

Just then, Angela's phone rang. It was Brett, calling with the details of his flight.

For the first time in a long time, Angela realized that it wasn't only Logan who missed Brett. She missed him too. This weekend would be all about family. Logan was thriving, Jason was happier than ever. Perhaps the pain and drama of the past few years could now finally be put behind them?

Tatiana stood up and shook hands with the three suited men across the table.

'Thank you all for your time,' she smiled warmly. 'I'll see myself out.'

In the grand eighteenth-floor lobby at Angel Court, in the heart of the City, it was all she could do not to hug herself and jump for joy as she waited for the lift. She was glad she'd restrained herself, however, when one of the suited men followed her out and tapped her on the shoulder.

'Marcus.' She jumped. 'You surprised me.'

Marcus King was only thirty-nine, but he was the most senior of Tatiana's trustees. A handsome Oxford graduate and former rowing star, Marcus was a practical and serious man, as steady in his private life as he was in his job. Happily married with three children, he was one of the rare heterosexual males able to look on Tatiana Flint-Hamilton solely as a client.

'I want to be completely clear with you, Tatiana,' he said, in his usual sober tone. 'While we support this investment, there are risks involved. Significant risks.'

'I understand that.' Tati nodded gravely.

'Forty per cent loan to value is our absolute limit,' Marcus went on. 'That means you need to find considerable seed capital on your own. We won't release funds without it.'

'I understand that too,' said Tatiana. 'And I appreciate the trust's support.'

'If you don't mind my asking,' Marcus pressed her. 'How

241

do you intend to find the money? Six million dollars is a very considerable sum.'

'Marcus.' Tatiana smiled sweetly, stepping into the elevator. 'I never mind you asking.'

The doors wheeshed closed behind her.

Marcus King shook his head. *She's grown up immeasurably in the last year,* he thought. The proposal she'd presented to him and his colleagues today had been impressive. Well researched, balanced, compelling. But for all her confidence and newfound maturity, Marcus wondered whether she fully understood the risks.

If she pulled it off, she could potentially make a fortune.

If she didn't, she could lose a fortune, one that her father had spent a lifetime struggling to preserve.

Yet there was something in Tatiana's eyes that seemed to suggest that to her, this was all a game.

With a lingering feeling of unease, Marcus King returned to his desk.

Brett Cranley sat bolt upright in his first-class seat as the British Airways flight roared upwards, dwarfing the New York skyline before disappearing above a blanket of cloud.

Brett could have afforded a private plane. Most of his peers in the real-estate business had one, once their net worth got above a certain level, but it had always seemed like a waste of money to Brett. At least his yacht, the *Lady A*, paid for itself through expensive charters when he wasn't using it. Besides, yachts were built for pleasure. Jets, in Brett's view anyway, were for business, for getting quickly from A to B, and as a business proposition, they sucked, burning through money faster than a Russian hooker in Cartier. There was also a faint whiff of insecurity about the owning of a private plane – the very rich man's version of the shiny red Ferrari. Jets were for short men who wanted to be noticed by beautiful women. Brett Cranley was a big man who beautiful women noticed anyway.

Not that they always gave him what he wanted. As they reached cruising altitude, Brett sipped on his champagne, but it tasted sour. He ought to be happy, but he was not. Eight months after their fiery, passionate encounter at his London flat, Tatiana Flint-Hamilton still had the power to dampen his mood. She took the sweetness out of his successes and sharpened the sting of his failures, simply by existing. Brett resented her for exerting such an irrational power over him. For remaining important in his psyche when she ought to be supremely unimportant, just another girl he'd been to bed with. Deep down, however, he knew it wasn't Tati who was the problem, but himself. Why couldn't he let go?

It was hard to put his finger on it exactly, but ever since last summer in France, when Ange had walked in on him and Tricia in bed on the yacht, Brett's personal life had slid off kilter. Angie had changed afterwards. She'd forgiven him, and stayed with him, like she always did. But something was different between them. It made Brett feel profoundly uneasy.

He loved Angela as much as he always had, maybe more. He'd felt genuinely guilty about the Tricia thing – a stupid, opportunistic fuck if ever there was one. And yet that day at the High Court, when he saw Tatiana again, there had been a desperation about his need for his young 'cousin' that he wouldn't have felt six months earlier. Back then, Angela's blanket acceptance of his infidelities, of all his frailties and weaknesses, had given him the confidence to go forth and conquer, be it in business or in bed. Back then, he was pretty sure, he could have slept with Tati, enjoyed it and moved on, as he had with countless other beautiful young women before her. But now, unsure of Angela for the first time in his life, he'd come to Tatiana in a position of weakness, of need. Brett Cranley hated himself for that. He was sure it was the reason that Tatiana had spurned him afterwards. Ever since, a part of him had been feeling like Samson after his hair was cut. Preposterously, he found himself angry at Angela about it, as if she were somehow responsible for what had happened. He'd barked at Ange and bickered with her more in the last eight months than at any time during their marriage. Brett hated himself for that, too.

And now it was Jason's birthday party, and the two women would be under the same roof, his roof, a prospect that made him feel guilty, anxious and enraged all at the same time, not least because he was powerless to stop it. Worse still, Tati was rumoured to be debuting her boyfriend at the party, a sure sign that things were becoming more serious between the two of them.

Feeling like a schoolboy guiltily thumbing through *Playboy* beneath his bedcovers, Brett turned on his iPad and opened the file on Marco Gianotti. There was Tatiana's boyfriend, smiling professionally in his official Goldman headshot. Other pictures from Facebook showed him playing beach volleyball in Miami, or laughing with friends around the lunch table in Forte dei Marmi. No doubt about it, Marco was a great-looking kid. Twenty years younger than Brett (and less than half his net worth, but Brett sensed correctly that Tatiana Flint-Hamilton couldn't give a shit about that), he was also both well born and well connected. Although raised and educated in America, Marco's mother's family had been Italian aristocrats. Brett felt his chest tighten with envy and dislike. He closed the file. Everything he had, he'd worked for. Marco Gianotti, on the other hand, had been gifted his advantages on a solid gold platter. Just like Tatiana.

Spoiled brats, the pair of them.

'Do you know what you'd like for supper this evening, sir?' A pretty stewardess wearing far too much make-up appeared at Brett's side. Leaning over him, menu card in hand, she afforded him an excellent view of her ample cleavage, her large, milky-white breasts, pressed together beneath her blouse like two, perfectly round scoops of vanilla ice cream. In his younger days, Brett would have got the girl's number and bedded her as soon as they landed, or maybe even before. Air stewardesses had some wonderfully uninhibited habits, in Brett's experience – yet another good reason not to fly private. But tonight he had zero appetite, either for the girl or the food.

'I'm not eating,' he said curtly. 'I'll go straight to sleep. Please don't disturb me.'

'Of course, sir. Would you like to be woken for breakfast?'

An image of the breakfast awaiting him at Furlings popped into Brett's mind. Angela, pretty and smiling in her apron with the cherries on it, pouring fresh orange juice; Logan wolfing down some ghastly sugary cereal, regaling him about what had happened at school since he left; Jason, happier than he had been in years, evidently, reading the papers contentedly by the Aga.

I have so much to be grateful for, thought Brett. *Life doesn't get any better than this.*

Why can't I enjoy it?

He looked at the stewardess. 'No, thank you. I'll sleep till we land.'

In fact, he barely slept at all. The flight was bumpy, a fitting backdrop for Brett's turbulent emotions and the torrent of thoughts and fears racing through his head. Angela had called in him in high excitement earlier that day, overflowing with happiness about Jason.

'He was playing the piano for about an hour after work, and then again after dinner. I happened to catch a glimpse when he got off the stool to go up to bed, and the look on his face, Brett! I wish you'd been here. I don't think I've ever seen him so happy.'

'That's great,' said Brett, trying to sound as if he meant it. He *was* pleased that the depression that had dogged their son throughout his teens seemed to be lifting. But it was almost as if the dark cloud had transferred itself from son to father. Now it was Brett who seemed incapable of any positive emotion.

'His eyes were sort of half closed,' Angela went on. 'I can't describe it exactly, but he looked dreamy and peaceful and . . . content. I think he might be in love.'

'I doubt it,' said Brett. 'Love doesn't make you content. It makes you anxious and miserable.'

'Thanks a lot!' Angela laughed, trying to make light of this comment, but Brett could hear the sadness in her voice. It wasn't just his own happiness he was ruining with his black moods. It was Angie's too.

I'm bringing her down.

As ridiculous as it sounded, he almost felt as if Tatiana Flint-Hamilton had put some sort of curse on him, in revenge for him 'stealing' her inheritance. As if he were under a spell that meant he would never find happiness under Furlings' roof.

Finally succumbing to sleep as they prepared for landing, Brett had wild, vivid dreams of witches and moorland. Angela was old and wizened, leaning over a cauldron next to him, while Tatiana danced naked around them, a cold wind blowing through her long, streaming hair. In the background, Jason was playing the piano. Beautifully. But it was a melody that made Brett cry, a song he hadn't heard since childhood, since before his mother died.

'Welcome to Heathrow.'

The steward's voice woke him with a start. Looking down, he saw the front of his shirt was wet with tears.

CHAPTER FIFTEEN

The night of Jason Cranley's twenty-first birthday party finally arrived, and everyone agreed that Furlings had never looked more beautiful. In its last few years under Rory Flint-Hamilton's care, the old man's ill-health had meant that the house had been allowed to fray a little at the edges. Nothing dire or drastic. Peeling paint around a window here, crumbling brickwork there, the wisteria that snaked over half the façade allowed to explode unchecked, so that its roots worked their way into the stone, causing deep cracks, like lines in the mud of a dried-out river bed, or wrinkles in the face of a very grand, very old woman who had once been a great beauty.

Over the last year, however, Angela Cranley had begun to change all that, painstakingly starting to restore Furlings to its former glory with a combination of love, patience and good taste, all washed down with limitless money. She'd stuck to her guns and made sure that the theme for this evening was very much 'Birthday Party'. As well as the contested balloons, found everywhere in cheerful clusters of yellow, red, blue and green, and emblazoned with kitsch

248

gold sparkly number 21s, she'd ordered Jason an enormous chocolate cake in the shape of a grand piano, and had table-cloths made up out of photographs from Jason's babyhood and childhood years, printed against a background of the Australian flag. But despite these relaxed, youthful touches, the house itself radiated understated elegance and good taste, as every grand old English estate ought to. A wonderful smell of roses and gardenias, combined with beeswax wood polish, filled the grand state rooms. Bathrooms were lit by Jo Malone candles in mandarin or lime. Priceless antique rugs and solid, Jacobean English furniture shared space with modern sculptures and artwork, but it was a testament to Angela's skill with interiors that the juxtaposition never felt forced or awkward. Similarly, none of the guests seemed put off by the fact that, having approached the house through a formal lavender walk, accompanied by a violin quartet playing Handel, they walked into a brightly lit hallway throbbing to the beat of pop music.

The guest list was huge and eclectic, but somehow on the night it worked, with Jason's village friends and local schoolteachers rubbing shoulders happily with Brett's property-tycoon cronies and a decent smattering of celebrities, many with second homes in the idyllic Swell Valley. The age range was equally broad, with at least two ladies from the Fittlescombe Conservative Association topping the hundred mark, and Logan's posse of St Hilda's Primary School mates starting at just seven.

Max Bingley was one of the first to arrive, arm in arm with his new love, Stella Goye. In her late forties, with a sleek bob of dark hair that Max always thought made her look rather French, and a face that was attractive and intelligent rather than pretty (long nose, high cheekbones, small, expressive mouth and merry green eyes, deeply wrinkled from years of smiling), Stella had gone for a floaty, vintage look tonight. Privately, Max wasn't a fan of the gypsy look. (His daughters informed him it was known as 'boho' these days, but to Max Stella's tasselled patchwork dress and jangly gold bangles made her look as if she lived in a caravan and/or read tarot cards for a living.) Her graciousness and warmth more than made up for any fashion-related shortcomings, however, and Max felt proud introducing her to Angela Cranley.

'I've heard such a lot about you,' Angela said kindly as they shook hands. 'We're so glad you could make it.'

In a floor-length Calvin Klein shift dress in slate grey, low cut at the back, and no jewellery other than a plain diamond cross necklace, Angela looked stunning, as pared down and chic as Stella was colourful and eccentric. Max saw Angela regularly at school and in the village, once a week at least, but rarely remembered her looking quite as radiant as she did tonight. Indeed, the last time she'd seemed so completely happy was in the garden of The George Inn at Alfriston. They had never spoken about that day since, or about Angela's mystery Frenchman. True to his word, Max had told nobody, not even Stella, about running into her. In some unspoken way, he felt that his chance encounter with Angela Cranley that afternoon had deepened their friend-ship. It was a moment he wanted to keep for himself – rare and, in its own way, quite perfect.

Angela certainly appeared genuinely pleased to see him here tonight. As for Max, he was always happy to see Angela. She was one of those women, like Stella, who could light up a room simply by walking into it.

'Your house is breathtaking,' Stella was saying.

'Thanks. It might be more breathtaking if Gringo hadn't chewed up half the upholstery,' Angela joked. 'You don't want to buy a very poorly trained basset hound, do you?'

'Not really,' laughed Stella. 'Max said your son still lives at home. I must say, now that I've seen the place, I don't blame him. He's a lucky young man.'

'In some ways he is,' Angela agreed. 'He hasn't always felt lucky. But I think – I hope – he does tonight.'

'When I was twenty-one, my dad took me to the pictures and bought me a gin and tonic in the pub and my mum baked rock cakes with little silver keys on top made from sugar,' said Stella. 'I thought that was the height of sophistication.'

Angela smiled. *She's nice*, she thought. *Funny and genuine. No wonder Max looks so happy.* She felt a tiny, unworthy stab of envy, but stifled it. After all, she was happy too, wasn't she?

Brett had got home yesterday morning from New York and was clearly making a real effort to shake off his bad mood and get back into her good books. Business had gone well out there evidently. He'd arrived home from the airport with an enormous duty-free gift bag for Angela, as well as a hand-tied bouquet of flowers that he'd actually stopped off to buy from the flower shop on Brockhurst High Street. Logan had launched herself into his arms the moment he got through the door, claiming her father for herself as she always did. But Brett had made a point of putting her down and coming over to kiss his wife.

'I missed you, Ange,' he whispered in her ear, reaching down and grabbing her hand tightly for emphasis.

She'd felt happy. Relieved. 'I missed you too,' she told him. She looked around the room now for Brett, hoping to introduce him to Stella, but he'd disappeared off somewhere.

Angela made small talk for a few more minutes, mostly about Stella's work as a ceramicist and how she was finding life in the village. Then Max Bingley and Stella Goye drifted away, and another couple came up to talk to Angela; then another; then some business friends of Brett's . . . Before Angela knew it, it was ten o'clock. She hadn't seen Brett in hours and, other than catching a half-glimpse of him walking onto the dance floor with Logan, hadn't laid eyes on her son at all.

It was a relief when Mrs Worsley, tapped her on the shoulder. 'Could I have a word, Mrs Cranley? It's about the cake.'

'Oh God,' sighed Angela. 'What's that bloody dog done now?'

But for once, Gringo wasn't the guilty party. In a fit of exuberance, brought on in part by running around the tables drinking the dregs of the adults' cocktails, two little boys from Logan's class had apparently decided they couldn't wait for candles and speeches and had attacked Jason's beautiful piano cake with their bare hands. Dylan Pritchard Jones, eager to impress Jane Templeton, his putative future boss, had apprehended the culprits and, disregarding their protests of innocence ('You've got half a ton of chocolate cream icing round your mouth, William!'), dragged them to Mrs Worsley for punishment.

'I'm so sorry,' the housekeeper was saying over and over, wringing her hands despairingly. 'If only I'd *seen* them. Sixteen hundred pounds' worth of chocolate cake, ruined! Poor Jason.'

'Jason will be fine,' Angela reassured her. 'And I'm sure the cake's not ruined. It's as big as a house, they can't have eaten *that* much of it.'

The two little boys in question looked so terrified when they saw Logan's mother coming over, not to mention sick to their respective stomachs from the combined effects of cake and alcohol, Angela didn't have the heart to yell at them. Instead, instructing Mrs Worsley to put on a DVD in the playroom and dump all the under-elevens in front of it, she wandered outside into the grounds in search of Brett. Suddenly she wanted to be with him, wanted the two of them to be a couple on this special day, twenty-one years since their first child was born.

Outside, Furlings' rose garden was heaving with people. Most were having a wonderful time flirting, star-spotting and drinking copious amounts of Brett Cranley's vintage champagne. A few, however, were less than happy. While Angela Cranley ploughed her way through the crowd in search of her husband, Dylan Pritchard Jones stood rooted to the spot beneath a mulberry tree, listening to Jane Templeton tell a long and unremittingly tedious story about a friend of hers from Oxford who'd attempted a bicycle ride across the Asian Steppe, got lost in Mongolia and written a book about it. Dylan hadn't noticed it before, but St Jude's chair of governors was really quite spectacularly ugly. She had blotchy skin, a whiskery chin like a witch's, and the sort of thick ankles more normally associated with extremely elderly women in support stockings. Jane Templeton wasn't elderly. Dylan guessed she was in her mid-fifties. But there was a matronly quality about her, from her heavy, pendulous bosoms to her resolutely undyed grey hair that made her look far older.

What made it harder to bear was the fact that there were so many young, beautiful girls here, just waiting to be flirted with. Dylan had already spotted Keira Knightley, a regular in the valley during the summer months, and local model Emma Harwich, who looked spectacular tonight in a back-less white dress that clung to her bottom like shrink wrap on a perfectly ripe peach. Tatiana Flint-Hamilton had arrived late and – much to everyone's surprise after all the hype about her boyfriend – alone. She also looked stunning, much to Dylan's irritation, in a gunmetal minidress that barely skimmed the top of her thighs and black Alexander McQueen ankle boots. Her long hair was swept up and cleverly pinned so that it looked short. Combined with her dramatic dark eye make-up, the overall look was halfway between punk and rock chick, and spectacularly sexy.

'So she took it to Simon and Schuster. That was her first port of call,' Jane Templeton wittered on.

'Interesting,' said Dylan, stifling a yawn. Out of the corner of his eye he saw Maisie, his wife, being chatted up by a good-looking man in an immaculately cut dinner jacket. When the man turned his head, throwing it back to laugh at one of Maisie's jokes, Dylan saw to his fury that it was Danny Cipriani, the England rugby star and one of Maisie's long-time crushes.

'. . . But she didn't end up with them. There was a bidding war, you see. Even though the book wasn't finished. Anyway, you'll never guess what happened after that.' Jane Templeton gripped Dylan's arm with her bony, arthritic fingers.

'No?' He forced a smile.

He can't possibly fancy her, can he? he thought, trying to reassure himself as he sneaked another glance across at Maisie and the rugby star. *I'll bet she's boring on about the baby. He's probably just being polite.* No sooner had Dylan had this thought than Danny Cipriani rested his hand on the small of Maisie's back in a distinctly impolite, intimate gesture. The cheek of it!

Dylan longed to make an excuse and go over there, but Jane's grip on his arm was like a vice.

'Well, she went to New York . . .' Jane went on.

Dylan's eyes glazed over. Just then Tatiana Flint-Hamilton

swept past him. She had a flute of champagne in her hand and an amused glint in her eye. Whatever had happened to the boyfriend, it didn't seem to be fazing her. 'Hello, Dylan.' She waved at him regally.

'Hello, Ta . . .' he began. But Tati had already moved on, sashaying through the throng followed by scores of admiring male eyes, paying Dylan no more attention than a passing fly.

Self-important bitch, thought Dylan, watching her go. When he looked back to where Maisie had been standing with Danny, the two of them had gone.

This was not going to be Dylan Pritchard Jones's evening.

At the other end of the garden, outside the orangery, Brett Cranley was talking business with an old friend from Australia when he saw Tatiana talking to Jason. They were only together for a moment. Tati leaned in to tell Jason something, probably just, 'Happy birthday.' Jason smiled and hugged her, kissing her on the cheek before walking away to join a group of girls Brett didn't recognize. But even that momentary exchange, those few seconds of touching, felt like a razor blade stabbing into Brett's heart.

'Are you all right, mate?' his friend asked, frowning. 'You looked a bit crook there all of a sudden.'

'I'm fine,' Brett murmured. 'Excuse me.'

He walked over to Tatiana, like a moth drawn to a flame, even as it can feel the heat start to singe its wings.

'What happened to lover boy? Stood you up, did he?'

Tatiana spun around. Brett loomed over her. Black tie suited almost all men, but not Brett Cranley. He looked awkward and uncomfortable in his jacket, like a bear squeezed into performing clothes by some sadistic circus ringmaster. Tati made a point of avoiding Brett whenever possible, and it was months since she'd last seen him in the flesh. It bothered her the degree to which his presence could still unnerve her. She felt her stomach churn unpleasantly now, and a disagreeable sensation, halfway between attraction and revulsion, shoot through her.

'Maybe I got a better offer,' she smiled sweetly.

'You did,' said Brett, deadpan. 'Mine.'

'Marco had to work,' said Tati, deciding it was safer to ignore this last comment. 'His team have got a big deal closing. You know how it is.'

Brett raised an eyebrow mockingly. 'Uh huh.'

Irritated, Tati shot back waspishly 'Where's Angela? Shouldn't you be holding her hand, playing the doting husband and father? Today of all days?'

As soon as she'd said it she felt guilty. Tatiana liked Angela Cranley. She liked Logan and Jason too, and felt bad using them as verbal weapons. It was only Brett she had a problem with. What had happened between the two of them last year should never have happened. As far as Tatiana knew, nobody knew about it, and she vowed to keep it that way. Just because Brett wound her up about her love life, it didn't mean she should sink to his level. But that was what Brett did to her, every time they met: pulled her down to his level. With Brett Cranley she was the worst version of herself.

'I'm not playing at anything.' Brett spoke through gritted teeth. He was standing very close to her now. Tatiana could feel the anger coming off his body like heat rising from scorched earth. 'I love my family.'

'Uh huh,' said Tatiana, deliberately echoing Brett's sneering cynicism about Marco.

'At least I have a family to love,' Brett snapped. 'What do you have, Tatiana? An invisible boyfriend and a job at a school. Bully for you.'

For a moment, they stood in silence. Brett knew he was being a jerk. That it was only sexual jealousy and the pain of rejection that were making him lash out. But he couldn't seem to help himself.

Tatiana felt his eyes boring into her, stripping her down to nothing, to her soul. She looked away. At that moment Angela Cranley walked over, sliding an arm around Brett's waist.

'There you are!' she kissed him on the cheek. 'I've been hunting for you for ages. It's time to cut the cake and make the speeches.'

'Right,' said Brett, staring at the ground.

'Oh, hello, Tatiana.' Angela's smile was so genuine, Tati felt even guiltier. 'Are you having a nice time?'

'Lovely, thank you.'

'I'm so pleased you were able to make it. Pleased you two are burying the hatchet as well.' She gazed up lovingly at Brett. 'It's about time. Now, have either of you seen Jason? For some reason, I can never seem to get the men in my family in the same place at the same time. We'll be cutting the cake at midnight at this rate.'

'He was here a few moments ago,' said Tati. She looked back across the garden. 'Is that him, talking to Annalise Merrivale?'

'Bloody gold-digger,' grumbled Brett, glaring across the lawn at the two of them. Annalise was the very beautiful, very sought-after daughter of the lord lieutenant of Sussex, a frightful old bore by the name of Cedric Merrivale. 'She's only talking to Jason because she knows he just came into his trust fund.'

'Or *maybe* it's because it's Jason's birthday party, and she likes him?' Tati couldn't resist observing sharply. 'Not everyone thinks of nothing but money.'

257

'Come on,' said Angela, pulling Brett by the hand before another argument erupted between him and Tatiana. 'Let's go and hijack him together, before I lose one or both of you again.'

The speeches were mercifully short. Jason gave a shy, stammering toast of thanks to the guests for coming and his parents for laying on such a fabulous spread, while Annalise Merrivale hovered proprietorially behind him. Angela said a few words about how proud she was of her darling boy, tearing up almost immediately, and Brett told a couple of blue Aussie jokes that went down remarkably well, probably because ninety per cent of his audience were three sheets to the wind.

'Bloody crass.' Dylan Pritchard Jones, sober and in a foul mood, whispered in Maisie's ear after the roars of laughter subsided. 'Cranley should know better in mixed company. There are children and old people here.'

'Oh, do pull the stick out of your arse,' said Maisie, slightly more loudly than she'd meant to, triggering sniggers from Santiago de la Cruz, the famous local cricketer, and his fiancée Penny, who were standing next to them.

'Maisie!' Dylan flushed indignantly.

'Sorry, darling. But you can be such a teacher sometimes. Try and relax and enjoy yourself.'

'Like you, you mean?' snapped Dylan. 'Don't think I didn't notice you "relaxing" with Danny Cipriani. You made a complete fool of yourself, you know.'

Maisie shot him a look of utter disdain.

'Bugger off Dylan,' she said roundly, and stormed off.

'Dear oh dear.' Gabe Baxter, a late arrival, appeared at Dylan's shoulder like an unwelcome ghost. 'Trouble in paradise?'

Despite being teammates from the village cricket eleven, there was no love lost between Gabe and Dylan.

'Sod off, Baxter,' Dylan snapped back. 'I saw Chumley, the new bank manager, at the bar earlier. You'd better make a run for it, before he repossesses your dinner jacket.'

Gabe's financial troubles were well known in the village. Only last week he and Laura had had a furious row in The Fox, which ended in Laura storming out in tears and Gabe lashing out and causing a few hundred quids' worth of damage with a bar stool. Everybody in Fittlescombe knew that Gabe had overstretched himself to buy that huge chunk of the Furlings estate the year before ago. Now, mortgaged to the hilt, and under pressure to pay for private IVF for Laura, who still hadn't succeeded in getting pregnant, Gabe could barely afford to keep himself in baked beans.

'Go after your wife,' he told Dylan, choosing to ignore the jibe. Dick-Hard Jones was an arsehole, but his wife Maisie was sweet.

'Why should I?' Dylan pouted. 'She was flirting outrageously with that little oik.'

'So what?' said Gabe. 'You're the worst flirt in Fittlescombe.'

'Second worst.' Dylan looked at Gabe meaningfully. 'Talk about pot calling the kettle.'

'Whatever. Maisie's a bloody good wife to you and you know it. More importantly, if you don't go after her, the next time you'll see her she'll be in *Heat* magazine, falling out of China White at four in the morning with her knickers round her ankles and rugby boy in tow.'

Dylan hesitated, glared at Gabe, then hurried up the hill towards the house.

'Maisie! Maisie! Wait!'

His voice was swallowed by the roar of chopper blades overhead.

Gabe looked up.

'Who do you think that is?' he asked Laura, who'd returned from the bar to join him with two flutes of champagne. They were late because they'd had yet another row, followed by incredible make-up sex on the dilapidated farmhouse stairs.

'Paparazzi I should think,' said Laura, kissing him. She knew she looked flushed and dishevelled in a green taffeta evening gown that was a good decade past its prime, but she was too happy and sated to care. 'Trying to get a shot of David Beckham's new mistress, I imagine. *Alleged* mistress, I mean,' she added with a wink.

'The *Sports Illustrated* chick?' Gabe brightened visibly. 'Really? Is she here?'

Laura sighed. You couldn't teach an old dog new tricks. Even if it was your dog.

'Yes, darling. She was in the Ladies' loo a few minutes ago, boosting the Colombian economy. Either that or she'd had a serious accident with the talcum powder.'

Gabe grinned and hugged his wife tightly.

As the chopper noise faded, Logan Cranley sauntered over, doing her best 'grown-up' impression in a stunning, *very* short red dress.

'Logan.' Laura's eyes widened. 'I hardly recognized you.'

Over the past year Logan had become a semi-regular presence over at Wraggsbottom Farm, often popping in to 'help' or chat just when Laura was finally sitting down to write, or about to make an important telephone call to a producer in London. It was hard enough to carve out any time in the day for her own career. Life as a farmer's wife, especially a poor farmer's wife, meant early starts and constant mucking-in. Having to deal with Gabe's pre-teen groupies didn't make life any easier. But Logan was a sweet girl at heart, affectionate and funny and, Laura sensed, a bit isolated up at the big house with only her mother and much older brother for company. She felt sorry for her, and liked her, despite her all too obvious passion for Gabriel.

'My goodness, you look gorgeous.'

'Thanks.' Logan smiled.

'Doesn't she, Gabe?'

'Mmm.' Gabe nodded. 'Very sophisticated.'

The smile turned into a mile-wide grin. 'It's Topshop.' She tossed her long dark hair back with a devil-may-care insouciance that she hoped made her look like Selena Gomez. 'Mum thinks it's too short, but I like it.'

I'll bet she does, thought Laura.

'Can I have a sip of your champagne?'

'No,' said Laura.

'Sure,' said Gabe simultaneously, earning himself a reproachful look from his wife and an adoring one from Logan.

'She's eleven!' Laura protested.

'Nearly twelve,' Logan corrected.

'It's only a sip,' said Gabe. He handed Logan his glass. Laura could have sworn the girl's hands were shaking as she tasted the forbidden bubbles. Or perhaps it wasn't the champagne that was exciting her?

'Thanks,' Logan handed the glass back. 'I'll see you both later.'

'You encourage her,' said Laura to Gabe, once she'd gone. 'You do know that, right?'

Gabe nuzzled into his wife's neck. Sex earlier had been amazing, and a much-needed stress reliever. They were fighting too much. Gabe hated it. He shuddered to think where he'd be without Laura. 'Why don't *you* encourage *me*?' he whispered, sliding a hand down over Laura's taffeta-clad bottom. 'Just a little bit.'

'Get *off*!' she slapped him away.

'Come on,' teased Gabe. 'You know you want to.'

And of course Laura did.

On the verandah, where the cake was being dissected into slices and handed out, Jason Cranley pulled his mother aside.

'I've hardly spoken to you all evening,' he said, leaning back against the wall and feeling the cool bricks through the cotton of his dress shirt. He'd been dancing, very unusually for him, with Annalise and some other girls, and had discarded his DJ and bow tie somewhere in the vicinity of the dance floor. His blond hair was spiked upwards with sweat and his cheeks were flushed. Angela remembered this look from his boyhood, running to the car after soccer matches or cross-country runs, invariably the loser, but always cheerful in those days, before his teens and the depression that had blighted all their lives. She felt a pang of love for him so sudden and deep that it made her clutch her chest.

'I can't believe you're twenty-one,' she sighed. 'A grown man.'

'You're not going to blub again, are you?' teased Jason.

'No,' said Angela, brushing away tears.

'Listen Mum,' said Jason, suddenly serious. 'I want you to know I love you. And I'm really, really grateful for tonight. It's been amazing.'

'I'm glad you're enjoying it,' said Angela, slightly nervously. There was something about his solemn tone that she found jarring.

'I love you,' Jason said again, this time hugging her tightly.

Angela frowned. 'Is everything all right, Jase?'

'Of course,' he laughed, releasing her.

'You're quite sure? You'd tell me if something was the matter?'

'Nothing's the matter, Mother,' he assured her. Gringo, the family basset hound, picked the perfect moment to wander over, tail wagging, with the remnants of a priceless silk cushion wedged between his teeth. Seeing his mother about to explode, Jason grabbed the dog by its collar. 'I'll deal with this,' he said. 'You'd better go and rescue Dad.'

'What do you mean, rescue him?'

Jason pointed outside, to where Brett was standing by the bar, surrounded by a gaggle of local mothers from the church committee, no doubt hitting him up for a new roof. 'Come on, Gringo. Let's find you something to eat that's made of food, fella.'

Angela watched as Jason disappeared inside, with Gringo trotting merrily at his heels.

Banishing her worries, she headed back outside.

The party rumbled on into the night. At around midnight, Gabe Baxter began looking around for Laura, wondering if they ought to make a move. He realized guiltily that he hadn't seen his wife for almost an hour, and hoped she was OK. She'd commented earlier that one of the few advantages of finding you were *not* pregnant, yet again, was that you could drink as much as you liked at parties. Gabe suspected that Brett Cranley's assertion that it was impossible to get a hangover on really good vintage wine was going to be put to the test tomorrow morning at Wraggsbottom Farm.

He collared Max Bingley. 'Have you seen my Laura recently? I can't find her.'

'She was on her way up to the bathroom about fifteen minutes ago,' said Max. 'She looked a bit green round the gills to be honest,' he added. 'I daresay she was after some Alka-Seltzer.'

Gabe weaved his way upstairs and along a winding

corridor that led to a series of bedrooms. He'd been to numerous Furlings' parties over the years, but unfortunately he'd been drunk at all of them, so had no idea which door might lead to a bathroom.

'Laura? Are you up here?'

Opening the first door on his right, he was greeted by an ear-piercing scream. Emma Harwich, stark naked and sprawled out on a four-poster bed, was going at it hammer and tongs with an older, blond man whom Gabe vaguely recognized.

Wasn't he one of Brett Cranley's business partners? And didn't he have a wife downstairs?

'Sorry,' Gabe mumbled, hastily shutting the door.

After that he started knocking before he tried different rooms, calling out Laura's name, but no joy. At last he found a bathroom, with a packet of Alka-Seltzer open next to the sink, beside an empty bottle of prescription pills. Curious, Gabe read the label.

Lexapro. Wasn't that an antidepressant?

He saw that they were Jason Cranley's.

'I'm in here.' Laura's voice drifted through from an adjoining bedroom. Gabe found her perched on the edge of a neatly made bed. Not drunk, as it happened, but looking anxious. She was holding some sort of paper in her hands.

'You all right?' he asked her. 'I was thinking about going home. Max Bingley said you weren't feeling too chipper.'

'I'm fine,' said Laura. 'But I'm not sure Jason Cranley is. Look at this.'

Gabe sat down next to her as she handed him what she'd been holding – two sealed envelopes, one addressed to 'Mum' and the other to 'Dad'.

'This is Jason's room,' said Laura. 'When I came up looking for something for my stomach, I found an empty bottle of pills on the bathroom counter. His name was on the front.'

'Yeah. I just saw it,' said Gabe.

'Anyway, I was worried so I came through here and found these letters propped up on the bed.'

'Shit.' Gabe ran a hand through his hair. 'You think he's overdosed somewhere?'

'I think it's possible,' said Laura. 'I mean, look around this room. It's immaculate. Doesn't that seem odd to you? For a twenty-one-year-old boy?'

'Like he was putting all his stuff in order,' Gabe said quietly.

'Exactly. The pills. This room. He left notes.' She held up the envelopes. 'I think we should do something'

Gabe felt his stomach lurch. She was right. Jason had seemed very happy earlier, when he saw him downstairs. But hadn't he read somewhere that people were often calm and happy right before they topped themselves? As if, once they'd made the decision, they already felt at peace?

'I'll go and find Brett,' he said grimly. 'We need to open those letters.'

Angela and Brett were sitting on a bench together beside the lake when Gabe and Laura found them. After several large whiskys and two outstanding Cuban cigars, Brett had pushed his earlier encounter with Tatiana out of his mind. He felt calm again, and happy. Angie's presence soothed him tonight, the way it always used to in the old days. If it could just be the two of them again – if Tatiana Flint-Hamilton could somehow evaporate and Brett's sexual obsession evaporate with her – he felt sure that everything would be OK. Gazing out over the lake, with his wife's hand in his, cool and slender and lovely, Brett could taste the peace and contentment waiting for him.

Until Gabe Baxter came along and shattered it.

'Sorry to interrupt,' said Gabe. 'But we found these in Jason's bedroom.' He handed Angela and Brett their respective envelopes.

'There was an empty bottle of pills in the bathroom next door,' blurted Laura, 'and his bedroom seemed very . . . tidy. Not a thing out of place. We don't mean to pry and it's probably nothing. But we were worried . . .'

Angela Cranley went sheet-white. She let out a long, low moan of anguish. 'Oh God. I knew something was wrong. I knew it! I should have followed him.' The panic in her voice was palpable.

Instinctively, Brett reached over and squeezed her hand. 'I'm sure he's fine.'

In the distance, the chopper noise they'd heard earlier was back again. It grew louder by the second, making conversation impossible, then receded. Somebody, presumably, had got their shot.

Angela gazed down at the envelope in her hand, the neatly written single word – '*Mum*' – and let out a sob. Her hands were shaking. 'I can't open it.'

'Give it to me,' said Brett. He'd already torn open his envelope and glanced at the contents. Now he did the same with Angela's. Her letter he read more closely, carefully scanning every line. His face was set like flint.

Laura looked at Gabe and raised an eyebrow. Brett's expression was hardly that of a concerned father. If anything he looked irritated. Not for the first time, Laura wondered how her husband could like this cold-blooded, arrogant, compassionless man.

Turning to Angela she asked, 'Is there anything we can do? Should we call the police?'

'The little shit,' muttered Brett furiously. His voice was so quiet it was almost inaudible. Somehow that only served

266

to make it more menacing. 'The stupid, *stupid*, reckless little SHIT!' Standing up, he screwed both letters up into a tight ball and hurled them on the ground.

'What? What's happened?' said Angela desperately. 'Brett, for God's sake tell me! What did he say in the letter? Is he all right?'

'Not for long he isn't,' snarled Brett, already walking away from her back up towards the house. 'I'm going to kill him. I'm going to kill them both.'

Angela sat frozen with shock. Quietly, Laura bent down and retrieved the balled-up letter.

'Here.' She handed it to Angela. 'We'll, er . . . we'll leave you to it, shall we?'

Angela nodded. 'Perhaps that would be best,' she whispered. 'Thank you. Goodnight.'

'Goodnight.'

Gabe led Laura away.

'That was odd,' he said.

'Very.'

'What do you think's going on?'

'I have no idea,' said Laura. 'But I tell you what. I feel sorry for Angela Cranley. I wouldn't be married to that bully of a husband for all the tea in China. He didn't seem to care about his son at all.'

Gabe said nothing. It was hard to argue with her this time.

The view from the helicopter was spectacular. Furlings was already an illuminated speck in the distance. Below them the South Downs slumbered, silver-green and ethereal in the moonlight, undulating ever onwards towards the calm, mirrored stillness of the sea. Villages nestled between the hills, snaking their way along valley floors beside the river

Swell. Every now and then a church steeple punctured the skyline, reaching up boldly into the night sky with its magical blanket of stars.

Tatiana leaned across and squeezed Jason's thigh. She had to press her lips right against his ear to make herself heard. 'This time tomorrow we'll be man and wife,' she told him. 'How do you feel?'

'Wonderful,' Jason said truthfully. He placed his hand over hers.

'No regrets?'

'Regrets?' his eyes widened. 'God no. I can't wait. It'll be a whole new life.'

Yes, thought Tatiana. *It will.*

They were headed to Le Touquet, where they'd spend the night at the Château de Montreuil Hotel before marrying at the town *mairie* in the morning. It was astonishing how easy it had been to organize the paperwork. Tatiana remembered how much her father had loathed the EU, and particularly the French, and felt a stab of nostalgia and affection. She'd always imagined Rory would be there to see her married. Then again, she'd always imagined she would be married at home, at Furlings, on the lawn . . .

She looked across at Jason Cranley. He looked even paler than usual in this light, his skin practically translucent beneath the shock of red hair. *Will I ever be attracted to him?* She pushed the thought away, along with an image of Marco; Marco whom she'd been too cowardly to tell the truth to; Marco whom she'd hurt, badly. She did feel guilty about that. But the truth was, this was a war, a war against Brett Cranley, and in a war there was always collateral damage. Civilian casualties. She owed Marco a lot, not least for giving her the business idea that was going to make her rich and change her life. She would make it up to him one day.

Today, however, was about her and Jason. The one thing Marco hadn't been able to provide was the seed capital to get Tati's business off the ground and secure her Coutts loan. That, among other things, was where Jason came in.

Tatiana Flint-Hamilton might not be getting married at Furlings. But by marrying Jason Cranley, and securing access to his very sizable trust fund, she was one large step closer to eventually getting her beloved home back. She was also rescuing him from a miserable life, a life in which he'd been enslaved and belittled by his tyrannical father. By casting himself as their common enemy, Brett Cranley had unwittingly created a bond between Tatiana and his son. OK, so Tati wasn't wildly attracted to Jason the way that she was to Marco – or even, in some toxic, destructive way to Brett. But she liked him, genuinely. Tati and Jason were friends. She knew of many marriages that had been built on less.

'What about you?' Jason looked worried suddenly, a cloud of anxiety passing across his boyish features. 'You're not having second thoughts, are you? I love you so much, Tatiana, but I want you to be happy, more than anything.'

Closing her eyes, Tati kissed him on the lips. He tasted of chocolate cake and sweet wine. The kiss wasn't erotic but it was perfectly pleasant. She smiled.

'I am happy, darling. Very. I can't wait to be Mrs Cranley.'

Leaving England behind them, the helicopter swept out to sea.

PART TWO

The Reckoning

CHAPTER SIXTEEN

Five years later . . .

Logan Cranley ran a finger along her lower lashes, deliberately smudging her black eyeliner into what she hoped
was a sexy, rock-chick effect, and admired the results in the
mirror of the tack-room loo.

Perfect.

Logan wasn't especially vain for a sixteen-year-old girl.
But she was especially beautiful, a fact she understood and
accepted with the same calm appreciation that another girl
might feel for a sunny day, or a better-than-expected mark
at school. Her looks didn't particularly interest her. They
were a means to an end, a useful weapon in her romantic
armoury. At least, they were supposed to be. So far they'd
been no bloody use at all.

Tall, almost five foot eleven in her riding boots, with long,
slender legs, a tiny waist, and the sort of glowing, translucent
skin that rich older women spend their lives trying to recap-
ture, Logan Cranley was now officially employed as a stable
hand at Wraggsbottom Farm. It was, without reservation,
her dream summer job. And she had Laura Baxter to thank
for it.

'We may as well employ her, as she's here all the time,' Laura observed to Gabe over breakfast one morning, pushing away a plate of untouched scrambled eggs.

'I'll employ her if you eat something,' said Gabe sternly.

'I can't,' Laura groaned. 'Truly.'

After five long years of fertility treatment and three miscarriages, each more heart-breaking than the last, Laura Baxter was finally twenty weeks pregnant. It was the furthest along she'd ever been, and she felt sicker than the proverbial dog. Having Gabe flapping around her day and night like a useless chicken didn't help matters either, although Laura could see how delighted he was, and how terrified of something going wrong. They'd been through hell these past five years, but they'd been through it together.

Tired of passively watching while Gabe sailed their marital ship into bankruptcy, Laura had sat down at her computer one winter morning and not got up again, other than to eat and sleep, until she'd finished a new teleplay. An *Archers*-esque drama about farming life, it was the best thing she'd written in years. Within a month she'd sold it to Sky TV, and been commissioned to write a further two daytime soaps. The money wasn't spectacular, but it was decent, and steady, and it had meant the difference between the business surviving or Gabe's farm being repossessed. Deeply grateful, but with his manly pride more than a little wounded at having to be rescued by his wife, Gabe had thrown himself into diversifying Wraggsbottom to try and protect against another run of bad harvests. He'd begun by converting six outbuildings into holiday lets, a business that had started generating income almost immediately. Stage two had been to open up a livery stables and riding school. That had taken longer, but it hadn't required much investment to get it started. The stable blocks and paddocks were just sitting there, waiting for a lick of paint, and some fencing, jumps and a few tons of sand had been all he needed to create an outdoor 'school'. Within two years the stables had become the most profitable business on the estate, as Gabe proudly now thought of the farm, and not without reason. He and Laura now had almost as much land as Furlings, and were one of the most successful mixed farms in the Swell Valley, if not in all of Sussex.

The only downside to the great Baxter turnaround in fortunes was that both Gabe and Laura worked all the hours God sent, which left neither time nor energy for romance. When they did have sex, it was always under the gun of Laura's ovulation test stick, the pressure to conceive hanging over them like a dark, oppressive, profoundly un-erotic cloud. Between that and the exhaustion and Laura's wild hormone swings – the IVF injections were murder – it had been a gruelling time.

But now, at long last, all their hard work was bearing fruit, both literally and metaphorically. The farm was in the black, Laura's writing was ticking along nicely, and they were finally, *finally*, about to become parents. To someone other than Logan Cranley, whom Laura had come to think of almost as a surrogate daughter over the past few years. Albeit a daughter with a lot of attitude.

'You realize if we give her a job she'll be here every day,' said Gabe, removing the offending egg and handing his green-faced wife a ginger biscuit, one of the few foods she could still stomach. 'I don't want her bugging you when you're trying to rest.'

'I won't be trying to rest. I'll be trying to write. Besides, she'll be working in the yard, so it's you she'll be bugging.'

Gabe rolled his eyes.

'What's the matter?' Laura teased him. 'Tired of being the object of desire, are we?'

'I'm not any more,' said Gabe. 'She's over me. Brett told me she's going out with Seb Harwich.'

'Oh, is she?' Emma brightened. 'That's wonderful. I love Seb. He's so funny and sweet.'

'Hmm,' said Gabe, grumpily. 'I'm not a fan of all the beads. He's turned into a proper pothead since he got back from India.'

The younger brother of Emma Harwich, Fittlescombe's first home-grown supermodel and all-round brat, Seb Harwich was an easy-going twenty-one-year-old with a love of cricket and girls (in that order) whom everybody in the village adored. Including Gabe, for all his disapproval of Seb's year-off fashion stylings.

'Maybe Logan will get him back on the straight and narrow,' said Laura, tongue in cheek.

Gabe snorted with laughter. 'Yeah, *right.*'

'At least if she's working here she can't get into too much mischief,' said Laura. 'Will you tell her or shall I?'

That conversation had been a week ago. Now Logan was here, an official member of Gabe's staff. She'd had to pinch herself when she got up for work this morning. No more thinking up excuses to drop by. From now on she would see Gabe every day. More importantly *he* would see *her.* At some point he was going to have to realize that she was no longer the little girl he'd first met more than six years ago, when he bought that land from her father.

I'm a woman, thought Logan. If nothing else, she hoped that Gabe seeing her with Seb Harwich might change his perceptions of her, or even make him a little jealous. Seb was twenty-one after all. That made Logan part of a bona-fide, grown-up couple.

'Logan!' Gabe's voice shook her out of her reverie. Hurriedly slipping her eyeliner back into her pocket she emerged into the yard.

'Good morning,' she smiled cheerfully.

'Have you tacked up Jack and Cornflake yet?' Gabe frowned. He was wearing dirty jeans and a Guinness T-shirt. Two days' worth of stubble clung stubbornly to his chin, and from the bags under his eyes it was clear he hadn't slept well.

He's so handsome I could cry, thought Logan. *If I were his wife, I'd take better care of him.*

'Not yet.' She did her best to look smouldering.

'Well pull your bloody finger out. The first lesson starts in ten minutes and it's Lucinda sodding Prior. Her fat-arsed mother's always looking for a reason to complain, so you'd better not give her one.'

He turned and stalked off.

Logan bit back her disappointment.

She worked here now. She had the whole summer. *And* Seb Harwich to distract her in the meantime.

Now, where did she leave those bridles?

Angela Cranley sat alone at the dining table at Furlings, admiring the view over the rolling parkland. She rarely ate breakfast in the dining room. It was too big and grand and formal, especially for one. But this morning she felt in need of a pick-me-up, and the view across the idyllic Swell Valley never failed to provide it.

I love it here, she reminded herself. *This house, this village, this valley. It's my home now.*

Since Jason had left home, Angela rarely had any company at breakfast time. If Logan was home from boarding school, she was usually still in bed at this hour. Although this morning she'd started her new summer job at the Baxters' farm and had dashed off at crack of dawn. Brett had stayed in London last night, working. And the night before. He'd taken to staying in town more and more during the week. Angela oscillated between anxiety that once again the distance was growing between them, and relief at his absence. At least without Brett here she could enjoy her toast and Vegemite in peace, and without fear of a row erupting out of nowhere.

Recently the fights with Brett had been particularly bad. They seemed to come in waves, and even after so many years of marriage, Angela didn't really understand what triggered them, or why certain phases of their marriage were so much worse than others. Some of the flashpoints were constant – Jason and Tatiana being the most obvious one.

Furious at their elopement from day one, Brett had not spoken to Jason since the day of his twenty-first birthday party. Jason and Tatiana were officially and permanently banned from Furlings, and when drunk or angry, Brett was fond of observing that he 'no longer had a son', a statement that upset Angela terribly.

It made no difference to him that, against the odds perhaps, Jason and Tati's marriage had lasted. That they seemed happy together, had started a highly successful business and led an independent, one might even say a gilded life, in London. Jason was now the successful businessman that Brett had always wanted him to be. But it had happened on his and Tatiana's terms, not on Brett's. He couldn't forgive either of them for that.

For once, Angela had held her ground and refused to allow Brett to cut her off from her own child. It was bad enough that he had banned Jase from the house and cut him out of his will. (Not that Jason needed his father's money any more.) But he wasn't going to rob the boy of his mother as well. Both Angela and Logan saw Jason and Tati semi-regularly, although these meetings were always in London and never overtly discussed with Brett. He knew about them however, and resented them deeply, considering Angela's continued closeness to their son a betrayal.

For her part Angela thought Brett's grudge-holding was both childish and wildly unreasonable. The worst part was that he was hurting himself more than anybody. Angela could see how the distance ate away at Brett. How it made him feel abandoned and helpless, even though it was he who was perpetuating the rift. In the beginning she'd tried to comfort him and reason with him. But after a couple of years she abandoned the effort. Something had snapped in Brett the day that Jason married Tatiana. Whatever it was could not be repaired.

In the beginning Angela had spent a lot of time wondering about what would happen once Tati got pregnant. Would Brett acknowledge his own grandchild? And if he didn't, where would that leave the family? Leave her and Brett as a couple? But as the years passed and no baby arrived – no baby was even talked about, Angela learned to stop fighting ghosts. Jason and Tati seemed to be making a go of their marriage. It was up to her and Brett to do the same, what-ever their differences.

'Can I get you anything else, Mrs C?'

Mrs Worsley appeared in the doorway with a fresh pot of tea on a tray. The housekeeper had aged in the last few years and was now a properly old woman who walked with a stoop and spoke with that permanent tremor unique to the elderly. Angela had grown very fond of Furlings' house-keeper over the years. She dreaded to think how lonely she'd be without Mrs Worsley. There were days, weeks even, when she and Gringo, the arthritic basset hound, were the only living souls she spoke to. *I really must get out more. Join some societies or something*, she thought for the umpteenth time, relieving Mrs Worsley of the tea.

'No thank you,' she said. 'I'll have this and then I think I'll take Gringo for a walk. It's such a beautiful day.'

'It is,' the housekeeper nodded. 'Set to be a scorcher, I reckon.'

She was right. By the time Angela and Gringo reached the village stores, it was already eighty degrees outside, without a breath of wind to take the edge off the heat. Not that Angela was complaining. Fittlescombe High Street looked glorious, with its flint cottages and shops bathed in the amber morning sunshine, and its rows of front gardens full of hollyhocks and lupins and foxgloves and roses, their colours a dazzling patchwork against the bright blue backdrop of the summer sky.

Mrs Preedy at the stores had thoughtfully left a bowl of cool water outside for her customers' dogs. Gringo fell on it gratefully, his floppy ears swaying as he slurped away, while Angela went inside for a newspaper and an ice lolly.

'A bit early for a Twister isn't it?'

Penny de la Cruz, Seb Harwich's mother and one of Angela's few real friends locally, tapped her on the shoulder. In a scruffy, Indian-print dress with bells on the bottom of it that would have looked frightful on anybody else, and a fraying straw hat, Penny somehow managed to look eternally youthful and happy. Perhaps marriage to a younger love-God cricketer was the answer?

'I'm Australian,' said Angela. 'It's never too early for an ice cream in our book. Want one?'

'Oh, go on then,' said Penny. Angela paid for the lollies and they both went outside.

'We haven't seen you for ages,' said Penny. 'Logan's been over quite a bit recently, but you've been hiding yourself away as usual. What's going on?'

'Oh, nothing much,' said Angela. 'Logie got a summer job.'

'At the stables. I heard. And how's Brett?'

The question was asked out of politeness rather than interest. Brett had made no effort to develop friendships with any of the locals, other than the occasional beer or game of pool with Gabe Baxter, who for some reason he'd taken a shine to. This was another factor in Angela's isolation. If she'd been divorced or widowed, people could have invited her to dinner as a singleton. But no one knew what to do with a married woman whose husband never said yes to invitations, and who only entertained at home if he was throwing a party for hundreds.

'He's fine. Working,' Angela said numbly.

'You and I should get together.' Penny squeezed her arm kindly. 'Santiago's playing almost every day at the moment, so I'm on my own a lot. Let's have lunch.'

'I'd like that,' said Angela.

Dragging the reluctant Gringo away from his water bowl, she set off back towards Furlings. On a whim, she decided to walk past Wraggsbottom Farm and see if she could see Logan. She wouldn't go in and embarrass her. Everything Angela did seemed to embarrass Logie these days. She was at that age. She'd just take a peek and reassure herself that the job was going all right.

A few yards from the farm gates she stopped, ducking behind a parked car so as to remain out of sight. There was Logan, in a pair of jodhpurs that were far too tight for her and a half-buttoned white shirt, leaning against a wall and staring. Not doing anything. Just staring, like a hawk focusing in on a distant mouse, oblivious to everything else around it. Following her gaze, Angela saw Gabriel Baxter bending over the open bonnet of a tractor, a spanner in his hand.

Shit, thought Angela, a momentary panic rising up within her. She'd thought – hoped – that all that was over. But a few seconds later, the lanky, bronzed form of Seb Harwich emerged from the tack room. Walking up behind Logan, Seb slipped his arms around her waist. Angela watched her daughter smile and turn into Seb's embrace, standing on tiptoes in her riding boots to kiss him passionately on the mouth.

'Oy!' Gabe's voice carried across the farmyard. 'Get a room, you two. Better still, Seb, sod off. I'm not paying her to spend the morning snogging.'

Seb and Logan both giggled. Angela sneaked away, feeling happier than she had in a long time. At least one member of the Cranley family had a love life that was on the right track.

Gabe walked into the kitchen at seven o'clock that evening, dog tired.

'You look shattered.' Laura was shelling peas at the kitchen table. In a smocked maternity dress with little pink rose buds embroidered on the bodice, she looked quite different from her normal self, like something out of a Jane Austen novel. There was a serenity about her this evening, Gabe noticed, a sort of calm happiness that clung to her as she worked. As clichéd as it was, you might almost call it a glow.

'I love you,' he said, kissing her, suddenly feeling awash with happiness himself. 'You look beautiful.'

'You're blind,' Laura laughed. 'I look like a whale.'

Gabe pulled a cold beer out of the fridge and opened it. He started to tell Laura about his day, about Logan and the problems he'd had with the damn tractor engine going on the blink again, when he noticed she was staring smilingly into the distance and not listening to him at all.

'Are you all right?' He waved a hand in front of her glazed face.

'Oh, yes, I'm fine. Sorry. I had some news today. I went to the hospital.'

Gabe put down his beer with a clatter. 'The hospital? Why?' He looked worried. 'Was something wrong? Have you been having cramps?'

'No,' Laura beamed. 'Nothing's wrong. I went in for a scan and everything's fine.'

'Oh.' Gabe's shoulders slumped with relief. 'Good.'

'We're having a boy.'

He looked at her blankly.

'Gabe?' said Laura. 'Did you hear me? I said it's a boy. They gave me some pictures. They're a bit blurry . . .' Scrabbling around in her handbag, she pulled out a white envelope and handed it to him.

Pulling out the pictures, Gabe looked at the pictures one by one. He still hadn't said anything. 'Are you OK?' she asked.

Gabe looked up, his eyes brimming with tears.

'Oh, darling! What's the matter?'

'Nothing,' said Gabe. 'I'm just so happy. This is our son. Our *son*!' He looked at the pictures in wonder. Then, putting them down on the table, he took Laura's hand and pulled her up into a hug, wrapping his arms tightly around her and their unborn child.

'I'm taking you away next week,' he said suddenly. 'Somewhere romantic and amazing, where all you're going to do is lie in bed all day and eat chocolates.'

'Really?' Her eyes lit up. 'Sounds lovely. But who'll take care of things here?'

'Graham and the lads can manage things on the farm for a few days,' said Gabe. Graham Dean was Wraggsbottom's farm manager, a sort of first mate to Gabe's captain. 'And Logan can house-sit and feed the dogs.'

'Logan?' Laura raised a sceptical eyebrow. 'Really?'

'Sure,' said Gabe. 'I think the responsibility would be good for her.'

'Hmmm, maybe. But will it be good for our lovely house? What if she clogs up the dishwasher or forgets to water my tomato plants? She's not exactly domesticated.'

'Your tomato plants will be fine,' said Gabe. 'Stop fussing. My son doesn't like it.'

'Oh, so he's *your* son now, is he?' teased Laura.

'He'd bloody well better be,' said Gabe. 'I'll text Logan now to let her know.'

Up at Furlings, Logan was in the small family sitting room watching *The Big Bang Theory* when the text came through. She read it once, then twice, before hugging the phone to her chest and letting out a little squeal of delight.

'What's this? Romance blossoming?' said Angela, walking in with a cup of tea and a Bounty bar and catching Logan's gesture.

'Yes, actually,' said Logan, smiling back at her mother for once. She'd been terribly moody recently, no doubt picking up on the tension between her parents. 'I think it might be. I'm wiped out though, Mum, it's been such a long day.' Relieving Angela of the tea and the chocolate, she slipped the phone into her pocket and kissed her mother on the cheek. 'I think I'll go up to my room.'

She wants to text Seb Harwich without me looking over her

shoulder, thought Angela happily. *I must take Penny up on that lunch offer. See how Seb's feeling about everything.*

Upstairs in her bedroom, Logan read Gabe's texts another twenty times.

He trusts me! He trusts me to take care of his house, to stay under his roof.

He's starting to see me as an adult.

A friend.

It wasn't enough. But it was a start. More than that, it meant she'd be able to sleep in Gabe's bed, to wash in his shower, to smell the scent of his skin on the sheets. She would open his drawers and read his letters and uncover his secrets.

How on earth was she going to be able to wait another week?

CHAPTER SEVENTEEN

Jason Cranley sat on the therapist's couch, staring at the botanical prints on the wall. He didn't want to be here. But he'd promised Tatiana he would go. And the truth was, he had nowhere else to be this afternoon. Or any afternoon, for that matter.

'What have you got to lose, darling?' Tati had asked, in her usual confident, breezy, can-do voice as she rushed out of the door to work. It was the voice of someone who'd never been depressed, who'd never faced a challenge that she couldn't overcome. 'I mean, you're not happy. Are you?'

'No,' Jason agreed.

He wasn't happy.

'And the pills alone aren't working?'

'No.'

'So why not try something else?'

Because it won't work. Because I'm tired. Because I can't explain to a stranger how I feel when I don't know myself.

'I guess.'

'Give it a whirl.' The forced cheerfulness in Tati's voice

was the aural equivalent of having blinding light shone directly in your eyes. Jason winced.

'You have to take responsibility for your own life you know, darling. Let me know how it goes.' And with a slam of the door, she was gone.

So now Jason was here, on a stranger's couch.

The therapist looked at him kindly. 'Where would you like to start?'

She was in her fifties, slim and blonde and attractive, with an open, compassionate face that reminded him of his mother. Instantly, embarrassingly, Jason felt his eyes welling up with tears. He pressed his fingers against his eyelids to stop them from flowing.

'I don't know.'

'Well,' she said, confidently but with none of Tatiana's briskness. 'Perhaps we should start with your childhood? Family history, that sort of thing. Where did you grow up?'

'Australia,' said Jason. *About as far away from here as it's possible to be.* Sometimes he wished he could blame his current malaise on homesickness. He did feel it sometimes, that primal longing for sunshine and blue skies and the open, outdoorsy life he remembered from his childhood in Sydney. London could be so relentlessly rainy and grey. But then he reminded himself that he'd brought his sadness with him when his family relocated to England. Whatever was wrong with him had been wrong with him for a long, long time.

The truth was – and this was one of the hardest parts to understand – that his life now, with Tatiana, was everything he'd always wanted. At least on paper. Jason and Tati lived in a beautiful townhouse just off Eaton Gate, which Jason had renovated and decorated exactly as he pleased, with no arguments from his wife. Tatiana was too busy building up her business: a prep school called Hamilton Hall that had become an overnight success, both academically and as a money-making machine.

Tucked away behind Sloane Square, in a converted hotel, Hamilton Hall charged fifty per cent higher fees than all of its smart London rivals. For this astronomical yearly sum, it scooped up all of the wealthy London families whose offspring had been rejected by the traditional top-tier schools, often for such trifling reasons as low academic ability. Tatiana threw Oxbridge-educated teachers and a rigorously old-fashioned teaching style at the problem – she had basically copied Max Bingley's approach to the letter – and spat the children out at the other end with the top eleven-plus exam results in the country. Indeed, in the four years since Hamilton Hall had first opened its doors, it had leapfrogged to the top of the independent schools rankings with a speed that had astonished and horrified its competition in equal measure. What was Tatiana Flint-Hamilton *doing* with these kids? How could a non-selective school possibly achieve such consistently excellent results?

Tatiana was coy in her answers to these questions in the apparently endless series of profiles written about her and Hamilton Hall by the national press. *The Sunday Times*, *Vogue*, *Londoner Magazine* and even *Vanity Fair* had all featured Hamilton Hall's beautiful headmistress and her handsome, elusive young husband in their hallowed pages. The *Vanity Fair* article in particular had done wonders for the school's reputation abroad. When asked how long the Hamilton Hall waiting list was by the magazine's reporter, Tatiana had responded robustly:

'We don't do waiting lists. Never have, never will. We'll take anyone prepared to pay our fees.'

'But surely you'll run out of space at some point?' the reporter countered.

'Hopefully,' said Tatiana. 'And when we do, we'll expand.'

Just weeks after that interview was published, Tatiana sold eighty per cent of the Hamilton Hall 'brand' to an investment consortium, mostly made up of American hedge-fund and real-estate entrepreneurs, with a smattering of aristocratic Brits thrown in at board level for good measure. The money from the sale had bought the Eaton Gate house, with a comfortable cushion of cash to spare. Tati and Jason retained a twenty per cent stake in the business and a lucrative three-year contract for Tati as CEO. She no longer had time for any teaching, still less to run the Sloane Square school as a headmistress, so she poached Drew O'Donnell, the brilliant headmaster of Colet Court to take her place – yet another, much-talked-about coup.

New premises on Clapham Common were already under construction, a twenty-million-pound venture that was taking up immense amounts of Tatiana's time. In addition she was scouting opportunities for growth of the Hamilton Hall model abroad, everywhere from the US to Asia. The school had become so successful, so quickly, it was tempting to look back on its foundation as a sure thing, some sort of fait accompli. In reality, however, starting Hamilton Hall had been a huge risk, one which Tatiana and Jason had taken together. She'd sunk her own modest savings into the first, flagship school. But it was Jason who had put the real money at risk. Every penny of his sizable trust fund had gone into the business, despite Brett's best efforts to claw the cash back.

'Hamilton Hall is your business as much as mine, you know. Your success as much as mine,' Tati reminded Jason constantly. She was always very generous and inclusive in this regard. 'Without your trust fund, and your belief in me, this could never have happened. You believed in me when no-one else would.'

It was true. Yet to Jason, it always felt like a technicality. Hamilton Hall, both the school and the brand, had been Tatiana's baby from the beginning She'd worked herself into the ground building and running a business that was, quite rightly, synonymous with its foundress. All Jason had done was write a cheque. A cheque he hadn't even had to work for. As a result, their beautiful home, and his expensive clothes, and the free time he had on his hands, all felt as if they rightfully belonged to someone else. To Tatiana, in fact. Jason Cranley was a passenger in his own life again, just as he had been when he lived at home with his parents. The fact that the ship he was now sailing on was a super-yacht, and that his was the presidential suite, didn't make him feel any better.

'What about your parents?' the therapist prodded gently. 'Are you close?'

'I'm close to my mother,' said Jason. 'My father . . .'

The word hung in the air, like an unfinished road to nowhere. How to sum up his relationship – non-relationship – with Brett in a single sentence?

'My father doesn't approve of my marriage. That makes things difficult.'

'I'm sure.' The therapist nodded understandingly. 'Your loyalties are with your wife.'

'Yes,' Jason said thoughtfully, surprised as he said it by how true this was.

His loyalties *were* with Tatiana. And hers, he still believed, were with him. And yet there could be no denying that their marriage was not, and never had been, what a marriage should be. For one thing their sex life was close to nonexistent. Neither of them it seemed had the will or the energy to try to change this. Tatiana was consumed with the school, her expanding educational empire. And Jason?

I have my music. The thought was so pathetic it made him laugh out loud.

'Is something funny?' the therapist asked.

'Not really.'

Thanks to Hamilton Hall's huge success, Jason now had more than enough money never to have to work again. He was free to focus on his piano, to follow his dreams, just as he'd always longed to. In the beginning he'd given it his all, practising for hours each day, eventually working up the courage to put himself out there as a professional jazz pianist, looking for work. And he'd found it, sporadically, in third-rate bars and restaurants. But none of the jobs lasted. Put simply, Jason had learned the hard way that his father had been right all along: he simply wasn't good enough, talented enough, to make it as a professional musician.

If there was one single cause at the root of his current depression, Jason suspected this was it. He was a failure. Creatively. Professionally. Maritally. Meanwhile his wife, whom he loved despite their sexless marriage, his wife was a roaring success, the toast of London.

Jason's mother had visited him and Tati at the Eaton Gate house a couple of weeks ago and unwittingly brought all his negative feelings to a head. Normally Jason enjoyed Angela's visits, especially when she brought Logan along with her. Something about his sister's energy was infectious, and pushed all thoughts of the absent elephant in the room – Brett – from Jason's mind. Logan loved Tati too, which helped, and the feeling was mutual. Whenever his kid sister was around, Jason felt as if his two worlds, his two selves had collided. That made him happy.

But this last time his mother had come alone. And one afternoon, quite out of the blue, she'd asked Jason about children.

'You've been together five years now,' Angela probed gently. 'Tatiana's thirty. You must have thought about it.'

Well, they hadn't thought about it. The subject had never come up between them. Not obliquely. Not in a jokey way. Not at all.

Never.

Because we both know there's something missing.

Something wrong.

This realization – prompted by his mother's innocent question – had pushed Jason over some sort of mental edge into his darkest mood of many years. After Angela left he felt exhausted and tearful and defeated, unable or unwilling to get out of bed. All the old demons were back. Concerned, Tati had pushed him back to therapy. But he really wasn't sure he had the strength for it.

'Tell me a bit about your marriage,' said the therapist. 'How do you feel about your wife?'

Jason looked up at the clock like a condemned man waiting for the guillotine. Had he really only been in this room for fifteen minutes? The thought of another forty-five minutes of questions filled him with something akin to panic.

'I'm sorry,' he said, standing up suddenly. 'I'm afraid I . . . I have somewhere I need to be. I forgot. I'll pay you. Goodbye.'

He bolted out of the door and down the corridor as if the room were on fire.

Poor thing, thought the therapist, who'd seen it all before. So much for the Cranleys' glittering life and perfect marriage. That boy was proof, if one ever needed it, that money and fame could not buy one happiness.

She wondered if she would see Jason Cranley again.

Seb Harwich watched Logan Cranley's perfect body gyrating to the music. He wished he weren't so mesmerized by her.

But the way her hair swung around her shoulders, and her back arched as she moved each long, lithe leg to the beat of the godawful German dance track she was playing had a totally hypnotic effect on him.

They were in the barn at Wraggsbottom Farm, where Logan had decided to throw an impromptu party. 'They' included a gaggle of Logan's spoilt, sixteen-year-old boarding school friends, Seb, and a smattering of locals, mostly boys in their teens, who buzzed around the St Xavier's girls like horny bees around a honey-pot. At almost twenty-two, Seb was not only the oldest person present, but by far the most mature. He'd tried to convince Logan not to invite friends over.

'Someone's bound to get drunk and break something or have an accident. Gabe and Laura would hit the roof if they knew.'

But Logan had pooh-poohed him, in her usual headstrong, thoughtless fashion. 'Yes, but they don't know, do they? And there's no reason why they should. As long as *someone* doesn't rat us out.'

'Don't be silly,' Seb frowned. 'I'm not going to say anything. I just don't think it's a good idea, that's all. Laura and Gabe put a lot of trust in you.'

'*Gabe* put a lot of trust in me,' Logan corrected him sharply. 'Laura still thinks I'm an irresponsible kid. I know she tried to talk him out of letting me house-sit. She doesn't want him to see me as an adult.'

That's because you aren't an adult, thought Seb, watching Logan topple backwards onto a pile of hay bales, burst into a fit of giggles and pour herself another half mugful of Gabe and Laura's Grey Goose. Seb knew Logan was a child, and a spoiled one at that. He also knew that she had the hots for Gabe Baxter and was only using him to try to make

Gabe jealous. But he couldn't seem to help himself. She was so gorgeous, and, when she wasn't drunk or high or banging on about Gabe, such fun to be around. It was like asking a starving lion to walk away from a juicy gazelle that was practically throwing itself into his jaws.

'Light another joint for me, would you angel?' Logan blew him a kiss from the hay bales. 'I'm so hyper right now.'

'You're not hyper, you're drunk,' said Seb. 'And none of you should be smoking in here. One stray spark and this whole place would go up like a box of fireworks.'

'Oh, give it a rest, Granddad.' Liam Docherty, the new gardener's boy up at Furlings, sidled up to Logan with a fat, ready-rolled joint in his hand. Lighting it for her, he inhaled once deeply himself before handing it over. 'Who invited this killjoy anyway?'

Like most of the boys in the village, Liam fancied the pants off his boss's daughter. Unlike most of them, he had daily opportunity to get close to Logan, and hadn't given up hope of eventually charming her into bed. Liam was eighteen but looked younger, thanks to a pale complexion and freckles that gave him the look of a naughty schoolboy. But all Logan's friends agreed there was something sexy about him, a certain cocksure Irish confidence.

'I did,' Logan sighed, looking at Seb Harwich with studied boredom. 'But I'm beginning to wonder why.'

'Come on. Let's get this party started.' Lavinia Creek, a particularly obnoxious schoolfriend of Logan's, stripped off her T-shirt to reveal a bright pink bra. 'Everyone has to take off at least one item of clothing. Last person on the dance floor goes naked!'

Lavinia was blonde and might have been described as buxom. She was inordinately proud of her large breasts, despite the fact that they came as part of a package that also included a roll of belly fat and a big, wobbly bottom. Seb kept reading that men were supposed to go wild over figures like Lavinia's. Personally he found the sight of her white flesh spilling over the top of her underwear and miniskirt borderline repulsive, especially when she jiggled it around in what drunkenly passed for dancing.

'I'm game.' Not taking his eyes off Logan, Liam Docherty removed his shirt to reveal a surprisingly taut and toned six-pack. The other girls swiftly followed suit, the prettier ones shimmying out of dresses, screaming with laughter as they jumped around in only bras and knickers. Everybody was drunk, but no one more so than Logan. Not one to be outdone on the exhibitionist stakes, she staggered back to her feet, turning up the volume on Gabe's ancient boombox and dramatically peeling off her bra, which she proceeded to toss provocatively into Seb's lap.

'Come on, Sebby.' She threw her arms in the air and spun around like some Bacchanalian goddess. 'Dance with me.'

Seb stood up and pulled Logan into his arms, more to shield her naked breasts from Liam and the other boys than out of any desire to be there.

'You're hammered,' he whispered in her ear, trying hard not to be distracted by the silken soft skin of her bare back. 'And you're making an arse of yourself. Tell this lot to go home and I'll make us some coffee.'

'Can't hear you,' laughed Logan, shimmying out of his arms and bending down to turn the music up even louder. As she did so, one of the girls took a picture on her mobile phone.

'I bet that'll get a fuck of a lot of "Likes" on Facebook tomorrow,' whistled Liam.

'And I bet gorgeous Gabe will be one of them,' added

Lavinia, loudly and for Seb's benefit. Like most of Logan's friends, Lavinia fancied Seb Harwich madly and knew he was jealous of Logan's crush on Gabe. Lavinia would have liked nothing more than to see Seb and Logan break up. 'I could be his beaver to cry on,' she'd told the other St Xavier's girls with a cackle.

'That's it,' said Seb, grabbing his jacket angrily. 'I'm going home.'

It took Logan a few moments to realize he was serious. By then he was halfway across the farmyard. Grabbing her T-shirt, she ran after him.

'Come on, Seb. Don't go.' She did her best to sound conciliatory. 'It's only a bit of fun.'

Seb turned on her angrily. 'No, it's not. It's fucking irresponsible. Poor Laura thinks you're keeping an eye on the place.'

Logan's face instantly darkened. 'Poor Laura indeed. If she'd had her way, Gabe would never have let me house-sit.'

'Because she thought you might pull something like this' said Seb, exasperated. 'And she was right, wasn't she? Laura was the one who got you the job at the stables, you know.'

'That's not true.'

'It *is* true. Gabe told me. He didn't want you around every day, but Laura felt sorry for you.'

'That's a lie!' said Logan.

Seb knew he was hurting her but he didn't care. It was true, and besides, she didn't care how much she hurt *him*.

'She's so fucking kind to you,' he went on. 'And what do you do to repay her? Abuse her trust and spend every waking hour trying to get her husband into bed.'

'I don't have to *try* to get men into bed,' said Logan, blushing scarlet at Seb's accusation. 'It's easy.'

Seb looked at her, stricken. How could he have fallen so in love with such a horrible, selfish person?

'Go back to your friends, Logan,' he said sadly. 'I'm going home.'

Laura drove through the deserted lanes, blinded by tears of anger and frustration.

How had they managed to have a row, tonight of all nights? And over something so stupid, too.

Up until dinner tonight, her romantic minibreak with Gabe had been going perfectly. They'd slept and cuddled – after so many miscarriages they were both too scared to have sex while she was pregnant – and gone for long country walks along the river. They'd talked about the farm, and her idea for a new TV series, and their future together as a family. But then, this evening, the conversation had turned randomly to education. Gabe had mentioned something about boarding school; Laura had said she didn't like the idea of their son being sent away from home – a son who hadn't even been born yet, never mind expressed his educational preferences! – and before they knew it things had descended into a vicious, knockdown drag-out fight. Gabe had accused Laura of everything from snobbery to trying to turn their child gay. In response, Laura had branded Gabe a sexist and a moron, and it had all gone downhill from there. Gabe paid the bill and they returned to their room, but the fight raged on. In the end Laura got so angry she packed a bag, grabbed the car keys and drove off into the night back to Fittlescombe. Fucking Gabe could get a fucking taxi in the morning on his own. She hoped it cost him a fortune.

She first saw the smoke from about a mile away, as she rounded the top of the hill that wound down into the valley at Brockhurst. *Odd time for a bonfire*, she thought. *And no one burns stubble in July.* It was only as she drew nearer to the village that she saw the flames leaping into the night sky and realized with horror that the fire was coming from their farm.

Pulling up outside, she jumped out of the car and was immediately hit by a wall of hot air that made her gasp. Thick black smoke poured out of the hay barn. The two stables nearest to the barn were also on fire. Within minutes it would reach the house.

Instinctively Laura ran into the stable yard to check the horses, but all the stalls were empty. *Thank God.* Logan must have taken them out to the paddock already. That meant she would have called the fire brigade as well. But where the hell were they? Running back to the car, Laura pulled out her mobile and dialled 999.

'Fire!' she panted. 'At Wraggsbottom Farm in Fittlescombe.'

The operator assured her a crew was already on its way. They'd had two calls from neighbours, apparently. Laura hung up and ran into the house. Grabbing the fire extinguisher in the kitchen, she shouted upstairs for Logan, but there was no reply. Perhaps she was still out in the field, dealing with the horses?

Running back out as fast as she could with her pregnant belly, she heard the sirens of the fire engines coming down the hill from the main road. They would be here in moments, but the fire seemed to be intensifying and spreading with each passing second. Getting as close to the front door of the barn as she dared, Laura pulled the pin on the extinguisher and began to spray white foam at the entrance. The flames immediately receded, replaced by black smoke so thick it almost felt solid, like a deathly, choking cloth.

That was when she heard it. A scream, loud, shrill and terrified.

'Logan!' Laura yelled back into the blackness. Still spraying foam in front of her, and with a hand clasped over her mouth, she moved into the doorway of the barn. 'Logan! Are you in there?'

No words, just another scream. This one louder than before and blood-curdling. The sound came from somewhere very close, only feet away. But both the heat and smoke were utterly disorienting. On instinct, Laura moved to the right, coughing violently as she tried to hold the extinguisher aloft. She heard the sirens behind her, very loud now. Were they here?

'Hold on Logan,' she shouted. Just the effort of breathing was painful. 'I'm coming!'

It took Gabe about four minutes to realize he'd been a complete tool, and another twenty minutes to swallow his pride sufficiently to pack a bag, call a taxi and follow his wife back to Fittlescombe. Boarding school! He didn't even care about bloody boarding school. He wasn't one of 'those' dads, the kind who live vicariously through their sons. And he *certainly* didn't believe that boys needed to be sent away to be toughened up, or any of that nonsense that he may or may not have said to Laura, in the heat of the moment and after the better part of a bottle of Newton unfiltered Merlot.

As the cab made its irritatingly slow way through the deserted Sussex countryside, Gabe tried to understand what it was that made him pick these stupid fights with Laura. He loved her. He'd always loved her, and needed her, now more than ever. But it was a love tinged with fear. The truth was, Laura was the only woman that Gabe Baxter had ever truly loved. Deep down he still couldn't quite believe that she'd chosen him. As a result, he lived his inner life on a constant state of alert, watching and waiting for Laura to leave him, to trade him in for someone more worthy. Now that she was pregnant with his child, the stakes had got even higher. Angry at himself for needing her so desperately, and determined not to show his weakness, he ended up drinking too much and lashing out, pushing away the very person that he was most terrified of losing.

It was a crappy pattern, one he knew he had to knock on the head before the baby was born. All the flirting with other women – it was all a front, but it hurt Laura sometimes and he knew it. If he were honest with himself, Gabe even enjoyed Logan Cranley's obvious adulation. He still thought of her as a kid in most ways, but there was no doubt that physically Logan was all woman. And a seriously sexy woman at that. Her desire for him made Gabe feel comforted on some level. Relaxed. It made him feel as if he had options.

Options for what? he asked himself angrily, as they crested the top of the Downs and the Swell Valley spread out below them beneath a blanket of stars. *You're a sad bastard, Gabe Baxter, and you need to get a fucking grip.* He was in danger of turning into Dylan Pritchard Jones at this rate, and that was a fate worse than death.

'Something's going on down there,' observed the taxi driver. 'Look at all those lights. And the smoke. Must be a big fire.'

The hairs on the back of Gabe's neck pricked up. He knew he was being irrational, but he needed to get to Laura, now. To hold her in his arms and tell her he was sorry. To make sure she was safe.

'Can you go a bit faster?' he asked.

Laura found Logan just a few feet back from the barn door. She could barely make out her features through the thick smoke, but she felt the panic as Logan gripped her forearm, her nails digging in so deeply they drew blood.

'It's all right,' said Laura. 'Let's get you out of here.'

'I can't move!' Logan sobbed. 'My leg. Something fell on my leg.'

Reaching down, Laura felt around in the darkness. Some sort of timber, perhaps a beam from the collapsing roof, covered Logan's left leg near the ankle. One pull told her instantly it was too heavy to lift. But perhaps they could roll it off?

'Lean towards me. I'm going to try to push it forwards. You try too, on the count of three.'

'I can't!' Logan was hysterical. 'I tried! It won't budge!'

'Yes it will,' said Laura, with a confidence she was far from feeling. *Where the fuck were those firemen?* The heat was so intense it was hard to speak. Above them, the roof seemed alive with flames. If they didn't get out of here soon, it would collapse.

'All your strength now.' She squeezed Logan's hand. 'One. Two. THREE!'

Without thinking she closed her eyes and focused every shred of energy and strength on the beam. At first nothing happened. But then very suddenly, like a well of oil erupting from the ground, the heavy wood rolled forwards, releasing Logan and coming to rest a few feet away, between the women and the door.

'Come on!' Laura pulled Logan, who let out a hideous cry of pain. Her lower left leg was clearly badly injured. There was no way she could stand.

'Crawl!' commanded Laura, who was too weak to pull her out alone. 'I can pull you under the shoulders but you have to help me.'

'I can't,' Logan wailed. She obviously meant it. She was

trying to move, her face contorted with pain, but nothing happened.

For the first time, Laura felt a creeping panic. The barn could collapse at any moment. They may only have seconds. Glancing behind her, the flames that she thought she had put out around the doorway seemed to have fought back somehow. She could still see the way out, but only barely. She knew she had to get out now, but she couldn't leave Logan.

'Try again,' said Laura. But all her earlier confidence and surety had gone. 'Please.'

And then it happened. Like a miracle, Laura felt powerful male arms around her. She was being pulled backwards, out through the heat and flames and smoke, out into air that felt cold and strange and wonderful. She closed her eyes. Somewhere along the way she lost her grip on Logan's hand. But when she opened her eyes outside, she saw Logan's haggard face lying next to her. She was aware of a deep, wonderful, almost orgasmic sense of relief.

Then she closed her eyes again, and all was white and peace.

By the time Gabe arrived, the yard was swarming with firemen. The main fire in the barn was already out. Only a shell was left; a black, charred skeleton of the building that had once been. The flames in the stables and outbuildings – what was left of them – were being brought under control. A small crowd of villagers huddled together in horrified silence, watching the crews at work.

'My wife!' Gabe pushed his way through the crowd like so many skittles. 'My wife was here. Is she OK?'

'You're the owner? This is your farm?' The foreman of the fire crew came over, removing his hat and wiping the sweat off his brow with his arm.

'WHERE'S MY WIFE?' Gabe was shrieking like a madman. He looked ready to punch the guy's lights out.

'Is your wife pregnant? The foreman asked.

Gabe nodded.

'She's been taken into hospital.'

Gabe's knees literally buckled under him. Lunging forward, the fireman grabbed him under the shoulders and heaved him back up to his feet.

'She's all right, sir. She's fine. They're treating her for smoke inhalation. When we got here she was trying to rescue the other young lady who was trapped in the hay barn. Your wife was phenomenally brave.'

'The other lady?'

The fireman gestured towards a white stretcher, where paramedics were bent over Logan Cranley. Evidently they were doing something to her leg before loading her up into a waiting ambulance. Logan herself was conscious but clearly drugged up to her eyeballs. When she saw Gabe, she gave him a morphine-laden smile, with tears streaming down her cheeks.

He ran over, his face a picture of concern. 'What the fuck happened?'

'I'm so sorry,' Logan sobbed. 'It was an accident.'

Bending low so as to hear her, Gabe instantly smelled the alcohol on her breath.

'Were you drunk?'

Logan nodded miserably.

'I'm sorry. It was just a small party. The others left. I . . . I must have passed out. When I woke up . . .'

Gabe put a finger to her lips. The gesture was slow, almost gentle. Logan exhaled, waiting for him to say something comforting. That it didn't matter. That all that mattered was that she was safe.

Instead he looked at her with those piercing blue eyes of his swimming with hatred.

'If anything's happened to Laura, or our baby, I will never forgive you. I will fucking destroy you. Do you understand? You stupid, selfish, useless bitch?'

Logan nodded. She opened her mouth to say something but Gabe had already gone.

CHAPTER EIGHTEEN

Tatiana Cranley looked at the gold Cartier watch on her wrist and frowned. Seven o'clock. The first guests would be arriving within a few minutes and there was still no sign of Jason.

Where the bloody hell is he?

Pacing the drawing room of their stunning Belgravia townhouse, immaculately decorated and styled by her husband (interior design bored Tati to tears, but Jason had a real flair for it), she tried not to feel irritated. She knew Jason was feeling low at the moment, and that he dreaded these sorts of social occasions. 'Not quite business, not quite pleasure,' he called them, and he was spot on. Tonight's soirée was a small affair, with only twelve guests, for drinks not dinner. It would, Tati fervently hoped, be over by nine. But all twelve of the guests were important, either current board members or potential new investors, carefully culti-vated contacts with the wherewithal to take Hamilton Hall schools to the next level. Tati talked a lot about 'the next level' and always had an eye to the future. But she was sensitive enough to see that poor, sweet Jason found the present more than taxing enough.

'Do I really have to be there tonight?' he'd asked Tatiana this morning over breakfast. 'I feel like Denis Thatcher at these things. I'm a total spare part.'

'That's not true,' Tati said kindly, reaching across the table and squeezing his hand. 'You're an important part of the business and the Hamilton Hall brand. More than that, you're important to *me.*'

Sometimes she found it exhausting, the daily battle to repair her husband's self-esteem, on top of everything else on her plate. Tati hadn't fully realized till she married Jason quite what a number Brett had pulled on his son. Not that compassion was Tati's only reason for wanting her husband there tonight.

Hamilton Hall was very much a family school, a family brand, that brought old-fashioned values to everything they did, not only their approach to academics. Jason and Tatiana Cranley were a young couple and happily married, at least as far as the outside world was concerned. This was good. But, they were a young couple with no children, a fact that had raised a number of eyebrows, not only Angela Cranley's.

For Tati, the no-kids thing was simple. The business took up all of her time. Even if it hadn't, Jason was still little more than a kid himself. They weren't ready and that was that.

But from a business perspective, being childless made it even more important that she and Jason should present a united front to everyone from parents to investors. Their marriage had to come across as rock solid.

The front doorbell rang.

'Damn it,' said Tati, smoothing down her vintage Alaïa skirt and scoop-necked cashmere sweater. The guests were here and bloody Jason wasn't. After all the effort she made with Jason's family. All those long lunches with Angela and stepping in as the 'fun' aunt with Logan whenever life with her parents at Furlings got too much. Not to mention being so understanding about Jase's depression, sorting him out with a new therapist and all that crap. The least Jason could do was show her a bit of support in return. Didn't he realize she was running herself ragged with this business? That it was the school he complained so much about that had paid for this house and the mocha velvet B & B Italia sofas he'd had imported specially from Milan, and the maids who ironed his shirts every morning and poured his favourite fresh-pressed orange juice at breakfast?

The butler showed the first visitors through to the drawing room.

'David! Ilaria.' Tati beamed, opening her arms wide to greet the hedge-fund founder and his Eurotrash wife.

'Jason not here?' David Morgenstein asked, immediately.

'Not yet.' Tati's smile didn't waver. 'I'm so glad you could both make it. Champagne?'

By the time Jason rolled in at eight thirty, drinks were almost over. 'Rolled' was the operative word. One look at his glazed eyes told Tati he was tight as a tic, and no amount of crunched-up Polos could fully disguise the gin on his breath.

'Sorry I'm late,' he mumbled, not daring to meet Tatiana's eye. 'I got caught up. At, er, my club.'

'Not to worry darling.' Tati slipped an arm lovingly around his waist. 'You missed a lovely party, though.'

Jason knew that this display of affection was purely for the guests' benefit. She would let him have it later, once everyone had gone, and rightly so.

He'd been supposed to have another therapy session this afternoon, but had bottled it. Then, wandering aimlessly

307

around Earls Court, he'd made the mistake of answering a phone call from his mother.

Angela was desperately worried about Logan. After last week's fire at Gabriel Baxter's farm, understandably the talk of Fittlescombe, she was lucky not to have been criminally prosecuted. If it hadn't been for Brett's friendship with Gabe, and Laura's abject pleading on Logan's behalf, Gabe would have shopped her in for sure. As it was, Brett had paid for all the damages out of his own pocket in a private deal with Gabe and Laura, to avoid insurance investigators, and Logan was officially off the hook. Behind the closed doors of Furlings, however, World War Three had broken out. Understandably furious, Brett had pulled Logan out of her expensive private school, grounded her, and spent hours of each day demanding to know what the hell his daughter had been thinking. Unfortunately Logan was too heartbroken about Gabe turning on her even to notice her father. Brett did not take well to not being noticed.

'He literally yells at Logie from morning till night,' Angela told Jason despairingly. 'He can't see how guilty she feels, how cut up about it all. And when I try to talk to him, of course he bites my head off.'

Too depleted himself to deal with other people's problems, Jason hung up after twenty minutes and ducked in to The Prince of Teck pub for a quick drink. As so often these days, he ended up staying for several. There was a filthy old upright piano in the bar. Jason, his inhibitions loosened and his emotions suitably numbed, sat down to play a few numbers. He was good, and the customers liked it. As a result, the landlord kept plying him with free drinks and, before Jason knew it, it was eight o'clock at night and he was in no fit state to make small talk with Tati's potential Hamilton Hall investors.

'*Lovely* to see you,' Tati was saying, escorting an elderly earl and his young consort to the front door, admiring the girl's mink as they said their goodbyes. Soon there was only one couple left, George and Madeleine Wilkes. Already parents at the school, Madeleine was a vastly wealthy sugar heiress and George a Mayfair gallery owner and renowned raconteur. Unlike tonight's other guests, the Wilkes's were actually friends. Even so, Tati was ready to call it a night, and she could see Madeleine Wilkes yawning in the drawing room and sneaking furtive glances at the grandfather clock.

'George is in the kitchen,' Tati hissed at Jason, pulling him to one side in the hallway. 'Make yourself useful for once and go and find him. Mads wants to leave.'

'OK,' Jason said sheepishly. 'I'm sorry I missed the party.'

'Are you?' snapped Tati. 'Somehow I doubt that.'

'Really. It wasn't deliberate. I lost track of time. I . . .'

'We'll discuss it later. Just pull George out of the drinks cabinet and send him on his way.'

George Wilkes was in his early fifties, a gentle, funny, softly spoken man with the sort of mellifluous Irish accent that made women want to sleep with him and men want to buy art from him. He was one of the very few Hamilton Hall 'contacts' whom Jason considered a friend. Despite their difference in ages, and despite the fact that George was a successful self-made man while Jason was more of a lost boy, George Wilkes never treated Jason Cranley like an appendage of his glamorous, successful wife. Instead he talked to him about art and music, and the limitless possibilities of the future.

'You're young, Jason,' George Wilkes would tell him. 'You don't have to have it all planned out yet. Relax. Try new things. Life is long.'

A conversation with George Wilkes almost always left Jason feeling happier and more optimistic. He'd often wondered how different life might have been if he'd had George for a father instead of Brett.

'Ah! Jason. The prodigal husband returns. In the doghouse, are you? Come to hide out in the kitchen with me?'

From his ruddy cheeks, dishevelled hair and slurred speech, it was clear that George was even drunker than he was. Jason gently prised the bottle of Laphroaig out of his hand.

'Actually, I've been sent to summon you.' He gave a rueful smile. 'The girls are tired. Mads wants to go home and Tatiana wants to begin the long process of slicing off my scrotum with a rusty penknife.'

'Ouch.' George winced. Helping himself to a slice of chocolate cake from the leftovers on the kitchen island, he sank down into an armchair with the air of a man who had no intention of going anywhere. 'So come on then. What's your excuse this time? Where were you?'

Jason told him the story, such as it was.

'I should have been here. For Tati. I promised,' he finished, contritely.

'Sure, well, it's important to keep promises,' George agreed. 'But you had to talk to your mother.'

'That's not why I was late,' smiled Jason.

'No, well, you were late because you were at the piano, weren't you? You're a musician, boy! An artist. Tatiana knew that when she married you. Artists get carried away sometimes.'

The way George put it made Jason feel wonderful. Not like he'd got drunk in a pub and ended up banging out a few tunes on an old upright. But as if he were part of an elite group. As if he were 'other'. Special. Tatiana did her best to support him, but she never made him feel like that. Not the way George did.

Just thinking about Tatiana now brought Jason down to earth with a bang.

'Yes, well. It was hardly the Royal Albert Hall,' he mumbled.

George Wilkes looked at him, his head cocked curiously to one side. 'You see, why do you do that? Put yourself down all the time?'

Jason laughed nervously.

'It doesn't matter if it's the Albert Hall or the room over your mum and dad's garage,' said George. 'It's *what* you're doing that matters, not where you're doing it. And *what* you were doing was making music. Music that people enjoyed. You've got so much going for you, Jason. Open your eyes, boy.'

Jason looked into the older man's kind, understanding face with a gratitude that bordered on love. Perhaps he was drunker than he realized? Or George was. Or both. Just then, Madeleine Wilkes appeared in the kitchen doorway.

'Do get a move on, George,' she said briskly, like a mistress calling an errant dog back to heel. 'I'm knackered and I want to go to bed. And poor Tatiana's dead on her feet.'

Eventually, after some cake-related negotiation, George was dragged out of his chair and led to the front door.

'Thank you for everything, angel,' he said to Tatiana, kissing her on the cheek. In a whisper he added. 'Go easy on the boy, eh? I don't think he meant it.'

At last they were gone. Tatiana wearily closed the front door behind them.

'Well,' she said sourly to Jason. 'Thanks for nothing.'

Buoyed by George Wilkes's kindness earlier, Jason took the rare step of defending himself.

'Look, I've said I'm sorry and I am. But I was on the piano, and everyone in the pub loved it.'

'The pub?' Tati's voice was rising. 'You missed an important investor evening for our business because you were spending the afternoon in the *pub*?'

'Important to whom?' muttered Jason under his breath, instantly regretting it when he saw the white-lipped fury on Tatiana's face.

'Oh, I see. It's like that, is it?' she fumed.

'No. Sorry. I didn't mean . . .'

'Do you know what time I got up this morning?' Tati ranted on. 'Five fucking o'clock. The same as I do every morning. I had a thousand fucking emails to deal with, then a full day in the office at school, then a site meeting in Clapham. I didn't even eat lunch! Then back here to change and schmooze these people, *our* partners, who, by the way, we really, really need to keep sweet, especially now we're expanding. And you can't even be arsed to cut short your afternoon in the pub to help me.'

'I said I'm sorry,' Jason floundered.

'Yeah. You say that a lot,' Tati said bitterly. It wasn't like her to let loose like this on Jason. But for whatever reason, tonight was the straw that had broken the camel's back.

'I'm tired, Jase,' she said, with feeling. 'I'm bone tired, all the time, and I'm tired of being tired, and of doing it all on my own.'

'Then stop working all the time!' Jason blurted. He was surprised to hear the words come out of his mouth, and even more surprised by the angry tone they came out in. 'You know the irony is, you only started Hamilton Hall to try to prove something to my father.'

Tati groaned. 'Not this again.'

'Yes, this again. You wanted to show Brett that you could make money and be a success and beat him at his own game. In business, if not in the courtroom.'

'That's not true,' said Tati, although they both knew it was.

'But instead you've turned into his clone,' Jason pressed on, ignoring her. 'You haven't beaten him. You've become him. You and my dad are two peas in a self-centred, work-aholic pod.'

Tati drew back her hand and slapped Jason hard across the cheek. His skin was so pale, the livid red hand-print began to form immediately in an ugly tattoo of rage. For a few seconds the two of them stood in the hallway in stunned silence, staring at one another.

Then Tati gasped.

'Oh my God. I'm sorry. I'm so sorry.'

'Me too,' said Jason. Moving forward, he hugged her tightly.

'Yes, but . . . I hit you,' Tati said in disbelief.

'I shouldn't have provoked you,' Jason comforted her and himself. He didn't know what he would do if he didn't have Tati. Despite all their issues – his issues, really – he loved her so much. 'I didn't mean those things.'

It was an awful moment, but it was real, and brutal, and in a strange way it was the closest they had been to each other in a long, long time. Unfortunately, the intimacy wasn't to last.

The front door shot open, almost knocking Tati flying.

'What the hell . . .?'

A heavy leather suitcase came hurtling through the door, landing with a thud on the marble floor. It was followed moments later by its owner, wearing a ripped denim mini-skirt, Doc Marten boots and a T-shirt cheerfully emblazoned with the message 'Kiss My Ass'. She was carrying a hospital-issued crutch, but she showed no signs of actually needing it.

Logan looked at Jason, her big, baleful eyes red and swollen from crying.

'Can you pay my taxi?' she sniffed. 'It's fifty-something pounds and I've only got, like . . . four.'

'Fifty pounds?' said Tati, shooting Jason a *what's she doing here?* look. 'Where have you come from, the moon?'

'Sort of.' Logan wiped away a tear. 'Lewisham. A horrible train man threw me off for not having a ticket. Can you believe it? He wouldn't even let me stay on till Victoria and pay at the end.'

Tatiana dashed outside to pay the cabbie while Jason took Logan into the kitchen and put the kettle on. 'What are you doing here, Logie?' he asked her, not unkindly. 'Have you had another fight with Dad?'

'It's more than a fight.' She shook her head and the tears started to flow in earnest. 'He hates me and I don't blame him. I hate myself.'

'Dad doesn't hate you,' said Jason, laying a comforting hand on his sister's heaving shoulders. 'He's angry, that's all. It'll pass.'

'It doesn't matter,' sobbed Logan. 'I've left home and I'm not going back. I can't stay in Fittlescombe anymore, Jase. Not after what I've done. Everyone in the village knows. It's awful! Poor Laura.' Her face twisted into the very image of misery as she told him about the fire. 'Her baby could have died because of me.'

'Yes, but it didn't,' said Jason, stroking her hair. 'Nobody died. You made a mistake. A bad one. But running away doesn't solve anything.'

'*You* did,' said Logan. 'You ran away.'

'That was different,' said Jason, frowning.

'Who's running away?' Tati appeared in the kitchen doorway. She was extremely fond of Logan, and of course knew everything about the fire. A small, childish part of her was glad that Gabriel Baxter had been made to suffer. He'd done everything he could to keep her from getting Furlings back all those years ago, when she'd tried to challenge her father's will. To this day she was sure Gabe had bought those lower fields from Brett purely to spite her. Tatiana Flint-Hamilton never forgot a slight. However, even she could see that what Logan had done: getting drunk and passing out, leaving a lighted joint burning in a barn full of dry hay, was reckless and unforgivable. By all accounts Laura Baxter had saved her life, risking her own and her unborn child's in the process.

'I am,' said Logan. 'I've left home and I'm moving in with you.'

Jason and Tati exchanged alarmed glances. Jason spoke first.

'Logan sweetie, you can't live here.'

'Why not? I won't be any trouble.'

Tatiana couldn't help but grin. That was like a sex addict turning up at a nunnery and promising the mother superior that they 'wouldn't be any trouble.' Logan Cranley was nothing *but* trouble. She couldn't seem to help it. It was part of her genetic make-up, just as it had been part of Tati's at sixteen.

'You can stay for the time being,' said Tati, earning herself a look of frank incredulity from Jason.

'Really?' Logan's eyes lit up. Getting up from the table, she threw herself into Tatiana's arms like a grateful puppy.

'We'll see how it goes.' Tati looked at Jason and smiled.

She's trying to make it up to me, he thought, smiling back.

Although somewhere in his chest the anxiety was already starting to gnaw away at him, like a dog with a bone. Logan living under their roof could only mean one thing: more drama.

As if they didn't have enough already.

CHAPTER NINETEEN

Tatiana Cranley sat back in the red leather armchair and flicked through the property particulars for a third time.

'Jasmine Farm, immaculate Grade II-listed retreat in the heart of the Swell Valley. £3.25 million.'

Too small, thought Tati, slipping the wisteria-clad, six-bedroomed farmhouse to the bottom of the pile. Completely secluded within its own land and almost eight miles from Fittlescombe, Jasmine Farm wasn't in the heart of anywhere. One of the many perfect things about Furlings was that it boasted both privacy and grandeur, whilst remaining part of the village. Isolated splendour was overrated, in Tati's opinion.

'Wesley House, lovingly refurbished former manse over-looking Fittlescombe village green.'

The Shenleys' old house? Far too small. This was going to the opposite extreme. *I'd be able to see Furlings from the bedroom windows. No thank you.*

She lingered a little longer over the third set of particulars. The picture showed a stunning, small stately home, its ancient stone walls half covered with ivy. The cover page read:

'Brockhurst Abbey. Idyllic country estate of medieval origins, complete with moat and maze. £5 million.'

That was more like it. A country house to be proud of. A statement house, historic, beautiful and on a suitably grand scale. Tatiana remembered Brockhurst Abbey from her childhood, back when elderly nuns still lived there. The estate was famous for its orchards, the apples from which produced a popular and very strong local cider called Abbey Dry, a rival to nearby Merrydown. Tati and her friends used to get horribly drunk on it in their early teens, before the more sophisticated pleasures of London beckoned. But as a small child, she remembered how the nuns used to terrify her. With hindsight she could see that they were perfectly sweet, harmless old women. But at the time, something about their grey habits and the silent, shuffling way they moved, crunching along the gravel paths, had caught Tatiana's childish imagination and given her the creeps. She had an irrational fear of becoming one of them, locked up forever in a lonely world of prayer, without conversation or life or company or *fun*. Even as a child, a life without fun had been the worst thing Tati could imagine.

How much fun am I having now? she wondered idly.

There were aspects of her grown-up, married life that she loved. Having money was good. Being successful and, in her own small way, famous, was gratifying. But happiness, true happiness, was as elusive for her now as it had ever been.

Sitting in the first-class Virgin Airways lounge at Heathrow, alone, waiting for her plane to New York, she tried to think about the positives. Despite Jason's late and drunken arrival at their recent drinks party, Hamilton Hall's board and investors were happy with her performance as CEO. That allowed her a lot of freedom, to develop the business as she saw fit – but there were still battles to be fought and won. Most of the board, and in particular Arabella Boscombe, still baulked at the idea of further overseas expansion, at least until the second London school was up and running at a profit. But Tatiana wanted to move now, while US interest rates were still low and the New York real-estate market had yet to fully recover from recession. She'd booked today's trip with her own, private money, and was excited at the prospect of scouting out possible locations for a Hamilton Hall NYC. It was a first step forward towards realizing a long-held dream. So was buying a country house back in the Swell Valley with Jason. Yet for some reason, Tati seemed incapable of feeling happy about any of it.

I don't want to live at Brockhurst Abbey, she thought moodily, flipping through page after page of glossy photographs showing stunning wood-panelled rooms and formal gardens. *I want to live at Furlings*. It didn't matter how much money she accumulated. Tati knew that it would be a cold day in hell before Brett sold that house, to anyone. As for selling it to her, she doubted her father-in-law would make that trade for a billion dollars. *That* was true power. What Brett Cranley had: control over something that other people wanted and that you would never, ever give up.

When she'd first married Jason, Tati had harboured vague, unformed hopes of somehow, in time, being accepted into the Cranley family. Perhaps she would have Jason's child, and perhaps that child would one day inherit Furlings? Then Tati could live out her old age there at least. But if anything her marriage to Jason had pushed her childhood home even further out of her reach. It had enraged Brett, as Tati knew it would. Hamilton Hall's success had only compounded that rage, which was gratifying in a way – irritating Brett Cranley had become one of the more constant pleasures in Tatiana's life – but it also meant that her banishment from Furlings was total and permanent. Proving Brett wrong by becoming a wealthy businesswoman in her own right was a victory, but a small one. In Tati's mind it was overshadowed utterly by Brett's triumph over her in the battle for Furlings.

According to Jason, unsurprisingly, Brett had gone ballistic about Logan's defection to Eaton Gate, accusing Jason and Tati of enticing her to come and live with them.

'That woman will stop at nothing to break up this family!' he'd raged at Angela. 'First Jason. Now Logie. And yet you still insist on treating her like one of us. It makes me sick.'

It pleased Tati to think of Brett Cranley feeling powerless, although she regretted the knock-on effect it must be having on Angela. On the other hand, she couldn't help but feel that Angela Cranley should stick up for herself a bit more. The more Tati got to know her mother-in-law, the clearer it became where Jason had got his passive nature from. Brett bullied them both because they let him.

'Flight VS 26 to New York is ready for boarding.'

The announcer's voice broke Tati's reverie. Putting aside her untouched gin and tonic, she stuffed the particulars back into her new Smythson briefcase and pulled out her boarding card and passport.

I'll feel better when I get there, she told herself. A change of scene, and some time out from the tension at home with Jason, would do her good. Ironically, Logan's impromptu invasion of Eaton Gate had made things easier between them at home. Her intense teenage emotions – she really did feel terrible about what had happened at Wraggsbottom Farm, and spent hours pouring her heart out to Tati about Gabe, Laura, Seb Harwich and all the people she'd let down – had put Tati and Jason's own emotions into perspective. Or at least thrown them into a more rational, adult relief.

Even so, the idea of some space and distance was appealing. And Tati had always adored Manhattan.

'Don't you just adore Manhattan? The life. The pulse. The energy. Where else can you find that, man?'

Brett Cranley smiled indulgently at Wilson Rainey. Rainey, a J. P. Morgan private banker from an old Boston family, had worked closely with Cranley Estates for the last five or six years and had become a personal friend. Not that the blue-blooded Wilson, with his impeccable manners and buttoned-down shirts and library full of first edition Mark Twains had much in common with a ruthless, ambitious street fighter like Brett, who never read anything other than the *FT* and *Wall Street Journal*. But sitting on the back seat of the limousine together now, on their way back to Brett's hotel after a successful meeting, Brett marvelled again at Wilson's positivity. The man was literally never unhappy. Never moody, or tired, or dissatisfied with his lot. Wilson Rainey had lived in New York for the last twenty years, yet he still spoke about the city with all the awe and wonder and adoration of a young man talking about a new and exciting lover. It was contagious.

'It's not Manhattan, Wilson. It's you,' said Brett. 'I don't know how you do it.'

He looked out of the window at the frazzled commuters, heading home after a long day toiling away on Wall Street. It was six o'clock, still relatively early, and the air outside was unpleasantly hot and muggy, like soup. This wave of workers were either secretaries and support staff, or traders and salespeople, all of whom would have been at their desks since five this morning and who got to clock off when the markets closed. The M&A guys started later and would work till midnight or beyond. 'The meeting went well though, didn't it?'

'The meeting went awesome.' *Awesome* was a word that Wilson Rainey used a lot. He might read like a professor and sit on the boards of God knows how many museums and art galleries and cultural institutions, but when Wilson got enthusiastic about something, his vocabulary was pure high-school jock. 'You totally owned them, man. They loved you. They wanna do it, for sure.'

'They didn't say that,' Brett cautioned.

Wilson was having none of it. 'Didn't have to, man. You could see it in their eyes. I'm telling you, it was a slam-dunk. You ruled.'

By the time they reached the Trump International Hotel, where Brett was booked into one of the Executive Park View suites, Brett got out of the car feeling uplifted and confident once again. He had two more days in New York, but today's meeting had been the most important, and Wilson was right: it *had* gone well.

Walking into his palatial suite, he kicked off his shoes, dropped his briefcase on the floor and loosened his tie. The floor-to-ceiling windows offered spectacular views of the city and the furniture, all velvet and leather in various shades of cream, coffee and chocolate, was masculine and luxuriously impersonal, exactly to Brett's taste. Flipping the television on to CNN, more out of force of habit than for any desire to catch up on the day's news, he flopped back on the bed, opened his laptop and began skimming through emails.

His mind kept wandering back to Furlings, and to Angela, rattling around the house on her own, or with only Mrs Worsley and the useless Gringo for company. Things were worse than usual between them at the moment. Ange clearly blamed him for 'driving Logan away', as she put it. It drove Brett wild with frustration, as if he were living with a

Martian. Their daughter had just *burned down the neighbours' property*, for God's sake! If that didn't entitle him to be angry, to punish her and shout at her and demand explanations, what did? Angela seemed to expect him to tread on eggshells, tiptoeing around Logan's feelings. As if Logan were the victim here! Good grief.

They'd had the same battle over Jason years ago, with Brett constantly being painted as bad cop. If he'd moped around the way his children did, he'd have been given a good hiding and told to pull himself together, and quite right too. Angela was far too soft on them and she called that 'love'. But it did them no favours in the end. Brett loved his children every bit as much as she did. He loved them fiercely. But somehow he'd lost both of them, and now Angie was slipping away from him again too.

Brett wasn't an introspective person. He'd learned long ago, as a child, to contain his emotions and repress them, brutally if necessary. He always looked forward, never back. But at times of severe stress, his subconscious didn't always co-operate. For the last few nights he'd been plagued by unsettling, vivid dreams. Some were about his mother. The events were confused, but they always ended with his mother walking away from him, slowly and calmly, and with Brett calling out for her to return, shouting louder and louder, unable to make her hear him. He would wake from these dreams feeling quite desolate.

Others were about Tatiana. Those were similar and equally painful. Not erotic, which would have been something at least. Instead they mirrored the mother dreams. He needed to tell Tati something, but couldn't make himself heard. These he would wake from with clenched fists, and a jaw that ached from a night spent grinding his teeth.

Bizarrely, Angela didn't feature in his nightly torments at

all. It was almost as if she were disappearing, slipping away from him on every level. Becoming a shadow in his life.

With an effort he brought his attention back to the screen in front of him.

He would work for an hour, then go down for a drink.

Get a grip, Brett.

At seven o'clock the lobby was starting to get busy. The gold and marble atrium buzzed with people, most of them in suits, heading either to the triple Michelin-starred Jean-Georges restaurant or the bar at Nougatine. It was resolutely a business, rather than a fashion crowd, which put Brett at his ease and was one of the reasons he had chosen this hotel over its many trendier, West-Village rivals. Brett liked the *clack, clack* of expensive stilettos on marble, and the way the sound echoed upwards, ricocheting off the high ceilings. He liked the ringing of mobile phones, too important to be switched off for something as trivial as dinner, and the constant, efficient tapping of the keyboards behind the concierge desks. It was a symphony of distraction, a scene dipped in wealth and privilege and comfort, like a strawberry dipped in warm chocolate.

Taking a seat at the bar, Brett ordered a Scotch on the rocks, which arrived immediately in a beautiful cut-crystal glass. The viscose amber liquid tasted as smooth as it looked. Brett already felt a little better. A couple of beautiful young women in skintight jeans and mink jackets sat together at a table in the corner, eyeing him in an overtly predatory manner. He felt better still, ordering a second Scotch, but deciding against sending a bottle of champagne to the girls' table. They were clearly semi-pros, working models who supplemented their earnings with 'gifts' from rich men such as himself, but (oddly in Brett's view) did not consider themselves hookers. New York was full of such women, and London was catching up fast. Not that Brett was averse to the occasional hooker. But he didn't have the energy tonight, physically or emotionally.

Turning away from them, back towards the lobby, he'd just shovelled a handful of warm cashews into his mouth when he saw her. Tatiana Flint-Hamilton, as he would always think of her. But, to the world now, Tatiana Cranley, his daughter-in-law. *Jason's wife*. The words still stuck in his throat, like poison.

What the fuck is she doing here?

In jeans, flat ballet pumps and a loosely cut beige cashmere sweater, Tati looked far more casual than any other woman in the hotel and infinitely more desirable. Her hair was piled up in a messy topknot, with strands escaping everywhere, and she wore dark glasses to hide what Brett assumed were tired eyes. She had clearly come straight from the airport. A porter was busy taking her luggage while she checked in at the desk. Despite her slouchy clothes and half-hidden face, she still managed to radiate sex appeal, like a tigress casually sauntering into a room full of sheep.

Brett tightened his grip on his glass.

He hated her.

'Cheque please,' he said to the barman, spinning back around on his stool suddenly as if he'd been stung.

'Certainly, sir. Is everything all right?'

'Everything's fine. I just want my bill.'

The bar was no longer an anonymous sanctuary. Slipping his black titanium Amex card across the polished rosewood, he signed the cheque and left a hefty tip. He would go upstairs, pack and check out before Tatiana saw him. The last person on earth Brett wanted to run into in his current, unsettled state of mind was Tatiana. Tatiana who had toyed with him and used him and weaselled her money-grabbing way into his family, to the point where she now had *both* of his children living under her roof. Even in his goddamned dreams she tormented him.

But he was too late. Walking towards the bank of elevators with a bus boy in tow, weighed down with her Louis Vuitton luggage, Tatiana saw him. Her upper lip instantly curled with distaste.

'My, my,' she drawled. 'Look what the cat dragged in. And I thought this was an exclusive establishment.'

'It was until you got here,' Brett shot back, deadpan.

The lift arrived. Tatiana stepped inside. Brett followed.

'Going up, sir?' the bus boy asked Brett.

'Yes. Fourteenth floor.'

The doors closed on the three of them and the elevator swooped upwards with stomach-splitting speed. It was a large lift, but Tatiana's mountain of luggage meant that she and Brett were squashed at the back like two sardines, while the bus boy was practically flattened against the doors. Tati could feel Brett's body next to hers, bristling with tension and resentment, like a coiled cobra ready to pounce. She hadn't seen him in the flesh in a long, long time. Years. But he hadn't changed. Nor had the unsettling effect he always had on her.

'Does Jason know you're here?' he asked gruffly.

'Of course. I don't have secrets from my husband,' Tati said virtuously.

Brett guffawed. 'Of course not. Only from your board members. Right?'

Tati's eyes narrowed suspiciously. What did Brett Cranley know about her relationship with her board?

'You're here to look at sites for a new school, I assume?' he elaborated. 'They won't like that.'

'If I were you, I'd make it a belated New Year's resolution to give up assuming,' Tati said waspishly. 'You're not very good at it. You assumed Jason would spend the rest of his life as your punch-bag. That didn't work out too well, did it?'

The bus boy shifted uncomfortably from foot to foot. This was starting to get ugly.

'He escaped, he's with me, and he's *very* happy,' Tatiana went on. 'So's Logan by the way. In case you were wondering. All she needed was someone to listen to her for a change. But listening isn't your strong suit either, is it Brett?'

Brett tried hard not to show how hurt he was. He missed his daughter, and his son for that matter. Underneath the bravado he was all too well aware of his failings as a father. But he couldn't let Tatiana see that. 'Save the Mother Theresa spiel for someone who doesn't already know you,' he said gruffly. 'You used my son for his money. Jason may not know it, but I do, and so does the rest of the world. He'll see through you eventually. Logan too.'

'There you go again. Assuming. You *assumed* it meant something to me when we slept together, didn't you?' Tati goaded him, laughing cruelly. 'You couldn't believe that the great Brett Cranley was just another insignificant one-night stand. But that's all you ever were. Unlike Jason.'

'That's a lie!' Brett flung out his arms in frustration. Mistaking the gesture, thinking that he might be about to hit her, Tati's hand shot out, grabbing him by the wrist.

'Don't you dare,' she hissed.

'Dare what?' said Brett. 'You think I'd hit a woman?'

'I don't know what you're capable of,' said Tati. 'Just remember, I'm not a passive little woman like your wife. I'm your fucking equal, Brett.'

'Fourteenth floor!' the bus boy's voice rang out loudly, a note of panic clearly audible. 'This is your stop, sir.'

Shaking his arm free, easily breaking Tatiana's grip, Brett straightened his jacket and walked out. He had to fight the urge to run. Ridiculously, he felt tears stinging his eyes. Being around Tatiana felt like sticking his hand into a naked flame.

Did he really mean nothing to her?

No. He didn't believe that. Couldn't believe it. Although the mere idea that it might be true, that Jason might be the one she *really* wanted, burned like acid on his skin. Even now, after all these years, Tatiana had the power to get to him the way no other woman ever had.

But she wasn't his. She would never be his.

Tati was Jason's wife now. Whatever her true feelings, Tatiana belonged to his son.

In the past, Angela had always been able to heal the wounds Brett suffered from other women, or from knock-backs in business. If Tatiana was fire, Angie was water, the cooling comfort of lapping waves, washing away Brett's pain. Brett could bring Angela his failures, his rejections, like a cat dropping a mouse at his mistress's feet; and she would make them insignificant with her love. With her patience and forgiveness. With her kindness that seemed to have no bottom, no limits.

But perhaps that was part of the problem, Brett realized now. He needed limits.

What had Tatiana said to him just now? *I'm not your wife. I'm your equal.*

The words played over and over in his head as he made the lonely walk back to his room.

CHAPTER TWENTY

On her hands and knees in Furlings' garden, weeding one of the kitchen garden beds, Angela Cranley watched a bumblebee going about its business. There was something intrinsically comic, but at the same time sad, about the way that this fat, round, awkward ball of a creature flew from flower to flower. As if it were drunk, or blind, or both. Everything it did seemed haphazard and clumsy, as if its very design were one of nature's private jokes: the gluing of gossamer-thin, fairy wings onto a graceless, sumo wrestler's body.

It's like me, she thought. *Blundering through life looking ridiculous, doing the only thing it knows how.*

She and Brett were both trying. A few days ago, Brett had brought her flowers, unsolicited. Later that same evening, he'd suggested they play cards, something they used to do a lot when they were first married but had given up once the children were born. Aware that Brett was making a huge effort, Angie tried to respond in kind, cooking him his favourite meals – beef Wellington and French onion soup – and agreeing to do things together as a couple, from walking down to the village shop to watching television programmes together in the evening. Simple things, obvious things. Things they hadn't done for one another in many, many years.

Perhaps, Angie thought now, her eyes following the bee as it buzzed noisily away towards the hollyhocks, *perhaps that's the problem? Perhaps we feel so stiff and awkward and stilted because we're out of practice?*

Because it *was* awkward. Painfully so at times. All the 'pleases' and 'thank yous' and 'would you mind awfullys?' were choking her, choking them both. Intimacy, it seemed, could not be switched back on like a light after such a long time. Even if both parties really, really wanted it.

As for sex, Angie was seriously starting to wonder if there might be something physically wrong with her. She couldn't seem to bring herself to let Brett near her. It was almost like an allergy. Whenever Brett touched her, she froze. Her entire body stiffened from toes to neck, like a corpse going into rigor mortis. Brett had been unusually patient and kind about it, but she knew it hurt his feelings and made him anxious. This in turn made him try even harder with the romantic gestures, and so the dance of forced affection and excruciating awkwardness went on.

The one subject they had been able to discuss more normally was Logan – a good thing, as term time was looming. Brett had yanked her out of St Xavier's, but she still had nowhere to go in September. Brett still wanted her back home. 'She can damn well go to the local comp and like it.'

But for once, he listened to Angela when she told him this was impractical.

'I wouldn't mind her going to a state school. Brockhurst Comprehensive is actually fine academically. It's her living back here that's the problem. She won't do it.'

'She'll do what she's bloody well told,' said Brett.

'It's all very well saying that,' Angie sighed. 'But the fact is, she won't. She went to Jason and Tatiana's because she was miserable here after the fire. She can't face Gabe and Laura, or Seb, or all the whispering in the village. She's mortified.'

'As she bloody should be.'

'I agree,' said Angela patiently. 'But if we drag her back, she'll only do another runner.'

'Maybe,' Brett admitted grudgingly. 'But I don't like her under that woman's roof. I don't like it one bit.'

As ever when Tatiana was mentioned in a conversation, however tangentially, Brett's temperature started rising. Only by using every ounce of her tact and diplomacy had Angie been able to persuade Brett to allow Logan to stay on at Eaton Gate for now. By shamelessly dropping the Hamilton Hall name, Jason had managed to secure Logan a place at MPW, the famous sixth-form college on Queensgate. It wasn't a perfect scenario. Privately Angela shared some of Brett's fears about Logan living with Tati and Jason. What if they let her run wild? If the fire had proven anything, it was that Logan needed boundaries. Jason was depressed, and Tati was always working, which made them far from ideal as parental substitutes to a troubled teenage girl. Plus, if her own teenage years were anything to go by, Tatiana was hardly the best role model for Logan.

Still, beggars couldn't be choosers. Jason was convinced Logie had learned her lesson after the accident at Wraggsbottom and turned over a new leaf. And maybe some time alone together at Furlings would help her and Brett to resolve the problems in their marriage?

At five o'clock, tired of gardening and with a sore lower back from so much bending down – *I'm getting old* – Angela decided to take Gringo for a walk. Grabbing the lead from a hook in the kitchen, she waited for the elderly, arthritic basset to waddle over to her, tail wagging excitedly.

'You're even older than I am, boy.' She ruffled his floppy ears affectionately. 'Don't worry. We won't make it a long one.'

It was a pretty afternoon. The air was still warm and the light had faded from its harsh noon brightness to a mellow, honey-coloured glow. Walking down the driveway from Furlings towards the village, Angie could smell wood smoke from the cottage fireplaces. Rooks cawed overhead, and a sweet scent, either honeysuckle or jasmine, wafted over from the hedgerows, mingling with the smell of freshly mown grass from the village green in a heady cocktail. Closing her eyes and breathing in deeply, Angie felt suffused with peace, and gratitude. Whatever mistakes she'd made in her life, whatever heartbreaks she might face, this place remained beautiful and unchanging.

She took a left turn at the start of the High Street, up Foxhole Lane, towards Wraggsbottom Farm. A number of long walks started here, with footpaths snaking up into the Downs, some going almost as far as the coast, although Gringo was too decrepit for such far-flung adventures these days. Taking one of the gentler paths through the woods, towards Brockhurst, Angela soon became lost in a daydream about Australia and her childhood friends. It was only after about twenty minutes that she looked down and realized that Gringo was no longer trotting faithfully at her heels.

Irritated, with herself more than the barmy old basset, she began calling his name, whistling and clapping loudly. The dog was so deaf, he wouldn't hear her unless she made a serious racket, and even then the odds weren't good if he'd gone too far.

Ten minutes passed. Then twenty. Then an hour. Angela crisscrossed all the paths in the vicinity and had gone twice up to the main road. She'd passed a number of fellow walkers in that time, but none of them had seen Gringo.

It was cooler now, but Angela dripped with sweat, a combination of exertion and anxiety. As much as she moaned about him, she'd never forgive herself if anything happened to that dog. In desperation she was about to head home – perhaps he'd somehow made his way back there, and if not she could call around locally and put the word out that he was missing – when a piercing scream stopped her in his tracks.

'No! STOP IT! I said get *off*!'

She recognized the voice as belonging to Penny de la Cruz. Come to think of it, she must be near Woodside Hall, Penny and Santiago's idyllic house nestled deep in the Brockhurst woods.

'Penny!' she shouted out, hurrying down the track. 'Are you all right?'

Moments later, she saw what the commotion was about. Penny, wearing a pair of men's pyjama bottoms, Ugg boots and a Greenpeace T-shirt covered in motor oil stains was standing in the garden at Woodside Hall waving a broom and shrieking at the top of her lungs. At first glance, she looked like a card-carrying lunatic. However, closer inspection revealed that the object, or rather objects, of her ire were Gringo, and Penny and Santiago's wire-haired dachshund bitch, Delilah. Gringo, God bless him, was enthusiastically humping Delilah, who seemed by no means displeased by his attentions.

Catching sight of Angela, Penny waved frantically. 'Can you get him off? If she has another litter of mongrels, Santiago'll hit the roof.'

Angela giggled. 'It seems rude to interrupt them. Poor Gringo.'

'Poor Gringo my arse,' said Penny, also laughing despite herself. 'Your bloody dog is the Jimmy Savile of Fittlescombe. He must be ninety years old! Delilah's only two.'

'And living up to her name already, the hussy,' said Angela. 'She enticed him.'

'Seriously, please help me!'

With both women in fits of giggles, and neither dog minded to cut short their happy union, a farcical few minutes of collar-tugging, barking and snarling ensued. Once they were finally separated and Delilah had been locked in the study while an exhausted Gringo collapsed contentedly in front of the Aga, Penny made herself and Angela a deserved pot of tea.

'Do you think we caught them in time?' Penny asked nervously, plonking a plate of Hobnobs down on the kitchen table on the one spot not covered with newspapers and half-finished works of art. 'I really will cry if Delilah's up the duff again.'

'I don't know,' said Angela. 'I can't imagine Gringo's sperm are up to much at this point. He is, as you say, ancient, though Brett and I like to think of him as more of a Bamber Gascoigne – "I've started, so I'll finish".'

Penny grinned. 'How is Brett?'

Angela's face visibly clouded over. 'He's OK. He's travelling a lot.'

'Do you miss him?' asked Penny.

'Sometimes,' said Angela cautiously. 'Not always. Things haven't been . . .' she left the sentence hanging, not sure herself quite what she wanted to say.

'It's not easy when you're apart a lot,' said Penny, understandingly. 'Santiago's gone for months at a time on cricket tours, or doing promotional stuff for sponsors. I long for him to come back, but as soon as he does we start getting on each other's nerves almost immediately. He calls it the "bumpy re-entry period". It doesn't mean you don't love each other.'

'No,' said Angela. 'I suppose not.'

She suspected that her twenty-plus-year union with Brett, complete with all the scars of his many betrayals, bore little resemblance to Penny's honeymoon-stage marriage with England cricket's most lusted-after hero. But it seemed ungracious to say so, so she didn't.

As if reading her mind Penny said: 'Listen, I was married to a complete shit before Santiago. It wasn't Paul being gay that I minded. It was him being a selfish, heartless, cheating liar. Not to mention a skinflint.'

'He sounds terrific.' Angela smiled over her mug of Earl Grey. 'A real winner.'

'Yes, well, he gave me two lovely children. Or one lovely child and Emma, depending on how you look at it.'

Angela gasped, 'You can't say that!'

'Oh yes I can,' said Penny. 'Believe me, Logan's little stunt at Wraggsbottom is nothing compared to some of the shit Emma's put us through. If I didn't have Sebby, I think I'd have wound up in a loony bin long before now.'

It was awful, but Angela felt better hearing someone else complaining about their children, especially someone as lovely as Penny.

'What about Santiago? Doesn't he support you?'

'He's lovely,' Penny sighed. 'But you know, I'm a realist. He's a lot younger than me. Girls throw themselves at him all the time. And he's away a lot.'

'You don't trust him?' Angela was surprised. She'd always thought that Penny and Santiago de la Cruz were the epitome of marital bliss.

'I do trust him,' said Penny after a pause. 'But I don't rely on him, if that makes any sense. At a certain age, and after you've been burned once, or more than once . . . I think you develop a certain self-sufficiency. Wouldn't you say?'

Angela nodded.

Later, walking home with an exhausted but visibly chipper Gringo, she thought again about what Penny had said. *Am I self-sufficient?* she wondered. *Or do I still rely on Brett? I might fantasize about it sometimes. But would I really survive without him?*

She realized she had no answer.

Back at Furlings, Brett sat at the desk in his study, a full tumbler of whisky in his hand. He was drinking too much. At some point he'd have to get a handle on that. But not today. Not now.

Angie wouldn't let him touch her. She jumped and shuddered whenever he came near, as if his fingers had turned into red-hot pokers. Downing his drink in three swift gulps, Brett poured himself a second, then a third, nursing his hurt feelings like a parent nursing a child. Outside it was growing dark, the gathering twilight reflecting the creeping blackness in Brett's heart. The oak trees lining Furlings' drive looked bleak and sinister in the shadows.

Brett turned back to his computer.

He wasn't sure what time it was when he heard the front door open and close again, indicating that Angela was back.

Brett walked downstairs to meet her, gripping tightly to the banister rail for support. He was fully drunk now, conscious of the adrenaline coursing through his veins and of Furlings' grand hallway spinning like a fairground ride around him.

'Where've you been?'

It was an accusation, his tone ugly and raw. Angela looked up. She could tell immediately that Brett had had too much to drink. His dishevelled hair, flushed cheeks and heavy-lidded, scowling expression all spoke volumes. Her heart sank. She hadn't seen this side of him in quite a while, and had dared to hope it might have been gone for good.

'Out for a walk,' she said briskly, letting Gringo off the lead. 'Gringo ran off. It took me forever to find him.'

'You've been gone for hours.'

'I just told you. The dog ran away. I found him having it off with Penny de la Cruz's bitch and we ended up having tea together.' She resented the fact that she was forced to explain herself. *So much for self-sufficiency.*

'Why are you lying to me?' Brett had reached the bottom of the stairs by now and stood swaying in front of her. He looked curiously vulnerable, like a young tree in the wind. 'You never used to lie to me, Ange.'

'I'm not lying to you,' she replied, with a calmness she didn't feel. 'Don't do this, Brett. It's degrading to both of us.'

'Don't do what?'

'You're drunk.'

'Are you having an affair?'

She almost laughed, but the furious look in Brett's eyes stopped her.

'Don't be ridiculous.'

'You are, aren't you? You're fucking cheating on me! That's why you won't let me touch you. Have you just been with him now?'

'Let go of me!' The anger in Angela's voice masked her fear. Brett was a big man, and though he'd never hurt her, there were many times when she'd felt intimidated by him.

'Let go of you? Why? So you can run to your lover? I don't think so.'

'I don't have a lover, Brett,' said Angela, thinking of Didier and how easy it would have been all those years ago for her to jump into his arms and into his bed. Perhaps she should have? But she didn't. Like a fool she'd put her dysfunctional wreck of a marriage first, as she always did. And for what? For this?

'I said let go!'

They were three-quarters of the way up the stairs now, but Angela was still resisting Brett, trying to wrestle free from his vice-like grip.

'How could you?' Brett demanded, ignoring her. 'How could you cheat on me?'

'I haven't cheated on you ever!' Angela shot back angrily 'But my God, why *shouldn't* I, Brett? You tell me that. After all your bloody affairs! Why shouldn't I cheat?'

'It was different with me,' mumbled Brett.

'How? How was it different?'

'Because I never loved them. If you had an affair it would be for love.'

'This is ridiculous,' Angela muttered.

'I never loved any of those women,' Brett went on.

'Well, they were lucky then, weren't they?' said Angela. 'Because you loved *me*. And I can tell you, Brett Cranley, that being loved by you is a crock of shit. Being loved by you *sucks*.'

With a sharp cry of effort, she finally wrenched herself free from his grip.

'I'm not cheating on you. I've never cheated on you. But I could have, once. And I *wish* I had. I *wish* I had, you selfish bloody hypocrite!' She screamed at him, all the pent-up emotion of the past few months spewing out of her like lava. 'Go to hell, Brett!'

'If I'm going to hell I'm taking you with me,' Brett yelled back. He lunged out, trying to catch hold of her wrist again. Angela leaned back to avoid him. As she did so, she slipped off the lip of the stair, losing her balance.

From that point on, it all happened in slow motion. Brett watched in horror as it dawned on both of them exactly what was happening. Angie began to windmill her arms frantically, trying to regain her footing, her fingers clutching vainly for the banister rail. Brett reached forward, trying to grab hold of her and stop her from falling, but it was too late. She tumbled backwards down the steep stairs, limbs flailing like a puppet whose strings have just been cut. A piercing scream was followed by a series of sickening thuds as her skull cracked down against the hard wood, *boom, boom, boom*. Brett closed his eyes. When he opened them, Angela was lying in a foetal position at the foot of the stairs, as still and lifeless as a ventriloquist's dummy.

No!

Brett clutched at the handrail, feeling his own knees start to give way.

Dear God, please no.

Stella Goye had been enjoying a typically relaxed evening at home with Max when the doorbell rang. Max and Mutley had returned from a long afternoon walk, and Stella had whipped up a chicken and chorizo risotto, which was rather a triumph – even if Stella did say so herself. She and Max had washed it down with a decent bottle of claret before retiring to the sofa to watch their DVD box set of *The Bridge*.

Stella's relationship with St Hilda's Primary School's headmaster was not what one would describe as passionate.

Both Stella and Max had been married before, Max very happily, Stella less so. But at this point in their lives, neither of them had much appetite for the whipsawing emotional rollercoaster of an intense, sexual love affair. What they had instead was warm and comfortable and easy. They cared for one another, were interested in one another, and they made each other's lives less lonely and infinitely more convivial. It was, by and large, enough for both of them, and more than they had expected to find at this point in their lives.

. Every once in a while, Stella would feel a pang that there was something missing – a momentary flash of mourning for the deep love connections of her youth. But tonight she felt nothing but happy with her lot. She loved Max and Fittlescombe and their beautiful cottage and their scruffy little dog and the studio at the bottom of the garden where she could make as much mess with clay as she liked. She loved Scandi Noir DVD box sets, and mugs full of M&Ms to be scoffed while she watched them, curled up in front of the fire.

The ringing doorbell was an intrusion. Definitely not in the script.

'It's half past ten at night.' Stella looked at Max accusingly. 'If that's one of your sodding PTA members moaning about school business, I warn you, I might be quite rude.'

'Not as rude as I'll be,' grumbled Max. A small group of this year's parents had been getting their knickers in a twist about everything from the most recent OFSTED report to the colour of the girls' changing room. Max had kept his temper so far, but there were limits. He opened his front door with his shoulders squared, ready for battle.

'Good God.' His face went white. Angela Cranley stood on his doorstep, an overnight bag at her feet. Her face was grotesquely bruised and her arm was in a makeshift sling.

'Can I come in?'

An hour later, having put Angela to bed in the guest room with a strong sleeping pill, Max and Stella finally collapsed into their own bed.

'What do you think?' asked Stella, staring at the beamed ceiling. 'Do you believe her?'

Max sighed. 'I don't know.'

Angela had told them tearfully that she and Brett had had a terrible row. He'd convinced himself she was having an affair and had gone off the deep end. But she insisted her injuries were accidental, the result of a fall down the stairs.

'I was lucky. It could have been much worse. The nurse at the cottage hospital said nothing's broken.'

Too drunk to drive, Brett had called a taxi to take Angela to A&E. According to her, he had wanted to come with her, but she'd refused. 'I needed some space, to think. So I packed a bag and, after they discharged me, I came here. I'm sorry, I just . . . I didn't know where else to go.'

She'd started sobbing then and shaking, poor woman. Evidently she was still in fairly serious shock.

'I think she's covering for him,' Stella muttered furiously. 'I've a good mind to call the police. Arsehole.'

'I couldn't agree more,' said Max. 'But it's not our place to get involved.'

'How is it not our place?' Stella's voice was rising, along with her feminist hackles. 'There's a battered woman in our spare room, for God's sake!'

Reaching across the bed, Max took Stella's hand and squeezed it.

'The police can't act unless she presses charges. You know that as well as I do.'

'Hmm,' Stella grumbled. He was right, of course. But the anger inside her refused to be quelled.

'We'll talk about it more in the morning.'

Max turned out the light.

'Why do you think she came here?' Stella's voice drifted sleepily through the darkness. 'I mean, we're hardly close friends.'

'No,' said Max.

'She must be very lonely, if we're the only people she could think of to turn to.'

Max paused.

'Yes.'

Stella drifted off to sleep. But Max Bingley stayed awake for a very long time.

The next morning, Angela didn't wake until almost ten. The sleeping pill had completely knocked her for six. Max had long since left for school by the time she came down to the kitchen, wincing with pain at every step.

'Gosh, here, let me help you.' Stella jumped up from the table and her half-finished *Times* crossword and helped Angela into the armchair next to the Aga. 'You poor thing. Can I get you some breakfast?'

'No, thank you. You've been kind enough,' said Angela.

In a loose-fitting white sundress and flip-flops, she looked even more tiny, bird-like and fragile than she had last night. Big, ugly purple bruises on her arms and legs matched the ones on her face.

'I don't think I could eat a thing anyway. I must call a cab.'

'There's no rush,' said Stella. 'You only just woke up. I'll put on some fresh coffee at least, and then you can see if you can manage a piece of toast.'

'Really,' Angela insisted. 'I have to get home. Brett and I need to talk.'

Stella stopped scooping coffee into the cafetière and looked at her pityingly. 'You should report him, you know. You can't let him get away with this.'

Angela sighed wearily. 'It was an accident.'

'You could have been killed!' said Stella. But it was clear that Angela wasn't going to change her mind. 'Fine. Well if you really want to go home, I'll drive you.'

'Really, there's no need,' Angie started to protest. But Stella was having none of it.

'I insist. I'll drive you to Furlings and I'll wait outside until I know you're safe.'

Too tired to argue, Angie nodded. 'OK. Thank you. I'm so sorry for dumping my problems on you and Max like this. I should have gone to a hotel. I don't think I was thinking clearly.'

'Yes, well. Most people aren't when their husbands have just tried to kill them,' Stella said archly. 'Anyway, you're very welcome. Max is terribly fond of you, you know.'

Angie tried to smile, but the effort was too painful.

'He's a lovely man,' she said.

'He is,' agreed Stella. 'Now where did I put those car keys?'

It took Brett almost half an hour to get the bloody, hippy Goye woman to leave. She insisted on walking Angela to the door, glaring at him all the while as if he were some sort of axe-murderer, and made an elaborate point of reminding Angela that she was just a phone call away and would 'check in' on her in any case over the next few days, 'just to make sure you're safe.'

343

But any irritation he felt towards Max Bingley's girlfriend was instantly overwhelmed by the mixture of guilt and anguish that engulfed him when he looked at Angie's face. Last night he'd been so happy she was alive and, OK, he'd barely noticed the bruises. Of course, he'd also been drunk as a skunk, which probably hadn't helped his powers of observation. And it was dark. But today the full scale of Angie's injuries hit home, each cut and bruise and swelling cruelly illuminated by the daylight.

'Jesus Christ, Ange.' He choked up. 'I'm so sorry.'

She could see that he meant it. 'I'll live.'

She took his arm and they went inside. Brett made some sweet tea and brought it to her in the drawing room.

'I never meant to hurt you,' he said softly, his head in his hands. Quite apart from the guilt, his hangover was brutal. He felt as if his cranium might explode at any minute. 'I'm sorry.'

'I'm not having an affair,' Angela said wearily. 'I almost did, once. But I decided not to.'

Brett winced as if a wasp had just stung him in the eye. 'When? Who with?'

'A long time ago. In France. Does it matter?'

'Not really,' Brett agreed. 'But I'm curious.'

'His name was Didier Lemprière. He was a lawyer. We had him to dinner on the yacht in St Tropez, the night before I walked in on you and Tricia.'

Brett groaned. He didn't want to be reminded of that trip.

'I'm sorry,' he said, awkwardly.

'Me too.'

They sat in silence for a while. Then Brett asked. 'So why didn't you have an affair with this guy? After all I put you through. Like you said to me last night, you'd have had every right.'

'I'm not sure one ever has a "right" to an affair, exactly.'

Angela's mind flashed back to the day in Alfriston, when she'd run into Max Bingley at the pub where she and Didier were having lunch. She'd often wondered what might have happened had Max not been there that day. Would she have taken the next step with Didier? Had Max's presence somehow shamed her into doing the 'right' thing? Into resisting temptation? Probably. She remembered strongly the feeling of not wanting to disappoint Max Bingley. Of not having Max think less of her.

'Anyway, a friend talked me out of it in the end,' she told Brett.

Silence descended once again.

'So what happens now?' Brett asked eventually.

Angela looked him in the eye. 'I think we need some time apart.'

'A separation?' Brett sounded stricken.

'It doesn't have to be formal. But we need to think,' said Angela. 'Both of us. We can't go on like this, Brett. I mean, look at us!'

They both turned to their reflection in the huge gilt-framed mirror that dominated the west wall of the room. Angie looked as if she'd done ten rounds with a champion boxer. As for Brett, unshaven, green-skinned and with bloodshot eyes, he looked more like a down-and-out than a property mogul.

'OK,' said Brett, defeated. 'I'll move out. I'll go to the flat in London for now. I've got a lot of business coming up in New York too, so maybe I'll spend some time there . . .' His words trailed off. 'I love you, Ange,' he said, his voice cracking with emotion. 'I'm sorry.'

'I love you too,' said Angela truthfully. 'But I don't know if that's enough any more. And I don't think you do, either.'

Brett stood up. Angela didn't think she'd ever seen him so broken.

'I'll pack a bag,' he said gruffly. 'Can I get you anything? Painkillers?'

'No, thank you. I'm fine.'

He left the room, closing the door gently behind him.

Only then did Angela give way to tears.

CHAPTER TWENTY-ONE

Autumn seemed to come and go in a blink that year. One minute Hyde Park was a riot of flowers and butterflies and sunshine, crammed with shirtless sunbathers and children leaping excitedly into the Princess Diana Memorial Fountain; and the next it was stark and bare, swathed in a grey blanket of frost and empty save for the few brave joggers prepared to endure the winter cold. There must have been a period in between, when the sycamore leaves turned to rust and fell, and a gleaming brown sea of conkers covered the ground. But Jason Cranley couldn't seem to remember it.

In any event, winter had arrived now, and with a vengeance, plunging London into a cold snap that had already seen a few flurries of snow, and the inevitable delays on public transport that any change in the weather always seemed to bring. Walking up the King's Road from his house on Eaton Gate, for his usual breakfast at The Chelsea Bun, Jason pitied the poor commuters crammed onto the number 19 bus, which was going nowhere fast.

Jason himself felt unusually cheerful. Swaddled in a heavy, black cashmere coat and scarf, he was protected from the cold, and could enjoy the childish thrill of watching his breath plume out in front of him, like a dragon's smoke. The sky above him was that magical crisp, bright blue you only ever saw in winter, and the Christmas displays in the shop windows, put up preposterously early as usual, lent everything a cheerful, festive and happy air.

Or perhaps it was tonight's concert that had put him in such a good mood? He'd landed the gig of a lifetime, playing a full hour-long set at the legendary Ronnie Scott's jazz club. Well, perhaps it was a stretch to say that *he'd* landed it. The truth was that George Wilkes, the Cranleys' art-dealer friend, was a close mate of the new manager there, and had pulled a veritable orchestra-full of strings to get Jason a slot.

'Listen. They're a business with a reputation to maintain. They heard your tapes. They wouldn't have hired you if they didn't think you were good,' George had assured him, scores of times, as the date drew nearer and Jason's nerves began to amp up. Jason clung to the idea that there must be some truth in what George said. This was Ronnie Scott's, for God's sake. Ronnie Scott's! They weren't in the business of disappointing paying customers.

I can do it.

George believes in me.

I just have to believe in myself.

Tatiana had been really sweet and congratulatory about it, and had promised to try to be there. Her work had been so manic lately, even more so than usual since the arguments with her board over a US school had begun to escalate, so nothing was certain. Secretly, Jason prayed that his wife didn't make it. Not because they were at loggerheads. They'd been getting along better recently, arguing less and supporting one another more. In a weird way, they had Logan to thank for that.

Having a needy teenager in the house had turned out to be a far more positive experience than Jason had anticipated. For one thing, Logan's presence had turned Jason and Tati into an instant family, albeit a rather unusual one, removing the unspoken pressure to think about having children of their own, at least for the moment. Then there had been the pleasure of seeing Logie mature and grow right before their eyes. Being away from Fittlescombe, from Brett and Angela, and village gossip, and that snobby school of hers, had done her the world of good. In so many ways, the fire at Wraggsbottom Farm had been the wake-up call that Logan needed. In the immediate aftermath she'd been too frozen with guilt to learn anything from her mistakes. But now, settled and happy in a new school, the changes were beginning. She barely drank any more and had given up smoking altogether. She'd written touchingly sincere letters of apology to Gabe and Laura, and to Seb Harwich, whom she knew she'd treated appallingly. Best of all, she seemed finally to have broken the spell of her obsession with Gabe Baxter and to have fallen in love properly with a sweet kid from school, Tom Hargreaves.

Today was a big day for Logan too. Laura Baxter had had her baby, a little boy they'd named Felix, and had emailed Logan, inviting her to come and see the baby. It would be the first time Logan had gone back to the village since storming out of Furlings, and the first time she'd seen Laura face to face since the fire. Jason had watched her set off to Victoria Station this morning looking white-faced with nerves. But she'd gone, and he was proud of her. He prayed things went OK.

His mind swiftly flipped back to tonight's concert, and the likelihood of Tati showing up. The thing was, as much as Jason loved his wife, she had a way of making him feel nervous. It was his fault really, not hers. Somehow Tati always seemed to remind him of his own inadequacies. There she would be, poised and confident and beautiful and successful, willing him on. And there he would be, frightened and sweating and useless and disappointed, letting her down.

George Wilkes, on the other hand, was a face he desperately wanted to see through the smoky clubroom tonight. With his gentle manner, his unquestioning acceptance of all that Jason was, good and bad, George was like a human quilt. Either that, or a fortifying shot of whisky for good luck. Jason wasn't sure which simile fitted his friend better. George, too, had promised to 'try' to make it.

Jason glanced at his watch.

Nine o'clock. *Ten hours to go.*

Tonight was going to be his night.

Laura Baxter wrapped the blanket more tightly around her infant son's shoulders and stared at his face lovingly. She wondered if his little nose and permanently pursed mouth would ever seem less than magical to her. She couldn't imagine that they would. Lots of people said he looked like Gabe, but Laura couldn't see it at all. Felix didn't look like anyone. He was himself: tiny, unique and quite perfect.

'Would you like to hold him?'

'Oh, no. Thanks.' Logan looked terrified. She and Laura were ensconced on the sofa in the drawing room at Wraggsbottom Farm, with Felix's Moses basket wedged in between them. Gabe was out on the farm and would be gone all day, so the two girls were alone. Laura had made tea and cut some slices off the enormous Battenburg cake that Mrs Worsley had brought over from Furlings 'in case you get a bit peckish, while you're feeding.' Everyone in the village had been so kind, but at this rate Laura stood no chance of losing her baby weight. Logan, by contrast, looked skinnier than ever and positively fragile in the black skinny jeans and baggy, cover-all sweater she'd chosen for today's visit.

'He's lovely,' she stammered, 'but I . . . I wouldn't know what to do.'

'There's nothing to "do",' Laura laughed. 'You just pick him up and cuddle him. Like a doll.'

'I'd rather not,' said Logan. 'My hands are shaking just thinking about it. I might drop him.'

Reaching into the basket, Laura lifted her son herself and leaned back against the sofa cushions, allowing Felix to rest against her while she chatted to Logan with both hands free.

'Pass me my tea, would you?'

Logan obliged, and Laura could see her hands actually were shaking as she rattled the cup against its saucer.

'It was sweet of you to come.'

'Nonsense,' said Logan, blushing. 'It was sweet of you to ask me. I should have come a long time ago. But I couldn't face it.'

'Couldn't face what?' Laura asked gently.

'You. Gabe. What I'd done.' Logan looked down at her hands and kept her eyes resolutely fixed there.

'It was an accident,' Laura reminded her. 'You didn't set fire to the barn on purpose.'

'Yes. But it wouldn't have happened if I hadn't got drunk and invited all those idiots over, and smoked weed even after Seb told me how dangerous and stupid it was.'

'We all make mistakes,' said Laura. 'Thank goodness the others had already gone home when it happened.'

Logan nodded. 'And thank goodness I'd been too lazy to bring the horses inside that afternoon, or they'd all have been baked alive in their stalls.' Her hand flew to her mouth, imagining the horror of what might have been. She let out a little yelp of distress, and had to force herself to look up at Laura. 'I wanted to come before, to say sorry. But "sorry" just sounded so inadequate, under the circumstances.'

'I think sorry sounds fine,' Laura said kindly. 'Now do eat some cake, for heaven's sake, or I'm going to turn into the fat one from *Bridesmaids*.'

Logan tried to laugh, but it wasn't working. If anything Laura's sweetness was making this harder.

'You saved my life,' she said. 'After all the mean things I said about you . . . you saved me.'

'Did you say mean things about me?' Laura looked surprised more than offended.

'Sometimes,' Logan admitted. 'But none of them were true. The problem was I was *poisoned* with jealousy.'

Laura laughed. She had missed Logan's melodramatic, teenage turns of phrase.

'I loved Gabe so much,' Logan went on seriously. 'And you had him, and I couldn't bear it. That's also why I behaved like such a prat. I think I thought if I were a bit more cool, and drank a lot, and did adult things like smoking weed and going out with Seb . . .'

'Is going out with Sebby Harwich an "adult thing"?' Laura couldn't help interjecting.

'You know what I mean,' said Logan. 'I thought it might make Gabe see me in a new light.'

'I see,' said Laura.

Poor girl. It had obviously taken a good deal of courage for Logan to come back to the farm today and face her. Laura wondered if she'd been brave enough to confront her father as well; she asked her.

Logan shook her head. 'I think I'd be shot on sight if I went back to Furlings.'

'I'm sure that's not true,' Laura frowned. 'I know your

mother misses having you at home, and I'm sure your dad does too. Men aren't always great at showing these things, you know.'

'Hmmm,' said Logan, noncommittally.

'I ran into your mum yesterday as it happens,' Laura went on. 'Gringo had fallen into some sort of silage, I think, and she was dragging him back across the field for a bath.'

'Oh, Gringo!' Logan pouted. 'I think I miss him most of all.'

'Yes, well, you've got a lot in common,' teased Laura. 'He's definitely the naughtiest dog in Fittlescombe.'

'Perhaps he'll reform?' grinned Logan. 'Like me.'

Laura laughed. 'Perhaps he will.' Felix wriggled sweetly against her chest, disturbed by her laughter. He then emitted a fart so loud and long it was impossible to believe it had come from such a tiny person. Logan erupted with giggles.

'What on earth have you been feeding him?' she looked at Laura aghast.

'Just breast milk, I swear! What can I tell you? Flatulence runs in the Baxter family, I'm afraid. Gabe may seem perfect from a distance, but I can assure you he has his faults – and plenty of them. You've never seen him in Speedos.'

'Oh God, really? No. He doesn't, does he?' Logan gasped.

'Not any more. But he did before I married him,' said Laura. 'Then there were the snowflake socks.'

'Stop!' pleaded Logan.

'The goatee that made him look like Noel Edmonds.'

'Oh, now, come on. I don't believe that.'

'I have photographic evidence!' Laura squealed. 'Hold Felix and I'll get it for you.'

Logan demurred. 'There's no need. The truth is, it's sweet of you to say all that, but I'm not in love with Gabe any more.'

It was such an endearingly honest comment that Laura wasn't sure what to say. She eventually opted for 'Oh.'

'I probably never was. It was just a crush gone a bit, you know . . . mad.' Logan pushed her hair out of her eyes. She'd cut it shorter since Laura last saw her, but it suited her face, and her new, more mature manner. Then again, a crew-cut would have suited Logan Cranley. She really was disastrously pretty. 'I'm in love with an amazing boy now. Tom,' she gushed. 'Tommy. You'll meet him one day. If Gabe's OK with it.'

'I'll meet him whether Gabe's OK with it or not,' said Laura robustly. 'Free advice for you, angel. Never let a man tell you who you can and can't hang out with. Not that Gabe would dare.'

'I'm sure he wouldn't!' giggled Logan. Laura Baxter really was the nicest woman she knew. She somehow combined all Tatiana's fun side with all her mother's kindness.

'Felix is so lucky. Having you for a mum,' she blurted out suddenly.

Laura was so touched she felt tears prick her eyes. 'Logan. Thank you. What a lovely thing to say. And you mustn't worry about Gabriel. He'll come around eventually, I promise.'

Back at her office at Hamilton Hall, Tatiana reached into her desk drawer and scrabbled around for a headache pill. She usually kept Nurofen in constant supply, as well as Alka-Seltzer for those mornings-after-the-nights-before, and (slightly embarrassingly) Rescue Remedy bottles for everything from stress to fatigue. Obviously they didn't work. But there'd been a fad for them in her A level year at school years ago, and Tati had got into the habit of using the little glass bottles; rather in the same way as she still read her horoscope at the back of *Vogue* every month.

354

Today, irritatingly, she was out of everything. And boy, could she use a pill right now.

Unlike Jason and Logan, Tatiana was having a horrendous morning. Hamilton Hall's headmaster, the brilliant and eminently sensible Drew O'Donnell, had called her to the school to fire two teachers. As chair of governors, and CEO of the parent company, hiring and firing were still officially Tatiana's job. The problem was that both today's fire-ees were lovely people: genuine, vocational teachers with decades of experience in their respective subjects of Chemistry and Maths.

'Look, I don't like it any more than you do,' Drew O'Donnell told her. 'But Miss Watkins' class all did poorly in their mocks last week – we've had several complaints from parents. And David Brinton can't focus on anything since his wife died. His head's a mess.'

'Can't we give him compassionate leave or something?' Tati protested. 'It seems awful to sack someone for grieving.'

'We offered.' Drew threw up his hands. 'The old boy won't take it. He's stubborn as a mule. I feel terrible for him, I do, but it's not fair to leave our Year Sixes with substandard teaching. Besides which, our policy's clear. Poor performance is cause for dismissal.'

Tatiana knew. She wrote the policy, a document abhorred by the teachers' unions who viewed it as the educational equivalent of *Mein Kampf*. Hamilton Hall staff were paid twice the salaries of their unionized peers at other schools. But their jobs came at a price.

Tati buzzed her secretary. 'How long do I have till Janice Watkins' appointment?'

'About ten minutes, Mrs Cranley.'

Tati used the time to check her schedule for the rest of the day, then wished she hadn't. *Fuck*. She'd totally forgotten, but she'd agreed months ago to go to tea with her elderly godmother this afternoon.

Beatrice Radley-Cave – Bee, or Queen Bee, as she had always been known to Tatiana – was ninety years old, sharp as a tack and lived in a mansion flat in Westminster that had been frozen in time at some point in the early 1950s. This was probably also the last decade in which it had been properly cleaned. Despite her somewhat shoddy surroundings, Queen Bee herself remained as regal as ever. She was not a woman one disappointed – or rescheduled – lightly.

Tati adored her godmother, and in other circumstances would have looked forward to a visit. But things were so preposterously hectic at work, between the firings and the ongoing boardroom battles over a New York school, she had neither the time nor the energy for Bee today.

Not that work was going badly, per se. Tati's last trip to New York had been wholly positive, from a business point of view. Not only had she found a great potential site for Hamilton Hall NYC, but she'd met with two potential new investors who might be willing to step in and provide funding, should Tati's chairman and CFO really stick to their guns and try to block her. She ought to have returned to London in high spirits. But for some reason her unexpected run-in with Brett Cranley the evening she arrived had both heightened her stress levels and depressed her.

How had Brett known about the infighting amongst the Hamilton Hall board? There was no way he'd have heard anything through Jason. Relations between father and son were as bad as they'd ever been, nonexistent at this point, in fact. Was it just coincidence that Brett had been staying at Tati's hotel? Somehow Tati doubted it. She didn't trust him an inch.

The thought that Brett Cranley might be up to something,

and that she didn't know what it was, accounted for part of her anxiety. The other part was harder to explain. She hated Brett with a passion, felt repulsed by the very thought of him. And yet she couldn't seem to *stop* thinking about him. In some dark, sinister way, Brett seemed to be all around her, a shadowy ghost hanging over her marriage, her career, her future. Worse, since bumping into him in New York, Tati had started to have dreams about him, some of them embarrassingly sexually explicit. She awoke from these dreams panicked and drenched in sweat, gripped by a sensation that was part arousal, part disgust and part fear. And then Jason would lean across the bed and ask her what was wrong, and a new torrent of emotions – guilt, shame, resentment – would wash over her. She hadn't even told Jason or Logan that she'd run into their father in New York. Which was ridiculous! Why not tell them? It wasn't as if she'd done anything wrong. But somehow, every time it might have come up naturally in conversation, Tati couldn't bring herself to do it.

'Mrs Cranley?' The secretary's voice crackled over the loudspeaker. 'Janice Watkins is here to see you.'

Tatiana sighed. Running a successful business was good for the ego, but both the self-esteem and the financial rewards came at a cost. Brett Cranley had been paying it his whole life and it showed. Was Tati really becoming just like him, as Jason had said? She hoped not.

'OK Caroline,' she said grimly. 'Show her in.'

CHAPTER TWENTY-TWO

Beatrice Radley-Cave scowled as her goddaughter walked in.

'You're late.'

'Only five minutes, Bee.'

'Only? There's no "only" about it. Late is late, Tatiana. Who in their right mind sits down to tea at *five* past four?'

Tatiana grinned. She was glad she'd come after all. Her godmother's flat in Ashley Gardens was as familiar to her as her own body, and one of the few reminders of her childhood that made her wholly happy. She loved everything about it, from the sweet, musty smell that lingered in every room (part Garibaldi biscuit, part Gauloise tobacco smoke, part Chanel Number 5 and, Tati assumed, part mould) to the dust-covered ornaments along the mantelpiece, to the frayed Knole sofa still covered with its original William Morris fabric, now more hole than cloth. She loved Queen Bee's face, a crumpled mishmash of folded, wrinkled skin, like crepe paper, but brought alive by the two twinkly, bright blue eyes, blazing with intelligence and wit and warmth amid the wreckage. She loved the fact that Bee had known her father, Rory, all of *his* life, and that she still dropped his name into conversation with Tatiana freely and easily. As if he were still alive. Or as if father and daughter had never grown apart, never hurt and disappointed each other and left it too late to put things right.

Tatiana made the tea, scrubbing out a pair of filthy bone-china teacups in the chipped Belfast sink in Bee's kitchen, and risking electrocution at the hands of Bee's ancient kettle. She brought everything through on a tray, complete with teapot and cosy (Bee was a stickler for these things) and a plate of ginger nut biscuits a mere two years past their sell-by date.

'Now,' said Bee, cheering up at the plate of ginger nuts, which she proceeded to devour enthusiastically like an arthritic Pac-Man. 'What's going on in your life, my dear?'

'Well, the school's going well, but things have been completely frantic,' began Tati. 'I had to fire two teachers today, which was horrid, and I'm battling with—'

'Tatiana, my darling girl, you really must *listen*,' Bee chided gently. 'I asked you about your life. Why are you telling me about your job?'

Tati laughed. 'What would you like to know, darling Bee?'

'Well. We could start with your unsuitable husband. The Cranley boy. How's he?'

'He's well, I think,' said Tati. 'Better than he was, anyway. Less depressed. His name's Jason, by the way Bee.'

The old woman shuddered. 'Must you? I've been trying so hard to forget.'

'Don't be such a snob,' said Tati, plainly delighted.

'Why was he depressed?'

It was a good question, and one to which Tati didn't really have an answer. 'I'm not sure. It's complicated. Jason's quite a sensitive person.'

'Piffle. He's fed up because his wife's always working I 'spect.'

'Yes, well. One of us has to earn a living,' said Tatiana, a little piqued by this brisk assessment of her marital issues.

'Why?' countered Bee, with her usual directness. 'From what I read in the Sunday papers, you've got pots of money. Far more than Rory would have been able to leave you, even if you hadn't been so difficult and forced him to cut you out of the will. To want even more money seems a bit vulgar. Can't you just retire?'

'I'm thirty-one, Bee. Jason's only twenty-six.'

'There you go again. "Only" twenty-six. There's no "only" about it, child. Roger and I had three children by the time we were twenty-eight. Why haven't you and . . . Cranley . . . had any babies yet?'

Tati rolled her eyes. 'You sound like my mother-in-law.'

'That's not an answer,' said Bee, helping herself to more Lapsang from the pot.

'Maybe I don't want to retire and have babies,' said Tati. 'Maybe Hamilton Hall *is* my baby.'

She was starting to feel quite emotional. It had been a rotten, stressful day. Firing people was the worst part of the job. She simply didn't have the strength for one of Queen Bee's grilling straight afterwards.

'I see.' Sensing perhaps that she'd upset her goddaughter, the old woman sat back in her chair and paused for a moment. But only for a moment. 'May I give you some advice, my dear?'

Tati knew Bee well enough to understand that this was a rhetorical question.

'Don't take marriage for granted. If you love this husband of yours . . . . I assume you do love him?'

'Of course,' Tati said quickly. She could never explain her feelings about Jason to Bee. He was more like a brother, or a son, than a husband. But she did love him.

'Then don't ignore him. Especially not for the sake of your career. A career is not a life, Tatiana. It is not a family. You must take an interest in his life, his aspirations, as well as your own.'

Tati thought about Jason's music, and the set he was playing tonight at Ronnie Scott's. She hadn't intended to be there, and she was sure Jase didn't expect her. But perhaps Bee was right? *Perhaps I will show up, and surprise him.*

'And give the man a child,' the old woman added, draining her teacup.

'Jason doesn't want a child, Bee,' Tati said patiently.

'Nonsense. All men want children. Some of them just don't realize it, that's all.'

Since 1959, Ronnie Scott's Jazz Club, on Soho's Frith Street, had been *the* place to watch live jazz in London. An old-school establishment in every sense of the word, with dimly lit red leather booths and tables crammed into tiered circles around a central stage, Scott's was still unparalleled not just for ambience and clientele, but for performers. The food was average, the drinks warm and the prices high. But the music was sublime, and that alone had kept the club on the top of its game for more than half a century.

Tatiana slipped in late. The doorman and hostess both recognized her. Tati was, once again, the toast of London society these days – not that that mattered much at Ronnie Scott's, where celebrity patrons were ten a penny. But few looked as beautiful in the flesh as Tatiana Cranley. In a red Victoria Beckham cocktail dress, with a Rick Owens black leather bomber thrown casually on top, she'd abandoned her usual elegant businesswoman image. As a result she looked both sexier and younger, her long hair left loose for once and her flawless face betraying no trace of the day's stresses or her earlier exhaustion.

'My husband's playing tonight—' she started to explain, but the manager cut her off.

'Of course, of course. Good to see you, Mrs Cranley. If you'd like to follow me I'll make some space for you up front.'

'Oh, no no no, please.' Tati sounded mortified. 'Don't disturb anyone. I'll slip in at the back.'

The manager tried to protest but Tati insisted. 'Really. Jason would prefer it that way, anyway. He doesn't know I'm here. I wouldn't want to throw him off stride.'

Sliding into a tiny table at the very back of the room, it took her eyes a moment to adjust to the darkness. The room was packed, and loud, with people drinking and dining and socializing while the musicians performed. Jason was playing some sort of complicated freestyle number, accompanied by a saxophonist. Secretly Tati loathed this sort of jazz. Atonal, fast-moving and loud, it sounded to her as if a cat were being strangled. But Jason was clearly in his element, eyes closed, head rocking, his entire upper body swaying to the music. Tati watched as he leaned into the keyboard, a look of ecstasy on his face, then swung up and out and away, like a surfer riding some imaginary wave of sound.

The saxophonist, who was black and looked to be in his early seventies, was if anything in an even deeper state of bliss, his elderly body jerking around in paroxysms of musical pleasure. Tatiana could hear her father's clipped vowels in her head, as if he were sitting next to her. 'The poor fellow looks like he's got St Vitus's dance.' She smiled to think how vehemently Rory would have disapproved – of the music, of Jason, of everything. And yet had it not been for her father reneging on her inheritance, she would never have met Jason, or any of the Cranleys. How strange life was.

She ordered a double gin and tonic, and was mentally calculating how much longer she was going to have to sit through this cacophony, when something caught her eye. In the very front row, a man, sitting alone, was on his feet, swaying to the beat and applauding wildly as Jason reached the end of a brief piano solo. Tati watched as Jason opened his eyes and beamed back, acknowledging the man's applause. It was only for a split second, but his face looked utterly transfixed, suffused with happiness in a way that Tati didn't think she'd ever seen it before. That in turn made Tati happy. But her broad grin was replaced by a lurch of surprise when the man in the front row turned and she saw who it was.

A few moments later, she weaved her way down to join him, slipping into the empty seat at his side.

'George!' she said warmly. 'How sweet of you to come. Do you know, I hardly recognized you in those trousers. How trendy you look!'

For a moment George Wilkes's face froze in shock. Then he forced a smile. 'Tatiana. I didn't expect . . . I mean . . . I didn't know you were coming tonight.'

'Last-minute decision,' she shrugged. 'Where's Maddie?'

'Erm, she's at home. With the children.'

Is he blushing? Tati was confused. It was unlike George to be so awkward. He was normally such a smoothie, with the right line for every occasion. *Perhaps he feels embarrassed because of his clothes?* Tati knew George Wilkes as a slightly scruffy, corduroys and brogues man, but tonight he was looking unusually dapper in tight drainpipe jeans and Doc Marten boots, paired with a seventies-style floral shirt, open to the top of his chest. He actually looked good, just . . . different.

'It's so sweet of you to come and support Jason,' she said. She had to lean in very close to make herself her heard. Her lips were almost touching George's ear.

'Not at all,' said George, regaining a little of his usual composure. 'It's the least I could do. Besides, I love jazz.'

'Do you?' Tatiana raised an eyebrow. 'I must say, George, you are a dark horse. I always had you down as a classical man.'

Glancing up, Jason saw his friend and his wife together. He briefly registered his surprise at Tati's presence, then smiled at the two of them. It wasn't quite the rapturous grin Tati had witnessed a few minutes ago. But it was enough to tell her he was pleased to see her.

She was glad she'd made the effort; glad she'd taken Queen Bee's advice. Perhaps it was easier to make Jason happy than she'd realized?

In the cab on the way home she took a step further and leaned into her husband, resting her head on his shoulder and her hand on his knee.

'You were wonderful, darling,' she enthused. 'How do you feel?'

'Good,' said Jason. 'Tired. Relieved. Good.' He smiled shyly. His face was flushed from heat and exertion and his hair was damp and stiff with sweat.

'Were you surprised I came?'

'Very,' said Jason, truthfully.

'Were you happy?'

'Of course.' He stroked her hair, gazing out of the window at the Soho streets, still crammed and buzzing with people at almost two a.m.

'And what about George Wilkes?' said Tati. 'How adorable of him to come and see you. I couldn't believe it when I spotted him in the front row, jiving away like a teenager.'

'Hmmm,' said Jason.

'He's terribly kind. He and Madeleine both are.'

'Hmmm,' Jason said again.

They rolled on in silence for a while, Tati enjoying the sensation of having Jason's arm around her, of being the protected for once, rather than the protector. Out of the blue she heard herself saying:

'Jason? Would you like us to have a baby?'

She could feel his body stiffen, like one of those heat packs where you click a button and the surrounding liquid suddenly transforms into a solid, hot mass. When he spoke, his voice sounded different too. Higher pitched. Strained.

'Of course,' he said. 'That would be lovely. One day.'

'Yes,' Tatiana agreed happily, lying down across his lap. 'It would, wouldn't it? One day.'

She'd been worrying about nothing. She and Jason were on exactly the same page.

Next time she saw her godmother, she must make sure she told her so.

CHAPTER TWENTY-THREE

Angela Cranley trod her way gingerly across the Wetherby Garden Centre car park, being careful not to slip on the icy tarmac. Winter had arrived in the Swell Valley in earnest about a week ago, but last night's ground frost had been the coldest and deepest so far. All the lanes around Fittlescombe were slick with black ice, a biting east wind whistled in across the Downs and heavy snow was confidently forecast for later in the day.

'Morning, Mrs Cranley. You all ready for Christmas, are you, up at the big house?'

Janice Wetherby, who ran the garden centre with her husband Jim, greeted Angela with the same relentless good cheer she showed to all her customers, especially at this time of year. The Wetherbys loved Christmas, not least because the business tripled its usual takings in the three weeks leading up to the big day. As well as trees and mistletoe, the garden centre stocked every conceivable kind of light, bauble, crib ornament and decoration, from outdoor reindeer sculptures to novelty snow globes at two pounds a pop. The café shifted tons of mince pies and Christmas cake, and this year had introduced homemade Yule log, a roaring success that was selling out daily at almost four pounds a slice! And if that didn't fill one with Christmas cheer, then the glorious sounds of carols from King's College wafting over the loudspeakers was surely enough to melt even the hardest and most cynical of winter hearts.

'Sadly not, Mrs Wetherby,' said Angela. 'My daughter came home for the holidays last night from London with her new boyfriend, Tom. They've already complained that Furlings isn't looking Christmassy enough. I'm here in search of supplies, the gaudier the better, apparently.'

'Well you're in the right place, Mrs Cranley, you're in the right place!' Janice Wetherby looked fit to burst with excitement and happiness from beneath her cheap fur-trimmed Santa hat. A house the size of Furlings would take a *lot* of decorating. Janice could already hear the festive sound of ringing tills.

'Can I offer you a free mince pie?'

'Thank you,' said Angela, suddenly remembering that she'd had no breakfast as Logan and Tom had polished off the last of the milk, cereal and bread.

The mince pie was delicious, warm and sweet and satisfying. But pushing her trolley through row after row of tinsel and garlands and tasteful felt robins, Angela couldn't help but feel a twinge of sadness. She'd been reading a book about separation and divorce in middle age – *Michaela's Journey* it was called, written by an irritatingly earnest New Zealander. According to Michaela it was important to 'walk through' one's feelings of sadness and loss, and not to try to ignore them. Angela Cranley disagreed. Thinking about Brett didn't help. Nor did crying. It wasn't cathartic, it was miserable. Angela was determined not to be miserable, whatever the future might hold. Especially not at Christmas.

She still found it hard to come to terms with the fact that Brett would not be home for Christmas this year. Part of the problem was that the decision had been taken almost accidentally. A conversation about nothing much – travel arrangements and some debate over Logan's A-level choices – had ended with Angela agreeing that it 'made sense' for Brett to accept an invitation to Mustique with some old friends of theirs from Australia, rather than come home to Furlings.

'You'll be more relaxed without me,' Brett said breezily. 'It's the first time Logan's been home in months, and she's bound to make a fuss if you and I sleep in separate bedrooms.'

'I suppose so,' Angela agreed vaguely, forgetting that Logan would make at least as much fuss about Brett not showing up at all.

'I'm assuming you're not ready for us to share the same bed again?' said Brett.

'Well . . . not yet.' The truth was they hadn't talked about it. Angela wasn't sure how she felt. But Brett seemed to have all the answers.

'If I go to the Listers', we can say it's work-related. She'll accept that. Then you and Logie can have some mother-daughter time together. You and I can both have a relaxed Christmas, and then we can regroup and talk about things in the New Year. Sound good?'

It didn't sound good. It sounded awful and clinical and like they were already divorced. Angela didn't want to 'regroup'. She wanted her life back. But she hadn't protested at the time, and all of a sudden it was done, agreed, decided. That was the way things had been since the separation. Cold and businesslike and with Brett firmly in the driving seat. At least that was how it appeared to Angela.

The irony was that *she* had been the one who'd asked for

time apart. She'd thought they both needed space, a cooling-off period after the drama of her fall. But the cooling-off period had quickly become too cold for comfort. Brett, as always, had had his work to distract him. But with Logan still living up in London with her brother, and Furlings empty, Angela had had nothing but time on her hands. She felt as if her life were in constant limbo, with no end in sight, no certainty, no plan. Were she and Brett headed for divorce, or reconciliation? Did they *want* divorce, or reconciliation? Angela didn't know. If Brett knew, he certainly wasn't sharing those feelings with her.

A week after the Mustique phone call, the prospect of a lonely Christmas at Furlings with just her and Logan around the tree suddenly sank in with bleak and terrible force. So Angela did the obvious thing and called Jason, inviting him and Tatiana to join them. They accepted at once, and the next day Logan announced that Tom, her first serious boyfriend, would also be coming down. 'If that's all right, Mum?'

For forty-eight hours, Angela was happy again and looking forward to a family Christmas. But when Brett heard the news he hit the roof and they'd ended up having an almighty row. Whatever *entente cordiale* had been reached between the two of them unravelled like a ball of yarn flung carelessly over the edge of a cliff. Once again, tension reigned.

Sod it, Angela thought, tossing gold, red and green ornaments into her trolley willy-nilly until it was overflowing with Christmas tat. *I'm going to enjoy the time with my children, whether Brett likes it or not. He was the one who decided to bugger off and leave us to it.* Logan was already here, floating around the house in a fog of love with her new 'man'. And Jason and Tatiana arrived the day after tomorrow. Michaela was always telling her to 'live in the present'. Angela decided she was going to do just that.

A few hours later, back at the house, she was putting up the Christmas tree with Tom.

'How's that? Better?'

Perched precariously on top of a ladder, Logan's boyfriend was attempting to secure the top of the enormous Norwegian pine to the upper balustrade with a length of garden twine.

'Yes, I think so. That looks straight to me,' said Angela. 'Come down and take a look.'

Logan had driven off to Tesco in Chichester to buy more milk and bread and family-sized tins of Quality Street chocolate – 'basic supplies', as she put it – leaving her mother and boyfriend to put up the tree alone. Angela was glad of the chance to get to know Tom, whom she'd already decided she liked immensely. He was short and stocky and not particularly handsome, but there was a boyish charm about him that she immediately warmed to, and he had the best, loudest, most infectious laugh she'd heard in years. More importantly, it was clear that he worshipped the ground Logan walked on, and the feeling appeared to be mutual. Angela had been very fond of Seb Harwich, and sad when Logan's fling with him had petered out in the wake of Fire-gate. But Tom was definitely a better fit for her.

'So what are your family up to this Christmas?' Angela asked, hoping she didn't sound too nosey or demanding as she handed Tom a packet of red blown-glass baubles with reindeers on them. 'Won't they miss having you around?'

'I shouldn't think so,' said Tom cheerfully. 'Pa's just got married for the fourth time and is on honeymoon in Indonesia, I believe. And Mum's in Scotland with husband number two and my three vile stepsisters.'

'Oh dear,' said Angela. 'Why are they vile?'

'Well, they're Scottish,' said Tom. Sensing this might not be explanation enough he added, 'They're spoiled, too. And not wild keen on Mum. Probably because she broke up their parents' marriage.'

'I see,' murmured Angela.

'Also,' said Tom, through a mouthful of green plastic hooks, 'they're called Kendra, Kyla and Kate. Can you imagine?'

'Really?' Angela giggled.

'Really. Like the bloody Kardashians. I can't be dealing with that. Can you pass me the snowflakes?'

Angela did as she was asked. She learned that Tom had a total of six half-siblings and five step-siblings; that his parents had divorced when he was three; and that he'd been away at boarding school since he was six years old, only recently moving to London to live with his godfather while he attended MPW.

'I've never really lived at home or had that stable-family thing,' he told her. 'Not like Logan. I think the situation's much harder for her.'

'In what way?' asked Angela. She was desperate to know what Logan had said to Tom. Like Brett, Logan did a good job of concealing her true feelings. Since she'd moved in with Jason and Tati, Angela felt as if she'd lost her completely.

'She misses her dad,' Tom said simply. 'I think she assumed he'd be home for Christmas. She was really cut up when she heard he wasn't coming.'

She's not the only one, thought Angela.

'She thinks it's her fault.'

'Why on earth would she think that?' said Angela, shocked.

'Because of the fire. Because she left home and moved in with Jason and Tatiana. I don't think she planned on that

371

being a permanent thing. She thought some distance might calm her dad down, that's all. And maybe, you know, her not being in the house might give you and him more romantic time. Or something.' Tom blushed, fearing he might have overstepped the mark. 'But now she thinks her leaving is what made everything worse. I told her it doesn't work like that.'

'What doesn't work like that?' Logan appeared in the hallway, weighed down with Tesco bags.

'Nothing,' said Tom, scrambling down the ladder and relieving her of the shopping. 'Do you like our tree?'

'It's gorgeous,' Logan beamed, successfully distracted.

He's so gentlemanly, thought Angela, watching her daughter gaze lovingly into Tom's eyes. *So sweet. I do so hope they stay together.*

The things Tom had told her worried her deeply. She knew that the thought of Logan blaming herself for her and Brett's current estrangement would upset Brett as much as it upset her. That gave them some common ground, at least. After Christmas she and Brett absolutely must sit down together and sort things out. For all their sakes.

'Oh God, which ones do you think I should bring?'

Jason watched, perplexed, as Tatiana ran a frazzled hand through her long, tangled hair. She was naked in their bedroom in Eaton Gate, surveying the bed, which she'd littered with just about every dress she owned. Shoes of all shapes, colours and sizes were strewn across the floor. It was mayhem.

'It's Christmas at home, not the Oscars,' Jason said gently, handing her a dressing gown. He had never quite got used to Tati's total lack of inhibition about her body, perhaps because he had never felt comfortable in his own skin.

'You don't understand.' She bit her bottom lip and looked close to tears.

Jason put an arm around her and pulled her down onto the bed beside him. It wasn't often he saw her so vulnerable.

'Explain to me, then. Do you not want to go to Furlings for Christmas?'

'No, no. I do.' Tati shook her head.

'Because we can stay in a hotel if the house is too much for you. If it brings back too many memories,' Jason said kindly.

'No,' she said firmly. 'It's not the house. It does bring back memories, of course. But they're good ones. Most of them, anyway.'

'Well what then? You know Mum loves you. She couldn't care less what dress you wear or what presents we bring.'

This was also true. It was hard for Tati to explain to Jason how she was feeling, hard to admit it fully even to herself. They might be spending Christmas with Jason's family, or what was left of it. But it was Tati's home they were going to. Furlings, but also Fittlescombe: the village, the church; her old colleagues from the school; people she'd grown up with and who had known her in all her various incarnations – from a sweet little girl to an obnoxious wild-child to a lowly village schoolmistress to her current role of über-businesswoman. Tati knew that her marriage to Jason was still considered a scandal by many in the village. Plenty of locals still felt that she'd corrupted the naïve young heir to her family's old estate. That she'd used Jason shamelessly for his money and hijacked the Cranley name in an act of revenge, to spite his father. The fact that there was at least a grain of truth to these accusations only made Tati more paranoid about them. Rory Flint-Hamilton might be dead but, on some unspoken level, Tatiana still yearned for his approval. Going back to the Swell Valley for Christmas made that yearning more acute.

Mrs Worsley would be there, of course, another face Tatiana hadn't seen since her marriage. Would the old woman have softened towards her former charge? Tati didn't know, but prayed so. In her current state, she wasn't sure she could cope with Mrs Worsley's hostility. The very idea of seeing Furlings' housekeeper again filled her with a torrent of mixed emotions she could barely contain.

'I've told Mum we're looking at houses down there,' said Jason, once it was clear Tati wasn't able to articulate her fears. 'She's so excited about it. I thought maybe, after Christmas, she could come with us on a couple of viewings?'

'Sure,' said Tati, collecting herself. 'Of course.'

She was grateful to Angela for defying Brett and inviting them back to Furlings, and for backing off about the baby. Mercifully, that subject had been dropped, for now at least. The least Tatiana could do in return was to show willing and include Angela in their house-hunting trips.

'I love you, you know,' said Jason, pushing back a stray strand of hair from around Tati's face. They'd actually made love last night, for the first time in many months. Or at least they'd tried to. Tatiana was so tense she'd found it hard to get into the mood, and perhaps as a result Jason had lost his erection halfway through. But a first step had been made. Tati had reassured herself this morning that it was the intimacy that counted, not the quality of the performance. This was marital sex after all, not high-diving at the Olympics, with a panel of judges holding up scorecards.

'I love you too,' she said, truthfully. 'But please, pick me out a dress for church on Christmas day.'

374

'Fine,' Jason laughed. 'The green DVF wrap dress. You can't go wrong with that.'

'Really?' Tati looked as if the weight of the world had been lifted off her shoulders.

'Really.' Not for the first time, Jason Cranley marvelled at the mess of contradictions that made up the woman he'd married. Part superwoman, part little-girl-lost, after nearly six years Tatiana still had the capacity to surprise him. Watching her put her dresses away, it struck him that he was actually looking forward to Christmas this year. Something had changed, something good. He found himself praying that it would last.

'Is there anything else I can get for you, Mr Cranley? Anything at all?'

Brett's new Serbian secretary smoothed down her skin-tight pencil skirt and flashed her boss a look that needed no translation. She was exceptionally pretty in a feline, high-cheekboned, Slavic way. Brett could not have been less interested.

'No. Thank you.'

The girl left the room with a disappointed pout. Brett picked up the plane tickets and itinerary she'd left on his desk.

Mustique. He didn't even like the place. More posers in a few measly square miles than you could find anywhere else on earth. He'd been on the point of cancelling, of swallowing his stupid pride, calling Angela and telling her enough was enough, he was coming home for Christmas and he wanted everything to go back to normal. But then she'd dropped the bombshell about inviting Jason and Tatiana and he'd dug himself a hole so deep he had no idea how to get out of it.

His own wife, inviting that little witch to Furlings, after everything she'd done to try to hurt them and destroy their family! Wasn't it enough that Tatiana had brainwashed and married Jason? That she'd now enticed Logan to live under her roof as well? That she made no secret of her desire to get Furlings back eventually, by fair means or foul?

If Angela really loved him, she would never have done it. It was an insult, designed to wound him. And it had wounded him. Deeply. All Brett had ever wanted, deep down, was a family. A place where he could be safe, where he could feel like a true insider for once in his life. He'd worked like a dog to create that, and to provide for his family. And now here he was on the outside, looking in. It was hard not to feel bitter.

Brett re-read his itinerary gloomily. He left London in three days. What the hell was he going to do until then? He'd have liked to work, but the real-estate market was dead as a doornail now and would be until after the New Year. Everybody else, apparently, had families to go home to or Christmas parties to attend. Not that Brett was short of invitations. What he lacked was desire or enthusiasm or even physical energy. Ever since he heard the news about Tati, he'd felt desperately tired. He felt like a champion boxer, hotly tipped to win, suddenly collapsing against the ropes in the tenth round through sheer fatigue.

Tatiana Flint-Hamilton was beating him, against all the odds.

She was wearing him down.

There was only one thing Brett Cranley wanted for Christmas. And neither his Serbian secretary, nor anyone else, could give it to him.

Logan Cranley ran up Furlings' drive with flushed cheeks, as delighted as a child on its birthday. It had snowed last night: not just a pale, half-hearted dusting, like icing sugar on a waffle, but a fully fledged dump of thick, heavy snow, like the frosting on a wedding cake. She and Tom had rushed out onto the lawn as soon as they'd woken up and made snowmen. Logan had given Tom's an enormous erection, which they'd both thought screamingly funny, especially when it kept falling off. Tom had been more successful moulding a pair of tits onto Logan's effort, complete with holly-berry nipples. Snow brought out the kid in everyone. It was impossible not to feel happy and Christmassy and excited on a day like today, and Logan was indulging her inner child with shameless delight.

The village also looked utterly magical, like a ravishing Christmas bride. Its snowy rooftops, punctured only by smoking chimneys and St Hilda's stone spire, topped cottages cheerfully decked out with wreaths and berries and brightly twinkling strings of lights. Children sledged on the Downs, their shrieks mingling with the beautiful sound of the church bells pealing. And on the snowy green, an enormous Christmas tree hung with baubles of every size and colour sparkled enticingly, a cheerful reminder of the celebrations and feasting to come.

Logan had forgotten how much she loved it here. Or rather, how much she used to love it, before the fire at Wraggsbottom Farm and the humiliation that followed. But this Christmas, for the first time, she felt better. Laura Baxter's kindness, inviting her down to meet Felix and forgiving her for everything, had been a huge step forward, relieving Logan of part of her guilt. Then, yesterday, she'd run into Gabe in the village stores. He was buying tinsel and, after a moment's hesitation, had smiled broadly when he saw her and given her a hug.

'Hello you,' he grinned. 'How's London?'

'Erm, nice.' Logan blushed, but it was out of awkwardness

rather than desire. In dirty jeans and a thick fisherman's sweater, Gabe looked as craggily handsome as ever. But he no longer had the mesmeric hold on her that had consumed her through her early teens. 'It's lovely to be back, though. Fittlescombe's so perfect at Christmas.'

'Isn't it?' Gabe agreed. 'I hear you brought a boyfriend down.'

My goodness, thought Logan. She'd forgotten quite how fast gossip travelled in this village.

'You should bring him over to the farm some time. See what we've done with the place. Everything's been rebuilt since the fire, courtesy of your pa.'

'I'm so sorry,' Logan blushed again.

'Don't be,' said Gabe. 'All's well that ends well. You should see the stables now. They're so state of the art, they look like something out of *Buck Rogers*.'

'Who's Buck Rogers?' asked Logan.

'Never mind,' Gabe laughed. 'I'm old. Good to see you anyway, kiddo. Merry Christmas.'

Logan had stood and watched him dart out into the cold with the last of Mrs Preedy's tinsel under his arm and felt a profound sense of relief. Gabe didn't hold a grudge. And she didn't fancy him. Well, not much anyway. It was the best Christmas present she could have wished for.

Or perhaps it was the second best. What she really wanted, deep down, was to have her father back. Not that she necessarily wanted to move back home permanently – she loved her life in London, loved MPW, and most of all loved Tom. But she wished she could wave a magic wand and heal the rift between herself and Brett, along with her parents' foundering marriage. That she could come down to Furlings at weekends and holidays and that everything would be back to normal. Everyone was glossing over it, but Logan wasn't

378

stupid. Brett not coming home for Christmas was a big deal, the biggest. It had to be the beginning of the end.

Finally reaching the house, she burst in through the kitchen door, red faced and panting.

'What on earth's the matter?' said Angela. Wearing a reindeer apron, and with her hands and arms elbow-deep in flour, so thick that she looked as if she were wearing white gloves, Angela was rolling out the pastry for another batch of mince pies. Yesterday's attempt had been, as Tom rather tactlessly put it, 'a bit cement-y'. Not that this had prevented him from eating an entire bowlful.

'Gossip!' Logan breathed heavily. 'You'll never guess.'

'Gringo's got the vicar's bitch pregnant and he's suing your dad for damages,' suggested Tom, who up till that point had been deep in last week's *Sunday Times* Sudoku at the kitchen table.

'Wrong,' beamed Logan. 'Besides, anyone would be ecstatic if their dog had Gringo's puppies. He's a legend.'

The legend farted quietly from his basket by the Aga.

'Terrorists have moved into Fittlescombe and are turning the village hall into a jihadi training camp.'

'No, stop being silly,' said Logan. Turning to her mother she announced, 'Mr Bingley's got engaged!'

Angela tightened her grip on the pastry cutter she was using for the mince-pie lids. 'Who told you that?'

'He did!' said Logan. 'He was at the WI stall buying pars- nips or swedes or something horrid – I think she's vegan, his fiancée – and he said hello and then he just told me. I mean really, at his age! What's the point?'

'He's not that old,' mumbled Angela.

'Oh *Mum*.' Logan laughed. 'He's ancient.'

'Who's Mr Bingley?' asked Tom, not looking up from his puzzle.

'My old headmaster,' said Logan. 'He's nice but he's terribly strict and sort of, stiff. You can't imagine him getting married. Can you, Mum?'

'Well, I . . . yes, I can imagine it,' said Angela. She was surprised by how thrown-off she was by Logan's news. 'I'm a little surprised. He and Stella have been together for years. I suppose I thought, assumed, that they were happy as they were.'

'Living in sin, you mean?' said Logan. 'I can't imagine old Bingley doing that either.'

'Must you talk like a tabloid reporter, darling?' chided Angela. 'Damn it!'

She looked down. Blood was gushing from her finger where she'd sliced it on the pastry cutter, staining the pastry pink.

'Quick, put it under the tap,' said Tom, leaping up and thrusting Angela's hand over the sink while he turned on the icy water.

'I'll get you a plaster,' said Logan, opening the drawer next to the fridge where the first-aid supplies, such as they were, were kept. Angela watched as the blood trickled onto the white porcelain and swirled down the drain. 'What happened?'

'I don't know. My hand slipped I suppose. I'm fine. It's nothing, really.' Drying her hand on a tea towel, she applied the proffered plaster and returned to her mince pies. She'd have to start again now, she thought with a sigh. All of a sudden, her heart wasn't in it.

'They'll be at the Live Crib on Christmas Eve anyway,' said Logan, returning to her gossip like a dog to an unfinished bone, now that the mini-drama was over. 'I said we'd see them there. Tati and Jason will be here too by then, so we can all ogle the engagement ring. Do you think he gave her a big one?'

'Nightly, I suspect,' Tom couldn't resist. Giggling, Logan came over and sat on his lap.

Everyone's happy, thought Angela wistfully. *Max and Stella, Logan and Tom. Even Jason and Tatiana seem to have settled down.* She thought about herself and Brett, and what they'd both somehow managed to lose. She missed him, or at least, she missed what they had once had together. Live Crib, Fittlescombe's annual Christmas celebration of the Nativity, complete with local farm animals, was truly a time for family.

Please God, she found herself praying, as she poured yet more flour into the mixing bowl. *Make me happy again. Show me the way.*

Outside the kitchen window, snow began to fall.

CHAPTER TWENTY-FOUR

Reverend Slaughter looked happily around his packed church and wondered if the BBC South East television crew would have a sufficiently good view of his new crimson robes when he gave the opening address.

Not that Live Crib was about him, of course. Like all St Hilda's services and celebrations, its purpose was to honour The Lord. Fittlescombe's famous Nativity-service-cum-carol-concert was also very much about the children, many of whom had already huddled excitedly around the altar-side pen that housed the goats, the sheep and Wilbur, Gabe Baxter's decrepit but ever-popular donkey. Even so, knowing that the event would almost certainly make the local news, Reverend Slaughter had splashed out on a new set of Christmas cassocks in crimson, magenta and gold that he flattered himself lent an air of pomp and ceremony to proceedings. Even if they couldn't quite match the glamour of some of the village's more famous parishioners, all of whom had turned out in force on this beautiful, snowy Christmas Eve.

Emma Harwich, a local beauty turned supermodel, currently gracing the front page of *Vogue* in an outfit that left little to the imagination, other than leaving readers to wonder how quickly its wearer might contract hypothermia, had turned up in a demure floor-length belted coat, to the vicar's immense relief. Admittedly she had teamed this with sky-high stiletto boots and sunglasses, no doubt to block out the glare of the softly flickering candlelight. Either that or so she didn't have to watch the very obvious public display of affection between her mother, Penny, and her second husband, the local cricketing heart-throb Santiago de la Cruz. Emma herself was hand in hand with a preposterously good-looking boy, a Hollywood actor apparently, although Reverend Slaughter had never heard of him. Axel something or other. In any event, he was rumoured to be the star of the new Gucci campaign and Emma's latest love interest, both of which facts drew him any number of lustful and/or envious stares.

A few rows behind the Harwiches sat the Drummonds, a famous British theatrical dynasty with an exquisite medieval mill house on the Swell just outside Fittlescombe. Reverend Slaughter couldn't quite see from the pulpit, but one of their Christmas house guests looked awfully like Dame Judi Dench, muffled up in red Jaeger coat. If it were Dame Judi, he absolutely must get her autograph.

Opposite the Drummonds, to the left of the nave, sat the local MP, Piers Renton-Chambers and his new young wife, a horsey-looking heiress from Hampshire called Jane Drew. In a floor-length mink that must have cost a not-so-small fortune, Jane was drawing plenty of attention, as were the other local soon-to-be-newlyweds, Max Bingley and Stella Goye, who sat beside them.

In the nearly seven years since Max had taken over as headmaster at St Hilda's Primary School, the village had taken him to its collective heart. Harry Hotham, the old headmaster, had been a tough act to follow. But Max had worked wonders with the tiny village school, transforming it into the highest-ranked state primary in Sussex. Property prices in the St Hilda's catchment area, already high, had skyrocketed, earning Max still more friends among the locals. It seemed funny now to think that Max Bingley had been a grieving widower when he'd arrived in Fittlescombe. He looked deeply content this evening. Little by little, local potter Stella Goye had brought Max back to life. Many people thought them an odd couple, with Max so straight-laced and conservative and Stella so hippyish and free-spirited. But clearly the relationship worked, and now their surprise engagement was the talk of the village.

Or at least, it had been, until Fittlescombe's own prodigal daughter had decided to return to the village fold, just in time for Christmas.

Looking at Tatiana Cranley, as she was now, throwing her head back and laughing in the front pew, dripping in diamonds like the Queen of Sheba, Reverend Slaughter tried not to think uncharitable thoughts. Everyone in Fittlescombe had adored Tatiana's father, Rory Flint-Hamilton. There were many who would never forgive or forget what Tatiana put the old man through in his declining years. The drugs, the sex, the scandals – all played out in excruciating detail by a salivating tabloid press.

Of course, that *was* a long time ago now. During her brief tenure as a teacher at the village school under Max Bingley, Tatiana had begun to win back the respect of the locals, only to blow everything up again by running off with the impressionable young Cranley boy on the very day he came into his trust fund.

Reverend Slaughter observed the two of them, Jason and Tatiana, leaning into one another, sharing a joke with Jason's younger sister Logan in the front row. He had to admit, five years in, the marriage did seem to be working, against all the odds. Much like Tatiana's schools empire – Hamilton Hall was rarely out of the papers these days. If things carried on at this rate, the younger Cranleys would soon be as wealthy as their parents. The vicar had already planned to approach them later this evening about a donation to the church roof fund, suspending his disapproval of Tatiana for the greater good of the parish, as a village vicar so often must.

'Good evening, Vicar. Marvellous turnout. You must be thrilled.'

Dylan Pritchard Jones, looking dapper in a new, expensively cut three-piece suit, sidled up to the Reverend Slaughter, flashing a mouthful of expensive white veneers. In the pew behind him sat his exhausted wife, Maisie, with their newest daughter, baby Ava, asleep in her arms, and a toddler slumped, bored, across her lap. Everyone, even the vicar, knew about Dylan's regular extramarital exploits. Rumour had it that he had a new, very young mistress, the third wife of one of the richest fathers at Lancings, the exclusive boys' prep school where he was now deputy head. Naturally the vicar disapproved, but as Dylan was chairman of the parish fundraising committee, and a damned efficient one at that, he kept his opinions to himself.

'Hullo Dylan. Yes, it's standing room only. You see the television people are here?'

'Are they?' Dylan feigned surprise. Ridiculously vain and attention-seeking, he'd dragged his family to church a full forty-five minutes early to ensure a pew that the TV cameras would cover. 'I hadn't noticed. I suspect they're here for Lady Muck, are they?' he nodded in Tatiana's direction, scowling disapprovingly. 'Some people have no shame.'

'Indeed,' Reverend Slaughter said archly.

The organist, Frank Bannister, struck up the opening chord of 'Once in Royal David's City'.

'I believe that's my cue,' said the vicar, scuttling up the pulpit stairs like an excited, bright red beetle. 'Merry Christmas, Dylan.'

'Merry Christmas, Vicar. Good luck.'

Every year at Live Crib, either an animal or a local child usually provided some sort of amusing distraction. Last year the baby Jesus had opened her lungs and howled piteously for the entire one-hour service. The year before that, an angel had fallen asleep in the rafters, falling twelve feet onto the stone church floor and breaking his arm, just as the three wise men were depositing their gifts. This year, brilliantly, dear old Wilbur the donkey had completely stolen the show, first by farting loudly immediately after the line 'And lo! An Angel of the Lord appeared', and then by lifting his tail and emptying his bowels dramatically during 'Hark the Herald Angels Sing', thereby eliciting a string of deeply unholy turns of phrase from both Mary and Joseph, not to mention howls of laughter from the congregation.

'That was priceless,' said Tati, wiping away tears of mirth as she and Jason filed out into the churchyard after the service. 'I do so hope it makes the BBC South East news.'

'If it doesn't we should send it in to *You've Been Framed!*,' said Tom. 'That's got to be worth two hundred and fifty quid. What the hell were they *feeding* that animal, that's what I'd like to know. Prunes?'

'Poor Reverend Slaughter,' said Angela. 'He looked mortified. We shouldn't laugh.'

'Oh, Mummy,' Logan poked her in the ribs affectionately. 'You were laughing as hard as the rest of us.'

'No I wasn't,' lied Angela.

'Then why has your mascara run all over your cheeks?'

'Oh, God. It hasn't, has it?' said Angela, stifling another giggle and hunting through her bag for a tissue.

Tatiana was already outside, standing at the bottom of the steps where a pool of parishioners had started to gather. It was a stunning evening. The sky glowed Christmas-card blue beneath a full moon, and a light shower of snow was beginning to fall, heavy, fat flakes floating gently down onto ground already thickly blanketed with white.

She recognized almost all of the families filing out of the church, and waited for people to come up to her and say hello, or Merry Christmas, but nobody did. One or two of them spoke to Jason, and acknowledged her curtly with nods or smiles. But there was no warmth, no recognition, no 'Congratulations on all your success, Tatiana,' or 'How have you been, Tatiana?' or 'Welcome home, Tatiana.'

Trying not to feel hurt, she slipped away from Jason and his family and wandered alone into the churchyard. She hadn't intended to do so, but she found herself walking towards her father's grave. Set about forty feet from the church walls, up a small hill, the Flint-Hamilton family plot consisted of a simple, unostentatious row of stone slabs lying flat to the ground. Rory lay next to his parents, Edmund and Hilda, on one side, and his wife Vicky, Tatiana's mother, who had died when Tati was just eight, on the other. His grave was only seven years old, but it was as worn and lichened as the others already. Behind her parents and grand-parents, a string of Tatiana's more distant ancestors were buried, with Flint-Hamilton stones dating back to the early 1720s. It was a peaceful place to be buried, particularly tonight, in the snow, and with the Christmas bells of the church pealing above them through the smoky night air.

'Tatiana.'

Max Bingley's voice made her jump.

'Merry Christmas.'

He smiled, that same warm, crinkly-eyed smile Tatiana remembered from her St Hilda's Primary School days. Ridiculously, she found herself welling up, and had to bite her lower lip hard to stop the tears from coming.

'Thank you. And to you.'

'I understand you and Jason might be buying a place down here. Missing the cut and thrust of Fittlescombe life, are you?' Max teased her gently.

'I do miss it,' said Tati. 'Terribly. Although I'm not sure many people around here miss me.'

Too honest to correct her, Max said simply 'Well, I do. I miss you at the school, for one thing. Now that you have an empire to run, I imagine you're far too busy to teach yourself. But you were very good at it, you know.'

'Thank you,' said Tati, touched. It was a sincere compliment, which meant a lot coming from a man like Max Bingley.

'Your father would have been very proud of you I'm sure,' added Max, nodding down at Rory's grave.

'I wouldn't bet on it.' Tati gave a short, brittle laugh. 'Pride in me was not something my father was known for.'

'You were very young when he died, Tatiana,' Max said kindly. 'You've achieved so much since then. A booming business, a glittering career, a happy marriage.'

Tati felt each word echo emptily inside her. Her life didn't feel glittering or happy. Looking at Max Bingley, newly engaged, completely content in his work and his life in his modest cottage in Fittlescombe, the truth was that she felt wildly envious. She'd have traded places in a heartbeat. And yet, when she'd lived here herself and taught at the school, she'd felt like a failure, miserable and trapped. She'd built

Furlings up over the years as some sort of talisman, the missing piece of the puzzle in her life – if she could just get that house back, she'd be happy. Standing here tonight at her father's graveside, the crisp night air biting at her face and hands, she realized what nonsense that was. Happiness wasn't made of bricks and mortar. It must come from within, or not at all.

'I do miss teaching,' she told Max, stamping her feet against the cold. 'I miss the children.'

'Well,' he put a paternal arm around her shoulders. 'I expect you and Jason will have your own one day. Believe me, Tatiana, no matter what you achieve in life, there's no sense of purpose quite like being a parent. Anyway, I'll leave you to it,' he kissed her on the cheeks. 'I just wanted to say hello and congratulations on everything. Oh . . . and welcome home!'

He walked off with a cheery wave. Tati watched him rejoin his fiancée and some other villagers outside the church, then head off to his car. He'd been so kind, but their encounter had left her feeling awful, a deep, crushing sadness weighing on her chest, making it hard to breathe.

'There you are.' Jason caught up with her. 'You disappeared on me. Everyone's waiting in the car. Shall we go?'

'You go on ahead,' Tati forced a smile. 'I'll stay here for a while and walk back.'

'Walk?' Jason frowned. 'It's freezing. And pitch-dark.'

'I'll be fine,' said Tati.

'You don't even have a torch.'

'I know the way. Anyway, I've got my phone, I can use that if I need to.'

Jason hesitated. 'I'll walk with you. I'll just go and tell Mum we're not coming . . .'

'No,' Tati said, more firmly than she'd intended. 'Thank

389

you, darling, really. But I prefer to be alone. I'll see you back at the house in half an hour.'

Reluctantly, Jason left. Tati stood and listened as the last of the cars from Live Crib pulled out of the church car park. She watched as the beams of the headlights melted into the night. At last she was alone in the churchyard. Only the moon and the distant lights of the village remained to guide her, but her eyes soon adjusted to her surroundings. An owl hooted twice, then fell silent. Tatiana listened to the crunch of her own feet on the snow as she paced back and forth, examining each of her family graves in turn. She ran her fingertips slowly over each rough stone, like a blind woman trying to read Braille. As if she could somehow find meaning in the dead, in the past.

A terrible emptiness threatened to overwhelm her, numbing her senses, making it hard for her to move or think or do anything. Tears would have been a relief, but they refused to come.

She wasn't sure how long she'd been crouching there, trance like, when the cold suddenly hit her. Her limbs ached, and it was hard to stand up. Glancing at the screen on her phone, she saw that it was past ten o'clock. She'd better get home.

Walking quickly up the lane towards Furlings, it took her less than ten minutes to reach the entrance to the drive. Once there she did have to be careful, as the trees arched above her, blocking out what little moonlight had been guiding her thus far, and making it hard to pick her way along the rough, icy track. Her phone made an inadequate torch as she picked her way over the potholes, and it took another ten minutes before she rounded the corner and the lights of the house hove into view.

Slipping her phone back into her coat pocket, Tati had

started to walk faster towards the lawn when something made her stop and slink back into the shadows. It was a figure, a man, heavyset and silent, his black coat and hat silhouetted in the moonlight. He was standing about twenty feet back from the drawing room, stock still in the darkness, watching the figures within. Not like a burglar, casing the joint. More like a friend or a visitor. It was as if he were considering going inside, but was afraid to.

For a brief moment, Tati wondered whether he might be a ghost. It seemed the right sort of night for it somehow. She wasn't afraid, just curious, half expecting him to walk a few steps forward then evaporate into the winter air like a wisp of smoke. But instead he moved his arm slightly and shifted position, triggering one of the garden lights to switch on and glare up at him. There must be some sort of motion sensor. In that instant, Tati knew that this was no spirit. This was a man, as human and alive as she was, and just as lost and sad on this snowy Christmas Eve.

The light only fell across his face for a moment before switching off, plunging him back into darkness. But it was long enough for Tatiana to see the abject misery in Brett Cranley's eyes.

CHAPTER TWENTY-FIVE

Tatiana smoothed down her skirt and checked her make-up in the mirrored doors of the lift. *Perfect.* She was heading up to the eighteenth floor of Number One Angel Court in the City of London, to Hamilton Hall's new business offices, for an important board meeting, and she felt terrific.

The morning had begun well, with a negative pregnancy test. Sitting on the loo in her master bathroom, with Jason still asleep next door, it was all she could do not to weep with relief when the single blue line appeared in the little plastic window. She knew she wasn't handling the whole baby thing well. She ought to sit down with Jason and tell him she'd changed her mind; that she categorically wasn't ready for motherhood. But some sixth sense told her that such a declaration would mark the beginning of a conversation about their marriage that neither of them had the strength for. Too guilty to go back on the pill in secret, Tati spent each month playing a ridiculous game of Russian roulette. Each time the test was negative, she experienced a wave of euphoria and renewed energy, like a condemned prisoner awarded a last-minute reprieve.

Today's result couldn't have come at a better time. This morning's board meeting was going to be a battle of wills. Tatiana's key opponent on the board, the infuriating Lady Arabella Boscombe, was implacably opposed to opening a New York school, and was spitting teeth that Tati had already verbally agreed a deal on a prime piece of Manhattan real estate without board approval. Lady Arabella used to be deputy editor of the *Times Educational Supplement*, and considered herself to be a grandee of the educational establishment. Her sense of entitlement wasn't hindered by the fact that her family owned half of Chelsea, with property holdings second only to the Duke of Westminster A little bird told Tati that Lady Arabella had been ringing round her fellow board members, trying to whip up support for a vote of no confidence in their CEO and foundress.

Tati, however, felt invincible. Not only was she not pregnant, but the figures had come in late last night for the new Clapham School. They were already at full headcount and running at a thumping profit. Meanwhile, the original Sloane Square School had just been nominated Private Co-Ed Prep of the Year by the *Times Educational Supplement*. Hamilton Hall Ltd's coffers were awash with cash like never before. Even the exchange rate was in Tati's favour. No one, not even that old battle-axe Lady Arabella, could argue that this wasn't an auspicious time for British companies to be buying up US assets. Expansion was the future and the key to Tatiana's next fortune. She wasn't about to let her lily-livered board of directors hold her back.

The lift doors opened and Tatiana strutted down the corridor to the Hamilton Hall reception.

'Good morning, Mrs Cranley.'

The receptionist looked nervous. Clearly the tension surrounding this morning's meeting was contagious.

'Good morning Tracy,' Tatiana smiled. 'Beautiful day, isn't it?'

The views from the seventeenth floor were spectacular. You could see the famed dome of St Paul's in the foreground, overshadowed by the phallic glass monstrosity known as 'the gherkin'. Beyond these were the river, and a panoramic view of East London stretching to the horizon. In the distance, the impressive towers of Canary Wharf punctured a bright blue summer sky, as rare in England these days as a UFO sighting. The offices had cost Tati – cost Hamilton Hall – a fortune. But they were impressive, the sort of space that both reassured and enticed investors. Tatiana was a firm believer in the mantra that money beget money; that one had to spend in order to earn. The problem with dinosaurs like Arabella Boscombe was that they had no vision. No vision and no balls.

'You're the last to arrive, Mrs Cranley,' said the receptionist meekly. 'Shall I show you straight in?'

'That's all right,' said Tati. 'I know where I'm going. I could murder coffee, though, if you wouldn't mind. Black, strong, three sugars.'

As it turned out, she was going to need it. The faces that greeted her around the table were almost uniformly disapproving. Lady Arabella, sweltering in a heavy tweed suit, looked the most thunderous of all, her bristly chin thrust angrily forward and her large matronly bosom heaving with indignation.

'You're very late, Tatiana,' she boomed.

She sounds like Queen Bee, Tati thought crossly. *Who does she think she is?*

She looked at her watch idly. 'Am I?'

The lack of concern in her voice was like a red rag to a bull.

'Yes. You are.' Arabella Boscombe looked ready to spontaneously combust. 'Some of us have been sitting here for forty minutes!'

'Yes, well,' Tati said dismissively. 'I'm afraid that's what happens when one has a business to run. A phenomenally successful business, I might add. I trust you've all seen the figures from HH Clapham?'

A begrudging murmur of assent rumbled around the room.

'Combine that new revenue stream with the figures from Sloane Square and you'll see we've never been in a stronger position to expand.' Tati walked around the table, handing printouts of the latest figures to each board member before returning to her own seat. 'I'm excited about the future for Hamilton Hall, and I know you all are too.'

'Tatiana.' Eric Jenkins, a senior partner at one of the largest City accountants, and usually one of Tati's most stalwart supporters, gave her a serious look. 'The Clapham figures are a boost, certainly. But a number of us have concerns.'

'Grave concerns,' Arabella Boscombe echoed.

'We feel that a period of consolidation is what the business needs.'

'Stagnation, you mean,' said Tati, rolling her eyes. 'Come on Eric. We've been through this a hundred times.'

'Yes. And you've ignored us a hundred times,' Michael Guinness, one of Hamilton Hall's largest individual investors, jumped in. 'New York represents a huge outlay and a huge risk.'

'The Manhattan site's forty per cent cheaper than what we paid in London,' Tati shot back.

'Yes, but we know the London market. We know the British educational system. All our experience, all our brand awareness, is here.'

'Because we're not there yet, Michael,' Tati said simply. 'And we need to be. New York parents are climbing the walls trying to get little Chip, Chuck and Rusty into a decent school. They'll pay anything. I'm telling you we could double our fees, maybe even triple them.'

'That may be so,' said Michael. 'But we can't just—'

'Yes we can,' Tati cut him off rudely. She addressed herself to the entire table. 'I've been to New York. I've spent time there. And I'm telling you, you can smell the desperation wafting out of the admissions office at Avenues. All those rejected millionaire families, spat out onto Lexington with nowhere to park their children, or their money! The risk is in *not* doing this now, when we have the cash on our balance sheet and a perfect site at a knockdown price.'

'A knockdown price?' Lady Arabella was shaking with anger. 'It's twenty million dollars, Tatiana! And that's before renovations. Then there's the marketing spend we'd need to raise brand awareness . . .'

'I know all that.' Tati waved a hand regally, as if swatting a fly. 'Trust me. It will be worth it.'

'But that's just it,' said Eric Jenkins, the light reflecting off his bald head as he leaned forward over the table. 'How can we trust you, when you keep making executive decisions behind our backs? We're your board, Tatiana. You need to trust *us*. You need to let us do our jobs and advise you.'

Tati bit back her irritation. She liked Eric, but really it was tiresome to be surrounded by such pygmies. All these people operated in a culture of 'no'. Their every decision was based on fear, on hesitation, on an ingrained pessimism that was the very worst side of Britishness.

'You have advised me,' she said through gritted teeth. 'But I know I'm right about this. I'm flying back to New

York this afternoon. I suggest we meet again at the end of next week when I'm back and I can update you all on developments.'

Eight mouths fell open simultaneously. Even Arabella Boscombe was rendered temporarily speechless. In the end it was Michael Guinness who found the board's collective voice.

'You're flying *back* to New York? You do understand that we unanimously oppose the purchase of this building?'

Tatiana stood up. '*I* built this business. *I* did. It was *my* vision, *my* hard work that you all bought into. There is no Hamilton Hall without me.'

Her arrogance was breathtaking, but no one contradicted her.

'Perhaps I should remind you that you all opposed opening a second London school too, in the beginning?'

'That's true,' said Eric Jenkins, reasonably. 'But that was a little different.'

'No it wasn't,' said Tati, arrogantly. 'It was exactly the same. I'm sorry, but you were wrong then and you're wrong now. I will return from New York armed with the figures to prove it. Now, if you'll all excuse me,' she picked up her briefcase, 'I have a plane to catch.'

It was a full minute after Tatiana left the room before anybody spoke.

'We have to do something.' Lady Arabella Boscombe's voice was calm but determined. 'You do see that now, don't you Eric?'

The accountant nodded grimly. 'Yes. I do.'

He'd always liked Tatiana. He admired her energy, her courage, her youth. By contrast he'd always found Arabella Boscombe to be a shameless snob, self-important and far too fond of her own voice. But Tati had gone too far this time. She was making fools of them all.

'She's right about one thing though,' he observed. 'There is no Hamilton Hall without her.'

As they filed out of the room, stony-faced, Michael Guinness could be heard muttering under his breath. 'We'll see about that.'

Jason Cranley watched Tati's black cab pulling up outside their house from the bedroom window. He felt a sickening churning in the pit of his stomach and ran to the bathroom.

Calm down, he told himself as he sank to his knees on the tiled floor. *For God's sake calm down.*

The nausea subsided, thank God, but was immediately replaced with a throbbing headache, the same one that had been coming and going all morning. Jason still couldn't quite believe that he was going to do this. His spirit was willing – desperate even – to tell Tatiana the truth. But his flesh was weak, his body rebelling in every possible way against the idea. Staggering back to his feet, he ran the cold tap over a flannel, wrung it out and pressed it to his forehead and temples, like a Victorian heroine in the throes of some sort of fit. His skin alternately burned and tingled and his throat felt dry. He had never been more afraid in his life.

This is Tati, he told himself. *Your wife. Your best friend. You can tell her anything.*

'Jason? Darling? Are you home?'

Tati's voice reverberated up the stairwell. Jason felt his chest tighten. For a moment he found it hard to breathe. Before he could reply, Tati burst into the bedroom.

'Oh, there you are,' she said, kissing him on the cheek and apparently not noticing his greyish-green pallor, or the flannel still clutched in his hand. 'I just had a bloody irritating board meeting. Really, there's no pleasing some people. You'd have thought, after the financial results we just got in from Clapham, they'd be patting me on the back, but oh no. Bloody Arabella Boscombe's whipped everyone up into a frenzy about New York and the price I negotiated on the Seventh Avenue site.'

Oh dear, thought Jason. *She's on a roll.* He knew this version of his wife well. Talking quickly, her voice raised, a ball of excitement and indignation and nervous energy.

Tati carried on, without drawing breath.

'I mean, don't these people read the sodding business pages? For a building that size in that position, twenty million's a fucking snip! We only got it because we're cash buyers and the vendor's desperate. And the exchange rate's never been better. Have you seen my cabin bag, by the way?' She began opening and closing cupboards without waiting for an answer. It was if a tornado had swept into the room. 'Ah, there it is. You know, sometimes I feel like screaming, "Wake up, morons!" Opportunities like this don't come along every day and they don't wait either. I can't just sit in London dithering until Lady Arabella untwists her capacious knickers and gets on board, can I?'

Jason watched silently as Tati chucked a suitcase onto the bed and began throwing clothes inside it, willy-nilly. Soon she'd be grabbing her passport from the bureau drawer and running out of the door again. He couldn't let her leave for New York without saying anything. By the time she got back, whatever small shreds of courage he had would have deserted him for sure.

'Tatiana, I . . . there's something I need to talk to you about.'

'Can it wait?' Tati asked absently, flinging a pashmina

shawl and a pair of red Louboutin pumps into the case before zipping it up. 'I'm super-duper late.'

'Not really.'

For the first time since she walked in, Tati noticed how ashen Jason was looking. It was a look she remembered well from before they married, back when Jason had been his father's emotional punch-bag. Each time Brett put Jason down, or imposed his will, ignoring the boy's feelings, Jason had worn the same bloodless, terrified expression.

Tati sat down on the bed. 'What's the matter? Has something happened?'

Jason opened his mouth to speak, then closed it again. He'd gone over this speech in his head hundreds, maybe even thousands of times. But now that the moment had finally arrived to deliver it, the words stuck in his throat. 'I-I-I . . .' he stammered. 'You see, the thing is . . .'

Tatiana's mobile rang. The noise was loud and insistent, as if an angry bee had flown into the room. She looked at the screen. It was Jenna Finch, her PA. Jenna knew better than to bother Tatiana if it wasn't important.

'Sorry, darling.' She made an apologetic face at Jason. 'I have to take this. I'll be quick, I promise. Standing up, she walked back to the window, cradling the phone in her hands. 'Jenna. What's up?'

By the time she got off the phone, Jason's mouth had turned to sawdust. Rivers of sweat poured down his back and chest.

'Sorry,' Tati smiled, swinging her suitcase down off the bed. 'You wanted to say something?'

'It's all right,' he said. 'It's not that important.'

He hated himself but he couldn't do it, not rushed and frantic like this. The moment had passed.

Tati kissed him on the cheek. 'I'm sorry. Today's just been

a crazy day, that's all. When I get back we'll spend more time together.'

'Sure.'

'We can talk properly then.'

'OK.'

He watched as she swept out, the lingering aroma of Chanel Cristalle the only sign that she'd been there at all, and listened as the front door slammed shut.

When she's back, he vowed. *I'll tell her when she's back.*

But deep down, not even he believed it.

CHAPTER TWENTY-SIX

Lying back on a blue and white striped sun-lounger at the members only Maidstone Club in East Hampton, Angela Cranley enjoyed the warm feeling of the sun on her legs. Truth be told, she hadn't really wanted to come on this trip. But Brett had insisted, and for once Angela was thankful that he'd bullied her into it.

Angela and Brett had reconciled for the umpteenth time in the New Year. There were a few awkward weeks when he first moved back to Furlings, but since then things had been much better between them. So much so that Logan had moved back once her A-level exams were over, along with the lovely Tom. They'd both taken summer jobs at a fruit farm near Fittlescombe to save up for their year-off travelling together. Angela had expected Brett to throw his toys out of the pram at the mere suggestion of Logan's boyfriend staying under their roof, but he'd surprised her. The time spent away from his family seemed to have mellowed him. Brett appeared to be as pleased as Angela that Furlings once more felt like a family home, and he and Tom got on well from the beginning. In return, Angela had respected Brett's wishes and agreed not to invite Tatiana to the house again. She would see Jason in London, or at his and Tati's new country house in nearby Brockhurst, a run-down Elizabethan manor that Jason was about to start renovating. It was a compromise that suited everyone.

The one lingering problem that remained was the amount of time Brett spent travelling for work. In particular he seemed to be spending more and more time in the States, with his business trips often extending for two weeks or more. After his last jaunt, he'd floated the idea of buying a home there, a place where he and Angela could both stay when he travelled.

'I couldn't live in Manhattan,' Angela told him. 'All those skyscrapers. I feel claustrophobic just thinking about it.'

The old Brett would have pooh-poohed her objections and pressed ahead regardless. But the new, more sensitive version had proposed a place in the Hamptons as a compromise solution.

Their current visit was part-vacation, part-house-hunting mission. If Brett's aim had been to sell Angela on East Hampton, she had to admit it was working. After the longest, greyest, most miserable spring and early summer in England that anyone could remember, it felt wonderful to wake up to blue skies and sunshine. And the town itself, with its pristine white sand beaches and idyllically understated shingle architecture, appealed to Angela immediately. They were staying with the Claridges. Dean Claridge, a business associate of Brett's, had made hundreds of millions in Russian oil, and his wife Lavinia 'Vinnie' Claridge lived in their sprawling East Hampton beach house full time while her husband spent the weeks in town.

'I just adore it here,' Vinnie told Angela, over a game of tennis on one of the Maidstone Club's many courts. 'The summer's a zoo, but other than that it's so peaceful. And the club's like a second home. The waiting list's over a thousand names long. This is *the* club out here. But Dean and I can easily get you and Brett in, if you like it.'

Angela *did* like it, slightly to her own embarrassment. She disapproved of the snobbery of private members' clubs. But she had to admit to herself that this was a very pleasant way to live.

A shadow falling across her body made her open her eyes. 'Lunch time.'

Brett stooped down to kiss her. Still in a business suit, he looked handsome and relaxed. He must just have returned from his meeting in Manhattan this morning. Judging by the broad grin on his face, it had gone well.

'Dean and Vinnie got us a great table inside. Why don't you change and meet us in there? I'll order you a drink.'

At lunch, talk was of nothing but real estate.

'I'm telling you, it's gonna be the Eighties all over again,' Brett said to Dean Claridge, over a steak so sinfully juicy it would have tempted Linda McCartney. 'More than twenty-five per cent of Cranley Estates' growth in the last year has been down to the boom in the New York market. Mark my words, the Hamptons are gonna skyrocket too.'

'Haven't they already?' asked Vinnie, between sips of her ice-cold Chablis.

'As high as prices are now, this is just the beginning,' said Brett. 'You watch.'

'Have you seen any places you like?' Dean Claridge asked Angela. A stocky, bulldog of a man with a thick neck and a pronounced under-bite that gave him the pugnacious air of a bulldog, Dean was in fact a kind and generous man, uniquely among Brett's work friends.

'I like all of them,' said Angela truthfully. 'I'm just not sure it's worth buying another big house.'

'Why not? Big houses are better than small ones,' said Brett with a grin.

'Yes, but it's so extravagant,' said Angela. 'Logan's about to leave home and Jason's long gone. We don't need all that space. Especially for a place I'm going to visit a couple of times a year.'

Brett reached across the table and covered her hand with his. 'Maybe we'll start spending more time here. You'd like that, wouldn't you?'

Angela smiled nervously. Brett had dropped a lot of hints in the last few days about them spending more time in the US. In the back of her mind, she wondered whether he might be growing tired of Fittlescombe and their sleepy country life in Sussex. The Hamptons were lovely for a holiday, but the last thing Angela wanted was to be uprooted from her home. She couldn't help but feel that Furlings was the glue that had held her and Brett together, through all the tough times and betrayals of the past seven years. Without it, things might slip back to the way they were before.

After lunch, Dean headed back to his home office to work and Vinnie and Angela joined some girlfriends for a game of doubles. Brett had another house to see at four, which made it hardly worth going home. He decided to catch up on some emails at the bar. Settling in to a quiet corner table, he ordered a grappa, the perfect postscript to a perfect meal, and opened his iPad.

So far, the trip was going exactly to plan. Angela was clearly taken by the Hamptons. Vinnie and Dean had been the perfect hosts. Thanks to them, Brett could see that Ange was starting to feel at home here. He must be careful not to push too hard and scare her off.

He'd decided that he wanted to move to New York back in the spring. He and Angela needed a fresh start: while Angela viewed Furlings as some sort of talisman of good luck for their marriage, for Brett it was the opposite. That house was a daily reminder of Tatiana, the one person above all others that he needed to forget. Cutting her out of their lives, physically, was all very well. But what good did it do him if she was still in his head and his heart, haunting him like some toxic shadow?

Christmas was a turning point. Having foolishly left his home unguarded, Tatiana had wasted no time moving in like a snake, coiling herself around each member of his family, warming herself by *his* fire in *his* drawing room while he, Brett, stood out in the dark and cold, looking in. Of course, it wasn't his family Tati wanted. They were just collateral damage. It was Furlings. That was the bait, the bricks-and-mortar bond that tied her and Brett together, eternally. He'd have sold the house tomorrow if he didn't know for a fact that Tatiana would call any new owner the moment a sale went through and offer them limitless amounts of money to buy it back. After the cynical manner in which she'd run off and married his son, Brett would rather cut off his own hand than see Tati get that house back. He'd already changed his will so that Furlings and the remainder of his estate was left entirely to Logan and her future children. If Tatiana thought that having a baby with Jason would change anything, she had another think coming.

He'd decided to let Furlings out, decamp to New York, and be rid of Tatiana and the past for good. All he had to do now was convince Angela.

'Your grappa, sir.'

A waiter set down the miniature tumbler of clear, viscose

liquid in front of Brett. Lifting it to his lips, Brett suddenly froze.

No. It's not possible.

It was almost exactly a year since he'd last seen Tati. On that occasion he'd also been in New York State, and in a bar. The encounter was seared on his memory like a cattle brand. And now here she was again, looking relaxed and happy in a white, twenties-style sundress with a dropped waist, arm in arm with an extremely attractive man.

Instinctively Brett sank back into the shadows. He did not want Tati to see him.

'Do you know that man?' he asked the waiter, sotto voce, nodding towards Tati's companion.

'Yes, sir. Of course. That's Leon di Clemente.'

Brett knew the name. Leon DC was a famous angel investor on the East Coast. He'd made a lot of money from a couple of apps, specifically one that let people pay off their tabs in a crowded bar from their phone, without having to wait for service. Leon's father, Andrea di Clemente, had made a small fortune in mining in the Congo and his son had turned it into a large one, inheriting at the tender age of twenty-one. All of which begged the question: *what the fuck was Leon DC doing here, with his arm around Tatiana Cranley?*

Tatiana was having a wonderful week. Not only had she persuaded the seller of the Seventh Avenue site to lower his price by a further ten per cent, but her meeting with Leon di Clemente yesterday had gone better than she'd dared hope. A mutual friend from London had set her up with Leon, and Tati's plan had been to approach him about joining the board of Hamilton Hall NYC. But the two of them had hit it off instantly, agreeing about everything from the unique opportunity currently presented by Manhattan commercial real estate, to the limitless possibilities for growth in the private education sector. Within forty minutes, Leon had been reaching for his chequebook and promising to underwrite the New York school in its entirety if necessary, should Tatiana's London board continue to stymie her proposal. After all the stress and confrontation of the last few weeks, Tati felt as if the weight of the world had been lifted off her shoulders.

She and Leon got on well personally, too. It was a long time since Tati had felt a sexual connection to anybody, but Leon's attentions, combined with the adrenaline rush she always felt pulling off a great deal, had set her libido on fire. A few years older than Tati, with curly, jet-black hair, dark brown eyes and the swarthy complexion of a pirate, Leon was a handsome man. But his sex appeal lay more in his confidence. There was nothing passive or subtle about his flirting.

'You're gorgeous,' he told Tati, apropos of nothing, halfway through their meeting in his palatial Park Avenue office. 'Have dinner with me.'

'I'm married,' said Tati, unable entirely to keep the disappointment out of her voice.

'So? I'll pick you up at your hotel at eight.'

He took her to L'Artusi, a trendy restaurant in the West Village that wasn't remotely discreet, and held her hand as they walked to the table, apparently not in the slightest concerned about who might see them together. Nothing happened. But after a few sour apple martinis, Tati felt a warm rush of happiness whenever Leon touched her back or paid her a compliment. Like a coma patient opening her eyes after years of nothingness, every sensation was heightened and wonderful. It was an effort to return to her hotel room alone.

Leon, however, seemed unfazed and happy to play the long game.

'I'm heading out to the Hamptons this weekend. You should come. If we're going to be business partners, we need to get to know each other better. And there are people there it would be useful for you to meet.'

Tati hadn't needed to be asked twice. After sending a brief, pithy fax to her board – she couldn't resist addressing it to Lady Arabella's attention – outlining the new sale price on the proposed school site and her decision to go ahead with the deal with or without them, she splurged on a new sundress and bikini at Barneys, got her hair highlighted at Garren and was sitting in Leon's helicopter sipping champagne by four that afternoon.

Steering her through the bar at the Maidstone Club, Leon commandeered a table by the pool and ordered oysters on the half-shell and Bloody Marys for both of them. Tati enjoyed the feeling of not being in control for once, of having the man make the decisions.

'So,' Leon said bluntly. 'What's the deal with you and your husband?'

'The deal?' Tati laughed. 'It's called marriage, Leon. It's where you stand up in a church and promise to be faithful and stay together forever.'

'Ah, yes. Because you love each other so much.'

Each word dripped with cynicism.

Tatiana said nothing.

'How long have you been together?'

'Six years.'

'No kids?'

'No.'

Leon sipped his drink slowly. 'Why not?'

'What is this, the Spanish Inquisition?' said Tati, crossly. 'Can we change the subject?'

'Absolutely not.' Leon grinned. 'I like this subject.'

He wasn't a tall man. Nor was he stocky, like Brett. If anything he was rather slight, which was usually a huge turn-off for Tati. But Leon's black eyes glinted when he spoke, with the sort of playful arrogance she'd always found irresistible. She noticed his hands on the tablecloth, slender and impeccably manicured, and found herself imagining what they would feel like caressing her naked body.

'Do you love your husband?'

'I do. Yes,' she said truthfully.

'Have you ever been unfaithful to him?'

'No.'

'I'm afraid that's the incorrect answer.' Picking up an oyster, Leon lifted it slowly to Tati's lips. 'The correct answer is "not yet".'

Their eyes locked. Tati swallowed the slimy, salty creature. She felt both aroused and afraid. Suddenly, irrationally, she wished Jason were there. Or that she was at home, in Eaton Gate, in the safety of her marriage bed.

I'm afraid of myself.

She stood up, aware of her legs quivering beneath her. 'Excuse me. I have to go to the bathroom.'

Leon sat back in his chair triumphantly, his perfectly chiselled face radiating the confidence of the victor.

'Take your time,' he drawled. 'I'm not going anywhere.'

Brett Cranley watched as Tatiana hurried back through the bar and into the Ladies'. The body language between her and Leon di Clemente had been unequivocal.

Little slut.

But this time Brett wasn't about to let his anger get the better of him. He must think, and strategize, before he made his next move. Dropping a fifty-dollar note on the table, he slipped out to the tennis courts and found Angela.

'Time to go,' he said forcefully.

'What? I can't leave now, darling,' she protested. 'We've still got another set left to play.'

'The vendors called and moved up our viewing,' said Brett. 'They got an offer this morning apparently, so it's now or never. I really need you to see this house, Ange. It's perfect.'

'But . . . I . . .' Angela hesitated.

'Go,' said Vinnie. 'It's fine. One of the other girls will step in. It's only a game of doubles.'

'See?' said Brett. 'It's fine. Now let's get out of here.'

Very late that night, Tati called Jason.

'I've decided to come home early,' she told him. She forced herself to sound upbeat but the hand that held her phone was shaking. 'I'll be on the first flight to London tomorrow.'

'Really?' Jason sounded surprised. 'Is everything OK?'

'Everything's fine!' Tati chirped.

'But I thought you said things were going really well over there.'

'They were. They are,' said Tati. 'I just . . . I miss you.'

There was a brief silence on the other end of the line. Then Jason said cautiously, 'OK. Well, I'll see you tomorrow then.'

He was about to hang up. Tati didn't know why, but she suddenly felt panic welling up inside her. She wanted to go back. Back to yesterday. Or farther back. Back to when she and Jason had been happy together. But did that time even exist? She didn't want to think about it, to lift the cover off her marriage and examine the yawning, terrifying fissures beneath. She wanted to put her fingers in her ears and hum. She wanted everything to be OK, everything to stay as it was.

But that could never happen. Not now.

'I love you,' she blurted out, close to tears.

'I love you too,' said Jason. Tati pictured his words as pieces of driftwood, floating out on an ocean of sadness. 'Goodnight, Tatiana.'

The soft click of the receiver sounded like the cocking of a gun.

Leon di Clemente was deep asleep when his mobile phone rang.

'Mmmm?' he said groggily, knocking books off his bedside table. His clock informed him it was 2.50 a.m. But when he realized who the caller was, it was as if a glass of cold water had been thrown in his face. He sat bolt upright, wide awake.

'What can I do for you?'

'The question, Mr di Clemente, is what I can do for you. I'd like to meet.'

'Of course. Yes,' Leon stammered.

'Good. Is tomorrow afternoon convenient?'

Twenty seconds later, Leon slumped back against his pillow, physically and mentally exhausted. Had that conversation really just happened?

Then again, after the day he'd had today, perhaps nothing should surprise him?

He slipped back into a deep and dreamless sleep.

CHAPTER TWENTY-SEVEN

Max Bingley's wedding to Stella Goye was Fittlescombe's most talked-about event of the summer. With the village fete and the annual Swell Valley cricket match both now over and done with (both had been drearier affairs than usual thanks to some dismal spring and summer weather), the wedding became the focal point of the entire village. In early August the skies had finally cleared, and a belated summer descended over the South Downs. Temperatures for the Saturday of the wedding were expected to soar into the high eighties, lifting local spirits still further and prompting a run on Pimm's, the like of which the village off-licence hadn't seen in a decade.

Rumour had it that the wedding would also be the first time since Jason and Tatiana's elopement that the entire Cranley family, both generations, would be gathered under the same roof.

'Poor old Reverend Slaughter only just got St Hilda's roof fixed,' Gabe Baxter joked to Seb Harwich, filling his vintage MG up with petrol at Vick's garage in the village. The MG had been an extravagant birthday present from

Laura, whose happy hormones seemed to have gone mad with breastfeeding Felix. 'Shame to see the top blown off it so soon.'

'You think there'll be fireworks then?' Seb asked, checking the oil on his decrepit Datsun. Seb was back in Fittlescombe briefly, in between trekking in the Andes and going on what he reverently described as a 'cricket pilgrimage' to India, Australia and the West Indies in September. His so-called year off was beginning to look more like a decade, but he was such a nice lad, it was hard to hold his lack of industry against him. And at least he was finally over Logan Cranley. Gabe had caught a brief glimpse of Seb's latest squeeze in The Fox last weekend, a stunning blonde with the sort of legs guaranteed to cure any twenty-three year old of heartbreak within minutes. 'I don't think even the Cranleys would air their dirty laundry on Old Man Bingley's special day.'

'It's not the Cranleys,' said Gabe. 'It's Tatiana and Brett. They won't be able to help themselves. They're like two cats in a bag.'

'I thought you liked Brett?'

'I do,' said Gabe. 'But I also know him. He hates Tati Flint-Hamilton's guts.'

'I disagree.' Santiago de la Cruz, Seb's stepfather, came out of the garage shop looking thunderous with a copy of the *Daily Mail* under his arm. Yet another scandalous piece about Seb's sister Emma has been printed in the gossip section, upsetting poor Penny dreadfully. 'I reckon Mr Cranley's protesting too much. He fancies her.'

'Tatiana? No way,' said Gabe. Once cricketing rivals, Santiago and Gabe had become good friends over the years.

'Well, we'll see at the wedding I suppose, won't we?' said

Seb. Pulling the paper out of his stepfather's hand, his eyes widened at the piece on his sister. Emma's antics didn't upset him the way they did his mother, but this latest sex scandal was more salacious than most. Apparently she'd been caught on video trying to sell sex to a Middle Eastern sheikh for some insane amount of money.

'I'm not sure we'll be going to the wedding,' Santiago told Gabe.

'Why not? You must have been invited.'

'We were, and we accepted. But Penny can't face it. Not now.' Retrieving the newspaper from Seb, Santiago passed it to Gabe.

'Shit,' said Gabe, skim-reading the article.

'Yeah,' Santiago muttered darkly. 'Shit. I tell you, compared to my wife's darling daughter, Tatiana looks positively saintly.'

'I'm not sure anyone could make Tati look saintly,' said Gabe. But his mind was already wandering back to Santiago's earlier comment, about Brett Cranley lusting after her. If that were true, if Brett was secretly falling for his own son's wife, it would really set the cat amongst the pigeons.

Max Bingley's wedding was looking set to be one big fireworks display.

Gabe Baxter could hardly wait.

St Hilda's Church, lovely as it was, was tiny, only seating eighty at a pinch. Happily, the garden at Willow Cottage was big enough for an enormous marquee. Well over two hundred friends and well-wishers were there to welcome the bride and groom back from the wedding, and to begin the serious business of celebrating.

'Isn't it beautiful?' Laura Baxter, who'd left Felix with a

babysitter for the evening, wandered entranced through the white, candle-lit tables. Stella had gone for a 'summer's orchard' theme, with tall glass vases holding blossom-laden branches, and smaller, simple jam jars stuffed with cottage garden flowers: sweet peas and roses and softly overblown peonies in various shades of dusky pink, white and purple. 'It's like *A Midsummer Night's Dream*.'

Willow Cottage's lawn sloped down to the river, and the end of the marquee was open so that the bottom tables nestled right on the banks, by the water's edge. The central beam holding the tent aloft had been decorated as a maypole, painted in bright candy stripes and with silk ribbons tied around it. Max's granddaughters, Celia and Martha, danced around it in their bridesmaid's dresses, along with some of the village children, like a scene from a Kate Greenaway book, while their parents got stuck in to the Pimm's and fresh mint cocktails on offer.

'Half the price of champagne and ten times as delicious!' proclaimed the bride, helping herself and handing one to Max as she kicked off her church shoes and let down her hair. 'Are you happy, darling?'

'Of course.' Max kissed her, a trifle stiffly. All the bare feet and fairies weren't really his thing, but he was glad Stella was happy.

He was happy too. Happy and relieved. The run-up to the wedding had been stressful. What had started out as a low-key, intimate affair had somehow ballooned in the planning into a major social event, with pretty much the entire village invited. Quite apart from the expense, the scale of the thing made Max feel faintly embarrassed. They weren't young, after all. Truth be told, he'd only proposed in the first place because his daughters had confided in him that Stella really wanted to get married. Max had been quite happy muddling along as they were. The last thing he wanted was a big hullaballoo.

'You should take it as a compliment,' Stella told him. 'It shows how much the village has taken you to its heart, the fact that everyone wants to share your happiness.'

Privately Max thought it showed how much Fittlescombe villagers appreciated a free bar. But now that the ceremony was over and the party was under way, he determined to enjoy it.

Brett Cranley was enjoying it too, until he saw the seating plan. In the two weeks since he and Angela had got back from New York, he'd been working flat out. He'd been looking forward to the Bingley wedding as a chance to relax and unwind a little, until he learned that Jason and Tatiana had also been invited and had accepted, damn them both.

Angela had calmed him down, assuring him that it was a huge reception and he'd be able to avoid Tati easily enough if he wanted to. But someone, presumably the meddlesome Max Bingley, had other ideas.

'You've got to be kidding me,' Brett hissed in Angela's ear. 'Have you seen this? Some maniac's put us all on the same bloody table.'

Angela looked at the hand-drawn plan in dismay. All the tables were named after Shakespeare plays. There, on *Hamlet*, were she and Brett, Logan and Tom and Jason and Tatiana, along with Dylan Pritchard Jones and his wife Maisie. If this were Max's idea of diplomacy, a well-meant attempt at family bridge-building perhaps, it was as subtle as a sledgehammer.

Still, there was a chance that fireworks might yet be averted. Jason and Tatiana had been invited to both the service and the reception, but had been no-shows at the church. Angela had tried Jason's mobile twice since, but it went straight to message.

'Keep your voice down,' Angela chided Brett. 'They're probably not coming anyway. Something's obviously happened or they'd have been at the church.'

'You were saying?' Brett scowled.

Angela followed his gaze to the marquee entrance. There was Jason, standing hand in hand with a green-looking Tati. Angela felt her stomach lurch with a combination of love – Jase looked so handsome in his morning coat – and nerves. Today was Max and Stella's day. It mustn't be allowed to become about the Cranleys and their internecine warfare.

'Don't make a scene, Brett. Please. You promised.'

'I'm not going to make a scene.'

Brett squeezed her hand. The last thing he wanted was to upset Angela now. Last week the purchase had gone through on their house in the Hamptons, a stunning nine-bedroom beachfront estate with gardens to rival Furlings'. Brett had anticipated a long, protracted battle to get Angela to even entertain the idea of moving to the States, but to his astonishment she'd already agreed to consider a trial period of a year. They could rent Furlings out and 'see how things go.' It was more than Brett had dared hope for. Now was not the time to rock the boat.

He pulled a Cuban cigar out of his jacket pocket.

'If you want me I'll be outside by the river, having a smoke.'

'Thank you,' said Angela, visibly relieved. 'I know this is hard for you, darling, but it's only for one night. I know it would mean a lot to Logan too if we can keep things civil.'

Brett nodded. 'Just see if you can shuffle the name cards

around while I'm gone, so I'm not right next to them. All right?'

'All right,' agreed Angela. 'I'll try.'

'Can I get you anything?' Jason asked Tati. 'A glass of water?'

She shook her head miserably. 'Go and talk to your family. I'll find a quiet corner and die somewhere. I'm not fit to be seen anyway.'

'What are you talking about? You look lovely,' Jason lied loyally.

'I look horrendous,' said Tati.

It was true. The nausea had come out of nowhere. From the moment she woke up this morning she'd felt like death, not just sick but puffy and bloated, her skin sallow and sweaty. The dark green, brushed silk dress that had looked so cute and eighties retro in the changing room in New York, now made her look like a tree-frog that had somehow ingested its own poison. Her hair stuck limply to her head beneath a wilting green-feathered fascinator, and her swollen feet felt like pigs' trotters squeezed into black patent Manolo pumps.

Of course she had to get stomach flu on the one day she was certain to run into Brett, not to mention all her old friends and colleagues. She'd felt judged enough at Christmas, but the pitying looks she was receiving now were almost worse than the envious glares she'd got then. *Look at Tatiana Cranley*, she imagined them all thinking. *Talk about losing her looks!*

Having missed the entire wedding ceremony doubled over on the verge of the A3 puking her guts out, Tati had insisted on soldiering on to the reception, despite Jason's objections. If she didn't show up, Brett would think she was running scared, and she couldn't have that. Now though, dizzy and seasick and wilting in the afternoon sun, she was already starting to regret her decision.

'Are you sure I can't get you something?' Jason sounded worried. 'Max is bound to have some Alka-Seltzer in a bathroom cupboard somewhere.'

His concern only made Tati feel worse. Ever since she'd got back from New York, Jason had been kindness personified, cooking her meals and listening for hours while she poured out her frustrations about her board, who *still* hadn't signed off on the Manhattan site and were using any excuse to stall the deal. In return, Tati had tried to be affectionate, and had even attempted to kick-start things sexually between them, with disastrous results. Their lovemaking was so awkward and forced it was mortifying, like a scene from a bad *Carry On* film. At least Tati's sudden mystery illness would buy her a few days off sex, she thought guiltily. *I must try harder.*

'I'll be fine,' she told Jason. 'I might go and lie down for a bit, see if I can rally for dinner.'

Dinner was a living hell.

Tati forced herself to sit down and eat, but by now she had spots in front of her eyes and felt borderline delirious. Brett and Angela, thankfully, were on the opposite side of the table, far enough away to make conversation impossible. The downside was that this left Tati between Tom, Logan's adorable but by now completely drunk boyfriend, and Dylan Pritchard Jones, her old enemy from St Hilda's.

'Hullo, Tatiana.' Dylan smiled smugly. 'It must be ages since we last saw each other. Do you know, if I hadn't read your place card, I don't know if I'd have recognized you.'

Clearly this was code for 'you look like shit.'

Arsehole.

Tati decided to take the high road.

'Hullo Dylan. How are things going at St Jude's?'

'My lord, you are out of date!' Dylan laughed, a loud, braying, donkey-like sound. *I'm sure he didn't used to laugh like that*, thought Tati. *Wasn't he quite attractive when I first met him?* 'I left Jude's years ago. Got the headship at Lancing. I'm having the time of my life.'

With his sun-bed tan, mouthful of white veneers and once naturally chestnut curls now dyed blonde to cover the grey, Dylan looked more like a television presenter than a headmaster these days. He reminded Tati of a Ken doll: vain, obnoxious and above all fake. If it hadn't been for the gallon and a half of Gucci aftershave he must have sloshed over himself this morning, Tati was sure she could have smelled the insincerity on his skin.

'You should drop by some time. It's a gorgeous campus.' Under the table, Dylan slipped a hand onto Tati's bare thigh and squeezed, while flashing his teeth. 'I'd be happy to show you around, for old times' sake.'

Oh my God! She shuddered. *Is he serious? He actually thinks I might be interested?*

'How kind,' she said brusquely, removing his hand and inching her chair as far towards Tom's as it would go. 'Unfortunately I'm rather busy with Hamilton Hall right now. Both the London schools are oversubscribed. In fact, business is booming so much that we're opening our first American school next year,' she couldn't resist adding.

'So I hear,' said Dylan, refilling his wine glass.

Tati frowned. 'What do you mean?'

No one knew about their planned New York expansion. She hadn't even officially cleared it with her own board yet, although now that Leon DC had effectively underwritten the new school, their approval was a formality.

'Did Jason say something to you about New York?'

'Jason? No, no. It was your beloved father-in-law.' He nodded across the table to where Brett was deep in conversation with Seb Harwich's extremely young, extremely beautiful blonde girlfriend. 'I gather he saw you there last month. Funny how your paths seem to keep on crossing, isn't it? Now that Brett and Angela are moving Stateside, I expect you'll be running into each other all the time. Like one big, happy family,' he added snidely.

Tati put her head in her hands and squeezed her eyes shut, willing the nausea to dissipate. She felt so ghastly it was hard to concentrate, but what Dylan was saying was important. He must be wrong.

'Brett and Angela aren't moving,' she said slowly. 'They'd never leave Furlings.'

Dylan shrugged. '*Au contraire*. They're upping sticks. It's the talk of the village. Well, that and Emma Harwich dropping her knickers again, although quite how that's still considered news, I couldn't tell you. Ask Brett yourself if you don't believe me.'

Tati stared at him mutely. He had to be mistaken. Or perhaps he was saying it just to get a reaction out of her? Dylan had always been a shit-stirrer.

'Funny, isn't it, me knowing so much more about your family's business than you do?' he smirked.

'Hilarious,' said Tati.

As soon as dinner was over, Tati dragged Jason off to one side.

'Dylan Pritchard Jones told me your parents are moving to America. Is that true?'

'Apparently so,' said Jason.

Tati exploded. 'Why the fuck didn't you tell me?'

A number of guests turned around to stare at them. Dizzy with the effort of shouting, Tati slumped down onto the nearest chair.

'For God's sake, calm down,' said Jason, pulling up a chair next to her. 'I didn't know myself till tonight. Mum told me at dinner.'

'Don't you understand what this means?' said Tati, running her hands through her hair.

'I don't think it means anything,' said Jason. 'Other than Mum and Dad wanting a fresh start.'

'Of course it does,' snapped Tati. 'It means they'll sell Furlings. Which means we can buy it.'

'Don't be silly,' said Jason gently. 'Dad wouldn't sell to you – to us – if we were the last buyers on earth.'

'Of course not. But he'll sell to someone else. Then we can swoop in and make them an offer they can't refuse.'

Jason sighed. He wished, for her own sake, that Tati would let go of her fantasies about Furlings.

'According to Mum they're not selling at all,' he told her. 'Dad's renting it out. They want to keep their options open. I think Mum would like to come back, eventually.'

While Tati sat in brooding silence taking this in, Logan, looking ravishing in a gold brocade dress and with her long dark hair swept up in Cleopatra-esque coils, came over and accosted Jason. Since she and Brett had buried the hatchet, she had been back living at Furlings over the summer holidays. Both Jason and Tati missed her presence at Eaton Gate and had been looking forward to seeing her today at the wedding.

'Can Tommy and I cadge a lift back to London with you tonight?' Logan asked. 'A friend from college has two extra tickets to the Venom concert tomorrow at the O2.'

'Sure,' said Jason. 'We'll probably be leaving soon, though. Tati's not feeling too chipper.'

'She looks all right to me,' said Logan, pointing to the far corner of the marquee. Tatiana was talking to Brett. Judging by her body language, she was letting him have it. 'Perhaps she's rallied?'

'Oh, God,' sighed Jason.

'You don't even want the house.' Tati was shouting, waving her arms around like an air traffic controller trying to bring a plane in to land whilst in the throes of an epileptic fit. 'Why can't you just admit it?'

'Look,' said Brett. 'I'm not selling Furlings and that's that.'

'Yes, and why not? Out of spite, that's why. Because you know Jason and I *do* want it.'

'Leave Jason out of this,' said Brett. 'This is between you and me.'

'Fine. So sell the house back to me. You can name your price.'

'It's not for sale.' His eyes were glittering but Tati couldn't quite get a handle on whether it was with amusement or something else. 'And it never will be. Why can't you just accept the fact that your father didn't want you to have that house? He cut you out of the will, and left it to me, and there is nothing you can do to change that. *Nothing*.'

The truth was that Furlings was the one thing, the only thing, he controlled when it came to his relationship with Tatiana. He couldn't have her. He couldn't stop wanting her either. But he *could* hold on to something he knew she wanted, and would always want. Furlings was the unbreakable chain that bound the two of them together. The only ace in Brett's hand. That made it priceless. Because as much as Brett yearned for escape from the misery of his feelings for Tati, the thought

424

of actually breaking that chain and letting her go filled him with terror.

Of course, Tati couldn't see Brett's fear. She was too blinded by her own, by her deep need to get Furlings back and right the wrongs of the past.

'He cut me off because I was a mess back then.' She pleaded with Brett's rational side. 'He wouldn't have made the same decision if he could see me now. I rarely drink and never touch drugs. I have Hamilton Hall. I'm rich and successful. I'm happily married.'

Brett let out a snort of derision at this last claim. 'You're delusional.'

'And you're a fucking arsehole,' Tati shouted, loudly enough for a number of nearby wedding guests to shoot her disapproving looks.

Brett leaned in closer. His voice in her ear was like the hissing of a snake. 'I saw you at the Maidstone Club last month. With lover boy.'

The hair on Tati's forearms stood on end and the greenish colour drained from her face.

'You can tell me that was a business meeting till you're blue in the face,' Brett went on. 'But I know what kind of business you've been doing. So you can spare me the "happily married", saintly wife act. I know who you are.'

Tati looked him in the eye defiantly. 'You have no idea who I am. You don't even know who *you* are.'

'Don't try to change the subject,' said Brett.

'Why not?' said Tati. 'You don't like it when people hold up a mirror and force you to look at yourself, do you Brett? Who the hell are you to pass judgement on my marriage? Take a look at your own.'

They stood in silence, squared off and staring at one another, like two duellists who'd forgotten to bring their

425

guns. *She's so like me*, thought Brett. *She keeps fighting, even when she's cornered.* He wondered how different his marriage to Angela might have been if she'd ever challenged him the way that Tatiana did? If she'd ever stood up to him. Would he have been faithful? He didn't know. He supposed it didn't much matter now anyway. Angela was a better person than Tatiana, and a better person than him. He knew it, but he couldn't forgive Tatiana for calling him on it.

'Read my lips,' he said slowly, savouring each word. 'You will Never. Own. That. House. Not while I'm alive.'

'You're evil,' whispered Tati. 'I hate you.'

She threw the words at him like a cup full of acid. But Brett could see that her eyes brimmed with tears. He'd intended to wound her. And yet a huge part of him longed to pull her into his arms and comfort her, to hold her till she stopped crying and never cried again.

At that moment Jason appeared at her side. He put one arm around Tati's waist and the other comfortingly around her shoulder, drawing her in to a hug. Brett felt a stabbing pain in his heart so acute he wondered for a moment if he were having an attack.

'You should get your bitch on a tighter leash,' he snarled at Jason.

Ignoring him, Jason turned back to Tati. 'Come on, darling, let's go. He's not worth it.'

Tati allowed herself to be led away. As she and Jason passed the dance floor, she saw the bride, barefoot and beautiful, twirling around with her new husband. Stella's smile could have lit the marquee on its own, and powered the rest of the village as well. Tatiana tried to remember the last time she had felt that happy, but her mind drew a blank.

She'd told herself that spending more time in the Swell Valley would lift her spirits and be good for her soul.

Brockhurst Abbey, which she'd bought on a whim, sight unseen, would be ready to move into in a few months. But she realized now that, however hard her architect and interior designer worked, it would never feel like home. While Furlings was still standing, and while that bastard Brett Cranley kept it from her, she was condemned to wander the world like a lost soul, an eternal refugee.

Jason kept telling her she was fooling herself. That getting Furlings back would not solve all her problems, the way that she imagined it would. That it would not right the wrongs of the past because, as Jason succinctly put it, 'Nothing can do that.' With her rational mind, Tati knew he was right. And yet emotionally that house, her dead father and Brett Cranley formed some sort of mystical triangle from which she could not break free. From which, on some deep, subconscious level, she didn't *want* to break free.

But tonight, for the first time, she asked herself the question: Was it Furlings she wanted? Or was it Brett Cranley?

The truth was she had unfinished business with both of them.

She felt a little better on the car journey home. The Range Rover was warm and comfortable, and Jason's Handel CD soothed the throbbing in her head. The nausea that had plagued her all afternoon was finally gone now too, a relief so sweet it was impossible to remain entirely unhappy.

Glancing over her shoulder into the back seat, she smiled. 'Look,' she said to Jason. Logan and Tom were both fast asleep, their arms wrapped around one another. 'They're like puppies.'

'They are,' Jason agreed.

They lapsed into silence for a few minutes. At a red light, Jason turned towards Tati and rested a hand on her leg. It was the first truly calm moment they'd had together since Tati's return from New York. The moment Jason had been waiting for.

'There's something I have to tell you,' he said quietly.

Tati felt her heart rate quicken, but she didn't flinch. It could not be avoided forever.

She was ready.

'I'm sorry, Tatiana.' Jason looked her squarely in the eye. 'I've fallen in love with someone else.'

CHAPTER TWENTY-EIGHT

Back at the house on Eaton Gate, Tati settled Logan and Tom into the blue guest room and waited till all was quiet upstairs before joining Jason in the kitchen.

'I thought I'd make us some tea.'

He'd carefully set a pot and two mugs down on the table, along with a plate of chocolate Hobnobs. Another couple might have opted for a stiff drink, but actually tea was exactly what Tati wanted. Something normal and soothing, something that was going to make everything all right.

'Thank you.'

They both sat down while Jason poured. After a few moments' silence, Jason was the first to speak.

'I'm sorry,' he said simply.

'Don't be,' said Tati. 'We both knew things weren't right. May I ask who it is?'

Jason looked down at the table, his whole body suddenly rigid with tension. Tati watched the way his fingers coiled nervously around one another, like trapped snakes. Reaching out, she put her own hand over his.

'It's all right,' she said. 'Really. And if you're feeling guilty, for God's sake don't. I slept with someone else myself last month. In New York.'

Jason looked up, surprised. 'Did you?'

Tati nodded, blushing.

'Someone serious?'

The question was more curious than accusatory. Tati thought how odd it was, to be sitting here discussing infidelity over a cup of tea in their kitchen, as if it were the most normal thing in the world.

'No,' she shook her head. 'Not serious. At least, I don't think so. I wouldn't want you to think I made a habit of being unfaithful,' she blurted. 'This was the first time. A one-off.'

Jason squeezed her hand tightly. 'You don't have to explain.'

'I do,' said Tati. 'We're married.'

'I know,' said Jason. 'But we never should have been.'

Tati let out a long breath. 'No,' she agreed softly. 'We never should have been. We should have stayed friends.'

'We *have* stayed friends,' Jason said, suddenly impassioned. 'We *are* friends, Tati. And I hope we always will be.'

Tati's eyes welled up with tears. She blinked them away, wrapping her hands around her mug, allowing its warmth to comfort her. The irony was, it wasn't sadness that she felt. It was pure, unadulterated relief.

'Of course we will,' she said at last. 'Always. So tell me. You *have* found someone serious?'

Jason nodded.

'You said you were in love?'

'I think I am,' he smiled shyly.

'Do I know her?' asked Tati.

Jason was quiet for a moment, his eyes fixed on the table. At last he forced himself to look Tati in the eye.

'That's the thing,' he said softly. 'It's not a her. It's a him.'

It took a lot to render Tatiana speechless. But this, temporarily at least, had done it. She looked at Jason for a long time. At least twice she opened her mouth to say something, then closed it again, an expression of frank astonishment written on her face.

'A him?' she said at last.

'Yes.'

'So . . . you're gay?'

'I'm in love with a man,' Jason replied. 'So I suppose so, yes.'

'But . . . you were in love with a woman before. With me.'

'That's true,' agreed Jason. 'It was never quite right, though, was it? Something was always wrong. Right from the beginning.'

Tati nodded. It was a shock. She hadn't suspected, not at all. But it *did* explain a lot. Something had always been missing between them. She'd just always assumed that she was the problem.

'I adored you,' said Jason. 'I wouldn't want you to think I married you under false pretences. But as time went on, I knew something was wrong. I was very depressed.'

'I remember.'

'I just didn't know why until I met George. After that it all made sense.'

'George . . .' Tati rolled the name over in her mind. She tried to picture this 'George' but all she could think of was an image of Matt Damon from the Liberace movie, all blond hair and tight trousers and rhinestones. To her dismay, she found herself starting to giggle.

431

'I'm so sorry,' she said, blushing. 'I'm not laughing at you. It was brave of you to tell me. I think I'm just in shock.'

'It's OK,' said Jason. 'I'd rather you were laughing than crying. I truly am sorry.'

They hugged each other.

'So,' Tati said, once she'd regained her composure, 'what happens now? Presumably you and . . . George . . . want to be together?'

Jason rubbed his eyes wearily. 'Actually it's complicated.'

Tati raised a questioning eyebrow.

'He's married,' said Jason. 'He has kids.'

'Oh.' Tati winced. 'I see.' Suddenly she felt immensely tired. 'Why don't we go to bed?' she said to Jason. 'I know there's a lot to talk about. But we don't have to rush into any decisions right away.'

'All right,' said Jason, visibly relieved. 'Thanks for being so good about it, Tati. I'll move my stuff into the spare room.'

'Don't,' she said. 'Not yet.'

He gave her a puzzled look.

'I realize it probably sounds ridiculous,' she explained. 'But I don't want to sleep alone tonight. I don't want to lose you. Not completely. Not yet.'

Jason wrapped his arms around her. 'Nor I you,' he said truthfully. 'I'll always be there for you, Tatiana. Whatever you need. I promise.'

When Tatiana woke the next morning, it was almost noon. A single shaft of brilliant sunshine pierced a crack in the curtains, throwing a laser-bright slice of light onto the bed and into Tati's eyes.

Groaning she rolled over onto her stomach, as the events

and revelations of last night gradually came back to her. Jason lay next to her, still deeply asleep, his chest rising and falling like a baby's. Looking at him, she felt a wave of affection. It was an immense relief to have the truth out in the open at last, at least between the two of them. The future would be different, and complicated. She assumed they would divorce at some point, but she felt no sense of urgency, only a deep peace that somehow, things would all work out all right in the end. All the guilt she'd been carrying around about her one-night stand with Leon DC in the Hamptons had been blown away like a dandelion seed on the breeze in the light of Jason's revelations. She felt lighter this morning, renewed and happy to a degree she hadn't felt in years. Like Scrooge on Christmas morning, after all the ghosts had gone.

Creeping out of bed so as not to wake Jason, Tati slipped into the bathroom and switched on her iPhone to check her emails. Twenty-two new messages, unusual for a Sunday. The last two were from Leon di Clemente, both overtly flirtatious, and the latter, sent very late New York time, positively graphic. Tati smiled. Just twenty-four hours ago she'd have deleted any overtures from Leon in a fit of guilt. Now she allowed herself to enjoy the feeling of being wanted by a man that, if she were honest with herself, she knew she wanted too. She'd told Jason it wasn't serious with Leon, and that was the truth. But now that she was to be a free woman, she allowed herself to entertain the possibility that it *could* be serious, one day. Once the New York deal had cleared escrow and the business side of their relationship was over and done with . . . well, who knew what might happen? Tomorrow was another day.

Tati's good mood soon evaporated, however, as she scrolled further down her inbox. Having not returned a call or responded to an email in weeks, it appeared that the Hamilton Hall board were now peremptorily summoning her to an extraordinary meeting first thing tomorrow morning. It did not bode well that the note had been written by Arabella Boscombe and sent from her account, despite being undersigned by the entire eight-man board *and* the three non-executive directors on the advisory committee. Clearly they'd all been plotting against her. Lady Arabella's tone was direct to the point of rudeness:

'An extraordinary meeting will be held . . . You are required to attend . . . By unanimous agreement of the board . . .'

She thinks she can bully me into submission, Tati thought furiously. *But I'm going to have the last laugh. With Leon's millions behind me, I can take Hamilton Hall Stateside, with or without them. Whatever coup she thinks she's got planned, she can stick it up her capacious, aristocratic arse.*

'Good morning.' Jason had walked up behind her, naked, and wrapped his arms around her waist. Tati smiled at him in the mirror. 'Everything all right?'

'Yes, fine. Some crap at work but it's nothing.'

'How about brunch at the Wolseley?' said Jason, 'My treat. I'll take you shopping on South Molton Street afterwards if you like. They've got the new autumn collections in at Browns.'

'Perfect,' said Tati.

She could get quite used to having a gay husband.

At seven thirty on Monday morning, Tati walked in to the boardroom at Hamilton Hall's City offices, braced for confrontation. Instead she found herself looking at a circle of smiling faces.

'Tatiana!' Lady Arabella Boscombe's smile was the broadest

of all. She stood up to greet her. 'Good of you to make it. Please. Sit down.'

Tati took her seat warily, looking for the glinting dagger blade behind Lady Arabella's smile. She did not appreciate being 'invited' to sit in her own boardroom.

'I've never missed a board meeting, Arabella,' she said pointedly, pouring herself a glass of water. 'Even one called so suddenly and, if I may say so, secretively. And at such an ungodly hour. I'm hardly likely to start now.'

'Yes, well, today's a day for celebration, not for dwelling on our differences.' Michael Guinness, Hamilton Hall's largest individual stakeholder and a thorn in Tati's side in recent months, looked positively aglow with bonhomie. 'There have been a number of interesting developments while you've been away, Tatiana. We called today's meeting to update you, and to take a vote.'

'I'm sorry,' Tatiana stiffened. 'What do you mean "while I've been away"?'

'In New York,' said Michael breezily.

'I got back to London days ago,' said Tati. 'Since when I haven't been able to reach any of you.'

There was a moment's silence, during which the smiles wilted just slightly. It was no more than a breath. But it was enough for Tati to realize with sinking clarity: Their silence had been more than a collective fit of pique. Something was up.

It was Eric Jenkins, her longtime ally on the board, who spoke up. 'You've been distracted with the New York school for some time now,' he observed, calmly. 'At our last meeting you made it very clear that that was your priority. So we've been holding the fort and handling things here.'

Tati sat rigid-jawed. 'What things?'

'Relax.' Michael Guinness was still beaming like a stadium floodlight. 'It's good news. Firstly, you'll be happy to hear that we're all now on board with the new American school. You were right. It's time for the Hamilton Hall brand to extend its reach globally.'

Tati hesitated for a moment, then smiled. 'Well,' she said, leaning back and exhaling for the first time since she'd walked in, 'that is good news. I must say I'm surprised. And delighted.'

'Good. So are we. And so is the acquirer who's made quite an astonishing bid for the business. Tracy, be an angel, would you, and pass Mrs Cranley her copy of the offering memorandum.'

A slim sheaf of papers appeared in front of Tati.

'What the hell is this?' She glared accusingly around the room, without touching them.

'It's an offer,' said Arabella Boscombe.

'For over a hundred million dollars,' added Michael Guinness. 'Your personal share would be north of thirty million.'

'No it won't be,' said Tati furiously, pushing the papers away like a plate of rotten food. 'Because Hamilton Hall is not for sale. How dare you approach buyers behind my back? For *my* schools!'

'Nobody approached anybody,' Eric Jenkins said reasonably. 'This was an unsolicited offer, from an American consortium. It would include the planned New York school. Read the papers, Tati. By any standard they're offering far more than the business is worth today.'

'I will not read the papers!' Tati shouted. She sounded borderline hysterical. 'We're not selling. It's completely the wrong time. We're on the cusp of becoming huge. This buyer can see that, even if you're all too blind to be able to.'

'Sit down, Tatiana,' Michael Guinness said firmly. 'Insulting your board is not going to help matters.'

'Oh really? And why shouldn't I insult you, Michael? You're a bunch of two-faced snakes!'

'Really!' Lady Arabella thundered.

'I don't need you anyway,' Tatiana ranted on. 'It just so happens I have a private investor prepared to fund the New York school in its entirety. So you can stick your stinking takeover bid where the sun don't shine.'

'I'm afraid it's too late for a white knight,' Michael Guinness said smoothly. 'If you'd talked to us about a private investor sooner, things might have been different. As it is, we're all in agreement. This is an offer we can't afford to refuse. We've come here today to take a vote on it.'

'I'll veto,' hissed Tatiana.

'A veto requires a minimum of two board votes,' said Arabella Boscombe.

'You're with me, aren't you, Eric?' Tatiana wished her voice didn't sound so desperate.

'If you'd read the memorandum, you would see that this is a wonderful offer,' the accountant said awkwardly.

Jennifer Engels, another of Tatiana's former supporters, backed him up.

'This truly isn't personal. What they're offering is a full forty per cent more than the takeover bid that Avenues turned down last year, from Innovation Private Equity. We'd be mad to decline.'

Tati sat down, shocked and deflated. This couldn't be happening. How had she allowed this to happen?

'I'm going to call a vote,' said Michael Guinness.

'No, you can't!' she shouted. 'Not yet, please. We need to discuss this properly.'

'We have discussed it,' said Lady Arabella pitilessly. 'And we're all in agreement.'

'You can stay on and work with the new owners if you

choose to.' Eric Jenkins clearly felt bad. 'The terms for your continued involvement are outlined on page six.'

'But you don't need to,' said Michael Guinness. 'You'll be so wealthy, you'll never need to work again.'

I don't care about the money! Tati wanted to scream. *Hamilton Hall was never about the money. It was about building something that was mine. Something that no one could take away from me, the way they took Furlings. It was about proving Brett Cranley wrong. Brett, and my father, and everyone else who ever wrote me off as a failure.*

'I'd like a show of hands, please.'

Michael Guinness's voice sounded distant suddenly, like a voice in a dream. *A nightmare. Why can't I wake up?*

'All those in favour of accepting the HCL bid.'

Eleven arms fluttered towards the ceiling.

'All those against.'

Tatiana closed her eyes and lifted her hand, alone. More alone than she had ever been in her life.

There was noise after that, people coming and going. Some of them stopped to talk to her. She heard conversations about press releases and legal fees. She heard excitement and happiness, the platitudes washing over her, like scum on the tide.

'It was a terrific offer, Tatiana. Once the dust settles, you'll see that.'

'It's for the best.'

'Time for a new challenge. You're still so young!'

At last the room was empty and she was alone.

Her head started to throb. She stood up to get some water, and the nausea that had plagued her the other day at Max Bingley's wedding suddenly returned with a vengeance. Running out of the room, her hand over her mouth, she only just made it to the loo in time, throwing up again and again until her stomach was so empty it ached.

Splashing cold water on her face, Tati looked at herself in the mirror and was shocked at the pale, ghostly face that stared back at her.

Something's wrong with me.

She just managed to dial Jason's number before she collapsed on the floor.

CHAPTER TWENTY-NINE

Madeleine Wilkes was exhausted.

School started again in a few days, thank God, and like most London mothers Maddie was counting the seconds. The summer holidays had been one gruelling round of activities after another. One son had cricket camp in Battersea Park, another went to karate and swimming classes in Notting Hill, and her daughter Caitlin had enrolled in some ghastly drama course in North London that meant Maddie spent her entire day in the car, shuttling between the three of them. Then there were the playdates sleep-overs and non-stop meals to be bought, prepared, cooked and washed up afterwards. Needless to say her husband had suddenly found himself *desperately* busy at the Mayfair gallery, as he did every summer. George Wilkes had a lot of lovely qualities, but nobody could describe him as a 'hands-on' dad.

Staggering through the front door, weighed down with Waitrose bags (miraculously Caitlin's modern dance recital had been moved to next Wednesday, giving Maddie a chance to go to the supermarket on her own, without screaming children), she dumped the frozen stuff into the freezer before switching on the kettle for a cup of tea. Magnus's Beyblades were all over the floor, and Hannah, the Wilkes's cleaner, clearly hadn't bothered to show up this morning, judging by the pile of dirty washing-up still festering in the sink. *I really must fire her*, thought Maddie, for the umpteenth time, poking at Frosties stuck to the side of a bowl with a cat-food encrusted fork. The kitchen clock said three o'clock, a whole hour till she had to be at Battersea to pick up Henry. Leaving the groceries in their bags on the floor, Maddie made her cup of tea and retreated upstairs for that rarest of treats, a siesta.

She heard the laughter when she reached the landing, but didn't think anything of it. Henry and Magnus were always going into her bedroom and leaving the television on. Pushing the door open, she froze.

Jason Cranley was lying on her bed, stark naked and in a very obvious state of arousal.

'Jesus Christ!' Seeing Maddie, he grabbed a pillow and hastily covered his groin.

Maddie just stood there, open mouthed. A few seconds later, her husband came sauntering out of the master bathroom, his hair slick from the shower and with a towel wrapped around his hips. 'Did you say something, darling?'

He was addressing Jason. But then he, too, saw Maddie. Every ounce of blood drained from his face.

'What are you doing here?' he blurted.

'I live here,' said Maddie on autopilot. She was still holding her tea, very carefully, so as not to spill it. She looked like a rather bedraggled, British version of the Statue of Liberty.

'I thought you were at Caitlin's recital.'

'It got cancelled.'

For a moment all three of them remained in stunned, horrified silence. Then George made the mistake of saying

'I can explain . . .' and all hell broke loose. Maddie was screaming and crying, the most awful noise, like an animal being tortured. Jason watched as the mug flew across the room, shattering on the wall just above George's head and spraying scalding tea everywhere. George moved towards her, and as he did so the towel dropped. It was dreadful, watching him bent and cowering, naked, while Maddie literally flew at him, scratching and kicking, her arms and legs flailing. Jason tried to pull her off but she spun around and bit him on the arm, so hard he screamed and let go.

'Get out!' George yelled at him through the melee, his voice half shout, half sob. 'Go home.'

Not knowing what else to do, Jason pulled on his jeans, scooped up the rest of his clothes and ran, blood streaming from his arm from where Maddie had bitten him.

Outside he ran barefoot down the street before flagging down a cab and jumping inside. 'Eaton Gate!' he panted.

'You all right, mate?' the cabbie sounded concerned. 'You been mugged or summink?'

'I'm fine,' said Jason. Tears streamed down his cheek and his heart was pounding so violently he thought it might be about to leap out of his ribcage. 'Just . . . hurry.'

He needed to talk to Tatiana.

Tati would know what to do.

As soon as he got home, Jason ran straight upstairs. Tati had been in bed all week, struck down with some sort of violent flu. Between her illness and her despair at having Hamilton Hall sold out from under her, the poor thing was at her lowest ebb. He hated having to break the news to her like this: that 'George', his George, was actually George Wilkes, one of their oldest and closest friends. But it couldn't be helped. Maddie, understandably, had gone completely off the deep end. Anything might happen. Jason desperately needed Tati's advice, not to mention her forgiveness.

Walking into their bedroom, however, he found the bed was made and Tati nowhere to be seen. Hurriedly changing his clothes and pressing a clean damp flannel to the bite mark on his forearm, cleaning away the dried blood, he went down to the kitchen.

'What happened to you?' asked Logan. 'You look terrible. Did you get in a fight?'

Jason had totally forgotten she was staying with them. Her night at the O2 with Tom after Max Bingley's wedding had turned into two weeks. Now that their parents were packing up Furlings for the big Hamptons move, Logan had been talking about moving into Eaton Gate full time. Jason didn't have the heart to tell her that yet another of her homes was about to implode around her.

'No, no. I'm fine. I got bitten by a dog in Holland Park,' he lied. Pulling the largest plaster he could find out of the first-aid drawer, he stuck it over the gash on his arm. 'Have you seen Tatiana?'

'Nope,' said Logan. 'Isn't she in bed?'

Jason shook his head.

'Oh well then. I guess she must be feeling better,' said Logan. 'If I'd just sold my company and pocketed thirty million dollars, I think I'd be feeling fabulous.'

Jason watched his sister as she pottered around his kitchen, helping herself to a large slab of Dairy Milk chocolate from the top shelf of the larder and washing it down with the last of the full-fat milk. She was humming a tune to herself under her breath, her feet tapping to the rhythm in her head. It struck Jason how happy she looked.

'You're in a very good mood today.'

'Yes.' Logan twirled across the room and kissed him on the cheek. 'Shouldn't I be?'

'I don't know.' His eyes narrowed suspiciously. 'Should you be?'

He had enough problems of his own to worry about, not least whether Maddie Wilkes was about to barge through the front door armed with a meat cleaver. But something about his sister put him on his guard.

'Has something happened?'

'No! Nothing's *happened*.' Logan laughed. 'I'm happy, Jason. I'm in love and I'm enjoying my life. You and Tati should try it some time.'

And with that she swept out, leaving Jason clutching his bleeding arm.

Where the hell was Tatiana?

Brett Cranley was in his office, running through the checklist from the East Hampton removals company with his new PA, when the door swung open and Tatiana stormed in.

'You bastard.'

She stood in the doorway quivering with rage. In a bottle green T-shirt and grey cigarette pants with kitten heels, she looked tiny to the point of frailness. Thanks to her recent illness, not to mention the intense stress of the past week, she was fifteen pounds lighter than usual. Her frame, always slim, now looked gaunt, and though she was less obviously unwell than she had been at Max and Stella's wedding, it struck Brett how very pale she appeared. He pushed the thought away.

'I'm busy,' he said, not looking up from the furniture lists. 'What do you want?'

'I know it was you,' said Tati, marching over to the desk and snatching the lists out of Brett's hand, to the dismay and embarrassment of his new assistant.

444

'It's OK, Linda,' Brett told her. 'You can go. We'll finish this up later.' As soon as the PA had gone, he turned to Tati. 'So. What is it this time? A few days ago it was Furlings you were up in arms about, and my move to New York. That's old news now, is it?'

'You know it is. And you know exactly why I'm here,' seethed Tati. 'HCL's nothing but a shell company. Laid up in bed these last few days, I've had plenty of time on my hands. So I did a little digging.'

'I commend your work ethic,' Brett purred.

'Go fuck yourself,' snarled Tati. 'You're the one who bought Hamilton Hall. It was you all along! You turned my board against me.'

Brett laughed, a low, throaty chuckle, and began playing with a wooden puzzle on his desk. He sounded genuinely amused. 'I didn't need to turn them against you. You'd alienated everybody on that board long before I came on the scene.'

This was true, of course, but Tati was damned if she was going to admit it.

'You're not even interested in schools. You know nothing about the business, nothing about the education sector.'

'Very true,' mused Brett. He was clearly enjoying himself.

'So you admit it? You did it just to spite me.'

'Do you really think you're that important to me?' Brett mocked her. 'You think I'd waste a hundred million dollars to make some sort of point?'

'Yes,' said Tati.

'Then you're even more of a fool than you look.' Brett stood up and walked over to the window, admiring his view of the London Eye and the winding river Thames below. 'You're quite right I know fuck-all about the education sector. But I do know about real estate. That was quite a deal you struck in New York. That site was undervalued by at least forty per cent, perhaps more. Combined with your London assets, I'd say Hamilton Hall was worth every penny I paid, and more.'

Tatiana's eyes widened, then narrowed with hostility.

'How did you know the price I'd negotiated on the New York building?'

Brett grinned from ear to ear. 'I have my sources. You know, I was disappointed you didn't take up our offer to stay on board and run the schools.'

'Work for you?' Tati sneered. 'I'd rather starve.'

'You'll hardly be starving. Not after the cash I've just shelled out. Still, it's a shame,' Brett mused. 'I'd have enjoyed watching you close the business down.'

Tati frowned, confused. 'What do you mean, close them down? You just paid a fortune for them.'

Brett cracked his knuckles luxuriously. 'You said it yourself: I know nothing about education. Why waste time and money on a business I don't understand? No, no, my dear. Real estate, that's my bag. Hamilton Hall's Clapham site is just begging to be turned into apartment blocks. I thought Seventh Avenue might make a nice little boutique hotel. At the price you negotiated, it's a steal.'

Tati gasped. 'You bastard. You're going to strip the assets!'

'You make it sound so dirty,' chided Brett.

'You lied to my board!'

'I did nothing of the kind. It's hardly my fault if they couldn't be bothered to do their due diligence. Blinded by the pound signs in their eyes, I imagine. Don't look so shocked, Tatiana.' He laughed. 'All I'm doing is maximizing the value of my acquisition. It's not personal. It's business.'

'Like fuck it is.' Walking over to where Brett stood, she faced him down, drawing herself up to her full height. 'It couldn't be more personal. You're a hateful, immoral,

446

disgusting man. You don't care about anything or anyone but yourself.'

Brett's smile wilted. 'You bloody hypocrite,' he snarled. 'Look in the mirror some time, Tatiana. You rode roughshod over your own board, then you cut a deal behind their backs. You think you can swim with sharks and not get bitten?'

'You don't know what you're talking about,' quivered Tati.

'You deserved to lose those schools. My only regret is you made so much damn money out of it.'

'I don't care about the money.'

'Oh, bull*shit*,' said Brett. 'Money's all you care about. That's why you married my son. You're a greedy, lying bitch. And you have the gall to stand here and lecture *me* about betrayal! You thought nothing about betraying Jason with that slimeball Di Clemente. I saw you, remember.'

'For fuck's sake. Jason knows about Leon,' said Tati.

'Oh really? And I suppose you're going to tell me he's fine with his whore of a wife sleeping around, are you? That the two of you have an "open marriage"? Do you think I was born yesterday?'

'He's gay, you idiot!' Tati blurted out in anger. 'Your precious son plays for the other side. Didn't know *that*, did you, Mr "I have my sources" Cranley?'

Brett looked at her with utter revulsion.

'You'd make up something like that, just to excuse your own behaviour?' He shook his head. 'You're ill, Tatiana.'

'And you're blind,' said Tati. 'Then again, when it comes to Jason, you always have been. Enjoy America. You won't be missed.'

She strode out, slamming the door behind her.

The euphoria and adrenaline she'd felt, getting the last word and leaving Brett so utterly blindsided, soon faded. She'd just outed Jason to his own father. She should never have done that. But, as usual, Brett had pushed her to the brink.

She jumped into a black cab, her thoughts racing, and switched on her phone. The voicemail symbol was flashing.

'*You have . . . nine . . . new messages,*' the familiar, automated voice informed her. '*To listen to your messages, press one.*'

Nine? Her phone had only been off for twenty minutes, while she was in Brett's offices. Nine calls seemed a bit excessive.

Pressing one, Tati immediately held the phone away from her ear. The voice was a woman's and she was ranting hysterically. It took a few moments for Tati to realize who she was, and a few more to make any sense of what she was saying.

But when she did, all thoughts of Brett Cranley and Hamilton Hall flew out of her head.

She had to get home.

Now.

'George is George Wilkes?'

As soon as she got home, Tati pulled Jason into her study and closed the door.

'Yes.'

He looked so bleak, Tati couldn't help but feel sorry for him.

'Why didn't you tell me?'

'I couldn't. I wanted to, but . . . George has a family. It's complicated.'

'I'll say.' Tati sank down onto the sofa. 'So Maddie really had no idea?'

'None at all. Till today. It was awful.'

Jason sat down beside her, pale and shaking, as if he'd just stepped out of a car crash. Which, in a way, he had.

'I still can't believe George Wilkes . . .' Tati shook her head in astonishment. Bizarrely it felt much more shocking to learn that George was gay, and not just gay but Jason's lover, than it had been to find out about Jason. 'How long have you two been together?'

'A long time,' said Jason. 'There are people in the art world who know. But George has always been very discreet. We both have. We never took risks.'

Tati remembered the night in Ronnie Scott's, when she'd made a surprise appearance to hear Jason play. George Wilkes had seemed horrified to see her there, completely thrown off stride. Now she knew why. Perhaps it should have been obvious, but she'd only ever known George as half of George and Maddie. She'd missed the signs completely. Apparently so had poor Maddie.

'Maddie's beside herself,' she told Jason. 'Her messages are hysterical. She's threatened to go to the papers.'

Jason blanched. 'Do you really think she will? Poor George.'

'Poor everyone. I doubt she'll go through with it,' said Tati. 'It would hurt her children more than anyone if she did. But she's not very rational at the moment and I can't say I blame her. You and George both need to be prepared for anything. Unfortunately the fact that I'm in the public eye means it will be a story. "Wholesome Hamilton Hall Husband Revealed As Gay Homewrecker".'

'Oh God, don't.' Jason put his head in his hands and groaned. 'But we don't even own Hamilton Hall any more.'

'No,' Tati said bitterly. 'Your father does.'

Jason's eyes widened. 'What?'

'It's a long story,' Tati sighed. 'But it seems your father was the brains behind the takeover bid. He founded the company specifically to acquire us.'

'But . . . why?'

'So he could strip the assets and close the schools. To hurt me, basically. That's where I was today. I went to his offices to confront him.'

Jason digested this in silence. Since his parents had reconciled, and particularly with their upcoming move to America, he'd begun to think that Brett's obsession with Tatiana and fury over their 'secret' marriage had finally begun to fade. Clearly he was wrong.

'There's something else.' Tati bit her lower lip nervously. 'I'm so sorry, Jason, but we got into an argument and I . . . I told him you were gay.'

'Ah.' Jason sat back, winded. 'I see.'

'I truly didn't mean to,' said Tati. 'It just slipped out. He was attacking our marriage and moralizing and I just saw red.'

Jason took her hand. 'It's fine. I understand. After what I did today, I'm hardly in a position to throw stones. How did he take it?' he added as an afterthought.

'I don't really know,' said Tati. 'I sort of dropped the bomb and left. And then I got in the cab and heard Maddie's messages. Brett's reactions didn't seem so important after that.'

For a few moments they both sat quietly, each trying to process their emotions. Then Tati said, 'I think you should tell your mother. And Logan. They should hear it from you, not Brett. Or even worse, read it in the *Daily Mail*.'

She was right, of course. But the thought terrified him. Coming out to Tati had been so easy and comfortable. Jason realized now that the two of them had been living in a cocoon of false security ever since, both of them happy to postpone their inevitable parting and the seismic life changes that would have to come. After today, there could be no more hiding, no more pretence. Maddie knew. Brett knew. The dam had broken.

'I think I'm going to throw up.'

'No you're not,' said Tati. 'You'll be fine.' She suddenly felt a wave of nausea herself. Excusing herself to go to the bathroom, she left Jason sitting there, desolate. He tried George's mobile again.

'You've reached George Wilkes . . .'

No I haven't, thought Jason, and hung up.

When Tati returned, she looked white-faced and ill again.

'I have to go out,' she told Jason. 'I should be back in time for dinner. We can talk more then. Will you be all right?'

'Yes,' lied Jason. 'But are you sure you should go out? I think you ought to go back to bed, Tati. You don't look well.'

'I'm sure,' she said hurriedly. 'I need some air. I'll see you later, OK?'

She was gone before he could answer.

Jason paced around the room a few times, staring at his phone, willing George to call him. George was always so calm and certain. Like Tatiana, he never seemed to be at a loss what to do. Jason was the neurotic one, the bag of nerves who needed to be steadied and soothed. But now it was *his* turn to be strong, *his* turn to take decisive action as George's life and family imploded around him. Tati would support him as far as she could, but in the end this was Jason's crisis to solve. He felt frozen with fear.

Not knowing what else to do, he decided to go upstairs to the bedroom and pack. If George called, they might need to go away somewhere together quickly. Especially if Maddie fulfilled her threat to go to the press. He had to be ready.

Mindlessly folding shirts and placing them carefully in a

suitcase, he began to calm down. Doing something, anything, was distracting. Wandering into the bathroom, he saw that Logan had left her make-up everywhere as usual. Rushing out for a date with Tom, she'd left face powder and bronzer spilled all over the countertop; lidless pots of glittery eye shadow were cluttering up the space around the mirror and smeared on the washbasin. She had her own bathroom, but preferred to use Tati's for make-up. 'The light's better and there's more space. I need to *spread out.*'

Thinking about his little sister made him smile. She'd been so happy today, bursting with joy about something or other. He wondered how she would react when he told her he was gay, and that he and Tati would be separating? He couldn't bear the thought of hurting her, of wiping that carefree, eighteen-year-old smile off her face.

Picking up two used face-wipes, he was about to drop them into the bin when something caught his eye. Reaching down he picked up the white plastic stick and turned it over. Two pink lines filled the little window, like prison bars. Jason's stomach lurched.

So that's what she was so happy about, rushing out to meet Tom in such a hurry.

The stupid child had gone and got herself pregnant. At her age, Logan was too young and naïve to see the problems and obstacles. All she would see was a fantasy of her and Tom, riding off into the sunset and playing happy families.

Jason's head started to throb. How could so many things go so disastrously wrong in a single day? Running into the bedroom, he dialled Logan's mobile. But a few seconds later he heard it ringing downstairs. The stupid girl had been in such a hurry to tell Tommy the 'good news', she must have forgotten her phone.

Abandoning his packing, Jason went downstairs, poured

himself a large Scotch and downed it in two gulps. How the hell was he going to explain any of this to his mother?

By nine o'clock, Jason was happily drunk, curled up on the drawing-room sofa watching *Borgen*. Tati still wasn't back and George hadn't called, but the whisky had taken the edge off everything. He heard the front door open and close. A few moments later, Logan swept in, looking flushed with love and excitement.

'Oh, hi. You look better,' she beamed. 'Did you find Tatiana?'

Jason switched off the TV. With an effort he sat up and looked at her.

'What's wrong?' she asked, noticing his stern expression.

Wordlessly, he pulled the pregnancy test out of his pocket and held it up.

'What's that?' Logan asked guilelessly.

'You know very well what it is,' snapped Jason. 'It's a pregnancy test. And it's positive. How could you have been so stupid? So careless?'

Logan flushed red. 'I wasn't stupid. Or careless.'

'I suppose Tom knows?' said Jason, ignoring her. 'Don't tell me, he's as happy as you are.'

The combination of the alcohol and his own nightmarish day was making him unusually mean.

'Tom's very happy,' said Logan defiantly. 'But not because of some stupid pregnancy test. We're getting married.'

'Getting married?' Jason stood up unsteadily. 'Don't be ridiculous. You think marriage is going to solve this?' He waved the stick aloft, like a tiny plastic sword.

'It doesn't need "solving",' said Logan furiously.

'Oh really? So you and Tom are ready to be parents, are you?'

'Readier than you and Tatiana, evidently,' said Logan. 'Not everybody waits a decade to start a family, you know. But I'm glad you've finally done it. Congratulations.'

Her voice dripped with sarcasm.

'What the hell are you talking about?' Jason frowned.

'That test isn't mine!' Logan shouted at him. Her eyes were brimming with tears now.

'Of course it's yours,' said Jason. 'For Christ's sake, Logan. Lying about it isn't going to help.'

'Oh my God, are you for real?' She snatched the stick out of his hand, outraged. 'IT. IS. NOT. MINE. OK? I'm not pregnant, you self-righteous idiot.'

'Oh really. Then whose is it? The tooth fairy's?' snapped Jason.

'It's mine.'

In all the commotion, neither of them had heard Tati come in. Quietly taking the test from Logan, she looked at Jason.

'Dr Rowley just confirmed the result. I'm pregnant.'

CHAPTER THIRTY

Angela Cranley paused at the top of the hill to catch her breath. The path from Fittlescombe along Devil's Dyke and up to Saddlescombe Farm, once home to the Knights Templar and now a popular rest stop and tea room for walkers, was one of the steepest in the South Downs, affording spectacular views. Gringo was too old and infirm to manage such a long hike, so Angela had gone alone, heading out early on this beautiful, misty September morning.

I'll miss this place, she thought wistfully, gazing down at the ancient landscape, shrouded in mist like a grey veiled bride. The legends of the devil and his wife being buried beneath the seven grassy humps at the foot of the valley were almost as old as the hills themselves. On her way up to the summit, Angela had walked through an Iron Age fort and past a thousand-year-old water mill, the oldest still operational in England. The Hamptons were beautiful in their own way, a different way. But there was nothing there, nothing in the whole of America, like this. The chalk hills, steeped in myth, the ruins and the old churches, the villages and the woods and the burbling river Swell, unchanged over countless generations. To belong to a place like Fittlescombe was more than a case of knowing your neighbours or volunteering for the village fete. It was to feel a kinship with everyone who had gone before, every grave in St Hilda's churchyard, every soul who, like you, had been lucky enough to call this magic valley home.

She told herself every day that they were not leaving forever. Furlings was only on a one-year lease. It was still theirs. She and Brett would still return to it. They would live out their old age here, and be buried one day among those familiar St Hilda's graves.

Crossing the stile, she carefully made her way down the steep bank on the other side. A figure of eight would take her back through Brockhurst woods, past the Harwiches' hidden Hansel and Gretel house and back to Fittlescombe via Gabe and Laura Baxter's farm. As she walked, her thoughts drifted to Brett. He'd left for New York yesterday, to finalize things at the new house and 'tie up some business', whatever that meant. He'd seemed in an odd mood, tetchy and distracted, and a tiny note of anxiety had crept into Angela's heart. She didn't regret her decision to move with him to America. Brett felt they needed a new start, and he was right. The marriage had to come first, especially now, with an empty nest looming. But the fact remained, leaving Fittlescombe and Furlings was a sacrifice for Angela, a sacrifice she was making for him. The least he could do would be to acknowledge that, and act happy about it. Brett had a business to go to in New York, an entire life outside their marriage. Angela had Brett. Everything she'd built up here: her charity work in the village; the History of Art classes she'd started taking at an adult education college in Chichester with Max Bingley's encouragement; her friendships, with many of the locals but particularly with Max; all that would be gone. She couldn't face it if they got to East Hampton and Brett descended into another of his black moods. If he shut her out here, she had a support network to fall back on. In America she'd be utterly alone.

She walked on, trying not to think about it. By the time she reached the outskirts of the village, the early morning fog had cleared, and with it her doubts and fears. Jason was coming down for lunch today, an unexpected visit that had lifted her spirits immensely. Fittlescombe had already shed the last vestiges of summer, but now dazzled in its autumn colours of brown, yellow and gold. It was cold enough for a fire. Even at this hour there were trails of smoke rising from some of the cottage chimneys, the smell of the burning wood mingling deliciously with the crisp morning air. Angela had asked Mrs Worsley to make a shepherd's pie for lunch, one of Jason's childhood favourites, to be followed by apple crumble. Furlings' orchard had produced a bumper crop this year, the poor trees bent double with the weight of so much fruit.

In less than a month I'll be on a plane, thought Angela. *I must drink it all in. Relish every minute.*

Jason stretched out his long legs in front of the fire in Furlings' drawing room and waited for his mother to return with the tea.

He'd completely funked it so far. They'd spent lunch making small talk about Angela's upcoming move, Furlings' new tenants and the Hamptons house, which sounded beautiful, although Jason could tell his mother had misgivings about the whole American adventure.

It was two weeks since the awful, fateful day when Maddie Wilkes had walked in on him and George together. So much had happened since then, it felt like two years. Maddie had instigated divorce proceedings, which looked set to be bitter, but as Tati predicted she had backed off from the idea of making a public scandal out of her private family drama. George had moved out, and was staying at a flat in Sloane Gardens, a few yards from Jason and Tati's house.

Meanwhile, Tati's pregnancy had provided a further family drama. Sitting down to work out her dates, it seemed likely that Leon di Clemente, the guy she'd had a fling with on her last trip to New York, was the father. But there was a technical chance the baby was Jason's.

As Logan had been there when they found out, they'd had no choice but to tell her everything. To Jason's relief, his sister had been eerily calm about it all, hugging and kissing both him and Tati and assuring them that it would all be all right, somehow. They'd agreed that Logan could tell Tom, but that no one else must know for now. Not until Jason had spoken to their mother face to face, and Tati had informed Leon.

Logan's only question had been to ask Tati whether she was going to keep the baby. Jason found himself waiting for the answer with baited breath. The child probably wasn't even his, and God knew it complicated everything at the worst possible time. Yet he found himself willing Tatiana to say yes.

'I am going to keep it,' she said, more firmly than Jason had expected. 'It's the one good thing to come out of this mess. And you know, it's odd. I've dreaded being pregnant for so long, but when I saw those two lines today . . . I was happy.'

Two days later she flew to New York to see Leon. Jason had promised to break the news to his mother while she was away. He'd half hoped, half dreaded that Brett would have told her so he wouldn't have to. But no such luck. Perhaps his father hadn't believed Tati when she'd blurted out about his being gay? Knowing the two of them, he might have thought it was a lie Tati had thrown out in anger. Either way, her revelation had been followed by complete radio silence from Brett. Jason would have to tell his mother himself.

'Here we are, darling.' Angela walked back in bearing a tray of tea and biscuits. 'What a treat to have the afternoon to ourselves like this. I can't remember the last time it was just the two of us.'

Jason took a deep breath. 'Listen, Mum. There's something important I have to tell you. A few things actually.'

'Oh?' Angela looked curious rather than worried.

'I think you'd better sit down.'

Less than ten minutes later, Angela found herself staring into the fire, hypnotized by the glowing embers as she tried to take in everything that Jason had told her. Three facts leaped out at her from the series of bombshells he had just dropped.

My son is gay.

I may be about to become a grandmother.

My husband has been lying to me. Again.

She was aware that the first two ought to be the most important. And yet she found it was the third fact that ate away at her, and left her needing to know more.

'So, your father has known about this for *how* long?'

'About me being gay, you mean?' said Jason. 'Two weeks.'

'And it was Tatiana who told him?'

'Yes.' Jason looked confused. This wasn't the reaction he'd expected. Perhaps she was still in shock?

'But why? I mean, why would Tatiana do that? I didn't know they were even in contact.'

'They aren't, usually,' said Jason. 'You know that we were bought out of Hamilton Hall, against Tati's will?'

459

'Yes. Her board accepted a takeover bid. Brett told me it was a good offer. That the two of you have made a lot of money.'

'We have. But then again Dad would say that. It turns out he was the one who bought the schools.'

Angela went white. 'What?'

'Tati found out about it and went over to Cranley Estates' offices to have it out with him. They had an argument and that's when she told him about me. To be honest, I don't know if he even believed her. You know what those two are like when they start going at it. They fight like cats and dogs.'

Yes, thought Angela. *I know.*

Brett had promised her that his obsession with Tatiana was over, a thing of the past. Yet here he was, making a hostile takeover of Hamilton Hall without so much as breathing a word to her. Never mind the fact that he'd known about Jason and said nothing. *Nothing!* This was the old Brett in spades. Lying, conniving, concealing. And always, somehow, Tatiana Flint-Hamilton was at the centre of it all.

He's in love with her, thought Angela. *Deep down, under all the rivalry, all the hatred, all the stupid games.*

Why should I leave the home I love for a man who lies to me? And not just to me. To himself.

'Mum, are you OK?' Jason looked concerned. 'It's all right to be upset, you know. To be disappointed. Shocked, even. It's normal.'

'Oh, darling.' Angela looked at him suddenly, as if waking from a dream. 'I'm not disappointed. Not in you, anyway. You're my son and I love you. More than anything.'

Leaning forward, she wrapped her arms around him and hugged him tightly. To his embarrassment, Jason found himself starting to cry. The three people he'd dreaded hurting the most – Tati, Logan and his mother – had accepted him unquestioningly. It was more than he'd dared hope for.

'So,' Angela said brightly, kissing him on the cheek. 'When am I going to meet this George?'

'I don't know,' Jason sniffed. 'Somehow I can't see Dad inviting us for a family Christmas in the Hamptons just yet.'

'Don't worry about your father,' said Angela firmly. 'You leave him to me.'

CHAPTER THIRTY-ONE

Leon di Clemente straightened his silk Hermès tie and picked up his handmade Italian leather briefcase. He was about to leave for work. Glancing around his immaculate bachelor pad on the corner of Broadway and Bleecker, checking everything was in order before he set the alarm, he felt a surge of confidence and happiness about the prospect of the day ahead.

Life was good. Better than ever, in fact. Not only had he just pulled off a sweet deal worth a cool ten million dollars, but Tatiana Cranley was on her way to visit him from London, with 'something important' to discuss. They'd only spent one night together, but they'd been texting almost daily since, and Leon sensed that her interest in him might be growing. He hoped so. He couldn't remember the last time he had wanted a woman this much.

Not only was she wildly sexy and a fucking dream in bed, but Tatiana Cranley kept him guessing in a way that few women, even the married ones, ever did. Leon had sensed as soon as he met her that her marriage was in trouble. She'd practically admitted as much. And now she'd been bought out of her business, too. One by one the ties that were keeping her in London, and away from him, were falling away. If he played his cards right on this trip, he might be able to persuade her to move in with him.

Punching in the code on his alarm panel, he opened the front door and almost jumped out of his skin.

'What's the matter, Leon?' said Tatiana coolly. 'You look like you've seen a ghost.'

'Tati! No, I . . . I'm surprised, that's all. I wasn't expecting you till tonight.' He laughed nervously. He wasn't usually a nervous laugher, but Tatiana did that to him. It was six weeks since they'd last seen each other, and he felt as excited and unprepared as a schoolboy at his first prom.

The alarm was still beeping behind him.

'Let me just turn that off.'

He punched some more numbers into the keypad. The beeping stopped and they both stepped back inside the apartment.

'So,' Leon exhaled. 'I guess you got an earlier flight?'

Taking off his coat and dropping his briefcase, he moved forwards to kiss her but Tatiana sidestepped him, walking across the room to the window.

'Yes,' she said. 'I needed to talk to you.'

'OK, well, good,' said Leon. 'I want to talk to you too. Actually, I wanna do a lot more than talk. I've missed you, Tatiana. Like crazy. I—'

'I know it was you,' Tati interrupted him. She was wearing an immaculately cut Stella McCartney suit in navy blue, with her hair swept up in a neat chignon, and she carried a sleek black Aspinal's of London briefcase. Belatedly it struck Leon that she was dressed for business, not pleasure.

'What was me?' he frowned.

'You sold me out to Brett Cranley,' said Tati.

463

Leon opened his mouth to speak but Tati cut him off.

'Please, don't insult my intelligence by denying it. You were the only one who knew about the negotiations on Seventh Avenue. Brett was here that week. He saw us together at the Maidstone Club. After I left the Hamptons, after our night together, you went to see him and you sold me out, didn't you?'

Leon hesitated. 'It wasn't like that. Hear me out, OK?'

'Just out of interest, what cut did he give you?' asked Tati, her face displaying no emotion.

'Tatiana, please. It truly wasn't like that. Brett contacted me and—'

'What percentage? Humour me, Leon. I'm curious.'

'Fine,' said Leon. 'Ten per cent.'

Tati was quiet for a moment. Then, turning back to the window she said, 'You're a fool. You'd have made much more with me. Those schools were so well positioned. New York was just the beginning. We'd have expanded right across Asia and the Middle East. Shanghai. Singapore. Dubai. You'd have had a stake in all of it, not just the real estate. Brett sold you a pup.'

'I didn't do it for the money,' said Leon. 'At least, not only for the money. I wanted you out of that business. I wanted you to leave London and live with me, here.'

Tati looked at him incredulously. 'You wanted me to move to New York? To leave my husband and move here?'

'Yes,' said Leon. 'Why not?'

'*Why not?*' The arrogance was breathtaking. He and Brett Cranley were two peas in a pod. 'How about *why*, Leon? Apart from anything else, you just stole my fucking business here. I'd have had nothing to do.'

Leon walked towards her, grinning. 'I'd have given you something to do.'

464

But Tati wasn't in a playful mood. 'Don't touch me,' she spat, vehemently enough to stop even Leon in his tracks. 'You sold me out. You betrayed me, to the one man on earth who's hurt me more than any other.'

'I'm sorry you see it that way,' said Leon.

Tati did see it that way. It hadn't taken her long to figure out who Brett's 'inside source' must have been. But she'd wanted desperately to be wrong, especially now, with the baby and all the turmoil at home with Jason. Part of her had clung to the idea that she might have a future with Leon. That he could be her lifeboat, her means of escape from the wreckage of her life in England. She told herself she wouldn't know for sure until she saw him face to face and looked into his eyes.

Well, now she was here, looking. Now she knew.

With an effort, she reined in her emotions.

'There's something else I have to tell you. I'm pregnant.'

Leon took two steps backwards, staggering as if he'd been shot.

'Are you sure?'

'Positive. The likelihood is it's yours. Although there is a technical possibility it could be my husband's.'

'Fuck.' Leon leaned against the wall for support, loosening his Hermès tie. Suddenly he found it hard to breathe. 'OK, well don't worry. We'll take care of it.'

Tati raised an eyebrow. 'What do you mean?'

'I know an excellent doctor,' said Leon. 'He's very discreet.'

'Oh, I'm sure you do,' said Tati.

How many unwanted babies had Leon carelessly fathered over the years, she wondered? How many desperate girls had he sent to his 'discreet' abortionist? She imagined the beautiful flowers he sent them afterwards. *Don't worry, darling. You did the right thing.* What had she ever seen in him?

'I'm not having a termination, Leon.'

She watched his expression change from incredulous to hostile.

'You can't be thinking of keeping it?'

'I'm not thinking of keeping it,' Tati smiled sweetly. 'I *am* keeping it.'

'I won't accept paternity!' Leon thundered. 'Not without a test. For all I know you've slept with hundreds of guys. Even if it is mine, it's fucking entrapment. You won't get a penny out of me, sweetheart.'

Tati's lip curled with disdain. 'I wouldn't touch your money if I were starving to death. I came here to give you these.' Reaching into her briefcase, she pulled out a sheaf of documents and dropped them onto Leon's coffee table. 'They absolve you of all paternal responsibility. And rights.'

Leon eyed the papers suspiciously. Then he looked back at Tati. Was he making a mistake, letting her go? She looked terrific when she was angry, her eyes blazing like hot coals, her body taut and tense beneath her business suit, like a tiger ready to pounce. He tried to imagine her pregnant, that slender, toned, built-for-sex body growing rounded and soft and milky and full. A shiver of distaste ran through him.

'Pass me a pen.'

Tatiana walked into August, a faux-rustic Mediterranean restaurant in the West Village, feeling confident and calm. Bizarrely, her meeting with Leon had left her on a high. She'd been afraid that seeing him again might stir up unwanted emotions, of affection, or at least of attraction. That subconsciously there might be a part of her that wanted him to tell her he loved her. That he wanted the baby. That Brett had double-crossed him too, and the whole thing with Hamilton Hall had been a huge misunderstanding.

But he hadn't, and Tati's reaction had been unadulterated relief. She was free. Free from her marriage, free from Leon, free from the business, albeit in ways she wouldn't have chosen.

I'm young, I'm rich, I'm independent and I'm about to have a baby.

She allowed the happiness to flow through her. It was a wonderful feeling, warm and serene. *Not even Brett Cranley can take that away from me.* There would never be a better time to face Brett, she decided. Nor a better place than here in New York, on neutral turf, far away from the reality of their lives back home. Once today's lunch was over, Tati would at last have closure. Her freedom would be complete.

'Hello.'

Brett stood up to greet her. He too was formally dressed, in a dark suit and tie, with blue and gold cufflinks glinting at his wrists. Behind him, the flames of the pizza oven leaped and roared. *He looks like the devil, welcoming me to hell,* thought Tati, smiling to herself.

'Something funny?'

'No, not really.' She shook his hand and sat down.

Brett looked at her warily. He wasn't used to this version of Tatiana – the calm, contented, peaceful version. It made him nervous.

'I was surprised when my secretary told me you wanted to meet me. After our last encounter in London, I didn't think I was high on your list of lunch companions.'

'I was angry,' said Tati, pouring herself a glass of water and perusing the menu. 'That was a difficult day for me. I can look at things more objectively now.'

Brett said nothing. He was still waiting to see what she wanted. He didn't even know why she was in New York. He couldn't imagine she'd come here purely to talk to him.

Not unless she had some plan up her sleeve, or some proposal she wanted to make.

'I'm sorry I told you about Jason,' she said, helping herself to a bread stick. 'I mean, I'm sorry I told you in anger. It's not the way he would have wanted you to find out.'

Brett's face darkened and his body tensed. He'd tried to block out Tati's bombshell about Jason's sexuality. He'd even tried to convince himself that it wasn't true. As if by not admitting it, or thinking about it, or telling Angela, he could somehow *make* it not be true. But looking at Tati now, it was clear that she hadn't been lying. His son was gay. There was nothing he could do about it.

'I don't want to talk about Jason,' he said gruffly.

'He loves you, you know,' said Tatiana. 'All he wants is for you to accept him. To love him for who he is, not for who you want him to be.'

'Let's order,' said Brett, closing both his menu and the subject as firmly as possible. 'We'll both have the Caprese salads and the Greek pizza. It's very good here,' he added to Tati as an afterthought, sending the waiter away without asking whether she approved of his choice, or what she might like to eat. It was typical of his arrogance and over-bearing manner. In other circumstances Tati would have called him on it and summoned the waiter back at once. But today she let it go. She had bigger fish to fry and was determined, for once, to get through an hour in Brett Cranley's company without losing her shit.

'I wanted to see you to clear the air and to set a few things straight,' she said.

'Okaaaay,' said Brett, still distrustful. She looked particularly beautiful today, which somehow made things worse.

'Jason and I will get a divorce. It's all very amicable. Once the money comes through from the Hamilton Hall deal, I'll repay every penny from his trust fund, plus interest. What's left we'll split fifty-fifty.'

Brett couldn't conceal his surprise. This was a more than generous offer. Hamilton Hall had been Tati's business. It had been Tati who'd created the value, Tati who'd worked to make it what it was. No one, least of all Jason, would expect her to give half of her profits away in a divorce.

'Why would you do that?' Brett asked.

'For the principle,' said Tati.

'What principle?'

'To show . . . people . . . that I didn't only marry Jason for his money.'

They locked eyes. For the first time Tati felt her inner calm start to falter, replaced by the nervous churning of the stomach she always felt in Brett's presence.

'Also, because I love him. And it's the right thing to do.'

Brett's stare turned to a frown.

'What will you do with the rest of the money?' he asked brusquely. 'You could start another business, another school. You're good at it.'

'Thank you.' The compliment was so unexpected, for a moment it threw Tati off stride. 'But what I'd really like to do is buy my house back.'

Brett shook his head. So *that's* what this was all about.

Furlings.

Again.

The food arrived, providing a few moments' welcome distraction. Then Brett cut to the chase.

'I won't sell to you, Tatiana.'

'Why not?'

'Are we really going to do this dance again?' asked Brett, stabbing his cheese with a fork.

'I'm not angry,' said Tati. 'I'm curious. I genuinely want

469

to know. Why won't you sell to me? When you don't want the house, and you know I do?'

That's exactly why, thought Brett. *Because you want it and I have it. It's my only card, the single ace I have to play with you. The day I sell Furlings back to you, I've lost you forever.*

'I do want the house,' he lied. 'And Ange really wants it. She loves that place. She wants us to retire there. I wish you could let it go, Tatiana.'

'So do I,' said Tati truthfully. That would be true freedom. Not wanting Furlings. Not longing, constantly, for the past. For her birthright. But that was like not breathing.

'Would it make any difference if I told you I was pregnant?' She played her last card. 'I want my child to grow up there, Brett. I know that's what my father would have wanted too.'

Brett put down his knife and fork. He looked horrified.

'Are you serious? You're pregnant?'

Tati gave a wry smile. 'No need to look so happy about it.'

'But, Jason . . .? You said he was—'

'He is. But we've been married a long time. It hasn't been a completely celibate marriage.'

Brett held up a hand. 'Don't,' he winced. He didn't want to think about Tati and his son making love. Couldn't think about it. But if Tati was pregnant, carrying his grandchild, that was it. There could be no chance for them, not even in some distant, imaginary future.

Ever since he'd got back together with Angela, Brett had told himself that his feelings for Tatiana were dead. Acquiring Hamilton Hall had been a final act of revenge, the last piece of a puzzle that would allow him to get closure. That and moving to New York, away from Fittlescombe and Furlings and all the reminders.

Now he knew that he'd been fooling himself. Tatiana was

pregnant. Pregnant with his grandchild! The pain was indescribable, like swallowing a handful of razor blades.

'I don't think Jason's the father.' Her voice cut through the agony. Brett clutched at the sliver of hope, unable to stop himself.

'You don't?'

'It's highly unlikely.'

'So who . . .?'

'Leon di Clemente,' said Tati. 'But don't worry, he won't be involved. I know he was the one who helped you take over Hamilton Hall.'

Brett opened his mouth to speak, then closed it again. There was no point denying it now.

'I don't care anyway,' said Tati. 'That man is dead to me. All I care about is the baby. And Furlings. Please reconsider.'

Brett looked at her with genuine compassion. The truth was, in their different ways, they were both trapped, prisoners of desires they could neither deny nor fulfil.

'I'm sorry, Tati. I can't.'

'Why not?'

'I promised Angela. She . . . we . . . might want to go back eventually.'

This was true, but it wasn't *the* truth. The truth was that if he let go of Furlings, Brett would have nothing left that Tatiana wanted. He would be letting go of her, for good. Forever. That was what he couldn't do.

A look of dismay crossed Tati's face. At first Brett thought it was about Furlings. But a few seconds later it intensified into a grimace of pain.

'Are you all right?' He pushed his plate aside.

Tati clutched her stomach. 'No.' She let out a short, sharp cry and doubled over, so violently that her head hit the table. 'Oh my God. Help me!'

Brett ran around and scooped her up into his arms. Looking down he saw that blood had already stained her white skirt.

'Call an ambulance!' he bellowed at the waiter. 'Hurry!'

The doctors at Roosevelt Hospital on Tenth Avenue were efficient, compassionate and fast. Ectopic pregnancy was diagnosed less than ten minutes after Tati arrived. Ten minutes after that she was in an operating theatre, and an hour later Brett was by her side in the recovery room.

Stroking her forehead, gently pushing damp strands of hair back from her ghostly pale face, he had never felt so helpless in his life. She was still unconscious, the anaesthetic had yet to wear off, but her breathing was deep and steady, which the nurses assured him was a good sign. 'Some people take longer than others to come around. You did the right thing, bringing her straight in. Ectopic miscarriages are rare, but they can be fatal if you don't act fast. You probably saved her life.'

Brett didn't feel heroic. He felt terrible. Looking at Tati lying there motionless in her green hospital gown, he felt like crying. She was so small and fragile, so utterly vulnerable, it was like looking at a child.

Her eyelids began to flicker. She looked at him, peaceful for a moment, then winced with pain.

'I think she needs something,' said Brett.

A nurse brought water and some painkillers. Tati swallowed them, then slumped weakly back onto the bed.

'I lost the baby.' Her eyes brimmed with tears.

'It would never have survived, sweetheart,' Brett said gently. 'If they hadn't operated, you'd have died.'

Tati nodded. Her face crumpled.

'Please don't cry,' said Brett.

'I want my baby back.'

'I know.'

Tati's voice was slurred and sleepy. Brett looked anxiously at the nurse.

'It's the drugs,' she whispered. 'They're pretty powerful. She'll be up and down for a few hours yet. In and out of consciousness. Tearful.'

Tati murmured something that Brett couldn't hear. He bent closer, turning his ear towards her lips.

'What was that, angel?'

'I want . . . my house . . . back.'

She sighed heavily and sank back into a deep sleep. Brett stood over her, watching, as the nurses moved in and out of the room, going about their business. Under his breath he whispered.

'I know you do, Tatiana. And I want you. But neither of us can have what we want.'

CHAPTER THIRTY-TWO

Max Bingley watched the raindrops racing one another down his kitchen window, pushing the tension and anxiety out of his mind. He was alone at Willow Cottage this Saturday morning. Stella had gone to stay with her sister in Suffolk, ostensibly a painting trip, but they both knew it was more than that. She needed some time away from him, away from Fittlescombe and the school and the cottage and their life together. Or, as she would put it, *his* life.

'I feel like a guest here,' Stella told Max the day before she left. 'Like a visitor in my own marriage.' It hadn't been said in anger. One of the things Max loved most about Stella was her calm, even temperament. Theirs was a relationship that had begun quietly and without drama. If it ended, he hoped and believed it would end the same way. Not much of a silver lining, perhaps. But where there had been no great, passionate love, at least there could be no agonizing, passionate parting. Wagner's *The Valkyrie* was on Radio 3, its sweeping, triumphant refrain filling the tiny cottage with sound. *Perhaps, if I'd never been married to Susie, Stella and I could have worked.* But having tasted real love, no imitation would do. Max and Susie had both adored their opera. Rosie had been conceived to Wagner, if Max remembered correctly. Stella had tried to take an interest for his sake, but it was obvious opera didn't move her. When he'd taken her to Covent Garden to hear the sublime John Tomlinson as Hagen, Max had turned to Stella at the end of the *Götterdämmerung*, tears of emotion streaming down his face, only to find her fast asleep and snoring beside him.

He couldn't blame her for not being Susie. Stella was a wonderful, talented woman in her own right. Max respected her as much as anyone he'd ever met. The problem was he wasn't in love with her, nor she with him. Not really. They'd married to save themselves from loneliness, and because Max's daughters had so wanted them to. But the irony was they both felt lonelier now than they had before. Something had to change.

The knock on Max's kitchen door was so faint at first that he didn't hear it over the radio. It soon grew louder, however, an insistent banging that demanded an answer. Biting back his irritation – as headmaster of a village primary school, one was always on duty – Max turned down the Wagner and opened the door.

'Angela!'

His irritated frown vanished instantly.

'Come in, come in! You look like a drowned rat.'

This wasn't true, of course, and Max instantly regretted the turn of phrase. Mrs Cranley looked as beautiful as ever, her skin sparkling wet beneath a mask of raindrops and her blonde hair sticking to her cheeks and neck like a mermaid's tresses. She was wearing a scruffy old pair of corduroy gardening trousers and an army green macintosh coat that seemed to have done little to protect her from the elements on this foul, rainy morning. But even in her bedraggled state she was radiant, her smile lighting up the room and Max's heart in the same, glorious instant.

'Thanks.' She stepped inside, closing the door behind her. 'Sorry to drip all over your floor. I wanted some advice.'

'Of course, any time. And don't mind my floor, it could do with a wash.' Taking her wet coat he dashed into the downstairs loo for a towel. 'Here. You can dry yourself off with this.'

Angela took it gratefully, rubbing her wet hair beside the Aga.

'I thought you'd be packing,' said Max, filling an ancient cast-iron kettle and putting it on the hot ring of the Aga to boil. 'The whole village is agog about the new tenants taking over Furlings. Rumour has it you've let it to some pop star. Please tell me that's wide of the mark.'

'Actually, that's what I came to talk to you about,' said Angela. She pulled a letter out of her trouser pocket, carefully wrapped in a clear plastic sandwich bag to protect it from the rain. 'This came this morning. I'd like your opinion.'

Max took the letter and read it, slowly.

'But, that's wonderful!' he said to Angela. 'You've been accepted onto a Masters course in art history. The department at Sussex University is one of the best in the country. Congratulations!'

'Thank you.' Angela smiled shyly. 'It's rather a long commute from New York, though.'

'Ah.' Max put the letter down on the table. 'Yes.' He thought for a moment. Then, trying his best to sound upbeat, he said, 'Perhaps you can transfer to a US college? A lot of the universities have reciprocal arrangements these days. The main thing is that you're doing something for yourself. Something unconnected to Brett or the children. You deserve that, Angela.'

476

The kettle started to boil, a loud hissing sound that made them both jump. Max made tea and cut the last of Stella's home-made fruitcake into slices. He cleared a space at the table amidst the paintbrushes and newspaper supplements and they both sat down.

'I don't want to go,' Angela blurted. 'I . . . I think I've changed my mind.'

'Then don't go,' said Max.

Every time he looked at her, she noticed how piercing his eyes were, how intense. In every other way he looked his age. His face was lined, his hair grey and his back slightly stooped, the way that older men's so often were. In all these ways, he reminded Angela of her own father. But his eyes still danced with the light of youth and energy and intelligence. It was his eyes that made him attractive. That and the kind smile that, over the past decade, she had truly come to love. Max Bingley's smile was as much a part of Fittlescombe to her as the church or the green or the annual Swell Valley cricket match. Max Bingley's smile was home.

'It's not just America. It's everything. Me and Brett . . .' She tailed off. Max found himself waiting with baited breath for her to finish the sentence. When she said no more, he prompted her gently.

'You've changed your mind?'

She nodded. 'Yes. It's not that I want to end my marriage. It's that it *has* ended. I'm just watching from the sidelines. That probably sounds stupid.'

'No,' Max assured her. 'As it happens, I know exactly what you mean. Have you spoken to Brett?'

She shook her head. 'He's away in America. Finalizing things at the new house. He gets back tomorrow.' She looked at Max bleakly. 'What am I going to tell him?'

'The truth?' Max suggested, gently.

'It's not that easy,' said Angela.

'The important things in life rarely are,' said Max.

'Yes but purely on a practical level. Half our life is already on a boat! We have tenants supposed to arrive in a week. We signed a contract.' Angela grimaced.

'None of that matters,' said Max. 'Not if you're really not happy. It can all be undone.'

Can it? thought Angela. Could she really just accept this place at Sussex University? Start a new life, here in the village, on her own? At her age?

'You never know,' said Max. 'Brett may already be thinking the same thing you are. If you've watched your marriage crumble, isn't it at least possible that he has too? Perhaps you've both been too scared to say anything. It isn't easy to rock the boat, but sometimes it's the right thing. Sometimes it's worth it.'

Angela took a bite of cake and finished off her tea. She felt so safe here with Max Bingley, so comfortable and happy. But this was Stella's home, Stella's life, not hers. She remembered something that Penny de la Cruz had once said to her.

I mustn't rely on Max. If I do this, I have to do it alone. Start as I mean to go on.

'I'd better get back.' Reluctantly she stood up and took her mug over to the sink.

'All right.' Max sounded equally regretful. He'd have loved her to stay, but couldn't think of a reason to keep her there.

'Do you really think I can do it?' Angela asked at the door, shrugging on her still-wet raincoat. 'The Masters, I mean?'

'Of course,' said Max. 'Standing on your head. And the professors at Sussex obviously agree. Your problem is you don't have enough confidence. You can do whatever you want to do, Angela.'

478

'You see, *that's* why you're a teacher,' she joked, kissing him on the cheek goodbye.

Max watched as she disappeared down his garden path and into the lane. He stood at the doorway, watching the rain fall, long after she'd passed out of sight.

In the background, the muted strains of the Wagner drifted back to him. But they no longer lifted his spirits. Angela Cranley had gone.

Brett Cranley tied the belt on his silk Turnbull & Asser dressing gown and looked at his face in the bathroom mirror. Deep grooves fanned out from each of his eyes, like cracks in a dry river bed. The grey in his hair had spread from his temples all the way back to the nape of his neck, and deep shadows had inked themselves permanently beneath his eyes like two violet tattoos.

I look old.

I am old.

At Tatiana's request, he'd said nothing to Jason or anyone about her losing her baby. She wanted some time to grieve, alone, and she wanted to tell people herself. But the emotional trauma of his week in New York still weighed heavily on Brett. Part of him longed to share the burden with Angela. But somehow he found he couldn't talk to Ange about Tatiana. Nothing had happened between them, nor would it. Whatever feelings Brett harboured for Tatiana, she'd made it clear over many long years that they were not reciprocated. Even so, her very existence on this earth cast a shadow over Brett's marriage. As if his love for his wife were a plant that hadn't quite died, but could no longer grow or thrive. There was no more light for it to reach towards. However much Brett watered or tended it – fresh starts, beautiful homes, more time together – it remained stunted, a sad remnant of what it might have been.

Brett had got back to Furlings this afternoon. Angela had made him tea and he'd dutifully sat down and drunk it, laying out pictures of the Hamptons house on the kitchen table and talking to her about plans. An agent from Savills was coming in the morning to run through the inventory at Furlings before the big move-out. Life, their life, was marching on.

Brett splashed cold water on his face. *I have to get a grip.*

Angela was already in bed. Sitting propped up against two large pillows, her blonde hair brushed out and her reading glasses on, it struck Brett that she looked tired too. She was wearing an ancient Laura Ashley nightdress with pink rosebuds on it and reading a book about art history, but she put it aside when he came in.

'I think we need to talk.'

Brett perched on the edge of the bed. 'All right.'

Angela took a deep breath. 'I want a divorce.'

Brett stood up again, shocked. 'Are you serious? Why?'

Reaching for his hand, Angela pulled him back down onto the bed. She didn't look angry. And when she spoke, her voice was calm.

'Because I want to stay here and live here. And you don't.'

Brett said dismissively. 'Come on, Ange. We've been through this a hundred times.'

'I know. And I know I said I'd move to New York. But the fact is, I've changed my mind.'

Brett exhaled slowly, turning her fingers over in his hand. 'Fine,' he said at last. 'Then we'll stay. Together.'

Angela shook her head. 'It wouldn't work.'

'Of course it would work,' said Brett. 'It's worked for thirty-odd years, hasn't it?'

Angela raised an eyebrow but said nothing.

'This is crazy, Angela. Where we live is just geography. You don't divorce over geography.'

'No,' said Angela quietly. 'You don't.'

'Well what then?' He could hear the desperation in his own voice. Every word he said sounded like *please don't leave me*. 'I'm not cheating on you. I swear. Since we got back together there hasn't been anyone.'

'Brett.' Reaching up, Angela gently touched a finger to his lips, shushing him the way a mother might a child. 'We don't have so many years left that we can afford to waste them. I want to live a quiet, uneventful country life. And you're in love with someone else.'

'What? I . . . that's not true,' said Brett on autopilot.

'Yes it is. I think you loved Tatiana even before she married Jason. But ever since then you've been obsessed, and you know it.'

'You're wrong,' Brett insisted.

'You launched a takeover for Hamilton Hall without telling me.'

'Because I knew you'd be upset. Take it the wrong way,' said Brett. 'And you have. That was business.'

'Darling.' Angela looked at him reproachfully. 'Come on. And what about Jason? Was that business too? Tatiana told you about him being gay, but you said nothing to me.'

'I didn't believe her.'

'Even if that's true, she still came to your office to see you. Why did you keep that a secret?'

'Because I didn't know what to say!' Brett blurted.

'Because you didn't want me to know you'd seen Tatiana. That you'd spent the last three months trying to buy out her company because you can't help yourself. You can't stay away.'

481

'That's not true.'

'You can't even mention her name to me, Brett! I don't know why you're denying it.'

Brett pulled away and began pacing the bedroom, running his hands through his hair. 'Look,' he said eventually. 'Nothing's happened between me and Tati.'

'I believe you,' said Angela truthfully.

'Then why are you doing this? Why are you leaving me?'

Peeling back the bedclothes, Angela got up and walked over to him. Wrapping her arms around his neck, she kissed him on the cheek then leaned her head against his chest.

'We won't be happy in America if we aren't happy here,' she said. 'I'll always be here if you need me, Brett. We'll always be friends. Dear friends. But friends tell each other the truth. It's over. It's been over for years.'

Brett opened his mouth to protest, but realized he had nothing to say. Instead he wrapped his arms around her and held on tight. He wished he could freeze the moment. Stand there for ever and never let go. But he knew he couldn't.

It was too late.

CHAPTER THIRTY-THREE

Tatiana watched the thick flakes of snow falling outside the café window and sipped her hot chocolate contentedly. According to the BBC weather-forecasters, this was set to be the coldest December in London in fifty years. A white Christmas was now so likely that bookies had stopped taking bets on it.

For Tati, the snow was a fitting end to a tumultuous year. The blanket of white on the streets felt like a metaphorical clean sheet: a crisp, white piece of paper on which a new chapter of her life would be written. The pain of her miscarriage still walked with her. But after three months, she no longer felt the raw desolation that she had in New York. Back then, at the hospital, Brett Cranley had seen her at her lowest ebb. Mourning her baby, her marriage, her business and her birthright all at the same time had brought her to the brink, with the collapse of her relationship with Leon di Clemente the icing on a rotten cake.

But a lot could change in twelve weeks, and a lot had. The nation had belatedly caught up with the Cranley family's travails – the simultaneous divorces of Tati and Jason and

483

Brett and Angela had prompted a flurry of salacious rumour and gossip in the tabloids, while business analysts still argued over Brett's intentions for the newly acquired Hamilton Hall. Despite his threats to Tatiana in New York, Brett had yet to start selling off assets, and both the London schools were still operating – so privately Tatiana felt the worst was behind her. With the Eaton Gate house to herself, the country house on the market and a comfortable cushion of cash from the Hamilton House deal nestled in her bank account, she'd begun to feel her ambition returning, and with it her appetite – for food, life and business, if not for romance. Fate had decided she wasn't going to be a mother, or a wife. But she was too young to sit around doing nothing. Brett Cranley was right. She was free. It was time to start making the most of her freedom. Brett had also been the one who'd suggested that she start a new school. Tati could hear his voice in her head now. 'Why not? You're good at it.'

She *was* good at it. Just imagine what she could do without the millstone of a hostile board around her neck? This time around she'd be more careful. She'd make sure she kept control, total control. She'd find a silent partner, maybe someone in Asia or the Middle East . . . the possibilities were endless, and exciting.

Unfortunately, not everyone had emerged from the latest round of Cranley family drama unscathed, or with such a positive attitude.

Tati watched as the café door opened and Maddie Wilkes walked in. Scanning the room, waving cheerlessly when she saw Tati, Maddie came over to the table looking haggard and ill. Even in her thick coat and scarf she looked thin. When she took them off and sat down she looked positively emaciated. Her twig-like arms and gnarled, veiny hands dangled uselessly at her side, and the skin stretched over her cheek-bones was so paper-thin it was almost see-through.

'Thanks for seeing me.' She smiled thinly at Tatiana.

'Of course. How are you?'

'Oh, you know. Fine.'

Ignoring Maddie's protests, Tati ordered her a hot choco-late with whipped cream and a plate of warm cookies to share. Maddie left both untouched. She'd come here to talk to Tati about her divorce, not to enjoy herself. Talking about her divorce had replaced eating, sleeping and breathing for Maddie Wilkes as the number one priority of her existence. There was still so much anger and shock and pain. If she didn't lance the boil and let the bitterness out, she would die.

'He wants half the house but he won't get it.' Her thin lips moved quickly, powered by resentment. 'Can you imagine? After everything he's done, he thinks he's entitled to a share of my home.'

It was his home too, thought Tati, but wisely didn't say anything.

'And now, to top it all, he says he can't pay the school fees. According to George, the lawyers have cleaned him out.'

'Perhaps they have?' Tati offered meekly.

'I daresay, but whose fault is that? If it hadn't been for his sordid little affair, he wouldn't have needed lawyers. If he hadn't betrayed me and the children and broken every vow he ever made . . .'

Tati listened patiently while Maddie railed on. After a solid fifteen minutes, she finally ran out of steam.

'Anyway, I know you still talk to them. Face to face, I mean, not through lawyers. I wondered if you'd give George a message from me.'

'I'll help if I can,' said Tati warily.

'I want the house and the business.'

'You want the gallery?' Even Tati couldn't hide her surprise.

'Yes. If he gives me both I'll drop the claim for maintenance.'

'If he gives you both he'll be bankrupt!'

'Nonsense,' said Maddie curtly. 'His boyfriend can keep him. Jason's filthy rich now, thanks to you. George has made his bed and he can bloody well lie in it.'

'But Maddie,' Tati tried to be reasonable. 'That gallery is George's whole life's work. He built it up from nothing.'

Maddie shrugged. 'Our family was my whole life's work. I built *that* up from nothing. But he didn't think twice about destroying that, did he?'

There could be no reasoning with her. Underneath the anger and wild demands, it was painfully obvious that Maddie still loved George, that love and hate were two sides of the same coin.

'Will you ask him, when you see him?' said Maddie, standing up and pulling her coat back over her bony shoulders. 'It will have more impact coming from you than from my lawyers. Knowing George he probably just throws their letters in the bin anyway.'

'I'll ask him,' said Tati. 'But I can't promise he'll agree.'

'Yes, well. Tell him if he doesn't, he can wave goodbye to his children,' said Maddie. With an angry flick of her scarf she was gone.

'That's outrageous,' said Jason. 'She can't do that. I'll talk to her.'

'Noooo!' said Tati and George in unison.

'For God's sake, don't,' added George. 'It'll only make things worse.'

They were in Jason and George's new flat on Drayton Gardens, a beautiful first-floor apartment with views over the communal gardens and high, Victorian ceilings. Jason had bought it with his share of the Hamilton Hall money, and although it wasn't grand, it was warm and charming and perfect for the two of them. It also boasted a spare bedroom, which George had poignantly furnished with bunk beds in hopes that Maddie would eventually thaw about access to their children. Christmas was only three weeks away, and they'd yet to reach any sort of agreement.

'All right, sit down everyone. George, refill Tati's glass, would you? She's a nightmare when she's sober.'

Jason winked at Tati, setting down three steaming bowls of spaghetti vongole onto the immaculately laid table. He'd always been a good cook but, as with so many things, his culinary skills seemed to have blossomed since being with George. *He* had blossomed. It made Tati happy to see him so happy. *Although, I suppose it's easier for me, never really having been in love with him in the first place. Not like poor Maddie with George.*

They sat down to eat. George refilled Tati's glass and then his own. He looked relaxed too, and handsome, Tati thought, in a navy blue cashmere sweater and dark maroon corduroy trousers. Still, it was clear that the situation with Maddie was tearing his heart out.

'I think I'm going to do it,' he said suddenly. 'If she's serious about dropping this nonsense about access. I'll give her the gallery.'

'Don't be ridiculous,' said Jason, firmly. 'Why should she have that gallery?'

'Because she wants it, and I want to see my children before their twenty-first birthdays. Ideally without a bloody social worker present.'

487

'It's blackmail!'

'Ah, don't be so dramatic.' George waved a hand dismissively. 'She's had her heart broken. She's hurt and she's angry and she wants me to suffer. You can't blame her.'

'Can't you?' asked Jason.

'She'll get over it eventually. When she does, I daresay she'll give me the gallery back.'

Tati half choked on her spaghetti. 'I wouldn't bank on it, George.'

'Even if she doesn't, it's only a business. That's the problem with you two, both of you.' He pointed his fork towards Jason, then Tatiana. 'You take business much too seriously. If at first you don't succeed, try again, that's my motto.'

'Yes, but you *did* succeed,' said Jason. 'That gallery's worth a fortune.'

'It's not worth losing my family over,' said George. 'I'll open a new place. We can do it together.' Reaching across the table, he took Jason's hand and squeezed it.

This ought to be weird, thought Tati. But there was a rightness about the two of them together that somehow normalized everything. She thought back to dinners à deux with Jason at Eaton Gate. Those evenings had been far more stilted than this one.

'Jason's been doing a spot of family reconciliation of his own, haven't you, darling?' said George.

Tati looked suitably curious. 'Oh?'

Logan was away travelling in Australia with Tommy. Since news of her parents' divorce broke, and with Jason's sexuality and new living arrangements bound to hit the headlines at any moment, she'd wisely decided to spend as much of her time as possible very, very far away. As far as Tati knew, everything was peachy between Jason and his mother. Which only left Brett.

'I saw Dad the other day,' Jason confirmed. 'For lunch.'

Tati couldn't pinpoint the feeling in her stomach that this piece of news gave her, but it wasn't pleasant. 'How did it go?' she asked.

'OK,' said Jason. 'Better than I thought.'

'Was it his suggestion?'

Jason frowned. 'What do you think? No. Of course not. The only use Dad has for an olive branch is to hit people over the head with it. I called him. But, you know, he came.'

'And he didn't lecture you? About what a mess you've made of your life?'

'Amazingly, no.' Jason sipped his wine thoughtfully. 'I actually think he's mellowed, since the split with Mum. He does have a kind side to him, underneath all that rampant ambition and testosterone.'

Tati thought back to her miscarriage, and Brett's kindness to her in New York.

'Not that we talked about personal stuff. It was business mostly. You know he's decided to keep Hamilton Hall running as a business after all?'

Tati dropped her fork with a clatter. 'Are you serious?'

'Yeah,' Jason nodded. 'I guess he ran the numbers, belatedly, and decided not to slaughter the cash cow while she was in her prime. You'll never guess who he's brought in to run the schools.'

Whoever he thinks would upset me most, thought Tati bitterly, racking her brains.

'Arabella Boscombe?'

Jason shook his head. 'Dylan Pritchard Jones.'

'No!' Tati gasped.

'Who's Dylan Pritchard Jones?' asked George, helping himself to more pasta from the stove.

'He used to teach art at the primary school in Fittlescombe,' said Tati.

'Come on. That was years ago,' said Jason. 'He's been headmaster at Lancings for the last two years. Very ambitious. All the Swell Valley yummy mummies drool over him.'

'He's a little turd,' said Tati with feeling. 'I can't believe your father would choose Dylan of all people. He's duplicitous. He's smug. He has zero international business experience.'

'Nor did you when you started Hamilton Hall,' Jason reminded her.

'Whose side are you on?' Tati said crossly.

'I'm not on anybody's side. I'm just saying, we should give the man a chance.'

Tati got up from the table. Suddenly she wasn't hungry any more. 'You and your bloody father,' she muttered darkly at Jason. Grabbing her coat she stomped out of the flat, slamming the front door behind her.

George looked at Jason, perplexed. 'Did I miss something? What's she got her knickers in such a twist about?'

Jason rolled his eyes. 'I have no idea. When it comes to Tatiana and my father, you never know when the next land-mine's going to explode.'

CHAPTER THIRTY-FOUR

Brett was working late at his London flat when the buzzer rang.

Ten fifteen. Who the fuck rang people's doorbells at this time of night? Jemmying open the sash window of his office, he peered down to the street, expecting to see giggling kids or, worse, a tabloid reporter hoping to goad him into some sort of reaction that they could use to sell their trash.

Instead he saw Tatiana. Bundled against the cold in a full-length coat, scarf and hat, he recognized her mainly from her belligerent body language: arms folded, chin jutting forward, lunging angrily towards his doorbell.

'Come up,' he shouted down to her. 'I'll buzz you in.'

Moments later she was standing in his flat. The snow melting off her coat dripped onto the floor, making a dirty, damp stain on his Persian rug. But Brett had eyes only for her face, flushed with cold and anger, her eyes boring into him like twin green lasers.

'I've just come from Jason's,' she seethed.

'That's nice,' said Brett casually. Walking over to the drinks cabinet, he poured two fingers of whisky into a tumbler and handed it to Tatiana, before fixing one for himself. 'How was he?'

'He was fine.' She swallowed the amber liquid in one gulp, grimacing as it burned her throat. 'He told me you're going to keep my schools going after all.'

'That's right.'

'And that you've hired Dylan Pritchard Jones to run them?'

'Right again. May I take your coat?'

'No you may *not* take my coat, you Machiavellian little shit!' roared Tati. Peeling off her own coat, scarf and hat, she flung them in a wet heap onto one of Brett's ghastly cream leather armchairs. 'How dare you?'

'How dare I offer to take your coat?'

Brett looked amused. Still in suit trousers and a business shirt, with his tie loosened but not removed, he radiated confidence like a star pumping out light. *I hate him*, thought Tati.

'Everything's a game to you, isn't it?' she glared at him.

'On the contrary.' Brett took a step towards her, meeting her gaze steadily. 'I take many things very seriously indeed.'

'Like destroying my life?'

Brett was so close now she could smell the lingering, lemony scent of his aftershave and feel the heat coming off his body. Or perhaps it was her body? Maddeningly she felt the familiar rush of blood to her groin and drying of the throat that Brett always seemed to be able to arouse in her. But she wasn't going to let herself be sidetracked. Not this time.

'You hired Dylan simply to spite me.'

'Rubbish.' Brett sipped his own drink slowly. 'I hired him because I think he'll do a good job.'

'*I* was doing a good job!' Tati quivered with frustration.

'For fuck's sake,' said Brett. 'I offered you the CEO role, if you remember. I asked you to stay on and run the thing and you turned me down.'

'That's because hell would freeze over before I'd work for you,' spat Tati. 'And you know it.'

'Exactly.' Now it was Brett's turn to sound frustrated. 'That's why I hired Dylan.'

'Oh you are *full* of it!' said Tati, slamming her empty glass down on a side table so hard she almost broke it. 'Your offer to me was never genuine. You said yourself you were going to sell everything off. You only wanted to hire me so you could watch me fire all my staff and dismantle the business.'

'Right. So when I change my mind, and keep the staff and decide to grow the bloody business instead – you're *still* mad at me. You're impossible to please, do you realize that Tatiana?'

'How would you know?' Tati shot back. 'You've never tried to please me. You've never tried to please anyone but yourself, have you Brett?'

In answer Brett set down his own glass. Snaking one hand around her waist and the other at the back of her neck, he pulled her to him and kissed her, hard and passionately and for a long time. For a split second Tati stiffened, resisting him. Or was it herself she was resisting? But then she found herself kissing him back, her hands slipping underneath his shirt and clawing at the muscles on his back with a mind and life of their own.

He was kissing her neck now, moving down to her collar bone, then up again slowly till his lips brushed against the soft skin of her ear.

'You don't know what pleasure is,' he whispered.

Tati closed her eyes and moaned, lost in the delicious sensation of his warm breath in her ear and his hands sliding down over her buttocks. Somehow the belt of her jeans was already undone. They slid to the floor.

'What do you want?' Brett asked her. His hands were under her sweater now, expertly unhooking the back of her bra.

Pulling away from him just slightly, so they were looking into each other's eyes, Tati said slowly. 'Furlings. I want Furlings.' The faintest hint of a smile played at the corner of her lips. 'What do *you* want, Brett?'

'I want you and you know it,' he responded angrily. Grabbing her hand he placed it against his rock-solid erection, straining for release from his suit trousers.

Tati stroked it, firmly but tantalizingly slowly. Leaning forward, she whispered in his ear. 'Then sell me my house back.'

'Never,' groaned Brett, closing his eyes.

'OK then,' said Tati, wriggling out of his arms and refastening her bra. 'I'm going home.'

'No. You're not going anywhere.'

It wasn't a plea, or even a command. It was a simple statement of fact. Brett put his hands on her shoulders and walked slowly but determinedly forwards, pushing Tati backwards till her back was against the wall. Pressing down on her with the full weight of his body, he ran a finger along the line of her lips, then traced it up to her forehead, tenderly pushing back the stray wisps of hair that had fallen forward over her eyes.

'OK, I'll sell to you,' he said.

Tati's face lit up. 'You will? Why now? Why after all this time? I mean, that's wonderful. But I don't under—'

'For twenty million.'

Tati scowled. 'Don't be ridiculous. That's double what the house is worth.'

Brett planted a single kiss softly on her lips. 'Then don't buy it.'

Her eyes blazed with fury. 'You know I'm going to buy it. You arsehole.'

'That's right,' Brett smiled. 'And you know you're going to sleep with me. Because you want it as much as I do.'

Scooping her into his arms, he carried her into the bedroom. There was no more talking now. Laying her down on the bed, Brett removed the rest of her clothes piece by piece, taking his time, savouring every moment. Tati kept her eyes open. Watching him watching her was the biggest turn-on of all. Brett didn't admire her body, he devoured it, first with his eyes, and then with his fingers, lips and tongue, bringing Tati to the brink of release time after time but then pulling back right before she could climax. For so many years, ever since her marriage to Jason, she'd blocked out their last sexual encounter and the incredible sensations Brett had unleashed in her then. But what her conscious mind had erased, her body remembered in minute detail, every nerve and muscle arching towards him, straining to reach him and dance beneath his touch. No other lover, not even Leon di Clemente, could do what Brett Cranley did to her. He made her feel like a rare racing car that only he knew how to drive.

And he was right. He had always been right.

She wanted this as much as he did.

At last, as Tati lay writhing in a blissful agony of frustration, Brett slipped out of his own clothes and exploded into her. To her embarrassment, Tati came almost instantly. Feeling her warm, wet muscles spasm around him and her long legs tighten around his back, Brett came too. The first time was over in seconds. But after a few, blissful, silent minutes lying in each other's arms, he began making love to her again. And again. Tati lost count of how many times she came, or how long they spent exploring each other's bodies.

When it was finally over, Brett murmured, 'I love you. I want to be with you. To have children with you.'

'I love you too,' sighed Tati, drifting on a sated sea of bliss. 'But you're a terrible father.'

Her last thought before she fell asleep was of Furlings. How quickly she could sell enough shares to raise twenty million pounds?

'Rise and shine.'

Tati rubbed her eyes blearily. Brett, already showered and dressed and smelling of patchouli and toothpaste, drew back the curtains, flooding the room with bright winter light.

'Close them,' Tati commanded grumpily.

Brett climbed onto the bed and kissed her. 'No.'

Reluctantly Tati sat up and pushed the tangled hair out of her eyes. Brett looked so ridiculously handsome, and so happy, she couldn't help but smile.

'What time is it?'

'Half past eleven.'

'Fuck!' Tati threw back the covers. 'I have to get home.'

'You are home,' said Brett, grabbing her round the waist and pulling her into his lap, cupping her naked breasts in his hands.

Tati laughed. 'One step at a time. The first thing I need to do is make an appointment with my banker.'

Brett looked puzzled. 'What for?'

'What do you think?' said Tati. 'To figure out how I'm going to raise the extortionate amount of money you want for Furlings. Unless, of course, I can persuade you to lower your price?'

Turning around she straddled him coquettishly, coiling her long, lithe legs around his waist.

'Ah. About that.' Brett extricated himself from her embrace with infinite reluctance. 'I can't sell to you, Tatiana.'

'Ha ha,' said Tati. Wrapping the sheet around her, she padded towards the bathroom. 'Don't even joke.'

'I'm not joking,' said Brett. 'I can't sell to you even if I wanted to. The house is Angela's now. It was part of the divorce settlement.'

Tati turned around to look at him. She could see at once from his face that he was quite serious.

'But . . . last night,' she stammered. 'You said . . .'

'I'm sorry,' said Brett. 'I was afraid you'd leave if I didn't promise you something.'

'I would have left!' said Tati furiously.

'Yes, and then where would we be?' Brett walked over to her. 'I love you and I know you love me. I couldn't stand any more game-playing.'

'So you lied to me?' Tati shot back. 'You think that's how you stop playing games?'

She stormed into the bathroom and slammed the door.

Brett ran his hands through his hair in frustration as he heard the lock click shut.

'Don't be childish,' he said through the door. 'Come out and let's talk about it, like adults.'

'Fuck off,' said Tati.

'For God's sake, woman. It's "only a house,"' said Brett.

The door swung open. 'Only a house? Did you just say it's *"only a house?"*'

Tati stood there glaring at him, naked and furious. It was a look he remembered well from Greystones Farm, that awful house Tati had rented when he'd first arrived in England. The image of Tati that had haunted his dreams from that day to this. Instantly he felt himself getting hard.

Taking her hand he pulled her to him.

'You're a liar!' Tati screamed, wriggling. 'Let me go!'

'Not on your life,' said Brett. 'Not this time. I mean it, Tatiana. I am never letting you go again.'

Then he kissed her, and Tati realized what she'd known deep down all along.

She didn't want him to let her go.

Not now.

Not ever.

Angela Cranley crunched her way through the deep snow covering Furlings' lawn towards the apple tree that stood at the top of the drive. The air was so cold it hurt to breathe, but it was the sort of bright, joyful winter morning that couldn't fail to lift the spirits. The cloudless sky glowed as azure blue as a tropical lagoon, and the sun shone brightly, making the carpet of snow sparkle like a billion tiny diamonds. Against the white background, all the colours of nature seemed more pronounced. The green leaves of the holly bush were the deepest, most intense green Angela had ever seen them, and its red berries looked as plump and enticing as cherries.

She would be on her own this Christmas, for the first time ever. Unless you counted Gringo. Even Mrs Worsley had deserted her, to visit her sister (who knew?) in Edinburgh. But the prospect didn't daunt her. Indeed Angela had turned down numerous offers, from old friends, from Jason and George, even from some of her fellow students on her Masters course to spend the festive season with them.

'The first Christmas after divorce is always rough,' people told her. 'You mustn't be alone.'

No one seemed to understand Angela's explanation that Furlings was company enough. Now that the house was hers, really, truly hers, it felt like a fitting celebration to enjoy it by herself. After all, it was here that she had learned how to enjoy her own company. Here that she had discovered a place she truly belonged, a place where she might be alone, but she was never lonely. Unlike during the long years of her marriage to Brett.

Ironically, she and Brett were getting along better than ever now. But not for a moment did she regret their split. At fifty years old, Angela Cranley had at last understood the meaning of the word 'home'. It was the most wonderful Christmas present she could have asked for.

Clasped in her mittened hands was a large bag of birdseed. A bird feeder hung from the lowest branch of the apple tree. Reaching up, Angela carefully unhooked it and had just begun to refill it when a voice from behind startled her.

'Hello.' Max Bingley was wearing a Barbour jacket, teamed with a ridiculously bright, stripy woolly hat and knitted gloves, and a pair of black boots with green frogs on them. It was a ridiculous outfit – children's television presenter meets lunatic – but teamed with Max's trademark smile and unfailing bonhomie, it somehow suited him. 'On a robin rescue mission, are we? Not much fun for the birds, this weather.'

'I know,' said Angela, dropping the seeds. 'Poor things. They look so forlorn.'

She looked at Max and he looked at her, and for some reason she found her heart beating unpleasantly fast and her stomach starting to churn. All sorts of polite, conversational questions formed in her mind.

How are you?

Did you want to see me about something?

Can I get you a cup of tea?

But she couldn't seem to produce a single syllable. Staring back at her mutely, Max Bingley appeared to be suffering from the same affliction.

'Stella's left me,' he said suddenly, the words tumbling out of his mouth in a rush, like spilled marbles.

'Oh!' said Angela.

'Yep. She's run off with Dylan Pritchard Jones.'

'Oh!' Angela said again. She couldn't seem to come up with any other response. 'But isn't he, you know, a lot younger?'

'He is indeed.'

'And married?'

'Not so as you'd notice.' Max grinned.

'You don't seem awfully upset by it,' observed Angela. 'If you don't mind my saying so.'

'I'm not upset, really,' said Max. 'Stella and I have been on the skids for a while, to be frank with you. Although I was a little surprised by the Dylan thing. I fear that Pritchard Jones's interest in my soon-to-be-ex-wife has more to do with the preposterously valuable painting Stella's just inherited from her Great Uncle Stanley's estate than with her own, not inconsiderable charms. He's always been a prize shit.'

'Well, I'm sorry anyway,' said Angela. 'You and Stella always seemed so relaxed together. So content.'

'Hmmm.' Max rubbed his chin thoughtfully. 'Did we? The thing is, I was never in love with her. Not like I was with Susie.'

'Oh,' said Angela. She didn't know why, but she felt suddenly deflated.

'Stella and I married for companionship,' Max went on. 'But I realized after a while that that wasn't enough. I suppose this fling with Dylan is a pretty clear indication that she realized that too. It's for the best.'

Not sure what else to say, or do, Angela filled the bird-feeder and hung it back on the branch. As soon as she and Max stepped away, a flurry of sparrows, robins and tits swooped down onto the feast. Angela watched them, trying to regain her former happiness, but it seemed to have floated away on the wind.

She turned to Max. 'I suppose once you've had one true love in your life, it's hard to settle for less.'

'Exactly,' said Max.

'And two true loves is probably rather too much to ask.' Angela smiled.

'Do you think so?' said Max.

He looked at her, with those lovely eyes of his that Angela had always associated with laughter and fun. But they were deadly serious now. 'The thing is . . . I love you, Angela.'

Angela felt her heart drop into her boots with a thud.

'And I daresay that complicates things, and I don't expect you to feel the same, but I had to tell you,' Max couldn't seem to stop talking. 'I can't stand the thought of bumping into you in the village for the rest of my life and making small talk and you not knowing and—'

Angela removed her mittens and placed a finger gently on his lips.

'I love you too, Max,' she said. She thought about kissing him, but somehow it didn't feel quite right. Life with Max would not be about grand, romantic gestures. It would be about small, everyday joys, shared and cherished. It would be about peace. Slipping her bare hand into his gloved one, Angela turned towards the house – her other true love.

'Let's go inside and talk about it, shall we?' she said, happiness flooding through her as their fingers entwined. 'I'll make us a lovely pot of tea.'

ACKNOWLEDGEMENTS

Thanks to everyone at Harper Collins, especially my tireless editor Kim Young, but also Lucy Upton, Jaime Frost, Liz Dawson, Claire Palmer and the amazing sales team, Laura Fletcher, Sarah, Tom and Lisa. Also to my agents Luke Janklow and Hellie Ogden, and to everyone at Janklow & Nesbit, especially Kirsty Gordon in London and Claire Dippel in New York. Writing is the best job in the world and I am very aware of how lucky I am to be able to do this for a living. With this in mind, I would like to thank all my readers, new and old, and everyone who has helped me along the way, including: Lydia Slater who gave me a chance at the Sunday Times; Kate Mills, my wonderful first editor at Orion; the unique and lovely Wayne Brookes; Sarah Ritherdon, who had the original idea for a Swell Valley series; Fred Metcalf and my sister Louise, for telling me I could write in the first place; Tif Loehnis, for making it happen; and Luke Janklow (again) for continuing to make it happen, and more importantly, for making it fun.

Finally, as always, a huge thanks to my family for putting up with me, especially my husband Robin and our children, Sef, Zac, Theo and Summer. I love you all so much.

The Inheritance is dedicated to my lovely friend Sarah

Hughes and her husband Kris. Thank you for everything you have done for Sefi, and for me, this past year. You are friends indeed.

TB 2014

If you've enjoyed

THE INHERITANCE

read more Swell Valley stories from

Tilly
Bagshawe

One Christmas Morning
and
One Summer's Afternoon

Available to download now

Read more from

Tilly Bagshawe

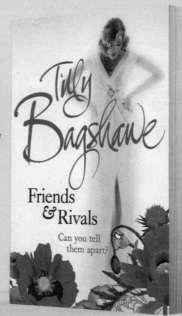

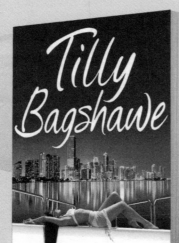

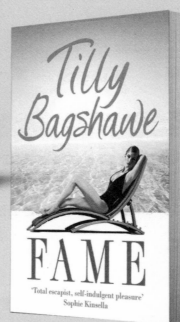

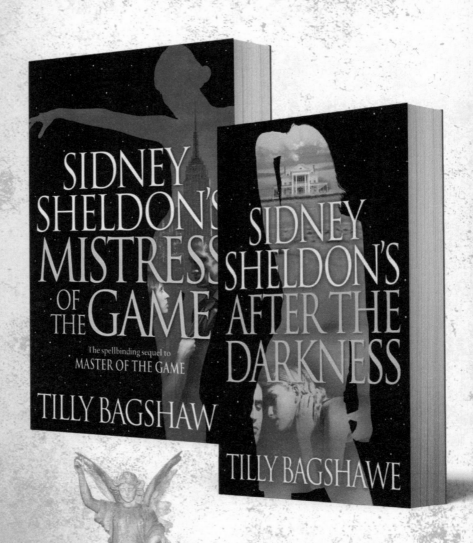

Master storyteller Sidney through

Sheldon's legacy continues
Tilly Bagshawe

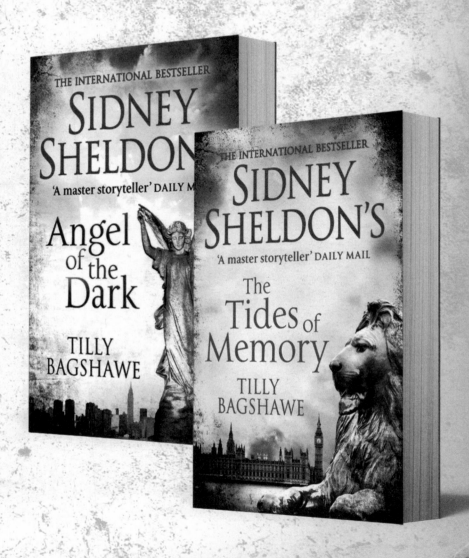

Keep up to date with

Tilly Bagshawe

www.tillybagshawe.com

Find Tilly on Facebook

 /tillybagshawebooks